PAX BRITANNIA

EL SOMBRA

And suddenly, without warning, there appeared on a neighbouring rooftop a man, naked but for a pair of black trousers, ragged and stained with desert dust. His hair was long, filthy and unkempt, his beard was wild and home to insects, and over his eyes, there was tied a red sash, coated with old, dry blood, with holes cut to see by, the tail-ends flapping in the wind like pirate flags. His skin was baked and hard from the desert sun and the burning sand. To Alexis, who bathed so meticulously and treated his skin and hair with a thousand products, he seemed like some ugly, savage monster.

In one hand, the creature held a sword. Razor sharp – gleaming and glittering in the light – it pointed directly at Alexis. The smile on the creature's face was powerful and confident and utterly unafraid. To Alexis, it seemed like the smile the devil might have in the deepest pits of Hell.

The moment seemed to last a thousand years.

An Abaddon Books™ Publication
www.abaddonbooks.com
abaddon@rebellion.co.uk

First published in 2007 by Abaddon Books™, Rebellion Intellectual
Property Limited, The Studio, Brewer Street, Oxford, OX1 1QN, UK.

Distributed in the US and Canada by SCB Distributors.15608 South
Century New Drive, Gardena, CA 90248, USA.

10 9 8 7 6 5 4 3 2 1

Editor: Jonathan Oliver
Cover: Mark Harrison
Design: Simon Parr & Luke Preece
Marketing and PR: Keith Richardson
Creative Director and CEO: Jason Kingsley
Chief Technical Officer: Chris Kingsley
Pax Britannia™created by Jonathan Green and Andy Boot

ISBN 13: 978-1-905437-34-4
ISBN 10: 1-905437-34-X

Printed in the UK by Bookmarque, Surrey

PAX BRITANNIA

EL SOMBRA

Al Ewing

Abaddon
Books

WWW.ABADDONBOOKS.COM

PROLOGUE

The Man And The Desert

The man walked across the desert.

And the desert destroyed the man.

The sun was a dragon that breathed fire on his neck and his back. Each grain of sand beneath his feet was a branding iron. He wanted to cry, but the desert had stolen his tears. Instead, his eyes wept blood.

In his left hand, he clutched a sash of silk, red stained black with spattered gore. His right hand gripped a sword. The knuckles on both hands were white and straining, almost bulging through the burned skin. He couldn't have opened his hands if he'd wanted to. But he didn't want to.

All the man wanted to do was die.

The wedding had been three days before.

And oh! What a wedding it had been!

The groom had passed the bride the thirteen coins and the rosary lasso was placed around their shoulders and then Father Santiago had blessed the couple – and when they kissed, you should have heard the noise! The whole town cheered and stamped their feet for joy! Everyone from old Gilberto, who'd crafted a pair of wedding-ducks, to little Carina, the madrina de ramo, nine years old and too shy to do anything other than giggle and punch the dashing madrina de laso on the arm. The cheer rang until the mariachis struck up their lively wedding march, and Heraclio led Maria – his Maria! – to his magnificent white horse, Santo. The noble beast stood quietly as his new mistress was lifted onto his back and then bore her with all the grace his old horse body could muster to the Great Square. Heraclio gave the venerable beast a gentle pat on the muzzle and fed him a lump of sugar from his wedding-coat, as the townspeople followed behind, led by the mariachi band, for dancing and laughter and food and good wine.

It was all the little town of Pasito had been talking of for months. The day when Heraclio, the handsome guardsman who rode through the town on his white horse and gave sugar-drops to the children from the pocket of his coat, would marry his Maria, perhaps the most beautiful girl the little Mexican town had yet produced and certainly the very finest dancer. To see her laugh and smile atop the gently pacing Santo was to catch a brief glimpse of what life could offer a man. Miguel the baker, forty-three years old and heavy and fat as his own loaves, drank her in with his eyes, and then turned those green eyes to his wife, with whom he had not shared a bed in more than a decade – and did those laughing green eyes not have a certain unidentifiable sparkle that said: *Come, mi amor! Let us forget the passing of years and find ourselves again under the desert stars!* Little Hector, the madrina de laso, who carried the coins and the lasso, all of twelve years old and looking very handsome in his miniature version of Heraclio's red wedding sash, looked at Maria as though he had never seen her before, never seen anyone before... and this time, when little Carina punched him in his arm, he grinned a cocky grin at her and said, "One day I'm gonna marry you!" Poor Carina, she blushed as red as that wedding sash, and ran to hide behind her father, the chubby jailer Rafael, who chuckled and murmured to his neighbour in the crowd: "That boy, he's muy caballero! Like a little Heraclio, hey? In ten years we'll be going to his wedding!"

"Ah, not if you can catch him first!" chuckled Isidoro the schoolteacher, and Carina blushed even redder but smiled secretly at Hector from the safety of her father's legs.

The only one who could look at Maria and not feel as though life was worth living was the poet Djego. Thin as a rake and soft as dough, with a mane of lank, black hair and a tiny pencil moustache, he might have been considered handsome – even debonair – if not for the air of misery and sorrow that he had carefully crafted to hang around himself like a funeral shroud. He was generally tolerated, occasionally even humoured, but there was not a soul in town who could possibly understand how Djego and Heraclio could be brothers.

The wise old women of the town nodded sagely in their rocking chairs when the question was put to them, and the reply was always the same. "Sometimes, a mother and a father put so much into that first child, that it takes a little out of the womb and the balls, and after that they don't work so good. So the first son is like a god, or maybe they have a princess for a daughter. And after that..." And at this point in the telling Djego would strut past with his nose in the air, frowning as though there was nothing to be enjoyed on a sunny day but his own secret and special pain. And the old wise women would chuckle. "After that... *blehhh*!"

And that was the reaction when Djego walked through the town, composing his awful poems, never turning his hand to anything of value, never allowing his heavy, leaden, rhymeless, metreless verse to breathe or represent something of beauty or worth. *Blehhh*. His brother looked after him, as he always had since their parents had died – because he felt sorry for him. "Djego is an idiot," he would say, "but he is my brother. And one day he will be able to laugh with me."

All of this is not to say that Djego could resist Maria's charms – quite the opposite. But when most men would see the most beautiful girl in Pasito and want to go out and live life, dance, sing, make great plans for themselves – Djego looked upon her and only wished to be transformed into stone.

The reason for this was simple. Djego had been hopelessly in love with Maria since the first moment his brother had brought her home.

The man in the desert fell to his knees and then fell forward onto his face.

Each breath was agony now. His throat was numb and his lips were swollen with the lack of moisture. His skin was like cracked parchment, burnt red. Blisters covered his feet from the red-hot sand that now seared his body.

In front of him, there was a small cactus, no larger than his head. His eyes could barely focus on it, but some switch in his mind triggered the thought that here was water. If you could question his conscious mind on the matter, he would tell you vehemently that he wanted no water; he wanted nothing but to die, and die soon. But his fingers crept forward, scrabbling at the spines of the cactus, drawing blood, then reaching for the hilt of the sword.

The conscious mind was all but dead. The brave desire to walk himself to death had boiled away in the furnace of the desert sun. All that was left was the instinct to survive. The sword flashed, carving the cactus open, the dry, cracked mouth making a terrible noise of despair and rage as a precious drop of moisture was lost to the sand. Then he was leaning forward to drink in what little liquid there was, eating the pulpy, wet flesh, swallowing and sucking it down, tearing at it with his teeth, breaking away the spines so he could devour the skin of the cactus itself.

When he began to choke on the cactus, he rolled to his side and slumped on the sand, unable to move, the pulpy meat of the plant resting in his arid mouth as the sun beat mercilessly down.

The cactus was of the Trichocereus variety. Originally from Ecuador, it had slowly migrated north through Central America, mutating as it went to survive the greenhouse effect brought down on the planet by Britain's runaway industrialism. Originally, the Trichocereus was used by tribal shamen to provide them with intense, often terrifying visions. Those botanists who had discovered this new variety termed it Trichocereus Validus.

This was because its psychotropic qualities were hundreds, perhaps thousands of times more powerful.

The man's eyes bulged. He began to convulse. Foam ran from his lips as from a rabid dog.

He could no longer recall his name, but he remembered very vividly that three days before he had been punched in the face by a woman, for the first and the last time in his life.

The procession had reached the great square, and there the dancing began. Heraclio danced with his beautiful bride to the strains of the mariachi band, and all around him, the whole town danced in the shape of a heart, as was tradition. Had there ever been a happier moment in the whole time that the town of Pasito had stood? Certainly none anyone could remember, although occasionally a husband would turn to a wife and squeeze their hand a little tighter, the glimmer in their eyes seeming to say: *Yes, I remember it well.*

And then the great circle broke up, and every man in the town took their turn to dance with the lovely Maria, and the women queued to be whirled around by the manly Heraclio, who danced well, but not as well as with Maria, and danced with consideration, slowing his pace where necessary – especially when gently escorting the ninety-five year old Consuela Vasquez, the town's oldest resident, from one end of the square to the other.

Occasionally, Maria would sit herself down in her magnificent white dress, and pass time with the old men and women who, unlike the beloved and venerable Consuela, were unable to dance – either through advanced age, physical disorder or, in the case of Toraidio DeMario, several bottles of good wine. She would also flash her stunning smile at Elbanco the singer and the rest of his band, who would not fail to play whatever song she requested. Even those they did not know, they would do their very best to attempt, plucking the words from the air and making up a tune which fit them. A song called The Dark Side Of The Moon, for example, had been the talk of London some ten or twenty years previously. It was a melancholy ballad with subtle undertones of laudanum abuse, and had become so famous that word of it had managed to spread even as far as El Pasito. In the hands of Elbanco's band it became a quick, jolly tune about a cuckold painting his wife's bottom black to discourage the many suitors who came running when she waved it out of the window. Maria laughed and danced to it regardless, and thanked each of the band with another sparkling smile, which they considered ample payment for their labours.

And so, when Djego finally deigned to take the floor and dance, Elbanco and his cohorts were busily attempting to perform an apparently famous European ditty called The Dancing Queen, which allegedly went something like:

She doesn't like to walk and she cannot ride a horse –
But the way she dances? Oh, it's a scandal!

Eyebrows were raised – the venerable Consuela gave a gasp of shock, which was a rare event as she had, it was believed, seen it all. Djego the poet, who was above all petty enjoyments, was moving to dance for the first time! It was scarcely believable. To her credit, Maria acknowledged the rarity of the event, and took him gently in her arms to start a waltz about the floor. Heraclio watched with a proud smile – Djego had never told him his feelings on any matter, and so he assumed he was simply watching his shy younger brother finally coming out of the thick shell he had so painstakingly built for himself. He accepted the hand of the chief bridesmaid, and led her into a stately twirl as Elbanco waved his guitarist into a spirited solo.

Of course, he had no way of knowing what was truly on Djego's mind.

Maria's green eyes sparkled as she looked into his, and the smile on her face held a hint of mischief. "So you've finally decided to enjoy yourself, hah? Is this the start of a trend or a momentary bout of insanity?"

Djego smiled stiffly in response. "I... would like it to be the start of something."

She raised an eyebrow. "A new career as a ladykiller? Well, in that case, you'll have to stop those hands shaking. Let me lead a little." She began to gently guide him around the floor, and soon they were moving almost gracefully, with Djego even managing a little smile. "There! Isn't this nice? Djego, if you can keep this up, I promise I will dance at your wedding. Come on, smile! You look handsome when you smile, my brother-in-law. You should do it more. Where's the harm? It might bring your wedding day closer, hah?"

Djego's smile faltered. "I do not see that I will ever get married now, Maria."

Maria laughed, and the laugh was strong and sure. "Oh, there's time yet. Look at your brother when I first met him! Remember how he used to spit out of windows? And then he hit poor Father Santiago in the eye!" She laughed again, but Djego's attempt at a smile was nervous. His hands were shaking. Maria sighed. "Djego, if you keep this up I'm going to abandon you to Consuela. She'll teach you a few more things than dancing, I warn you. You've not seen how she has her eye on you?"

Djego shuddered, but not because of Maria's mental image. He swallowed hard, then spoke softly, barely heard above the music.

"Maria... do you remember the poems that Heraclio sent you?"

She blinked at him, continuing to lead the dance more by reflex than anything else, cocking her head slightly to look at him. "How do you know about those? He showed them to you to get a second opinion, right?"

Djego shook his head. "I wrote those, Maria. Those were my words to you."

Maria said nothing, but she stopped the dance.

"Those poems I wrote to you – I gave them to Heraclio because I didn't think I was worthy. But those are my feelings, Maria. The poems that won your heart, that made you his – they were mine." He swallowed, searching her eyes. Her expression was unreadable, but he pressed on. "This... this should be my wedding day." His eyes welled. The sadness was almost too great for him to contain. "I... I know I've waited too long... but... perhaps one day..."

This was the moment that Maria pulled away from him, swung around and slammed one of her fists into his jaw, sending him tumbling onto the ground in a cloud of dust.

"Estupido!" she yelled, and kicked him in the ribs. Elbanco and his band stopped playing. The venerable Consuela gave another gasp of shock – it was doubtful whether her heart would be able to stand any more unthinkable happenings that day. Little Hector put his hand over his mouth, turning ashen – his juvenile meditations on the power of manhood shattered in an instant. Carina only grinned.

Heraclio stood dumbfounded, then found his voice. "Djego, what have you done now?"

Maria spat venom as she grabbed the lapels of Djego's unseasonal black shirt and hauled him up.

"You honestly think you can walk up to me on my wedding day and say such things? Those poems were terrible, Djego! They were desgraciado! It was nice that Heraclio thought of reading me poems, but in the end I used them to start a fire going! You cannot write, tonto!"

Djego sniffled, reaching to wipe the blood from his nose, looking at the blazing Maria with wide eyes.

"Seriously, idiota, what was your big plan, hah? Would

this be like one of those stupid books you read? Was I going to be the unattainable great love you pined away for for the rest of your life? Were we supposed to swap charged glances over the dinner table? Well guess what, retraso..." Her foot slammed into his groin. Hard. Djego gasped and collapsed, then began to retch, throwing up a puddle of half-digested wine onto the ground.

"I fell in love with a man. Not a bunch of stupid poems. So crawl off and hide away for a while? You're no longer welcome at my wedding party. Get the hell out!"

Silence rolled across the great square. All eyes were on the sobbing Djego, as he lay there, weeping openly. Had there been a more awkward moment in Pasito's long history than this? It was certainly the most public embarrassment anyone had suffered. Shocked, helpless eyes turned to each other, then to Heraclio, who shrugged, as if to say: *What can I do*? *She's right*! Not even the venerable Consuela could see a means of rescuing the occasion.

So in many ways it was a mercy when the stage exploded in a gout of fire and shrapnel, tearing Elbanco and his band into bloody shreds.

Djego convulsed on the sand as the sun fried his flesh. The memories seemed so clear. He could feel Maria's fist as it hammered into his jaw, again, again, again, the shame fracturing him with every impact, breaking him like glass. He could feel his soul filling with a black bile, hissing black acid that burnt and seared the walls of himself. The shame. The shame.

His throat burned and he retched. He could feel the bile, the shame, creeping slowly up his gullet. His eyes were wide, looking down at the glittering sand, and every grain seemed to him like a mountain. The sun was a jewel sparkling on blue cloth and in his ears there was a humming sound, as though he was a string that had been plucked – and it was deafening.

A shadow fell across him, hotter on his back than the heat of the sun. A giant shadow.

A giant.

Standing above him. He turned over and saw everything clearly.

His brother stood above him. A giant with his brother's face, looming like God. His brother, big as judgement above him, standing and looking down on him. Always. *Always.*

Djego closed his eyes and tried to breathe. His heart was pounding in his chest, a hot coal resting against his ribcage. Everything in his ears was still humming. Humming. His eyes were closed but the scene was the same. His brother, his judgement, looming over him, looking down.

Djego understood that this had always been happening. It would always be happening. His brother would always tower over him, always leave him in shadow, always look down. After what had happened he had no right to expect anything else.

After what had happened.

Djego shuddered and retched, more black-bile-memory flooding him, scalding him. He felt something hot on his face. Tears. Or blood. He shook like a child.

The giant's massive hand closed about him and squeezed.

Instantly there came the echo of similar blasts, a tidal wave of fire that seemed to sweep through the town, burning and destroying at random. The courthouse in the north of the town burst like an egg, sending showers of masonry into neighbouring houses, great shards of glass whirling like propellers as they smashed through walls into the cribs of children too young to enjoy the celebration. Then the screaming started.

The crowd scattered, running and trampling in a chaotic mass of bodies, as the crack and clatter of machinegun fire stabbed through the night air and bullets hit the ground around them. The venerable Consuela's head became a fine mist as a high-velocity round pierced her left eyeball, destroying, in an instant, the mind that held so much of the town in the amber of memory. Perhaps she would have died anyway – this was, after all, the third unbelievable event of the evening.

A bullet found Isidoro the schoolteacher, and he fell on his face in the dirt before flapping like a hooked fish, looking down at his right leg in horror. Mid-thigh, the flesh had been torn away and he could see bone and the spurting ends of the femoral artery. Isidoro taught biology among his many other subjects and he knew what that meant. But he did not believe. Even when darkness closed over his vision and he toppled backwards, shuddered and went still, he did not believe.

Who could?

Even Santo did not survive. He tried to run to his Master at the first sound of fire, but one of the bullets clipped a cannon bone, shattering it and sending the animal tumbling to the ground. Another shot slammed into his flank, ricocheted off a rib and exited his breast in a fountain of bloody horsemeat that cascaded over the screaming Hector. The boy's screams joined the cacophony from the agonised horse before a third volley of shots silenced them both. Santo's end was merciful – one of the bullets shattered his skull and he died in an instant.

Hector was not so lucky. For the next ten minutes he stared in mute horror at the seeping mass of offal that had toppled from his torn belly.

Maria's blistering anger fell away into confusion and horror. She looked up at the sky, unable to comprehend what could be doing this. And what she saw terrified her beyond measure.

There were men in the sky.

Men in grey uniforms, carrying great black iron guns, with grey helmets and grey expressions. On their backs were metal wings, flapping slowly in the air, great gusts of steam shooting from them as they clanked and groaned. *That isn't holding them up*, she thought madly, unable to comprehend. *Something else must be.* And then one of the men turned his gun on her, and she darted forward blindly.

Everything was happening very slowly now. Her feet, moving through thick molasses, hit Djego, who was still curled up on the ground, sobbing like a little child. Unable to stop herself, she fell forward, landing hard on the ground in her wedding dress. She looked up, winded and spitting dust from her mouth, and then there was a terrible sound and something hit her very, very hard in the side of her throat.

She couldn't breathe. There was something wet on her dress. It was spoiled. Everything had been spoiled. Somewhere, she could hear Heraclio screaming, but it was far away. Was he crying? *Don't cry, my love. I'll sort this out for you. I always do.*

The last thing she saw was the insignia on the shoulder

of the man who'd shot her. A red cross in a white circle, with broken ends, all the way round. Like four little L-shapes joined up.

Where have I seen that before? Thought Maria.

And that was that.

Heraclio looked up at the flying men and screamed... but that was in the past, wasn't it? Djego felt himself resting on sand, on the giant's palm. He could feel the flesh through the sand. He saw now the truth of it – Heraclio was looking down, not up, always looking down at him, and the opening of his mouth was in hungry anticipation.

Heraclio the giant was feasting.

The mouth of the giant hung wide open, then closed, and between the teeth were the bones of Djego's ankles, snapping, cracking like a chicken-bone, bitten through. Djego screamed. He was going to die. He was going to be eaten bite by bite. Eaten by the giant, the giant judgement, the giant reputation. The reputation he always had to live up to.

When they had been children, Djego had often been pushed over and beaten and his books taken and trampled in the mud. The boys in the village thought he was fat and doughy and pasty, and they kicked him sometimes until he pissed blood. And that was happening now. He was a child again. He was crying again. His brother was coming to rescue him again, wild swinging fists and shouts. Heraclio always came in the end, running and punching and kicking the bullies until finally the attacks stopped. Nobody picked on Heraclio's brother. Nobody. Djego heard his brother's confident shout again from the giant, the wind of it rushing in his hair.

And Djego felt shame again. Black bile. Again, his brother had done what he could not, his handsome brother, his popular brother who fought where Djego could only cower and weep. He had fought so hard. Never harder than that day, that day it had all ended between them. Heraclio had no brother now.

Djego hated him, and the hate brought more self-disgust that cut him open like a knife.

The giant bit deep. One of Djego's legs was torn from the pelvis, crunched and swallowed whole.

He looked up at the giant's eyes and screamed.

Heraclio looked up at the flying men and screamed. "Conchas! Get down here! Get down here and face me!" The sight of his beloved lying on the ground – the look in her eyes, the anger that was there – filled his vision with red mist. He gripped his sword in white knuckles, waving it at the sky-soldiers as they fired down, bullets cascading on the ground all around him. To those not running for any shelter they could find from the storm of men and bullets and death, he seemed a vision of bloody vengeance – righteous and pure.

One of the soldiers took notice.

He had been barking orders to his fellows, but now he handed command to a subordinate and swooped down, landing in the dust of the great square. As the soldier slowly removed his helmet, Heraclio's streaming eyes burned into him, as if seeking to destroy him with a gaze.

The soldier smiled. He was tall and blonde, barely nineteen, with sharp blue eyes that returned Heraclio's burning look with an audacious twinkle of his own. Heraclio was handsome, but this newcomer was beautiful – beautiful in the way that men can be, that dangerous, tempting perfection that comes in statues from Greece, or the rebellious teenagers who break their parents' rules in the kinema-films, the wild ones. An angel's face with a devil's eyes.

He smiled, and the smile promised terrible things.

And then he drew the sword from his scabbard.

Heraclio was not in the mood for niceties. He screamed and lunged, the point of his sword aimed at the heart of his enemy. The soldier, smiling softly, stepped back and swept his sword in a short arc, deflecting Heraclio's wild thrust easily before transforming the fluid motion into a strike. The point of his sword slashed across Heraclio's cheek, leaving a deep cut.

"Is that all you can manage?" purred the angel-face.

Heraclio screamed. His face was contorted in a fury nobody had ever seen there before, and yet his movements were precise now, as though the rage boiling in his belly was giving him focus. Djego, cowering on the ground, looked up at him through his wet eyes, and saw perhaps the greatest display of sword fighting he had ever seen. In Heraclio's white knuckles, the blade flashed and darted like a thing alive, seeking those gaps in the defences of his foe that would allow him to plunge the blade deep into flesh.

It found none. The defence was impregnable. The soldier flashed a mocking grin, the blades clanging as he parried each blow without effort.

Over their heads, the flying men circled like vultures, firing when necessary to herd the crowd into position, then landing and screaming orders at them in a foreign tongue.

The swords flashed and struck. Sweat fell into Heraclio's eyes, and he blinked, the sword jerking, leaving him wide open for the killing strike. But it did not come. In that heartbeat, the handsome young soldier looked straight into Heraclio's eyes. Heraclio blinked again. The pause seemed to stretch on forever, and the implication of it made Heraclio's blood turn to ice in his veins.

The soldier was choosing not to kill him... just yet.

The angelic face smiled again, like a cat. He had seen the realisation strike home, the fear begin to build, and so he lunged forward, sword flashing, pressing the attack, but keeping within Heraclio's skill. He was forcing Heraclio to work harder simply to keep from being skewered.

"Djego!" Heraclio shouted. "Help me!" The sound chilled Djego's heart. He could not move.

The angelic soldier pushed forward a little further, enjoying the fear. This was the moment he especially enjoyed – the moment when his foe realised that there was no hope of survival, that he was outclassed and outmatched. The sight of that knowledge blooming in Heraclio's eyes made his heart sing. Soon, there would come the other moment he savoured – the sweet moment of surrender, when the enemy knew he could no longer fight against his own death. He licked his lips in anticipation as his sword flashed, carving a line across his enemy's chest, then striking his blade through the muscle at the shoulder. Two quick strikes, designed to remove all hope. The end would soon come.

"Herr Oberst!" One of the other soldiers called over. "Wir haben die Verarbeitung beendet."

The angel-faced soldier nodded briskly. "Ich bin dort in einer Sekunde."

And then he moved very quickly, lunging and flicking with the tip of his sword. The blade carved deep into

Heraclio's belly, slicing up, opening out the guts, sending a tide of blood and offal and filth spattering onto the ground. Heraclio's eyes went wide, and then he looked down, and he saw – and the look of disgust on his face at his own body, so exposed and revealed for what it was, such a look was sweeter for the soldier than the look of surrender could have been. In its own way, it was perfect.

"Eine vollkommene Totung." murmured the angel face. And then he simply walked away.

Heraclio collapsed into his own offal, giving shuddering gasps punctuated by hacking coughs that sprayed more blood into the dirt.

Djego stumbled to his feet and ran forward to cradle his brother. "Oh God... Dios Mio... Heraclio, you have to keep still..." He tried to remove the red wedding sash, to use it as a bandage, but Heraclio gave a sharp twist, snarling like a dog, blood and spit dripping from his chin as he looked at his own brother with the same hate he'd had for the soldiers. The sash was left hanging in Djego's hand.

"Bastard!"

Djego recoiled as if he'd been slapped around the face, but Heraclio reached to grip his wrist, pulling him back, spitting blood on Djego's chest with every word.

"Corbarde. Spineless coward. You... you cower in the dirt while your brother is cut to shreds... while Maria, my wife, is murdered! Maria, who you make a big scene over, who you say you love – but you didn't love her enough to protect her, did you? A dog would have done that! But not you! You bastardo asqueroso!"

"Heraclio, please – I can get help..."

Heraclio gripped his sword and thrust the handle towards his brother. "It's too late to help, mierda. Go and run away. Run away like the bastard coward you are!"

"I... I won't run..." stammered Djego, taking the sword, horrified at the blood that coated the handle, that coated his hands, that flowed into the sand like a torrent and soaked his suit.

"You will, inmundicia. My brother, the shit. You will run away as you always do... but never far enough. Never far enough."

"Heraclio, please..."

Heraclio looked up then, and fixed his brother Djego with a terrible stare, a look which would never fade away, looking deep into his brother's eyes.

"No matter how far you run, Djego, my blood will always be with you. My ghost will always be with you. You can run from your home, your family, your responsibilities – you can run from your love – but you can never, never run from me. That is my curse upon you, brother. I will be with you until the day that you die."

Djego opened his mouth to speak, to plead, tears streaming down his face – but it was too late. Heraclio's grip relaxed. He slumped backwards, eyes rolling up into his head. Whatever strength had kept him alive long enough to deliver his terrible curse was gone. All that was left was a corpse at his feet.

Djego lifted his eyes, the sword and the sash in his grip, and he saw what was happening. The soldiers had landed and were herding the people through the square in a great mass, prodding them forward with batons. Old Gilberto was kneeling over the body of his son, looking dumbfounded. Two soldiers marched up to him in their black boots and, almost gently, forced him up and into the march. Then they turned towards Djego, and a terrible realisation ran through him that poured ice into his spine.

He would have to fight. He would have to lift his

brother's sword and run towards the soldiers and try to kill them. Most likely, they would shoot. The bullets would punch through his chest, his belly, his face and he would be left dead in the dirt. If he was unlucky, the baby-faced commander would swoop down and use Djego for sword fighting practice as he had used Heraclio. Cut him up like meat and leave his guts hanging out for the vultures.

Djego swallowed and took a step forward, tears streaming down his face, the sword a blur in front of him. He had to fight. It was the only thing left to do. If he didn't fight, then what did that make him?

The soldiers raised their guns with a chuckle, then a laugh – laughing at the man in the dirty black clothes, doughy and pathetic and lank-haired, with his wobbling sword and his streaming crybaby eyes.

The sound was enough to break Djego. He turned and ran, bullets kicking up the dirt at his feet.

He didn't stop running until he reached the desert and his breath gave out, and then he forced himself to keep walking as the town receded in the distance behind him.

The sword and the sash were clutched in his hands, his knuckles were white with the strain and he could no longer see through the tears, but he kept stumbling forward, breath ragged, one foot in front of the other. He was walking in search of death.

He walked for three days.

The teeth of the giant bit through Djego's stomach, severing his spine. Heraclio's perfect teeth. His perfect, handsome face. Crunching down into his chest. Djego understood then, as every piece of him was bitten away and crushed, how small and pathetic he had been. How meaningless. How futile and ridiculous. It was a pleasure to let go, to let 'Djego' be eaten and swallowed bite by bite, to let his ugly soul fracture and split into infinite pieces. Swallowed into something larger than he was.

He no longer felt pain, but something itched at him, at the back of his skull. The face. The face on the giant. He thought it was Heraclio's, but it had never been. The face on the giant was his own.

He heard laughter from his own throat, deep and rich, booming across the sands, a wonderful, joyous laugh of triumph and confidence. Whose laugh was that? Not Djego. He was dead and gone and he never laughed. But if not Djego... then who?

Who was lying in the sand?

He shuddered, convulsed once more, every muscle rigid. The eyes in his head rolled back. He gripped the sword and the sash tighter, until they seemed to pulse with a life of their own.

And then his heart stopped.

CHAPTER ONE

The Corpse Under The Sheets

Nine Years Later

Alexis woke up next to a corpse. He hardly noticed at first.

He lay there for a moment, blinking in the darkness of the room, feeling the cold mass in the bed next to him and trying to remember what it was. Who it was. Had been. There had been so many of them, it was always difficult for him to remember.

The Officers' Club, perhaps? He vaguely remembered a new waitress. Or some curfew-breaker? There was a tall, handsome youth he seemed to remember with some clarity. Was the lump male or female? He took men to his bed regularly, a healthy amount, experimentation – certainly not the same thing as the degenerates who ended up in the camps. Not the same thing at all. But it led to these frustrating mornings, when he desperately tried even to remember the gender or some distinguishing feature of the cold counterweight that balanced his own body on the mattress.

He racked his mind and clicked his tongue, in the very same way he clicked his tongue when he spilled his coffee or forgot his keys. And then he swung his legs out of the bed and stood. Enough time had been wasted by pointless musings. He left the corpse as it lay, under the sheets.

He was waiting for himself in the bathroom mirror. Still the face of an angel, clean and unblemished, with a mop of blonde hair and piercing blue eyes. The chiseled jaw and soft lips of a matinee idol. He had barely changed in the nine years since the occupation of the town began – when he took so much pleasure in gutting Heraclio like a fish. It was a face you could trust.

He took the opportunity to study the smile carefully. An easy smile. Good-natured. It was a useful tool for getting him what he wanted, which was the important thing. Idly, he looked down at his hands, examining the caked blood. He would have to get all of the dirt out from under his fingernails before he applied his facial scrub. These things had to be done efficiently.

Alexis Eisenberg had killed an average of one person per week in this fashion since he was seventeen.

The facial scrub was followed by a brief shower, and then a rub-down with an exfoliating gel that originally came from Corsica, and then another shower, and then Alexis walked back into the bedroom to do his exercises. One hundred press-ups. One hundred sit-ups. Ten minutes of aerobic exercise to work the heart and pump the blood. And the corpse lay under the sheets. It was probably a small man. Or perhaps a woman. It was hard to tell – the body seemed so shapeless and was in such a strange position. Several of the joints were most likely dislocated. The only way to know for certain would be to lift the sheet, but then he'd probably get blood under his fingernails again... ah well. It hardly mattered anyway. It wasn't important.

One hundred pull-ups, followed by a third shower. Cleanliness was next to godliness. Who could respect an Oberstleutnant of the Luftwaffe who did not bathe in a proper fashion? He applied a little aftershave before he put on his uniform. The aftershave came from Paris. The corpse lay under the sheets. Then on with the uniform, the dark grey of the Oberstleutnant, the second-in-command in this place, but taken in a little here and there to show off his figure. Was it five years ago there had been uniforms like this worn in the streets of Paris and Milan as the fashion? Post-modernism had a lot to answer for in those places where the world of art had not stood still, frozen in Victoria's gaze... and the Führer's. He wore the jacket open, and no cap. The solid silver cross that was his trademark hung over his chest, where the shirt hung open with no tie. Style was very important to Alexis.

On his way out, he smiled to the Gefreiter who stood guard on his room, returning the man's salute with easy familiarity. "There is some refuse in my bed, mein Herr. Could you see that it is disposed of, and my sheets cleaned?"

The private nodded. "Of course, Oberstleutnant. I shall attend to it at once."

He saluted once more and clicked his heels as Alexis walked on.

Once upon a time, before the occupation, the place had been called El Pasito. It went by another name now. Aldea. A clockwork-town, where no trains ran. And so the people would run on time instead. As Alexis strode through the town, his eyes passed over those who had once run this dusty collection of hovels. The subhumans. The Mexicans. They had been organised now – proud workers for a greater cause than their degraded notions of happiness. Subhuman they might be, but they were workers for the Fatherland and had thus earned a bare modicum of his respect. Alexis nodded brusquely to them as they filed to their labours, a number branded into the forehead of each. Men and women walking in lockstep to their work. The work that made them free.

Most of the work in Aldea was done in the middle of the town – the Great Square, where the Statue Of Freedom loomed. With the boot-heels locked in an eternal click, one arm raised in straight salute, it was a sight to bring pride and pleasure to the heart of every true Aryan. Every detail was exact, from the proud chest to the tall, straight legs, from the iron gaze to the perfectly trimmed moustache, this great stone statue of his magnificent Führer – Adolf Hitler himself!

In happier times.

Adolf Hitler was still Führer, of course, and he would be for a hundred years yet, perhaps a thousand. The propaganda painted him as immortal. But Alexis knew that if a statue were to be built of the Führer as he was now... well.

Best not to.

The sound of the work woke him from his reverie. Hammering and sawing echoed about the square as these fascinating, almost-human creatures worked on the scaffolding. The statue had been put up over the course of a year and according to the laws of Aldea, it must soon be taken down, for how could a statue properly represent the perfection of the Führer? The great Führer who, as any schoolbook in the town would tell you, was in all times and in all places, an ideology that had transcended the poor flesh to live forever? It was idolatry at best, a treasonous offence committed by these animals at worst. Thus, the statue would be slowly and painstakingly dismantled – and then the very next day the order would be given that it must be built again. Build and destroy. Build and destroy. The principle was easy to grasp – work should hold no significance for the worker, beyond the basic understanding that it was the worker's duty to work. All human feeling must be excised to create the pure detachment from self that would ensure eternal subservience.

The even numbers hammered and sawed and worked in silence on the great statue like a colony of ants. Like a machine colony. The odd numbers did the hundred and one other little jobs that needed doing. Farming the land. Cleaning the toilets. Waiting tables in the Officers' Club.

The corpse lay under the sheets.

On random days, the odd and even numbers would switch tasks. Then, a week, a month, a year later, they would switch back. It was best that the workers did not grow too attached to one particular task. Again, the work must hold no significance for the worker. You work until you stop – if necessary you work until you die. There should be no meaning to the work beyond that.

That did not mean that work should be entirely without reward, however, even for these half-human imbeciles. Alexis cast an eye restlessly about. Eventually his gaze alighted on a short, pudgy Mexican man, with a large handlebar moustache, dressed in a white ice-cream suit, a panama hat and immaculate shoes. Alexis smiled, a genial grin that seemed to light up his whole face. It never touched his eyes.

"Master Plus."

The fat little man in the white suit jumped, nearly losing the hat off his head and exposing his grotesque bald patch in the process. He turned quickly, eyes wide as he looked to the officer.

"Oberstleutnant... forgive me, I was woolgathering..."

"Heil Hitler, Master Plus."

The fat man turned pale and did a reasonable approximation of a proper salute. Alexis scowled. Nine years, this fat little half-man had been in a position of great responsibility with many perks – and he still couldn't manage a decent salute. His greasy brown hand was like a flailing fish jerking on the end of a line. Alexis shook his head slowly. Master Plus was the exception to the rule. No number was branded into his forehead. He never woke up to find that he was now expected to clean toilets. He owned a beautiful white suit and paraded it in front of his fellow aberrations. He had a diamond stickpin that flashed in the bright noon sun. He owned a beautiful house.

Master Plus was in charge of the concept of Reward.

A living carrot, dangled in front of his fellow subhumans, a symbol of how high in the ranks they could rise if they were to only play the game, follow the rules. In this capacity, he gave speeches to the workers, 'seminars' where he would tell them how simple it was to achieve his lofty position – if only they would work just a little harder. "If I can do it, why not you?" as he would say, over and over again, his diamond stickpin flashing into the eyes of the audience as they slaved in the pouring rain.

It was an illusion Alexis despised. You didn't need to trick the ox into pulling the cart, or butter up a sheep before you took its wool. So why play such games now?

The fat man swallowed hard. Alexis restrained himself from sneering openly in response. The creature was a natural coward – he'd turned on his own kind for fear that the Luftwaffe would do to him and his daughter what they had done to so many others. He'd grown dependent on the luxuries the new regime afforded him. And what was he now? A parrot on a jewelled perch, endlessly repeating the same empty phrases for fear of being denied his cracker. As he stammered his reply,

Alexis fought the irresistible urge to simply take hold of his fat Mexican head and twist it off. He had no doubt that such an act would provide more motivation than the workers had had in nine years.

"H-h-heil Hitler, Oberstleutnant. Heil Hitler." The moustache twitched as Plus forced an oleaginous smile. His eyes were those of a cornered rat.

"You only need to say it once, my dear fellow." Alexis smiled a little wider. "I've been watching the workers building the statue. Is it me, or do they seem a trifle behind?"

Master Plus blinked. He opened his mouth and then closed it, once, like a fish, before licking dry lips and summoning himself to speak. "Herr Oberstleutnant – I haven't observed any decrease in productivity..."

Alexis let his smile drop. "So it is me. My judgement is faulty. Thank you for bringing that to my attention, Master Plus."

"No!" The word was almost cried out. "No, I would never suggest such a thing, please, Herr Oberstleutnant, I merely meant to say that I have not seen any drop – I would never question you..."

"In that case, it's your judgement that's not up to par. Or your ridiculous speeches. Tell me – my dear friend – do you honestly think we need a Master Plus in this experiment? I don't wish to offend you – you do such necessary work. But do you truly think a colony of ants should have regular pep-talks? Are machines in great need of motivational speakers?" He was grinning now, a vulpine grin that was a world away from the cultivated, easy-going smile of the young, handsome officer. Here was revealed the beast, the carnivore, the killer who waited for his chance and struck once only.

Master Plus blinked. He spoke slowly, treading with the care of a man picking his way through a minefield. He was walking on the tongue of the crocodile.

"I would not dare to suggest that I was... indispensable, Herr Oberstleutnant. However, my function within Aldea has been... I do only what I have been directed to do by my superiors, Herr Oberstleutnant. By your father. The Generaloberst. My function is as a part of his larger mechanism, and as such... I would hardly dare to suggest that I was... dispensable, either. Such decisions are not up to me, Herr Oberstleutnant."

Your father.

There it was. Alexis could not help but feel a stab of admiration for the fat little animal's clever tongue. It was a stratagem almost worthy of a true man. Now, instead of tormenting a worthless subhuman raised far beyond his station, Alexis had been placed in a position where he was in danger of being seen to speak against the Generaloberst himself. The leader of the occupation force. His father. Alexis wasn't quite ready to make such a move.

Just yet.

Master Plus took the opportunity to steer the conversation towards less dangerous waters. "Perhaps we can discuss this at my house, Herr Oberstleutnant... it's been too long since you last made a visit."

Alexis flashed another lifeless smile. It had been barely three days. Still, had the half-man stood his ground and pressed the point, Alexis would have faced a choice between showing weakness and defying his father. Neither would have been conducive to his continued good health. The best thing to do now would be to graciously accept the change of subject.

Besides, there were far less pleasant activities on a hot

day like today than visiting the house of Master Plus. The greatest treasure in all of Mexico was kept there.

A few streets away from the statue lay the palatial house. In most respects, it was the same sort of house that many of the officers lived in – large rooms, nice furniture and what have you. But this one had an air of mystery about it not easily defined.

What officer of the mighty Luftwaffe did not show off his house? It was a symbol of status, and there was precious little of that to be found in Aldea. The house an officer was given was in direct proportion to their work for the Reich – the greater the work, the better the house, and so forth. So most evenings you would find a Staffelkapitan entertaining select members of the Staffel, or an Oberst showing off to a couple of Lieutenants – showing off his whisky and his gramophone records and his high ceilings. Thus, the inside of every big house in Aldea was common knowledge to all, from Udo Reimann's little bolt-hole with its wall of one hundred empty whisky bottles (always one half-finished) to the light, airy spaces of Oberst Mehler's residence, where he played Mozart on a little steam-player until late. But there was one house that was a mystery, and that was Master Plus' residence.

Few officers of the Luftwaffe would want to admit a desire to see the inside of a subhuman's dwelling, of course – even those who belittled the Führer's ravings in private were mindful of the effect such an admission would have on their careers – but by its very nature, the house of Master Plus invited comment and curiosity.

It was known as the House Without Windows.

Several of the windows on the upper floor were covered

with large sheets of canvas that permitted the light to come in, but blocked out all sight of the machine-town around it, and from these the house took its name. Occasionally people would swear they heard music from the upper floor – and more occasionally, singing, soft and sweet, an angel's voice. But nobody knew from whom it came.

Nobody except for Master Plus himself, the Generaloberst – and Alexis.

Master Plus ushered Alexis through the front door, looking left and right, up and down the street, before closing it behind them and turning the key in the lock. He turned to look at Alexis, the smile creeping up over his face underneath his caterpillar moustache.

"She's been asking after you, Herr Oberstleutnant... she's looking forward to the day of the wedding! Just imagine... the old church bells ringing again... the square alive with dancing! Why, we've not had a wedding in this town since... since..."

Alexis allowed the nervous prattle to tail off into silence. He cocked his head, gazing upon the smaller man with an undisguised sneer. Then, after a pause, he began to climb the stairs to the upper floor. Standing outside the heavy oak door, he waited as Master Plus bustled past him and ceremoniously withdrew a large jewelled key from his pocket, turning it in the lock with reverence. Alexis was half-amused at best by this – this undue ceremony, this imitation Blackbeard with his secret door. They'd been through this a hundred times. Surely by now he saw how ridiculous it all was?

"Are you decent, my little flower?"

The musical tones were muffled by the heavy oak of the door.

"It's all right, Papa. You can bring him in."

Master Plus gave a tight smile. "I've become a creature of habit, it seems." With that, he pushed open the heavy door, and the two men stepped into the room.

To say that Carina was beautiful was to call the noonday sun a flickering candle. This was not the only romantic cliché that applied to her.

Her skin was like coffee-coloured silk, her limbs long and supple, her lips soft and full, and so on and so forth, ad infinitum. But the cigarette advertisements on the hoardings in Berlin were as beautiful and similar songs were sung of the cabaret girls there, every night after ten. What those women lacked was the unique allure that comes with true grace in all its many meanings. Even if the rank and file were informed of the beauty that lived in the House Without Windows, they would never understand. Until one had seen Carina in motion, there could be no understanding.

As she padded across the carpet to meet her father her hips swayed gently back and forth like a cat twitching its tail. The hair that cascaded to her back flowed like water, tumbled like silk. It was a purely unconscious motion, without guile – Carina was an innocent in such matters, having been denied the opportunity to experience the heights and depths of human nature by her father. The intelligence that danced and sparkled in her green eyes was quick, and sharp, and alive – but caged. For the past nine years, Carina had lived the life of a fairytale princess. A princess locked in a tower.

The windows of her palatial rooms had canvas stretched upon them, painted with scenes of El Pasito as it had been in better days, before the occupation. These seemed completely real in every respect. The attention to detail was stunning, and the lack of depth was compensated for with a series of inbuilt optical illusions that made perspective appear where there was none. She had been kept in these rooms, looking through these trick windows, for nine years, with all possible luxuries provided for her – except the luxury of walking out through the hard oak door.

This bizarre set of circumstances had been created at the insistence of Master Plus, who had wished that his nine-year old child might be free of the horror that had befallen her world. The Ultimate Reich had been most co-operative in allowing him to realise this – for in many ways, Carina was as much an experiment as the rest of the town. Was it really possible to raise a human being to be so blind to reality? Was this the case with Carina, or was she only biding time? And if it could be done with her, could it be done with others?

As Carina moved to hug her father, Alexis moved to take hold of her hand and tugged sharply. Carina winced imperceptibly and turned to face him. He lifted the hand to his lips. They felt like a cobra brushing against her skin. Carina half-smiled, warily.

"Alexis. How pleasant to see you again."

"Carina. I've been counting the hours until our wedding day. I can hardly wait."

Carina's smile widened slightly, but it was a reflex action only. The hand in his grip tried to pull away. He did not allow it to. Her eyes narrowed.

Master Plus' wheedling voice shattered the moment.

"You will be wishing your life away, Herr Oberstleutnant! Come, have a pot of tea... or perhaps..." He tailed off, swallowing, as Alexis turned his cold eyes to pierce his. He stepped back, suddenly conscious of the way his forehead glistened, the clammy feel of his own skin. "That is to say... I did not mean..."

Alexis only smiled. "My life, Master Plus? Surely not." He smiled wider. Carina moved away, giving no sign that Alexis was even in the room, moving to pick up one of her books and settle herself down with it. At one time she had been flattered by Alexis' attentions. He remembered her adoring smiles, how she blushed when he looked her way, how her eyes once shone for his entrance. But those had been the reactions of a girl of fifteen who had never met a handsome young man before. In the years since she had simply grown to know him too well. She understood him now, and as a result she had become cold and distant. He could hardly blame her, but that was neither here nor there. The wedding would go ahead, or Master Plus and his daughter would simply vanish and never be heard from again.

Of course, it was mostly for the benefit of the locals and the psychologists, one more piece of data for the Great Experiment. It wouldn't be a true marriage of equals – the subhuman girl was sublime in her beauty, but that was merely an accident of genes and presumably masked imperfection elsewhere in her. The match would be very pleasant for him – for a brief while – but could not be expected to last any serious length of time. The only real question – one that had arisen in Alexis' mind in recent months as his respect for Carina's sharp mind had grown – was which of them would kill the other. But then, in such matters, Alexis was the superior.

"My apologies, Master Plus. I was... woolgathering." He smiled, turning his head, and slowly walked over to Carina, measuring his steps. "Until we meet again, Carina."

She did not look up. Master Plus coughed, then spoke up. "Come now, little flower, you can offer Herr

Oberstleutnant a kiss goodbye, can't you?"

Carina looked up at that, and looked at her father with a sweet smile, eyes like chips of green ice.

"Dear Papa, I am sure the dashing Herr Oberstleutnant will steal a kiss from my lips soon enough."

Master Plus almost choked. "Carina..."

Alexis chuckled. "I admire your... subtlety, Carina. It is, unfortunately, a skill I never learned... I will leave you with your father. Doubtless you and he have a great deal to talk about?"

Carina returned to her book as though he had said nothing. Alexis felt a wave of admiration for her, even as he nodded briskly to her coward of a father and silently walked through the oak door and down the steps. Admiration would change nothing, of course. It only made it clearer that Carina could not be underestimated. To allow himself the foolish cliché of the wedding night would be to sign his own death warrant.

He decided that she would not survive the carriage ride from the church.

After the meeting with Master Plus, Alexis needed something to take the taste from his mouth. It was always the same – the pleasure of seeing Carina's grace and beauty never lasted so long as the sickening feeling that came from standing in her father's obsequious, oleaginous presence. The man was like a ball of slime, a slug, a tainted creature who spread foulness – and worse, weakness – wherever he touched. The only way to cure himself of the pestilence that seemed to cover his flesh like a creeping tide of ants was to go to see Master Plus' opposite number.

Alexis strode purposefully towards the concrete bunker on the opposite side of the town, nodding to the menials as they performed their tasks. Already he began to feel better. Master Minus was a man after his own heart. Master Minus was in charge of Punishment.

The Palace Of Beautiful Thoughts, as it was known, was a grey concrete edifice that seemed like a simple blockhouse, but that was only what lay above ground. Beneath was a large complex of corridors and rooms – guesthouses for those who broke the rules of the town. There they were entertained by a man who was everything that the pathetic Master Plus was not – a true Aryan, a man who understood the meaning of iron will, an artist and a poet. By the time he reached the steel door, Alexis had a spring in his step.

"Hans! My good fellow. Is Master Minus inside?" It was a question that needed no answer – Master Minus was always inside.

Hans Bader smiled tightly as he performed the salute. "Jawohl, Oberstleutnant – the Master is in. He is, ah... working at the moment." Hans dropped his eyes to the ground. His duty for the past three years had been to guard the door of the bunker on the outside, and for this he was profoundly grateful. He had no desire to learn what lay inside.

"Ah, you are squeamish, Hans. Perhaps you could pass a little time with Master Minus yourself, hmmm? Help you get over these foolish attitudes. Open the door, Hans."

As Hans began to twist the handle that would open the heavy steel door, his hands began to shake. Alexis was not known for making idle threats.

Inside there was a small chamber with a number of leather suits hanging from pegs. Alexis stepped into the room and selected one of the suits as the door closed. The suits were baggy, shapeless and airtight, with a heavy faceplate, and every breath that Alexis took passed through filters over the nose and mouth, which cleansed the air of all impurities. It was a necessary precaution, for as the inner door slowly swung open, tendrils of sickly yellow seeped into the room, coiling around him like tentacles, attempting to catch him in their grip. Alexis stepped forward, lumbering in the bulky suit. He felt confined, weighed down. But he knew better than to discard the heavy leather. Only one man could keep his sanity in such a climate.

Stepping forward, Alexis entered The Palace Of Beautiful Thoughts.

The yellow mist contained massive doses of psychoactive chemicals – drugs designed to weaken the will, to bring paranoia, terror, euphoria and madness. This was the atmosphere a condemned man would breathe as he waited, chained and shackled, for Master Minus to reach him. Often, by the time Minus began his painstaking work on the flesh and psyche of his latest client, the victim would already be a broken, shaking wreck. Not that this would stop him.

Alexis wended his way down through the twisting corridors, listening to the unique sounds of the Palace – the sounds of screaming, sobbing, frenzied laughter, or that strange kittenish mewling, the guttural sound the throat made when all hope was lost. Beautiful thoughts, indeed! The spring returned to his step, even encased in the heavy leather, as he turned the corner to find himself in the main room that was reserved by Master Minus for the practice of his unique art.

The sight made him smile. An old man, more than sixty, was bound with iron manacles to a large metal rack, set at a forty-five degree angle. A corset of barbed wire had been wound around his stomach, and the bent, stick-thin figure of Master Minus was perched on a small set of steps, the better to reach his victim's face. Alexis watched the scalpel flash, the blade catching the light, reflecting as the blood seeped down across the neck and chest, which rose and fell like a bellows. Surely the man would have a heart attack at any moment! And yet, the touch of Minus was sure, and swift, and perfectly aligned with the planes of muscle and flesh, as the scalpel dug and carved and sliced. Scraps of pink and wet red, orange in the mist, flew with unerring accuracy towards a bucket reserved for such leavings. To Alexis, it was like watching a master sculptor putting the finishing touches to a great work of art.

"I will be right with you, Oberstleutnant, but I must not be interrupted at this critical stage. I'm sure you understand." The voice had the texture of old, dry parchment.

"Of course, Master Minus. Please, by all means – carry on." Idly, Alexis reflected that if Master Plus had spoken to him in such a manner, he would have been buried alive in a pit of caustic lime. But Master Minus was a different calibre of man altogether.

The scalpel flashed. The blade dug and stripped and cut. There were no screams – presumably either the victim was too far under the influence of the gas, or he had been properly anaesthetised beforehand. Pain was not the object, evidently.

Finally, Master Minus descended the steps, and the work was revealed – a shining skull. Eyes gazing without lids from the raw sockets, the jaw held in place with threads of muscle, still working, opening and closing, as the hands opened and closed at nothing and the barbed wire cut and tore at the flesh of the stomach.

Master Minus smiled softly.

"One of my better pieces. He will keep for a while, but it's important that I bring him to his daughter's house without too much delay. She must learn that spreading malicious gossip about Der Führer has certain... unfortunate consequences."

It was like conversing with an aged beetle. Master Minus must surely have been more than ninety years old. The flesh of his face hung in wrinkled folds and his body bent as he walked in slow, shuffling steps. The dark monk-like habit he wore covered most of his body, leaving only the shining bald pate of his head, and his wrinkled hands – his terrible artist's hands, that worked with such tender skill. Alexis smiled.

"You must forgive me if I fail to understand, Mein Herr. Why not simply take the woman for her crimes? It seems a somewhat roundabout method of punishment."

Master Minus chuckled, and the sound was like dry twigs cracking underfoot.

"I could not expect you to understand the concept of guilt, Oberstleutnant. I barely comprehend it myself except as one more colour for my palette. But take my word for it – there is no torture like that of guilt. Pain is useful, I will admit – as useful as a hammer, for pounding nails. But take a hammer alone to a block of purest marble and all that is left is rubble. The hammer must be used in concert with the chisel, and... but I am an old man, Herr Oberstleutnant. I could talk you into your grave and then wake you with my noise. Instead, let me give you a demonstration."

A flicker of light danced in the old man's eyes.

"Let me show you the true meaning of torture."

The yellow mist swirled in the air. Master Minus walked slowly to a rope hanging from one wall, and tugged. A small silver bell rang in the silence. Alexis leant forward, straining his ears, curious despite himself about what the old man would show him.

A door at the back of the room opened, and a shirtless boy of nineteen years walked through it. Subhuman, yes, but uncommonly handsome – perhaps as handsome as Alexis himself in his own inferior way. Alexis nodded in appreciation. "About to demonstrate your skill, Master Minus?"

"I already have, my dear Oberstleutnant. This man has been tortured. He has been broken, torn to pieces, placed beyond the limits of endurance and left there to scream until his throat gave out. He is a finished masterpiece."

Alexis frowned. "There is not a mark on him."

"Once again, you place too much importance on the physical world. Tell me, Oberstleutnant – what would you say is this young man's best feature?"

Alexis studied the boy's face for long moments.

"I suppose if I was forced to comment... I would say... his eyes. He has very striking eyes."

Without hesitation, the boy reached up to his face. Fingers scrabbled and dug at the flesh. A rivulet of blood ran from each of the sockets as he worked his fingers deeper... then tugged. There was a sickening popping sound – a wet suction – as his eyes were drawn from the bloody holes they'd rested in, still clinging to the stringy optic nerves. A further tug and those nerves were dangling on his cheeks amidst the blood.

The boy spoke a few words of halting Spanish, his eyeballs in his palms. Master Minus chuckled.

"He is offering them to you, Oberstleutnant. As a gift."

Alexis reached and took one of the eyeballs, examining it. Still very striking. "How did you manage it without marking the flesh?"

"Shame, Oberstleutnant. Humiliation. These are finely-honed skills. Guilt and self-hatred cut as fine and sharp and deep as a scalpel in the right hands... in my hands. When the soul is tearing at itself with hot claws, the body can be made to do anything the torturer wishes. Once that point has been reached, there is no more torture. There is only sculpture and poetry. Creativity worked in flesh. Do you understand me, Oberstleutnant?"

Alexis turned the eyeball around and around in his fingers with a half-smile. "I believe I do, Master Minus. I will have to visit you again soon. Perhaps I will try without my helmet, hmmm?"

Master Minus laughed. "I would not advise it, my friend. The air I breathe... I am adapted to this, yes? I breathe it every day. I'm used to the feelings it brings... the wonderful, heated shame. At this point, if I were to breathe the air outside – I would go mad. I have a suit myself for use when I leave the Palace."

"The black one. I remember it now. It's been some years since you've worn it."

"It has been some years since I've needed to leave, Oberstleutnant. But that reminds me – the General was asking after you. He and I have been in consultation over a difficult problem and now he requires your thoughts on the matter. If you'll proceed to the Red Dome, I will return to my patients..." He waved a hand towards the stripped skull of the man in the rack.

Alexis smiled, nodded, and moved back towards the airlock to strip the heavy leather suit off and return to the normal atmosphere.

As he walked back into the sunlight, he placed the eyeball in his mouth and bit down.

It was delicious.

In the centre of the city, within sight of the great statue, stood the Red Dome. Here sat the government for Aldea, the infernal heart of the terrible machine that drove the people to and fro on their tracks, that flew the flapping, hissing wingmen through their owned sky.

Here sat the Generaloberst.

Entry to the red dome was guarded by a platoon of soldiers below, and a flock of wingmen above, circling in formation, a halo of angels atop the devil's brow. Once all passes and permits had been checked, stamped and copied in triplicate for filing – a process that even Alexis was not excused from – the visitor was allowed to take the great spiral staircase to the waiting room. Here the soldiers would wait to have their leaves granted, to apply for transfer, to lodge a grievance, flirting with the pretty secretaries as the wheels of bureaucracy slowly turned and the clock ticked around to the time when they would be granted their belated audience. The General was a busy man.

Alexis needed no appointment, however. He nodded curtly to the secretary – a cool blonde of no more than twenty-two, most likely with a sweetheart among the officer class – knocked sharply on the oaken door and then walked into the main office.

This was the seat of power. An immense window dominated the east wall, looking out onto the town, and the statue. There was a red tint to the glass – plush red leather on the walls, the carpet a rich burgundy. Subdued lighting and gleaming gold furnishings gave the office an air of regality – a cross between the headquarters of a great banking company and the study of some deposed French king. The furniture itself, however, was paradoxically austere – a picture of the Führer (in happier times) and a picture of the General sat side by side on the wall, but neither were overly large or ostentatious. Indeed, the only things in the room which could properly be described as such were the desk of polished mahogany and red leather, and the sumptuous chair behind it, large and imposing, like the man seated in it. General Eisenberg.

His name meant 'Iron Mountain', and he was one of those lucky individuals for whom sobriquet and self unite in harmony. The General stood at six feet and seven inches. Even when sitting down, he seemed to loom over those he spoke to like some great outcrop of desert rock. A carpet of grey, close–cropped hair topped his great stone head, and his eyes were like hailstones. His face carried that certain touch of rugged fascination that came with the authority of war – in other aspects, it was like a fist, his stare or scowl a weapon to brutalise and subjugate those who dared oppose him.

His parents had died as part of an unsuccessful black operation on behalf of the Führer – the attempted coup, against the wishes of Victoria, which would have opened up Belgium and left Western Europe ripe for conquest. His first clear memory was being shown a lithograph of his father and mother hanging from a gallows in a Brussels jail.

An orphan at six years old, he had carried ammunition and medicine in the great assault on the Maginot Line, where so many thousands had died. He had seen men torn apart by the great Vickers guns, still living, men with bandaged eyes who eternally begged the orderlies to please remove their boots – they would do any favour if the doctor would only remove their boots and scratch that terrible itch that nagged even through morphine. Their boots were always a kilometer or more away, of course. With their feet. By eight, the boy carried a knife and pistol, and slit the throats of the wounded on the battlefield as they begged. No one had ordered him to do this – it was as logic dictated. While the French might take prisoners, and fatten them on good bread and cheese while their soldiery starved for bullets, Germany should never be so foolish. His voice was not yet broken, this boy, and yet he was stronger than grown men in this regard – or so the Führer would say, on the day they met.

Eisenberg grew to manhood and his place remained with the military. He participated in the bloody push into Italy, when Il Duce finally fell from favour. He had carried a clip of silver bullets in Hitler's terrible eastward push, fighting both the biting winter and the things that lurked on the Russian front. And he had returned alive to tell the tale when Der Führer finally had to choose between losing his face or losing his country under the terrible pressure of Her Majesty and her Soviet helpmeet, the man the British lovingly referred to as 'dear old Colonel K'. Be it the jungles of South–East Asia, the foothills of Spain or the endless deserts of Saudi Arabia, the Iron Mountain had been the Führer's implacable fist, his crushing hand. He had taken more and more power, greater and greater accolades, until finally his tireless work had led him here, to the plush, red leather chair, and the governance of the clockwork-town. This was the greatest reward – the most important duty. This was not just another of the Führer's plays at conquest, not a simple grab for more of the global pie. This was the future of Germany – and perhaps also the world.

It was hardly surprising, then, that he did not smile as his son entered the room. Such grave responsibility must preclude human feeling.

"Good afternoon, Father." Alexis displayed his very best smile, if only to provide a contrast. The red light that pervaded the room gave the easy grin an air of almost imperceptible menace.

Eisenberg's eyes narrowed, and the voice that echoed through the room was the sound of stone grinding upon stone.

"Within these walls, Oberstleutnant, I am the Generaloberst. Any biological relationship between the two of us is simply... coincidence. Nothing more. This constant lack of respect for my rank could soon become tiresome."

"My most profound apologies, Herr Generaloberst. Permission to stand at ease?"

The General leant back in his chair and sighed. "I should make you stand there all day and night. But I know it does no good whatsoever. My son and heir... I was informed of the mess you left this morning. Don't you worry that your proclivities might injure your chances at promotion?"

"The Führer shares my 'proclivities', Herr Generaloberst. I merely take a less efficient approach... more hands–on, as it were." Alexis grinned – that stage-star smile that charmed so many. The General only scowled in response and when he spoke, it was the low rumble of a glacier.

"I would not speak his name if I were you, boy." The huge man's eyes narrowed as his voice lowered to a whisper. "You are a deviant – and believe me, that is the kindest word for this fever that grips you. Without me to protect you, you would be bound for the camps. And I have no intention of protecting you at the cost of myself, Alexis. One day you will reach too far and I will be forced to choose between saving you or saving my career... and on that day..."

Alexis waved a hand through the air. "That day! That day has not come these past nine years, father! Nine years in a wasteland, driven to distraction by the boredom, the subhumans and the flies! I belong in Paris, or Milan, or on the Queen's Road, not cooped up with these animals! Is it any wonder I occasionally decide to amuse myself with their wretched bodies? It's either that or go mad!"

The General raised an eyebrow and gave the ghost of a smile.

"I could remark... no, no, I'd rather not start a fight at this hour. You're sane enough to be of use to me, put it that way. After all, if a wolf is in the woods, the sheep will more readily heed the bark of the sheepdog. Did you come for a particular reason, Alexis? Wedding plans, perhaps? I understand the lovely Carina is as taken with you as it is possible to be."

"Sarcasm ill becomes you, Herr Generaloberst."

"And your flippant attitude ill becomes an officer of the Ultimate Reich!" The General scowled as he rose from his seat and strode to the red-tinted window. "Do you understand the significance of what we do here, Alexis? Do you understand what Projekt Uhrwerk is? For decades Britain has loomed over the Reich like a vulture – allowing us to exist at her sufferance! And why? Because they have the technology to rule! A robot workforce to cater to their every need! While we – the superior race – must work with inferior robotics, clanking monsters of steel that can function only as terror machines! With an economy kept stunted by the cage Magna Britannia keeps us in! But no more! No more!"

Eisenberg's grey eyes flashed fire as he turned around. "Here is our laboratory, Alexis. Our testing ground. We have our robots now! Infinitely adaptable! Infinitely programmable! For they are crafted of human flesh! Our new robots will work tirelessly for the Führer – efficient, expendable and inexpensive. After all, we have been creating them since the apes came down from the trees. Imagine it, Herr Oberstleutnant! Berlin and Munich and Bonn running with the efficiency of Aldea! Cities ticking like well-made watches! A final solution to the tiresome individuality that leads to crime and perversion! An end to the twin burdens of free will and personal responsibility – the dirty and degrading chimera called morality! Can you see it, Alexis? Can you see the future?"

Alexis half-smiled. "This is a speech I've heard before, father. Besides, surely the experiment is a success by now? Time to go home, don't you think?"

Eisenberg sighed and turned back to the papers on his desk. "In six months, perhaps. A year at most. But there are still slight glitches in the machinery that must be set right... Come, if you're going to disrupt the peace and dignity of my office then you can put that twisted streak of yours to work. I'm deciding what to do with a special case." He beckoned, and Alexis walked around the desk. There, on top of the plush surface, lay a grainy sepia photograph of a man in his mid thirties, dressed in black with a shock of hair already shot through with grey. In his eyes was a look of weariness and infinite care, and at his throat was the small white square of a dog collar.

"It seems that for the past nine years, this man has been preaching the word of God to the citizens of Aldea. His name is Father Jesus Santiago."

Alexis shrugged. "Is that what a life of devout Christianity does to your looks?"

"Very droll. Very witty. But this sort of rabble-rousing is no laughing matter. When the good Father Santiago waves his God in the faces of good workers, it takes their mind away from their work and their Führer. Before very long, the people decide that perhaps his God would rather they did not obey. Perhaps his God would rather they rebel against us and martyr themselves to our bullets. We must not have that, Alexis. God cannot be tolerated."

"Master Minus will deal with Father Santiago, father."

"I think not. Oh, Master Minus is fine for destroying a man – or many men. But we are playing a different game today. It is not enough to finish Jesus Santiago, even if we string his guts between the houses like washing-lines and make the workers hang their clothes to dry on them. Our task is to finish God! We must kill him, grind his bones into dust, completely and utterly. We must rend the Almighty to shreds and hurl him from the rooftops like confetti! Even Master Minus admitted that this was a difficult task, although he's giving all his thought to the problem. But we felt your perspective might bring us some fresh insight."

The General looked up at his son, eyes narrowing. "Well, Alexis?"

Alexis smiled slowly.

The whip dug into Jesus Santiago's back as it roasted in the desert sun, leaving a red trail of bloody, ripped flesh. The crack was like a gunshot sounding over the crowd as the townspeople watched – and waited. Some of them were grinning, eyes glassy as they took in the show that had been laid on for them, while others looked at the ground, fearfully reaching into their clothes for hidden crosses. In the sky overhead, the Luftwaffe circled like vultures.

Santiago grimaced – but did not cry out. Not until the whip landed again, carving a bloody X into the flesh of his back. The priest was up on an improvised wooden stage, standing with his bare feet shoulder width apart, the tattered cuffs of his trousers held to his calves with rope – the rope that kept his ankles bound to the sturdy stage. He stood, stretched as through on a rack, his bare arms lashed together above his head with leather straps. A strong rope ran from his bound wrists through a pair of pulleys, and on the other side of that rope hung a wooden platform, the weight of which was enough to keep Santiago's body held up despite the blows of the whip staggering him.

Alexis held the whip.

"Where is God? Tell me, wretch. Where is God to be found here?" The whip whistled through the air again, marking the back twice, laying the flesh open. Santiago gritted his teeth, forcing his words out through the haze of red that shrouded his vision.

"In the hearts... of the people..."

"I see no people here, creature. I see subhuman scum! I see your executioners!" Alexis spat, and the whip landed another time, and another – cutting more slices out of the shaking flesh. Four shorter cuts now met the X at right angles.

Alexis had carved the swastika into Santiago's back.

He turned, addressing the crowd with a grin which would have befitted a wolf in the Black Forest. "Now, workers – you will show your obedience to the Führer! Each of you will take one stone – just one – and place it on the platform. Yes, the whole crowd of you will each take a stone... the penalty for doing otherwise will be death. By all means, think it over! But there is no shame in this act... How could anyone blame you? All you are doing is picking up a stone... a single stone..."

Santiago snarled. "Damn you!"

Alexis grinned. "Here is your God, Santiago. In these good men and women, each picking up their stone, because such a tiny act cannot possibly be unforgivable! Because everyone else is doing it – so why not they? Your God is dead! You see it now, and they see it too. Listen to the chink of the stones falling one upon another, Santiago – isn't it music? Sweeter than a hymn!"

The stones piled up, a small pyramid on the swaying platform, and the platform was weighed down by them, a little more, and then a little more... and with each stone, Jesus Santiago was stretched, bit by bit, as the agony built... until his joints and sinews screamed for mercy.

But no mercy came.

The men and women of the town shuffled forward, one by one, picking up a stone, dropping it on the platform, laying them reverently, gently. Then they wrung their hands, as though washing them clean. On and on it went. On and on, the silent procession of the shuffling damned, with only the sound of the clicking stones and the creaking pulleys echoing across –

Alexis snapped his head around.

"Who laughed?"

He scowled, raising his voice. The moment had been ruined.

"Who laughed? Tell me!"

It came again. The laughter. Rich and strong, echoing around the square, freezing the milling workers in their tracks. An awful laugh – a terrible laugh of hope and joy and strength! A sound that had not been heard in the clockwork-town for nine years!

In the Red Dome, Eisenberg heard the sound and blinked, unsure if he had imagined it.

In the House Without Windows, Carina looked up from her books with a gasp of shock, unable to stop herself from smiling wide. Such a laugh!

Deep in the belly of the Palace Of Beautiful Thoughts, no sound could penetrate, and yet a prisoner chuckled on the torture rack, as though amused by the great joke of life. Master Minus' scalpel clattered suddenly from numb fingers.

Such a laugh!

And suddenly, without warning, there appeared on a neighbouring rooftop a man, naked but for a pair of black trousers, ragged and stained with desert dust. His hair was long, filthy and unkempt, his beard was wild and home to insects, and over his eyes, there was tied a red sash, coated with old, dry blood, with holes cut to see by, the tail-ends flapping in the wind like pirate flags. His skin was baked and hard from the desert sun and the burning sand. To Alexis, who bathed so meticulously and treated his skin and hair with a thousand products, he seemed like some ugly, savage monster.

In one hand, the creature held a sword. Razor sharp – gleaming and glittering in the light – it pointed directly at Alexis. The smile on the creature's face was powerful and confident and utterly unafraid. To Alexis, it seemed like the smile the devil might have in the deepest pits of Hell.

The moment seemed to last a thousand years.

Far away, in Alexis' apartment, two enlisted men were beginning the grisly task of stripping Alexis' bed. They were preparing a large hessian sack for the corpse – it would then be taken to one of the pits on the outskirts of town reserved for the Aldean dead. The men did not speak as they worked...

...but as the sound of laughter echoed across the town, they shuddered and glanced at each other briefly, as though hearing the first sounds of an approaching storm.

The corpse lay under the sheets.

CHAPTER TWO

Beyond Thought

The moment ended as Alexis finally found his voice
– cracked and broken though it was.

"Kill him! Kill..."

He got no further. The masked man's foot slammed into
Alexis' angel face with a sound like a rifle shot. In the
time it had taken the Oberstleutnant to give the order,
the man in the mask had hurled himself from the roof,
landed on the stage with the grace of a cat, flipped onto
his hands and driven the ball of his bare foot into the
side of Alexis' jaw with enough force to loosen teeth.
For the crowd, it was like watching lightning in a bottle.
Jaws hung open and eyes that had been half-closed with
sullen anger or acceptance – or even a terrible ecstasy of
punishment – snapped wide.

Alexis stumbled back, his whip falling at Santiago's feet,
and he toppled off the narrow stage and hit the ground
beneath like a sack of flour, the wind driven out of him
in an instant. His head struck one of the wooden beams
that held the whole construction of the punishment-stage
up, and everything went dark.

The soldiers standing on the stage were still aiming
their guns, hesitant to fire – mere seconds had passed,
and besides, to pull the trigger would be to risk raking
the Oberstleutnant with bullets. As Alexis disappeared
from view over the edge of the wooden stage, one of
them – the sharpest – seized his chance. His name was
Udo Maurer and he was twenty-nine years old. He had
grown up in a small village just north of Lowenthal. His

grandmother smelled of cloves.

He had less than five seconds to live.

Udo Maurer squeezed the trigger on his MG-66, shooting a burst of lead directly towards the place where the masked man had stood an instant before. But by then he was no longer there. Udo's eyes lifted, and he watched the man turning a lazy somersault in the air – then his vision blacked out as the ball of the bare foot snapped down again, shattering his nose. He fell backwards, the gun still firing, muzzle veering to the left as it spat –

– Santiago flinched once as something stung his cheek and passed on its way –

– Anton Stroh, the other machine-gunner, felt nothing even as the bullet burst his head like a melon and lodged in the back of his helmet –

– and then Udo struck the ground, his gun clicking and clattering, out of ammo. His helmet had not been properly secured, and it bounced hard away from him. His eyes widened as he saw the masked man land like a cat on top of him, straddling him, his face a tight smile as his hand slammed down, the heel of the palm first, a hammer blow against Udo's exposed forehead that slammed his skull back into the stage with enough force to crack the wood.

All the lights went out in Udo. They weren't going to come on again. His heels drummed against the wood of the stage, but soon they would be still.

The masked man rolled and got to his feet, the sword still in his hand as he slashed, severing the rope that held up the heavy platform laden with its cargo of stones – the weight that was stretching the old priest like a bowstring. As the platform crashed to the stage, the stones clattering in a heap, Santiago fell forward with a gasp of released tension, slumping to the ground. The masked man swung his sword at the ropes binding his ankles, leaving only frayed ends.

"Move!"

Father Santiago knew that voice and did not know it. There was confidence there – an assurance that was unfamiliar, and yet... No. It couldn't be.

Heraclio was dead.

He rolled and ran, diving off the stage and then crawled beneath it.

Seconds had passed and the crowd were beginning to react. As was the Luftwaffe. The six wingmen above circled, moving into formation as their great metal wings clanked and whirred. It was often wondered how such unwieldy mechanisms could possibly keep the soldiers of the Luftwaffe in flight – as with so many things in Aldea, the truth was kept hidden, the better to promote a feeling of unease among the populace, as though the flying men had some terrible secret reserved only for diabolists. All magic tricks rely on a simple secret, and this one was achieved with a metal that could be bought in bulk from any industrial manufacturing firm in Germany – although at prohibitive expense: Cavorite, the 'nth metal' that powered Britain's economy, and to a lesser extent the Fatherland's. The clanking, hissing wings, driven to and fro by small jets of steam, were only for manoeuvrability – it was the cavorite that infused the metal of the wing-packs themselves, which allowed the Luftwaffe the freedom of birds.

Moritz Dresdner's voice carried above the clank and creak of his wings. "No machine-guns! If we fire on the crowd, we'll create more problems than we solve. Shoot him down with your Lugers! He's only one man!" Moritz Dresdner was the flight leader. He spoke from experience. Early in his career, he had fired an MG-62 into a small gathering of children – just as a warning, you understand – and that had indeed created a great many problems for him. He had been accused of wasting the resources of the Reich and given twenty days in the stockade.

He had also been fined thirty Marks, three for each dead child. So it was certainly no small matter.

The formation passed over the stage, firing directly down at the man in the mask, who tumbled forward, rolling like an acrobat, flipped nimbly onto his hands, then changed direction wildly as bullets raked the spot where he was – and where he would have been.

The eyes behind the red mask narrowed as he landed next to the fallen platform and its cargo of stones. Gripping one of them in his hand, he tested the weight. The flyers were wheeling back around in the sky for a second pass – playing it safe. He waited for his moment.

As the troops swooped towards him, he swung his arm around – his memory flashing back to countless hours, days, months in the heat of the desert, picking objects, testing, throwing, perfecting his aim into a skill, then a science. He had blocked so much from his mind, but it was all hidden inside him, waiting to be reclaimed at the proper time.

The stone left his hand.

Moritz Dresdner was not from Dresden, as his name suggested, but rather from the small village of Hegensdorf. In his twenty-five years, he had become used to a life of great and secure privilege – for Moritz Dresdner was a handsome man. In fact, to say he was handsome was to obscure the issue. Many men are handsome – it's a word that can mean a number of things. Moritz Dresdner had been the most handsome man in Hegensdorf from the age of thirteen onwards – and was loved for it, in that subconscious way that certain people are. It was far more than just phenomenal success with women – that old cliché clutched wistfully at by the monstrously ugly – no, this was a face which allowed its owner access to a world where anything could simply be had. Shopkeepers would smile at the handsome boy and laugh when he stole sweets from their counters. "Oh, that boy! He's a rascal. You can tell just to look at him!" Then they would turn around and give another child – who was not quite so handsome – a stiff clip around the ear for trying to sneak a look at the latest issue of The Pearl as it sat high up on the top shelf.

And so it went. Moritz was constantly showered with all the gifts, love and appreciation that regular, less photogenic children were denied. He would turn up at restaurants with the latest in a series of easy conquests – who, needless to say, thought of themselves as the one who could finally change his ways – and be shown to the best table, even though he had made no appointment. Despite his constant philandering and occasional trysts with married women (the husband of one of whom committed suicide), he was considered a pillar of the community – something of a rogue, perhaps, but certainly deserving of a free drink whenever he happened to be present in the bar. When he chose to join the army – tiring of his many luxuries, as those who have never tasted hardship often do – he was provided with a good overseas posting in the Luftwaffe, in a position of some importance on a vital mission for the future of the German Race. He had expected as much.

Moritz Dresdner had that quality, and it was most present in his smile – his clean, sparkling white teeth, arranged just so, not quite perfect but perfect in their very imperfection, his eyes that shined and twinkled. He could turn his smile on like a lamp, like the sun, and brighten the lives of any who came near. He had never imagined that it was possible to live any other way, but he had a dim understanding that his face was his fortune. As such, he kept very good care of his teeth and skin and occasionally laid awake at nights, with a fear he could not quite name.

It was the fear of this very moment.

The stone smashed into his face, knocking out his front teeth, chipping and shattering the rest, and breaking his nose. The impact cracked his jaw in two places and the sharp facets of the rock carved at his flesh, lacerating his lips. Moritz Dresdner, filled with panic and terror, bucked and jerked his body as he scrabbled at his destroyed face, and thus lost control of his wings.

The cavorite infused into the structure of the wing-pack was designed to compensate for the weight of the pack and rider, to enable the Luftwaffe to rise from the ground and make them mobile while in the air, but the cavorite ratio of each pack was carefully balanced for the individual rider's weight. Thus, if a wingman wanted to land, he could land. The downside was that if a wingman could not keep from crashing, then he would crash – as surely as a bird shot down from the sky.

He came down in the crowd. Up until this moment, the massed citizens of Aldea had been standing and watching the show, partly mesmerised at the display, partly afraid of the consequences of moving from the spot. But when Moritz Dresdner wheeled around towards them, desperately clutching at his ruined mouth, the assembled throng scattered in all directions, leaving him to crash down hard in the dirt, the crunch of impact breaking his jaw completely, crushing that handsome face beyond recognition.

Moritz would survive. He would be shipped out from Aldea, back to Germany, and spend six months in a treatment centre in Bremen before returning to the village of Hegensdorf. And twenty-two months after his return, friendless, deep in debt and awaiting trial for three counts of shoplifting, he would open his wrists with a pearl-handled straight-razor, still not fully comprehending exactly how it was his life could have changed so drastically.

The stone hit the ground, raising a little cloud of dust.

The man in the mask smiled. His voice was low and clear.

"Apologies. My hand slipped."

Under the stage, Father Santiago huddled and stared at the neatly punched holes, the sun shining through them. The holes where the bullets had gone right through the wood and into the dusty ground.

Soon, he thought, *they will happen to shoot at the piece of stage that I am under, and that will be the end. Or the Oberstleutnant will wake from his dreams and his first act will be to strangle me. Better than being stretched to death, I suppose. Oh Heavenly Father Above, look kindly on your foolish servant now. He did his best and now his life is in the hands of a madman.*

A familiar madman. Father Santiago sat under the stage, working at the ropes at his wrists, gnawing them, and tried to remember where he last heard that voice.

Dresdner had been the flight leader. There was a moment – a few seconds at the most after he smashed into the ground – when the five other wingmen simply looked at each other, flying in disorder, desperately trying to remember who would be next in line. Moritz, with his inbuilt certainty, had never prepared his unit for what might happen in the event of his face being smashed beyond recognition, and so there was no real second-in-command – it had never been fully decided.

So the masked man had a brief window of opportunity, and he used it. His hand took a stone, and then the stone left his hand. He picked up another and it left his hand too and then his hand found a third, as easily and quickly as thinking the words. It was beyond thought – as the action was conceived, it was carried out. Things merely were what they were and occurred in the order they occurred. Events took their place. He was in his element, and the world fitted around him like a glove. All past mistakes and triumphs were simply the causes that led to the current events. Things were what they were at any moment – and he filled that moment with the precise action needed.

Do you understand?

He did.

He had learned this concept in the desert, after his soul had shrieked at itself and torn itself apart with bloody claws for what seemed like a thousand years, and it was his total understanding of it that made him the most dangerous man on the planet.

The stone left his hand, joining the other two in flight.

The first stone hit Konrad Zumwald in the ribs, cracking one. The second smashed into the same rib, and the stabbing pain forced him to double over, aiming himself towards the ground. He saw the dangers and tried to pull up, against the screaming of his shattered rib, desperately attempting to right himself despite the agony.

Wolfgang Rader growled in anger, swooping forward

for the kill, readying his own pistol. He pointed the gun directly at the masked man's heart as the third stone flew.

This was the stone that did the damage. It hurtled into Konrad's balls, impacting hard against the testicles, ringing them like bells. Konrad gasped then screamed loud at the stabbing pain that ripped into his belly. He veered upwards, in front of Wolfgang Rader, at the same moment the other man pulled the trigger. A single bullet tore into the back of Konrad's neck, erupting through his throat in a gusher of hot blood, the crimson drops falling to earth like rain. Konrad's eyes went wide, glassy. He tumbled to the ground like a leaf.

Wolfgang was shaking, stiff, drifting in the air. Thirty minutes earlier he had been slapping Konrad on the back, promising him a beer in the mess hall to make up the rest of the debt he owed. A day before that, Konrad was grinning and pocketing the seventeen marks he had won from Wolfgang in the poker game and reminding his fellow wingman that he owed three more. Eight months before that, Wolfgang was teaching Konrad how the game of Seven Card Stud was played and the hierarchy of the winning hands. Three years before that, Wolfgang Rader was shaking the hand of Konrad Zumwald, originally from a district in Bonn, whose father was a doctor. "Welcome to the unit," he had said.

Konrad Zumwald hit the ground hard, the light fading from his eyes. The flesh of his throat flapped, ragged from the bullet that had torn through it. Wolfgang Rader dropped his gun and stared with eyes that didn't see.

He was thinking about a secret the two men had shared. A secret that would never be told to anyone, that was theirs alone. And now belonged to only him.

The man in the mask hurled himself left as three Luger

shots hit the wood of the stage, passing through the space he had so recently vacated. He reached out and let his fingertips find coiled leather – the bullwhip, still stained with Santiago's blood. His fist closed and jerked as he rolled up onto his knees, arm snapping out hard, the whip following –

– CRACK! The sound of domination! –

– and the tip of the whip curled around Marcel Renoux's Luger and tore it from his hand, fracturing the bones of the index and middle fingers. Marcel Renoux had been born in France, but moved to Germany at the age of eighteen with the express purpose of joining the Ultimate Reich. Life in Paris was too small, too chic, too petty. The obsession with Le Nouvelle Vague – it turned the stomach. Marcel dreamed of steel instead of silk, of fire and raised fists instead of cigarette smoke and clever words. He dreamed of what it might be like for the Ultimate Reich to march in his streets, to stride through Paris, to occupy it and bend it to their rule. His grandfather had died fighting back the Nazis on the Maginot Line, but there were always, and always would be, those who felt more than a little sympathy with the Führer's ideals.

He'd emigrated seven years ago, at the age of eighteen, head shaven, denim on his back, a cloud of contemptuous Gauloise smoke infesting his lungs. As he crossed the border, it was as though the air had become clean again. Immediately he marched into the nearest recruiting office and joined up. Sliding his feet into the jackboots had given him an erection, as is often the case when small men achieve small dreams of being controlled by big systems. The sound of domination was familiar and sweet to Marcel Renoux.

Two years ago, after a long, hard climb through the ranks, he had been transferred to Aldea. In his mind, it was his dream of a conquered Paris made real – and he strode through it with a smile of triumph, his leather boots creaking. He was a god, an Aryan, in a world that made sense to him.

Much more than a gun had been taken from Marcel Renoux. Such is often the way with men who worship power – they will bark and strut and snarl on command, but a crack of the whip will show them where the power really lies.

The whip cracked twice more, yanking the guns from the hands of the other two wingmen still airborne. The masked man caught the last one, whirled it around his finger and fired, a whirl of motion. The bullet sailed through the air, missing by a vast distance. The man in the mask looked down at the gun, a vexed expression on his face with the merest hint of humiliation.

The masked man had been in the desert for nine years. He had his sword with him. He had stones. He had his fists and his feet and the phantoms of his mind and he had time. Most importantly, he had the spark of madness, the fire of vengeance – and the understanding that all things were possible.

He had not had a gun.

Aiming one was a lot harder than it looked.

Perhaps in the future he would have a spare moment to practice. Not now. Now there was only time for action. His sword was in one hand, the whip in the other, and in the sky the wingmen were drawing their own swords, sharp as razors, swooping like eagles to move in for the kill.

He smiled, flicking the Luger back by its barrel.

The gun left his hand.

Underneath the stage, Father Santiago had managed to free his hands. His wrists burnt and ached from the ropes and the agony in his back was starting to make his vision blur. He could feel the trickle of fresh blood coursing down his spine every time he moved. He kept still, watching the bullets pound through the wood of the stage, getting closer to where he was, burying in the dirt inches from his feet.

Alexis murmured thickly, and began to stir.

Otto Baum was a simple man of simple pleasures. Out of all the members of the unit, he was the least complicated. He simply did as he was told. He was a big man, tall and skinny – if a soldier was too heavy, the cavorite would not be enough to help him achieve flight – and he packed a hard punch. His swordsmanship was proficient, and he had learned the hard art of air duelling with the simple, slogging perseverance with which he learned everything else. He was among the best of the Luftwaffe in this respect, which was obvious from his stance as he swooped in, ready to calmly chop off the masked man's head.

Which was why the butt of the hurled pistol slammed hard into the space between his eyes.

The masked man drew his own sword as Otto continued his fall, positioning the blade carefully. The gun hadn't hit hard enough to kill, but Otto's vision blanked and blurred and all he could think of was pain. It was only for an instant – three seconds at the very most.

That was long enough for Otto to fall onto the masked man's sword.

The point slid between the ribs and carved through one of the lungs, then slid out. Otto collapsed on the floor, choking blood before the blade chopped neatly down again, severing his spine at the base of the neck. After that, Otto Baum was even simpler, and he needed no pleasures at all.

The man in the mask looked up at his attackers and smiled. It was the kind of smile a gallant suitor might use to entice a fair señorita to dance, but it was contrasted by an icy gaze that promised quick death. Such a look might have worked to the swordsman's advantage had Wolfgang Rader not barrelled into him from the side, a mass of fists and tears, snarling and sobbing.

The death of Konrad Zumwald had driven Wolfgang to the brink of madness and beyond. Later, his fellow members of the Luftwaffe would wonder what it was the two men had shared that would make Rader attack so recklessly. Various theories would be expounded on the subject in the mess hall and in the dormitories, some of them scandalous, others simply scurrilous. The most common was that Konrad Zumwald and Wolfgang Rader had been having a sexual affair. Such things were uncommon among the soldiery for obvious reasons – the consequences for such a thing would be ignominy and death. But the very danger of such a punishment made such affairs, when they did occur, matters of deep and undeniable emotion. To risk death for a true love was something many soldiers could half-heartedly respect – even if they were, of course, disgusted and appalled and horrified, et cetera, that such a devil's practice could go on among proud soldiers of the Reich. They were quite wrong, anyway. Konrad Zumwald and Wolfgang Rader had not had any form of sexual contact whatsoever.

It was something quite different.

The masked man kept his grip on the sword, turning to meet the threat, slicing in a hard, quick, stroke, then sidestepping Wolfgang Rader's body as it flew on its way. The head of Wolfgang Rader arced up in a slow turn, lips working, gasping like a fish, then rolled along the stage to drop off the edge. The last thought in his severed mind before the blackness came was that he dearly wanted to tell his secret – the terrible secret, the long-held heart-deep secret that burned his lips every single day – but then there was the hard crunch of cracking bone and after that there were no thoughts at all.

So much for secrets.

Rader had sacrificed his life to give the two remaining men in the unit an opening. They took it, swords flashing, ready to carve up the masked man-like beef.

Father Santiago's mouth went dry as Alexis' eyes opened. At first there was confusion in the blue eyes, and then rage – terrible, burning rage, deep as the sea. He rolled over, and the expression on his face made Jesus Santiago clench his bladder for fear of wetting himself.

"Priest!"

Alexis snarled the word, spitting it. Slowly, he reached to his belt, gripping the sharp, cruel hunting knife he kept there. The blade was cut with seven notches. Seven kills. Alexis looked at it and grinned.

He smiled as the priest began to scramble backwards. "You like that swastika I drew on your back? There'll be another on your face in a moment, and two for your chest, and a nice big one for down between your..."

A severed head rolled off the stage and smacked hard into the back of Alexis' skull, hard enough to make a sound like bone cracking. Alexis went out like a light, slumping forward. He was lucky not to impale himself on his knife.

Santiago's eyes widened. He stared at the severed head, the eyes already rolling back. The lips twitched a couple of times, as though the head was trying to say something, to tell him something terrible and wonderful and strange.

It was down to Marcel Renoux and Hugo Stahl, and Hugo Stahl was the finest air duellist the Luftwaffe had produced.

The secret to air duelling is to combine the skills of the jousting knights of old with the killing instincts of the eagle swooping to catch prey. Two combatants dive, weave and spin on their metal wings, swords ready to murder, each aiming to strike their killing blow through the eye of their opponent's defence. The practice is bloody and savage, frowned upon by most of the officer class for its lack of discipline. The penalty for conducting an unauthorised air duel is six months in the stockade, or a year if there has been a fatality, with a fine of more than two hundred marks. Hardly small potatoes. Of his ten years with the Luftwaffe, Stahl had spent four years in the stockade for offences relating to air duelling.

That said, an air duel in progress is a strange and fascinating sight, a display of dazzling flight that requires the utmost skill from the combatants. So the Luftwaffe trained its wingmen scrupulously in the art of air duelling, and held mock-duels with blunt-tipped fencing foils each Sunday. Hugo Stahl routinely won these, and won the larger events that were held yearly (at least, during those times when he wasn't sitting in the stockade).

As a result, the wingmen of the Luftwaffe were accomplished swordsmen, used to the additional complexities and nuances of conducting sword-fights in the infinite arena of the sky. To face one of them on the ground and survive for sixty seconds would be a challenge that would push the finest duellist to his limits.

To face two was suicide.

The masked man smiled.

Renoux charged first, aiming his sword in a wide arc at neck height. The masked man held his ground, both hands gripping the pommel of his sword, shifting the blade to block the stroke and then aiming forward, attempting to plunge the point of the blade into Renoux's eye. Renoux reacted quickly, turning the masked man's blade aside and countering.

The blades rang as Stahl circled around like a hawk sighting a mouse. He grinned. At this angle it would be simplicity itself to thrust his sword into the masked man's back. The most beautiful thought of all to him was the knowledge that he would finally be able to kill – to spill blood, take life, stop the heart – and there would be no consequence. If anything, he would receive a commendation for a noble action in battle.

He was salivating at the thought as he swooped.

Marcel Renoux was sweating – his sword flashed and rang as his every blow was expertly parried and driven back by the man in the bloody mask. He was going about this the wrong way, he knew – treating it as a duel on the ground, hovering in close, barely a foot above the wood of the stage, not using the natural advantage flight gave him. Time to cut and run, recover his breath and then circle in for the kill... but then his eyes were drawn over the masked man's shoulder, to Hugo Stahl, diving, his sword up and ready to drive in, to kill.

Marcel Renoux allowed himself a tight smile as he suddenly pressed back his attack. In addition to the glance over the shoulder, it was too much of a signal.

The man in the mask suddenly flattened and spun, pirouetting out of the path of the plunging blade while deflecting Renoux's thrust from the front, leaving the Frenchman wide open. Stahl cursed as the point of his blade missed the masked man by inches, to pierce Marcel Renoux's breastbone – and then his heart.

The masked man grinned and swung. If Hugo Stahl had been any less of a fighter, he might have stayed still, wasting precious moments attempting fruitlessly to tug his blade from Renoux's chest, even as the killing blow cleaved the base of his neck. But Hugo Stahl was not a man who wasted moments. The moment his sword burst Renoux's heart, he let go, cursing once again, and flew out of reach of his enemy's sword-strike. The masked man's blade passed through the air where Stahl had been and buried in Marcel Renoux's neck.

It had taken less than half a second. The tight smile was still frozen on Renoux's face, as the second, bloody smile gaped wide beneath his chin, spilling blood down his chest. His eyes glazed as his knees buckled and he crumpled to the stage, his blood pooling and seeping between the wooden boards. Neither the masked man nor Hugo Stahl gave him a second glance.

Instead, they watched each other, Stahl circling, weaponless, the masked man with sword in hand but tied to the ground. Those few stragglers who'd remained in the square watched them. They held their breath. The whole battle had taken... three minutes? Four? Backup would be on the way at any moment, and then the masked man would be torn apart and killed. A flock of wingmen would descend on him, or a rush of ground troops armed with machine-guns. He was only one man.

One man who had killed five wingmen without breaking a sweat.

Some in the crowd held their breath in anticipation. One or two held it in wonder. These would be the ones who would begin to spread the legend.

Stahl circled, wings beating slowly, creaking in the still air. Then he swooped down. Not towards the masked man, but towards the Luger. Wolfgang Rader's Luger, lying on the dusty ground where it had fallen. One bullet had killed Zumwald, but there were seven shots still in the magazine. He could keep out of range and pick the masked man off at his leisure.

The man in the bloodstained mask dropped the whip and reached forward to take Stahl's sword from Renoux's chest. It did not come easily, but it slid out quickly enough, in the time it took Stahl to swoop down to the ground and grab the pistol.

A gun versus a sword.

Underneath the stage, Alexis blinked. The pain in his head was abominable – a hot, stabbing, throbbing pain, that threatened to make him vomit. There was something he had to remember to do. Someone he had to murder.

His eyes focussed on Jesus Santiago.

Hugo Stahl smiled. His aim with a bullet was not quite as perfect as his aim with a sword, but still, he was as proficient with a Luger in his hand as any man in the Luftwaffe. This time he would take into account his foe's seeming ability to dodge bullets. He would lead his pigeon, aim to wound. Perhaps one of the legs, or the gut, and then a shot to the head when the quarry was downed... Stahl's finger's closed around the pistol. He whirled, aiming carefully, watching to see which way his enemy would break.

The masked man's arm moved like lightning as Stahl's sword left his hand.

Stahl blinked, reflected light flashing into his eyes, spoiling his aim. Light reflected from something arcing towards him – a sword, his own sword. The sword he had polished and sharpened that very morning, flying towards him as straight and true as an arrow, thrown like a javelin –

– and then he was lying on the ground and his left side wouldn't move and there was pain right through him and blood in his eyes. His right hand reached up and touched the length of steel jutting from his forehead. He tried to remember what had happened and he couldn't think of the words. He couldn't think of anything but grey. Grey turning to black.

Hugo Stahl's body began to convulse, so hard that his sword began to teeter. It was lodged firmly between his eyes, in the folds of his ruptured brain, but its weight slowly turned his head to the side, as if he was settling to sleep.

The masked man smiled.

It had really been an excellent throw.

Alexis narrowed his eyes and snarled, like an animal ready to pounce. His head was clearing and the agony was subsiding somewhat, but the anger still held him in a red fog. He understood what had happened. He had been in control of the situation. He had been showing the worthless subhuman scum who was boss, who was in charge. And then he'd been thrown around like a child's doll by some lunatic caveman and – and this really was the icing on the cake – he'd been brained by the severed head of one of his own men.

He gripped the hilt of his hunting knife hard enough to whiten his knuckles. He would be revenged for this humiliation, and revenged now. The masked madman could wait – wait for backup to arrive and blow him into gobbets with sustained bursts of machine-gun fire, and never mind any workers who happened to get in the way. But the priest – the trembling, mewling Father Jesus Santiago – he would die now. He would die now and die in the ugliest manner. By the knife.

The snarl became a smile. Alexis crept forward.

Father Santiago was trembling, shaking like a leaf, a shell of a man, a wreck. His back was agony and his vision was beginning to grey at the edges through loss of blood. All he could do as Alexis closed in for the kill was try not to look into his eyes. If he didn't look, perhaps he could let himself believe in a quick death. He mumbled a soft, desperate prayer under his breath, for the strength to face what was about to happen.

There was a noise like a gunshot as the bullwhip cracked through the air. The leather tail laid itself on Alexis' face, snapping harshly, cutting it open down the cheek. Alexis screamed and fell back, clutching at his face with both hands, trying to stem the blood. His face had been broken. The film-star looks were gone in an instant, scarred, imperfect, ruined, gone. To Alexis it was worse than death. It tore through him on a level deeper than thought, and instantly his legs began to pump and work, scrambling him back, rolling him to his feet, carrying him away from that place. Tears and blood mixed on his cheek. When thought returned to him, he would feel worse than shame. And that would come to coalesce into a cold, hard, righteous anger, burning with freezing fire.

In time.

Now, he ran, and cried, and behind their windows and through their curtains, the town watched.

The man in the bloody mask dropped from the stage, sword coming down towards Alexis in a killing stroke, but he was already gone. In the distance, there was the sound of creaking, cracking steam-powered wings. A flock of predators.

Father Santiago looked up at the masked man, his vision blurring. He had seen him before somewhere... the day of the wedding... he knew if he could only remember who it was, then maybe he could ask him to help. His lips were moving but no sound came out. If he could only remember the name...

Slowly, everything went black.

Jesus Santiago collapsed.

Jesus Santiago sat up in his bed.

He was back in his little house, a tumbledown shack that looked abandoned from the outside – an illusion he'd carefully created to avoid detection. The shack had a large basement and it was here that Santiago slept. He often spent whole days down here, working by the light of one of the hundreds of old mass candles which he'd carefully stored and kept and rationed for nine years.

The shack was part of a long-abandoned satellite town of Pasito, a tiny knot of buildings nestled between cliffs two miles from the town itself. Even before the invasion, Santiago had been the only one who still lived there. Once it had been a thriving offshoot, a half-dozen strong new dwellings that might one day have become a town in their own right. But that was more than a century ago, and the cutting had failed to take root. Over a hundred years, families had moved back across the desert to Pasito, one by one, taking their belongings and often stripping their houses for wood until not even the frame was left. Even the old Santiago family home was in disrepair, so much so that it became a source of endless amusement to the townspeople. Indeed, Father Jesus very often began his covert sermons with a digression about how he really had to get around to fixing his roof or mending his windows or a hundred and one other small tasks that he never performed, drawing a little gentle mockery from his congregation before he moved onto more serious topics. Of course, they all knew the truth of the matter – Father Jesus Santiago was the most conscientious man you would ever meet, but he kept himself so busy with church and charity that he never had time to look after his dilapidated shack. It was only a place to get his head down for a few hours each night before he went back to the business of tending to his people. More often than not, he had spent his nights sleeping in the church.

The invaders had no way of knowing any of that. The one time they had bothered to search through the place, having stumbled across it while mapping a new patrol route through the desert, he had hidden in the basement, not moving, barely breathing, and they had missed the trapdoor that led down, underneath the rug. He had listened to them as they stood on top of it, discussing whether or not to burn the houses. Eventually they had decided to leave them be – it would be a waste of fuel and controlling the blaze would take away vital resources from the rest of the occupation. After four years of occupation, and with resistance at an all-time low, the scouting party had not even bothered to record the tumbledown shack on their map of the area.

And so Father Santiago's hovel became his hiding place, the base from which he conducted his own private war, without weapons or tactics – with nothing but his faith. It had turned his hair grey and driven deep wrinkles into the flesh of his face, and now it had carved throbbing scars into the muscles of his back.

His eyes focussed slowly, and he saw the stranger in the red mask looking at him with his head cocked.

"You've been out nearly two days, amigo. I thought you were a dead man."

Jesus swallowed, closing his eyes. He felt dead himself. The scars on his back still pulsed with heat. He reached to the bandages that had been wound carefully around his body. The wound had been dressed expertly. Where had the masked man learned that?

"How did..." he coughed hard, grimacing, as the swordsman handed him a cup of water. He drank in sips.

"How did I get you back? I remember where you used to live, Father Santiago. It's been a long time, but I still remember your battered old house."

"No, no... how did you know how to apply these bandages? The Djego I knew..." The stranger flinched as though he'd been struck. For a moment the only sound was the sound of the night wind in the desert above their heads. The priest was the first to speak again. "How did you know?"

The stranger rubbed the back of his head. "I forget. I forget so much, but it's all there for when I need it. I... I think I picked it up somewhere."

"Advanced first aid. Enough to save my life, and you 'picked it up somewhere'? What's happened to you, Djego?" Another flinch. Every mention of that name was a stab of a knife in his heart, a twist of a blade deep inside a wound that had scabbed and scarred over a thousand years ago. But the priest kept on. "I know who you are, Djego. What happened to you? What did you become?"

"Djego..." the masked man forced the word from his lip. "Djego is dead, Father Santiago. He was useless and stupid and pathetic. And he died and left good flesh behind. So I took his place." The eyes behind the mask met Santiago's then, and the priest breathed in sharply. There was nothing of Djego in them.

There was nothing human in them.

Something bigger had lodged there, something stronger and faster than a man, something with a laugh that could shake mountains and a spirit like hot iron and fire. Something better.

"I am his shadow. El Sombra."

This time the silence did not even have the benefit of the roaring desert wind to fill it.

Slowly, the priest began to smile.

"El Sombra. As good a name as any. All right, my friend, go and get us some coffee. We have a lot of work in front of us, you know?"

El Sombra relaxed, allowed himself a smile – one that promised great deeds and greater vengeance on the men who had stolen his life from him.

"Oh yes, amigo. A lot of work."

CHAPTER THREE

The Engine

Eisenberg was startled by the sound of the red telephone.

He had been leaning back in his creaking leather chair and watching the ceiling fan turn around and around. It seemed to him like four swords, cleaving the air with a regular slicing motion. He couldn't let go of the thought – the thought of the masked man, that bearded savage with his swords and his idiot grin and his terrible laughter, as though there was no finer thing to be doing on a hot summer's day than slaughtering good National Socialists. The masked man had killed his men, insulted his son and humiliated him. And now the red telephone. The red telephone that had never rung once, not in all the time he had been here, not until now.

Eisenberg took a morbid satisfaction in the thought that the ringing tone was as he had always imagined – like the rattling of metal bones, the jangling of some obscene talisman. He stared at the receiver as it vibrated in its cradle and considered ignoring it, but of course he could not. He might as well take the dagger from his belt and cut his own throat.

His arm seemed to reach on its own as he answered.

"Berlin calling, Generaloberst."

"Yes." His mouth was dry, his tongue like paper. There was silence at the other end of the line for a very long time.

"Generaloberst. Guten abend."

The sound.

A terrible chorus of clicking and crackling and buzzing, like some great mechanical insect from a child's nightmare slowly crawling up the telephone line to spit its venom. The scraping of metal on metal and glass on glass. And forever in the background the noise of the pistons, of hammers beating down in the foundries of Hell, the grotesque music of the machine.

This was the voice of his Führer.

"G-guten abend, Mein Führer." He swallowed. His temples throbbed. Fear took him. Perhaps he could bluff it out. The Führer surely would not yet know of –

"I understand there has been a disturbance of sorts."

There was no bluffing. He was a fool to even think it. The Führer knew, as he knew everything. *The lightning strikes the tall trees and not the blades of grass*, he thought bitterly. Which of the bastards had sold him out? Master Plus, perhaps, the fat little jailer, so aware of the precariousness of his position, so desperate to do anything to cement it. Or Master Minus, the sadistic little freak. The image of his son's face rose in his mind. Alexis, with his angel face, Alexis who left dead girls for the room service to pick up. The obedient second in command. Did he not have the most to gain? Would his own son be so ruthless as to – ?

"I am not used to being kept waiting, Generaloberst."

"I – I am sorry, Mein Führer. I was merely – merely gathering my thoughts so as to..."

The metal and glass made the approximation of a chuckle.

"You are afraid that this afternoon's little display will be the end for you."

Eisenberg closed his eyes, trying to ignore the whine and scream of the machine. "Jawohl, Mein Führer. Just so."

"Allow me to tell you a story, Herr Generaloberst. For a short time in Vienna, I had a room in a cheap boarding house. There were rats that came in the night to steal food and creep over my bedding. And so I put down poison. In the morning, I woke to find four or five dead around the skirting board, but there was one – as big as a cat. It was on its haunches, nibbling away at a lump of the poison – the same poison that had killed its brothers! Is it not a curious thing, Herr Generaloberst?"

Eisenberg's knuckles were white against the red of the phone. "Yes, Mein Führer. Very curious."

"I beat that rat to death with the heel of my boot, Herr Generaloberst. The poison had worked so well on so many, but there will always be one for whom it does not work. I learned that in my cold little room in Vienna, and many times since. You are learning it now. It is a fact of life, Mein Herr. There is always one."

Eisenberg could not breathe. The Führer was not relieving him of his post. There had been no order to return to Berlin. The great man understood. He sympathised! "I will crush him, Mein Führer. My men will not rest until he is in pieces!"

"Projekt Uhrwerk has come too far now to be allowed to falter, Generaloberst. By all means, make the attempt. But should the poison fail, do not feel offended if I provide you with the heel of a boot."

"Do you mean...?"

"Der Zinnsoldat is being readied for use."

"Mein Führer! I do not deserve such..."

"That will be all. Guten Abend, Generaloberst."

"Guten Abend, Mein Führer!"

The telephone clicked. The clatter and howl of the machine voice was replaced by silence. Gingerly, the General replaced the receiver in its crook, then leant back to once again contemplate the great ceiling fan as it swept in its measured circle. The blades of the fan no longer seemed to cutting the air of the room like a sword. Now, they seemed like four hands, extended, saluting in all directions. An endless salute, on and on forever.

Eisenberg was unaware he was smiling.

"I see you've got a new look."

A week had passed; the sun was again beginning its slow climb across the arc of the sky. In Jesus Santiago's cellar, El Sombra was eating a meal he had not had to skin himself, and eating it from a plate. The novelty of this situation was still so distracting to him that he barely heard the comment. He reached to run the tips of his fingers across his chin, the stubble scratching. All that was left of the wild tangle of beard was a rough moustache that stretched above his lips and down past the sides of his mouth. Similarly, the mass of hair above his temples had been chopped down to a manageable level. "The hair is getting into my eyes when I fight."

"It makes you look a bit less like a mountain man, you know? What's your next move?"

"I have no idea, amigo. Probably lots of stabbing. Is this lizard?"

The old priest smiled and shook his head. "Salt pork. You've been out a lot lately – I take it you're trying to draw some attention to yourself?"

The masked man was already tearing into the thin strip of meat hanging between his fingers. "Make a lot of noise and draw out the ones who killed my people – who killed me – who built this abomination on the bones of my home. When I meet them, they die, and this monster – this 'Aldea' – dies with them."

Jesus blinked. "That is... quite possibly the least well thought-out plan I have ever heard, my friend." He leaned over the table. "Do you know what will happen if you just charge in waving your sword?"

El Sombra was concentrating on a fried egg. "I'll kill the baby-faced bastard who murdered my brother, then I'll cut off his father's head and there'll be a parade."

The old priest chuckled humourlessly. "The only parade they'll hold in this town is for your corpse. The good men who watch over us from above will have killed the dangerous radical, the unmutualist with the mask and the sword, the serial killer, you know? You don't understand the power of the press around here. Besides, even if you do manage to kill ten wingmen, twenty, the General himself – there'll be another just like him here within the week, doing exactly the same thing. Also, you're going to need a knife and a fork to eat that."

El Sombra took hold of the egg, lifting it up like a wobbling white curtain, before biting into the yolk as it hung. It was a messy operation. Finally he spoke.

"Okay. Then I need to build a revolution. Drive those winged killers out and have an army ready if they come back. And for that I need the people on my side."

Jesus nodded. "That's more like it. Would you like another egg?"

"I couldn't possibly. You only have so many, and you're about to help me bring down an army of bastards. If the people are going to be on my side, I have to give them something. Something they don't have."

"Freedom."

El Sombra cocked his head. "A giant box of freedom? Where do I find one of those? I was thinking more of guns or medicine or strong drink, amigo. Start small. Is there some kind of storage depot or something the soldiers use?"

The old priest nodded again, taking a mason jug and uncorking it with his teeth. "Something better, my friend. Something much better."

Ewald Schenker had been in the Luftwaffe for twenty-two years, seven months, twenty-eight days and five hours. He had been inspired by stories of men who flew like birds, of honourable combat in the air, of modern-day Siegfrieds ruling the very skies. The recruiting officer who'd shaken his hand and led him away from his mother had promised him a world of action and adventure and the thrill of conquest, a life of opera and majesty. The reality had been a crushing disappointment.

Ewald Schenker drove the Traction Engine.

Oh, it was impressive enough. The Engine was an immense beast, fully forty feet long and sixteen across, with a crew of eleven. In appearance it looked much like an immense beetle. Twin treads at the side ran the length of the craft – the front ends raised to tackle obstacles – and a wide slit ran in front for the drivers to see out of. There were two levers, one for each tread, but in an emergency it was possible for one man to handle both, running back and forth between the massive.

Half of the space inside the beast was devoted to storage – this machine was first and foremost a transport for cargo and troops, though there were rumours that the Führer had considered mass-producing armed versions. Two men were tasked with guarding the cargo. It was an unenviable duty. They were allowed no distractions and simply stood to attention in the crushing heat. Were they even to engage in conversation – even look at each other – they would be taken off guard duty and made to work the firebox.

The firebox connected to a long chimney that rose from the centre of the roof and belched a never-ending torrent of thick black smoke into the sky, making the Engine visible for miles. Three strong men tended this furnace hour after hour, shovelling in coal and venting excess steam when necessary through pipes in the side of the craft. It was hot work – heat that made this chamber of the Engine resemble the fires of Hell. Working the firebox was a punishment detail.

The most pleasant job on the Engine was to be one of the four men riding up top, hanging onto the rails that ran around the outside of the roof. In the early days of the occupation, the Engine had been a target for rebels, but the roof guards, with their higher vantage point, were in a position to pick off any approaching raider from almost a mile away. Two of them carried sniping rifles for this very purpose – the others were armed with pistols. Up on the roof, they were free to hold conversations, and the burning heat of the desert sun was comfortable compared to the agonies endured by the men in the belly of the behemoth, men such as Ewald Schenker.

Ewald grimaced as he wiped more sweat from his brow and glanced over at his co-pilot. Bruckner seemed not to have a care in the world. Didn't he feel this accursed heat? Ewald felt a sudden wave of hatred for the chubby little wretch. How much longer would he be in this iron tomb, blasted by searing heat, chained to the odious Herr Bruckner? Herr Bruckner who had never read a book, who stuffed himself with day-old bratwurst and then farted the hours away in their confinement, who could not speak of a woman without giving a description of her imagined performance in the bedroom. Herr Bruckner, this oafish boor who was fifteen years younger than he, who had all his teeth and a full head of hair! Herr Bruckner, who joined the Luftwaffe only last year and would be his superior before this year was out! Herr Bruckner, who was constantly there, Herr Bruckner, Herr Bruckner, may the devil take Herr Bruckner! Ewald Schenker spat.

"This intolerable heat!"

Bruckner looked over with an amused grin. "There's nothing we can do about it, so we may as well ignore it." It was just the kind of mindless platitude that became him.

"We can take the route through the canyons again. That will give us some shade – the men up top will thank us for that, at least."

Bruckner frowned. "We shouldn't take the same route too many times. We could go around the mesa and be back at base in good time."

"Or we could go through the canyons and have an hour to spare. Perhaps even time to crack open one of those beers we're carrying when we get home, eh?" Ewald hated the wheedling tone in his own voice. Had it come to this? Begging Herr Bruckner for a moment's shade? For the illusion of shade – inside the guts of the engine, staring through the viewing slit, it would make little difference.

"Oh, very well." Bruckner sighed theatrically and tugged the lever, slowing his tread, forcing the machine to describe a slight arc that pointed it towards the distant canyons. "Why you want shade when you're already stuck inside a damned metal coffin is beyond me."

Ewald's face was crimson. He felt like a child. He stared straight ahead, watching the canyons slowly coming into view, and quite suddenly he wished Heinrich Bruckner dead. The thought was quite clear and distinct, almost as though it had been placed in his mind by another – *I wish Herr Bruckner were dead. I would not mind dying myself today, if I could first see him dead with my own eyes.*

Had he known his wish would come true within the hour, he may have thought differently.

For the most part, the rock walls of the canyon were high and steep, but in places they were only twelve feet off the ground. At those points it would be possible for a man to leap onto something passing below with only slight risk of injury. El Sombra waited patiently, pressed flat against the rock, listening for the unmistakable sound of the Engine as it chugged closer.

"You were right, they're going to come through this canyon."

Jesus nodded, taking a swig from a hip flask. "Mmm. When all this started, people used to try to attack the Engine, but anyone who attempted that died before they got close. They have sniper rifles on top, so they can pick..."

El Sombra smiled tightly. "Doesn't matter, amigo. This is close-up work. They aren't even wearing wings."

"I think they have some of their special flying-metal in the frame of the thing. To make it lighter, you know? Otherwise it couldn't move with the cargo in it. The guards on top used to have wings, but they probably figured they could cut corners. That's what it's all about – over time, they've got used to having no resistance. It's made them sloppy. Six, seven years ago, their routes were still all out in the open. They'd take the long way through the desert, so they could see for miles, pick off anybody they saw. Now they want to take shortcuts, get a little shade for the guys on top of the thing, you know? They've forgotten why they did it any other way."

"Let's remind them."

Georg Weber held the rail in his hands, enjoying the sudden cool as the engine passed into the shade of the canyon. It would be sausage tonight – sausage and potato and one of the beers that were down below, nestled between the bullets and the grenades. And then a patrol about the streets, watching the drones doing their work. And then – a letter to Gerda. He would tell her how much he was missing her, stuck in this backwater, and how he would be applying for a month's leave in the winter. He could take some work with old man Holtz and make them both a little money for extra fuel. They could sit together in her little apartment in Bremen and eat canned oysters, as they had done on their first night together, naked in the single bed, curled up with each other like a couple of playful kittens. Perhaps they could be married if her father had changed his mind. Best not to write of such things. It would only make it harder. Georg Weber glanced up as the shadow fell across him.

The point of the sword entered through his right eye, bursting it, diving into the soft tissue of the frontal lobe. Georg would think no more of Gerda now. His body hit the metal of the roof at the same time as El Sombra, his pistol clattering from its holster and over the side. The masked man stood, lifting the bloody tip of his sword from the corpse beneath.

"Good afternoon, gentlemen. Jump over the side and you might survive."

Rolff Waldschmidt was the first to react. Like lightning, he reached down to the holster in his belt, like one of the gangsters he used to watch every week at the old Kinema-house in Munich, bringing his pistol up to fire. El Sombra was faster, hurling his sword like a javelin, the point passing through the younger man's throat. Rolff pulled the trigger, but by that time he was falling backward in a spray of blood. The bullet soared into the sky.

Below, Bruckner looked up, one hand on the lever. "What are they doing up there? Was that a gunshot?"

Ewald shrugged. "Probably just horsing around, shooting at vultures. You know what Rolff's like. He's been warned about it before. This time tomorrow he'll be working the firebox instead of playing at gangsters, you mark my words." He looked sideways at the plump little man. "If you're so worried, go up and check, or get Stammler or Altmann to go."

"Stammler and Altmann have to guard the cargo – God in heaven!" There had been another heavy crash on the roof, followed by another crack of gunfire. "Damn it, I can't leave the steering until we're out of these canyons! I'm not trusting you to keep us from crashing. There'll be hell to pay for these idiots, I tell you now!"

Ewald gritted his teeth.

The loud crash had come from Klaus Mehlinger, a tall, reedy Austrian, who'd brought his sniper rifle up to bear before Jesus landed on his back, breaking his own fall by slamming the other man down into the metal. The two men immediately began rolling around the roof, attempting to trade punches and kicks, as the other sniper brought his gun up to his hip and fired at the unarmed El Sombra. Gunther Nagel was trained for long distances, and used to aiming from the shoulder, and so the bullet missed, passing within an inch of the masked man's cheek before smacking into the rock wall. The next shot would not miss.

As the engine swung out from the canyon exit, the sun blazed down on the roof of the craft, flashing into Gunther's eyes as his finger tightened on the trigger a second time. El Sombra lunged forward, the bullet passing harmlessly through the space where he had been one moment ago. His flat palms smacked against the hot metal of the roof and he flipped up, driving the ball of one foot against Gunther Nagel's forehead, smashing his head back into the chimney. The sound of Gunther's skull cracking mixed with the loud clang as the chimney buckled.

"Another gunshot! My God, what in hell is going on up there? I'm going to see what the matter is, Ewald. Try not to kill us all, will you?" Bruckner stood and moved to the small door that separated them from the firebox. As he opened it, clouds of black smoke swept into the steering chamber. "What in heaven..." Bruckner looked through, one arm in front of his face, ignoring Ewald choking and spluttering behind him. The smoke was backing up in the firebox! Two of the men continued to shovel, hacking up their guts – one had already vomited. "What in dear heaven's name is going on?"

Klaus Mehlinger, who was twenty-eight years old and whose fondest desire was to one day meet his four-year-old son, had managed to get his hands around Jesus' throat and was now pushing him back against the rail, attempting to tip him over onto the treads. Jesus attempted several ineffective punches into the larger man's gut, but this only made Klaus push harder. He had only been stationed here for two years, and when he'd made the long trip to Mexico, Aldea had a reputation as one of the safest postings in the Luftwaffe, and duty on the Traction Engine was the safest posting in Aldea. Klaus had never been in a situation like this in his entire life.

His uniform was soaked with sweat as he struggled, and his jaw was aching from where the priest has managed to get in a lucky punch. *A priest! Lord, this was madness! What was a priest doing here, doing this?* The unreality of it all made his head spin for a moment. He gritted his teeth. *A filthy Mexican priest. Push him onto the treads to join his subhuman God.* There was a noise behind him like someone sliding a butcher's knife through a cut of meat, but he did not dare to turn away – the priest was struggling too hard.

Klaus barely felt the sword as it sliced through the flesh and muscle of his throat, barely saw the spray of blood drenching the man he was fighting with, before strong hands had gripped his shoulders and hurled him onto the rushing treads. Suddenly he was moving very fast towards the front of the Engine. He tried to reach for the guard rail but his arms wouldn't move. In another moment there was a heavy thud and he was lying on desert rock and something was blocking out the sun. He tried to summon the breath to scream but could not. As his bones splintered, the memory of a cockroach being crushed underneath his father's shoe flashed in his mind – and then there was nothing at all.

The left-hand tread skidded suddenly on something wet, losing traction, the engine turning slightly as the opposite tread dug in. "Damn it, Bruckner! I can barely see! Bruckner!" Ewald shouted, eyes watering from the smoke, but there was no response. The clamour inside the Engine was too loud to shout through anyway. How long would he be expected to drive the machine by himself? He lunged over to the right-hand control, slowing it until the left-hand tread could dig in again. The sweat was pouring down his back, and he could feel a tightness in his chest. He was too old for this.

Bruckner was busy screaming at the men working on the firebox, doing everything short of whipping their hides to get them shovelling coal again despite the choking smoke. If the Engine ground to a halt in the middle of the desert, they were all dead. That ridiculous old windbag Schenker would have to suffer the indignity of doing his bloody job for a few more minutes – somebody had to take charge of this chaos, and that somebody was Heinrich Bruckner. His face was a mask of wrath as he began to undo the hatch leading to the roof.

El Sombra smiled. "Are you okay, amigo? For a moment it looked like you might be going overboard."

"I'll be fine, my friend. I just need to catch my breath." Jesus winced, shaking his head, his fingers feeling his throat. "That Nazi had a strong grip. I'm lucky to still have breath to catch – are we turning south?"

The masked man shook his head. "I don't think so. There's nothing to the south of us but a sheer cliff... ah, it's turning back again. Listen, amigo, you're not made for this kind of fight. You could get killed."

"And you can't?"

"Stay here. Leave the rest to me. In fact, you'd better take the sword. Both the pistols have gone over the side and I think we proved that these rifles aren't so helpful at close range."

Jesus opened his mouth to protest as El Sombra thrust the sword into his hand. The man was insane. God only knew what kind of hell they'd unleashed on themselves and he wanted to face it without a weapon! "You – you can't just give me your sword..."

The masked man smiled and shook his head. "It's okay, amigo. I trust you."

The sound of metal scraping against metal cut him short. On the other side of the buckled chimney, a hatchway swung open, emitting a belching cloud of black smoke. Turning away from the priest, El Sombra took a few paces towards it, then crouched down.

In the steering compartment, Ewald couldn't take any more. They were well away from the canyons now – he could stepping away from the controls for one minute to close the damned door and shut out the smoke. He was coughing his guts out and the pain in his chest was getting worse. He looked through the door, eyes slitted against the smoke, watching the men at the firebox, their bodies shuddering with hacking coughs as they loaded coal. Where was Bruckner, anyway?

There he was. Halfway up the ladder, his head poking through the hatch. Shouting something. Typical Bruckner. He wanted command of this whole...

Bruckner's shoulders twisted. One leg began to jerk, shaking and shuddering, slipping off the rung. His hands flopped, arms hanging limp at his sides. One of the men at the firebox turned as though he'd heard a sound, a snapping sound...

Bruckner tumbled off the ladder and crashed to the floor.

His head had been turned backwards on his shoulders.

Ewald slammed the door and drove the bolts home. He stood, blinking for a moment, trying to convince himself his eyes had played tricks. The tightness in his chest was unbearable.

El Sombra watched the body hit the floor, then jumped into the hole, his feet finding a soft landing on the dead man's back. The room was a mass of smoke, the noise unbearable – but he could make out three burly men armed with shovels. They were stripped to the waist, tattoos of naked women covering backs and arms, earrings glinting, teeth missing, noses broken and chins unshaven – tough guys. El Sombra grinned. It had all been too easy anyway.

"Call those tattoos? They make you look like Dusseldorf rent boys!" he barked in German, and laughed, the laugh turning into a hard cough in the smoky air. One of the men dropped his shovel in shock. Their eyes widened. "Oh yes, I speak your hideous language."

The first to react was the bullet-head with the swastika

over his right nipple. Snarling something in rural Bavarian, he swung his shovel for El Sombra's head. The masked man dodged beyond the range of the blow, his back bumping against the wall of the chamber. He wouldn't have been able to retreat any further, but then he didn't have to. As the momentum of Bullet Head's swing took him off balance, El Sombra gripped a rung of the ladder and swung his feet around, slamming both heels into the larger man's nose, breaking it for what was surely the fifth or sixth time. Bullet Head didn't fall. All he did was bellow, like some enraged animal. El Sombra jumped away, into the smoke, finding himself backing up against a bearded behemoth with a bandana wrapped around his head and a hoop dangling from his ear. The behemoth lunged, meaty arms wrapping around empty air as the masked man ducked, then rolled to avoid the sharp edge of a shovel being brought down with enough force to dent the metal flooring beneath. And things used to be so easy.

In the cargo bay, Stammler and Altmann listened. Stammler and Altmann had served in the cargo bay, day in, day out, for more than seven years. There was something of the hawk about these two men. For them, their duty was almost a pleasure – in their off hours they spent their time in almost total silence, sipping brandies in the officers' mess, looking out of the window. Waiting. Occasionally, one of the citizens of the town would hurry by on their way home, and then they would stand without making a sound, leave the mess and follow. Mostly, those citizens were never found. When they were – well, they had broken the curfew, most likely. And where would they find two men for the cargo bay on the level of Stammler and Altmann? It was best in the end to let such matters pass.

Stammler looked out of the corner of one eye at Altmann, who stared straight ahead. Scuffles up top. Three gunshots. Now some sort of fight was breaking out by the firebox. There had been episodes of roughhousing before, yes, and the roof guards had taken pot-shots at birds of prey in the past, then whined like children when the inevitable court-martial came. But this was a different matter.

Protocol stated that Stammler and Altmann were never to leave the cargo bay, from when the Engine started off from the supply depot, to when it pulled in at the base in the town. Even opening the door would lead to demotion and punishment – probably the firebox. Stammler looked at the door and listened. Then he nodded, very slightly.

Altmann unsheathed his knife.

Bullet Head struck lucky, catching El Sombra with a heavy kick at the end of his roll. The smoke was clearing through the hatch, and the masked man was easier to see now. The steel-capped boot slammed into his ribs with a noise like a side of meat being chopped by a butcher. El Sombra gritted his teeth, then let out a gasp as the wind was knocked out of him by the flat of one of the shovels, this one wielded by a huge Aryan thug with a facial scar that formed his lips into a constant sneer. "Hold him, Franz," murmured the scarred man to Bullet Head, as he twisted the shovel in a slippery grip, "I want to see the swine's face when I twist this inside his guts."

Ewald Schenker was shaking. His hand was slippery as it grasped the lever for the right-hand tread. His knuckles were white. He felt almost as though if he let go of the lever, he would fall. Would he ever stop falling if that happened? What was happening back there? What in God's name had those madmen done? The face of Heinrich Bruckner rose in his mind. The expression on the twisted corpse had been one of disbelief and outrage, as though Herr Bruckner was appalled that this should happen to him, of all people.c

It's my fault... I wished him dead.

Ewald swallowed, his eyes staring blankly through the slit at the front of the engine. He could not think like that. The barbarians were outside the door. They were killing each other. Bruckner was dead and he would be next. They would come through the door, and one would take Ewald's head in his hands, and slowly he would twist...

The pain built in his chest again. Ewald willed it away, but it would not stop. He could not breathe. Suddenly, the strength left his legs and he toppled, dragging the lever forward with his fall. The right-hand tread went into high gear with a terrible grinding noise, and with a hideous juddering motion the engine began to swing hard to the left.

In his mind, Ewald was still falling. He was falling and he could not breathe.

The sudden jerk threw Scarface off balance. "Was ist..."

El Sombra twisted off the ground, planting his hands

into the metal of the floor. Kicking out to the sides, he planted his right foot into Bullet Head's belly while the ball of his left foot slammed into Scarface's crotch. As the two men curled up, the Behemoth launched himself off the wall with a cry of rage. El Sombra brought his legs together to meet the charge, bunched them in – then kicked out, using the momentum of the Behemoth's charge, sending the attacker flying straight over him.

The aim was perfect. The Behemoth's head and shoulders jammed in to the open mouth of the firebox, his face against the blazing coal. His name was Gustav Dietz, and when he was seven his baby sister had giggled and called him 'funny face'. Funny face, funny face, look at the funny face. They called it a tragic accident when she fell into the river. At the funeral, he had barely masked his sense of victory, the flush of pride that he had stopped her teasing. Where was the funny face now?

His screams echoed around the engine.

Soon the funny face was gone.

Ewald's hand, shiny with sweat, slipped from the lever. As the lever snapped back to its normal position, the right-hand tread slowed. The engine came out of the turn and began to move straight ahead, towards the south.

The hand slapped against the chest and Ewald's corpse lay still.

Altmann turned to Stammler, who nodded again. The two of them moved to the door and took up positions either side. Their knives gleamed in the light from the window-slits.

Bullet Head recovered first, swinging his fists as El Sombra flipped onto his feet. The second punch connected – a blow to the side of the head that sent El Sombra stumbling back into the ladder, tripping as his feet tried to negotiate Bruckner's prone body. He fell sideways, clutching at the wall for support, seeing stars as Bullet Head moved in for the kill, reaching with hands like slabs for the masked man's face. "Eye for an eye, swine," he growled in his thick accent.

The sword came down hard through the hatch, the point raking down to tear open the flesh, carving a vicious trench through Bullet Head's skull, tearing off most of his nose and upper lip. As Bullet Head opened his mouth to scream, the tip of the blade tore his gum, scraped over the front teeth and drove into his tongue, then down through the bottom of his jaw into the hollow of his throat, to lodge in his chest. For a long moment, Jesus stared, pale and sick with horror, as he felt the sword vibrating in his grip with the heartbeat of the other man. Then Bullet Head jerked away, howling and choking on his own blood, the sword slipping from Jesus' slick palm and going with him.

El Sombra's vision began to clear. He took in the situation. Bullet Head was gurgling, choking on his own blood as he pleaded with Scarface. Was he pleading for help? For medical attention? To be put of his misery? It was impossible to tell. Scarface was bone white, frozen in place. El Sombra smiled.

Taking measured steps, he walked towards Bullet Head and spun him around, smiling as he looked into the wide, uncomprehending eyes.

"Amigo... that's my sword."

He took hold of the handle of the sword and twisted, driving down, bursting Bullet Head's heart, and then tugged upwards as though drawing the blade from a tight scabbard. Bullet Head tumbled to the floor, his blood dripping from El Sombra's chest, covering him in spatters down to his bare feet. The masked man grinned, like a cat with a bird. Scarface had shrunk back against the wall of the craft – now he swallowed, hard, as the point of the sword came to rest against his belly.

Jesus began to climb down the ladder. "Christ, it's a charnel house. I can't believe I did that."

"If you hadn't, it would have been my body at your feet." El Sombra smiled again, keeping his eyes locked on his enemy. The head of the shovel in Scarface's hand raised a fraction of an inch. El Sombra's smile widened and the sword shifted, digging into Scarface's flesh a quarter of an inch, making the larger man grunt in pain as a thin rivulet of blood crept down towards his belt. The shovel clattered against the metal flooring.

The priest spoke up again. "We should think about leaving, my friend. This thing's started heading south – and I think you said the only thing that way is a cliff? This beast doesn't seem to be slowing down much. We should grab what we can and bail."

El Sombra sighed. "That's a real shame. I was looking forward to taking this toy for a little ride. Can you imagine what this thing would do to a man if it rolled over him, amigo?"

"I don't have to."

"Oh, that guy. Well, perhaps he had an incurable disease. I bet we did him a favour. Hey, blondie!" He jabbed the sword again, another quarter inch. Scarface breathed in sharply, air laced with the stench of blood and the sickly-sweet smell of roasting human meat. "Which way to the cargo?"

Altmann and Stammler were listening through the metal door. They stood, muscles tensed, their combat knives ready, waiting for the next person to walk through.

The corners of Stammler's mouth twitched slightly before his expression resumed its natural state of blankness. It was as close as he ever came to smiling.

Scarface raised a finger and pointed. The finger shook.

Jesus took a step forward. "Okay, I'll go in there and get what I can..." El Sombra's free hand settled on his shoulder, stopping him in his tracks.

He shook his head. "You do that, amigo. I'll wait right here." He said, loudly.

El Sombra moved his eyes back to the scar-faced man. His finger raised to his lips. Then he gestured with the same hand in the direction of the door to the cargo bay: after you.

Scarface stood, and blinked. El Sombra twisted the sword, very slightly. Scarface begin to nod quickly.

When El Sombra tugged the point of the sword free of his body, he turned, casting a desperate glance behind him, and stepped towards the door, walking like a man condemned to the gallows. He raised his hand to knock, but the point of the sword jabbed into the small of his back. The hand moved to the handle, twisted, and pushed.

The door swung open, and almost immediately the blade of a knife seemed to grow through the back of Scarface's head. There was a sound like a heavy curtain tearing, his body jerked, and offal fell to the floor in a wet heap.

The blade at the back of the man's head vanished, and Scarface toppled backwards. The scarred face was split open, the torso ripped from chest to belly, and something that looked like wet red rope was trailing from the corpse to the offal on the floor. The offal that was preventing the door from swinging shut again.

In the doorway were two men with the eyes of hawks watching mice. Each held a dripping knife. "Unfortunate. The element of surprise is lost," said one, in a voice as soft and steady as a ticking clock.

"We can kill them both, no trouble." Murmured the other.

El Sombra smiled and replied in German. "Excuse me? I can understand you."

Jesus looked from one to the other. "What are you speaking? How do you know German?"

El Sombra shrugged. "I picked it up somewhere."

Jesus shook his head. "My Latin is a little rusty, you know? Maybe I should have a psychotic episode and wander the desert for nine years. What are they saying?"

"Nothing important. They're about to try and kill us both. Take a step back, amigo, I need room to work."

Jesus looked at the masked man for a second, and in that second Stammler moved. His arm became a blur of motion and in the next moment the knife was jutting from he priest's shoulder. It happened so fast that Jesus felt nothing. He looked at the knife as though it was something from a dream.

Stammler clicked his tongue.

The pain hit. Jesus cried out and stumbled back, landing with a thud on the metal floor. Gritting his teeth, he reached for the handle of the knife.

El Sombra spoke without taking his eyes off the two

men. "Don't take that knife out, amigo. That's what's keeping your blood in your body. Just stay down and leave this to me."

Altmann slowly raised his knife, taking the blade between finger and thumb.

El Sombra kept perfectly still.

Stammler's mouth twitched.

El Sombra tried to ignore his friend groaning in pain behind him. He tried to shut out the rumble of the engine. How long did he have before they went over the cliff? He breathed in. There was no sense thinking about that now. The important thing was to still the mind. Remember the desert. Remember the silence and solitude. Remember what was learned there.

Still the mind.

Altmann's hand moved. El Sombra's moved at the same instant.

The knife flew through the air, aimed directly at the masked man's heart –

– and ricocheted off the blade of El Sombra's sword.

Altmann blinked. "Unmöglich..."

El Sombra flashed a tight smile.

"Nothing is impossible."

He lunged forward, thrusting the blade into Altmann's heart. Altmann's jaw dropped and he took a faltering step backward. By that time, Stammler was already moving. He and Altmann had done everything together for seven years, and his death had meant less to Stammler than a drop of rain splashing against the back of his hand. For Stammler, the most important thing about Altmann's death was that it left El Sombra without his sword for a split second.

Stammler extended the knuckle of his middle finger and aimed for the masked man's throat with the speed of a striking cobra. First the trachea would be crushed. Then it would be a simple matter to remove the eyes. He would leave the optic nerves connected, so that pictures of what he did would continue to be sent to the brain. After that, he could retrieve his knife and begin work in earnest, as his foe writhed on the floor, gasping for a breath he would never take.

Stammler knew exactly how long a strong man took to suffocate. He knew what could be done in that time.

But El Sombra was still inside that silent place in his mind. He let go of his sword and shifted back so that Stammler's strike moved past into empty air, smashing against the metal of the open door. As Stammler's hand fractured with the force of the blow, El Sombra reached to grip it, closing his other hand around the forearm.

Less than a second had passed. Altmann was still on his feet, his reflexes keeping him standing. There was a foot of blade jutting from his chest. El Sombra brought Stammler's arm down onto it with all his strength.

El Sombra kept the killing edge of his brother's sword sharper than a razor. It was more than sharp enough to slice through the bone.

Altmann finally crumpled to the floor as Stammler looked down at the stump of his wrist. He held his other hand over the stump, but the blood continued to leak between the fingers, seeping out onto the floor. He let go and the blood came in quick pulses. As he stared at the mess that had once been his good right hand, Stammler was overcome with a feeling that some fundamental part of the world had gone terribly wrong. Some section of the world's great machinery had come loose. It was for him to take the hands and tongues and eyes of others. Not this. Not this at all.

El Sombra gripped his sword and pulled it free of Altmann's corpse, taking a quick look around the cargo bay. Then he stepped back into the main section of the Engine, leaving Stammler to it, and moved quickly towards Jesus. "Are you okay, amigo?"

"I've had some better days... Christ, this hurts!" the priest snarled through gritted teeth.

"There's a medical kit in there we can use, but mostly it's all guns, bombs, bullets... there are a couple of cases of beer. A reward for the troops, I think."

Jesus got slowly to his feet. "It sounds like the best... oww... the best place for all that is at the bottom of a cliff... speaking of which, we should move. Grab a case of the beer and the medical kit, I'll... I'll see if I can get up this ladder with one hand."

Stammler did not move as the masked man walked past him, grabbed two boxes and left. He felt grey, washed out. The pool of blood he was sitting in was getting larger no matter how tightly he gripped his wrist. As the masked man helped the other one up the ladder, Stammler realised that he was going to die. The notion did not trouble him in itself. But the thought that his killer – the masked man – would continue to live, with both his hands... that was an irritation. A splinter stuck in the corner of his mind. He should really do something about that.

Slowly, he stood.

El Sombra passed the medical kit and the case of beer up to Jesus through the hatch as the Engine rumbled on. Jesus picked up the beer with his good hand and hurled it over the side to land in a patch of sand. The kit followed. The priest winced, gritting his teeth. "I hope the bottles don't break – oww! Christ, I should have let you do that!"

El Sombra nodded. "You're lucky you didnt make your wound worse. Do I have time to get another load?"

The priest shook his head. "No. I can see the cliffs. We should jump now rather than take any risks. You're going to have to help me make the... oh my god –"

An arm without a hand wound around El Sombra's throat. Blood sprayed in his eyes. He lost his grip as Stammler's weight dragged him off the ladder and back into the Engine, the breath knocked out of him as he slammed into the floor. Blinking away the blood, the first thing he saw was Stammler's fist before it smashed into his jaw, loosening teeth. The stump smacking into the side of his head, sending more blood into his eyes. His sword had fallen within reach, he was sure, but he did not know where. His fingers scrabbled fruitlessly.

Stammler straddled El Sombra. Keep him off balance, that was the main thing. He aimed a blow at the masked man's forehead, but El Sombra swept an arm across and diverted the blow enough to crash it into the metal next to his head. Stammler ignored the pain. He only needed to hit once, and his own blood was proving a useful weapon. A few more seconds of life, that was all it would take.

Jesus' voice cut through the rumble of the Engine. "We're getting close to the edge! We need to jump now!"

It was true. There was perhaps six feet of distance between the front of the treads and the edge of the cliff. More than one hundred feet below, the Engine would make its grave.

El Sombra blinked blood out of his eyes as he somehow managed to redirect another hammer blow. His attacker's knuckles were smashed, fingers broken, and he had surely lost too much blood to stay alive, and yet here he was, readying another killing strike. El Sombra wondered if this was how he himself appeared to people, even as he saw the only opening he had and took it.

He reached down to grip Stammler's crotch through the fabric of the uniform, and he squeezed until something burst.

Stammler flinched.

It was enough. El Sombra drove the heel of his palm up into Stammler's nose, driving shards of bone deep into the brain, then rolled the convulsing man off him. His sword had been inches from his hand the whole time – how long had it been? Five seconds? Four?

The floor was beginning to tilt.

Jesus realised that this was perhaps his last chance to escape. The Engine was slowing even as it reached the edge of the cliff, but it would not be enough. If he was to survive, he had to leap, to hurl himself from the back of the beast before it tipped. The fronts of the treads were already in empty space. Instead, he fell to the roof and thrust his good arm through the hatchway. "Grab my hand! Quickly!"

El Sombra leapt upwards, feet on the rungs of the ladder, taking hold of the priest's arm as the older man used all the strength left in him to help haul his friend up through the hatchway. The angle of the roof was growing steeper.

The Engine was going over the edge.

El Sombra got to his feet, grabbed the old priest by the collar and hauled him up the slope, bare feet pounding the metal. The Engine should have tipped by now – but the cavorite in the frame of the machine was slowing things. Jesus was screaming something about dropping him – something self-sacrificing of that nature – but El Sombra was too busy making his legs move. It was like running up the side of a steel mountain.

Dragging Jesus with him, the masked man vaulted the rail and leapt, as the back of the machine left the cliff's edge, the mobile coffin starting a lazy descent towards the rocks below, accelerating as the force of gravity overcame the ingrained cavorite. He stretched out his arm –

And the point of the sword slammed into the sand, a foot from the edge of the cliff. He swung the priest up with his other arm, muscles straining and threatening to tear, and Jesus managed to catch the cliff's edge with his good hand. Slowly they began dragging themselves up onto solid ground.

"Damn," panted Jesus as he flopped onto his back, his legs dangling off the edge. "My shoulder really hurts. We should... we should go find that medical kit."

"Yes, we should." El Sombra spat a tooth out onto the desert sand. A molar.

"We should go find the beer as well."

"Oh yes, amigo. Most definitely."

Eisenberg leant back in the leather chair and looked at the ceiling fan as it turned. There was a report on his desk detailing the loss of the Traction Engine, and how supplies would now have to be marched across the desert for the foreseeable future. This would create rationing problems and ammo shortages. Already there was open insubordination caused by the lack of beer in the mess hall.

Curiously, there were rumours that curfew-breakers had been spotted with bottles of German beer in their hands, toasting to Old Pasito, and the gossip claimed that a man in a bloodstained mask had given them out to any bold enough to drink and toast openly. Eisenberg shut his eyes tightly and massaged his temples, attempting to disperse the oncoming headache.

The red telephone began to ring.

CHAPTER FOUR

How It Had All Started

The sun rose over the desert, on the man known as El Sombra. He sat cross-legged on a rocky outcrop, examining the small blisters that spotted the soles of his feet. His flesh ached and burns covered his arms and back. He still coughed occasionally, spitting out soot-coloured phlegm from the back of his throat. He was very lucky to be alive.

He did not feel it.

Drawing his sword, he examined the blade in the light of the dawn. He could still see the blood staining the metal, coating it in places. Normally he would have cleaned the sword by now – it was sacred to him, and he kept it as immaculate as he could. But this morning was different. He needed to be reminded of what he'd done the previous night, and whose blood was on the blade.

He needed to punish himself.

He remembered how it had all started.

Who was the man known as El Sombra?

He was a thousand different things in the clockwork-town, because there were a thousand different answers to the question. Since the raid on the Traction Engine the stories had been spreading like plague – even the most diligent worker, whose only thought was of the glory of the Reich, could not help hearing something on the matter. The stories fell on the ears and worked their way into the mind, past the conditioning and the programming and the thousand daily indignities designed to make human beings forget that they were alive. The stories brought back memories of how it was to live without the wingmen and their clattering metal wings, the guards and their guns, the jackboots. How it was to live without an alarm siren that woke you from your bed and forced you to march through blistering heat or freezing cold to do tasks without meaning for people who thought you less than human. For some, that was terrifying.

"El Sombra is a monster, a lunatic, a psychopath, a murderer, a cannibal. He ought to be hung from a gallows in the great square, in front of the statue! His innards should be defecated in by dogs. Dogs with diseases."

El Sombra looked up from the book he was reading – a copy of *Teresa's Temptation*, the latest from Dame Judith Cooper, a sizzling potboiler of sex, money, power, more money and sex set in the legendary fashion 'families' of Milan. He'd liberated it a couple of days before along with a few thousand rounds of ammunition, and had just reached the part where the beautiful fashionista was in the process of having it all, on top of her desk and in the company of the handsome chief designer who was secretly her brother.

The book was a hard-won luxury, the first one he'd read in nine long years. It wasn't the best thing to be caught reading by a priest.

"What did you say?"

Jesus cleared his throat and began again. "El Sombra is a monster, a lunatic..."

"I do have feelings, amigo. Is this about eating all your eggs?"

Jesus leant against the doorway with a grin. "I'm only repeating what I heard today. You have an image problem, my friend. The general populace sees you as supernatural at best, some kind of demon at worst... they actually make these little wooden stick-men to hang on the door to ward against you coming into their homes and eating their children."

The masked man shrugged, laying the book down open on the floor so as not to lose his place. "Supernatural I can live with, amigo. Besides, what can I do? I can't stop people talking about me."

"So give them something to talk about. Right now, all they have is that you run around half-naked with a sword in your hand killing people and stealing things and you're completely out of your mind, you know? You think that's going to endear you to anybody?"

El Sombra sighed, casting a glance down at the book. "So what can I do? Throw a street party? Maybe set up a puppet show for the little orphans?"

"I hate to deny such eloquent sarcasm, my friend, but you're thinking along the right lines. Remember what you said about getting the people on your side? Guns, medicine, strong drink?"

"It's harder to get anybody to take the guns than I thought. They're all terrified of getting caught and tortured. Same with the medicine – if I leave it for the people, it just goes back to the bastards. So I stash everything in little caches, places the bastards won't look, only it's no use to anybody there."

"What about the drink?"

"You drank it."

"Ah, yes. Well, I'm in recovery, you know? It's medicinal. Hey, maybe one of the reasons the people won't take any risks for you is because you're not doing anything for them."

"Guns, amigo! Strong drink!"

"That's all for you. When you wave a gun in some poor man's face – some guy who's lived only for that damned statue for nine years, who's maybe seen his family taken away to the Palace and coming back without any arms and legs, repeating Arbeit Macht Frei over and over like gramophones – what's he going to think? 'Oh, I will immediately join the violent struggle for revolution and die for this crazy man who doesn't seem to like shirts'? Of course not! He's going to soil himself and run away."

El Sombra blinked.

Jesus barrelled on, warming to his theme. "But if you've been doing things for them - not going out on sorties to kill people and steal things, just going out looking for people in trouble and helping them, you know? – then maybe the guy would think 'Yes! Now I'm being handed a gun by my friend who helps people in need! Why of course I'll get myself shot in the face for you, oh mysterious ghost with no shirt!'"

"I could wear a shirt if it would make you feel happier, amigo..."

"No, no, you're obviously very proud of your nipples, I wouldn't like to take that away from you. What I'm saying is that you need to bring some hope to these people. Right now, all you are is a story for parents to tell their children to get them to eat their vegetables, you know? Right now people trust the Nazis, because they control everything – they control how people think. The more you do for them, the more they trust you."

El Sombra looked at him.

Jesus swallowed. "Or something. It's not an exact science, you know?"

The masked man stood, stretched, and reached for his sword.

"So what you're saying is that I should run around all night, not killing any bastards, but checking to see if any old ladies need helping across the street?" He hefted the blade, then slid it through his belt. "Fine." He scowled, the thick moustache bristling as his eyes glared.

"But I don't promise to like it."

And he didn't. As he stalked over the low roofs, jumping across the alleys, eyes looking around for something to do, the wasted time hung heavy on him. He was used to striking quickly, with a specific target in mind – such as a raid on one of the supply depots, already badly understocked since the demise of the Traction Engine, or an attack on a small group of guardsmen to put the fear of God into the rest. This 'patrol', as Jesus had called it, was ridiculous. The chances of him coming across anything that he could usefully prevent were thousands to one. The most he could achieve would be to find evidence of some atrocity after it had occurred.

El Sombra was so fixed on his thoughts that he didn't notice the orange/yellow light flickering over the rooftops from the west. But he heard the screams. Changing course, he headed west, jumping across the rooftops, keeping to the shadows. The smell of the thick, black smoke hit him first, and beneath it another scent. A sickly sweet smell, like roasting pork.

The schoolhouse was burning.

The two-storey building had been deserted since the invasion. In the early days it had been used as a centre for administration by the Reich, but after the construction of the Red Dome, the schoolhouse had been abandoned. It was still occasionally useful, but for the most part it had been empty for eight years or more. There was no need for learning in Aldea. Every lesson of importance was taught as the children picked up their heavy stones for the first time, under the cracking whips of the overseers, struggling and hefting the rocks towards the great half-built statue.

The first lesson in Aldea was: You do not matter. The second was: You will obey. Anything else was superfluous.

El Sombra reached the conflagration, looking at it from the edge of a rooftop. It was like something out of Hell. The wooden schoolhouse was the wick of some terrible candle, burning and flickering, and around it was a circle of soldiers, armed with long metal batons, with their backs facing the blaze. As the masked man watched, one of the townspeople rushed forward with a tin bucket filled with water, screaming something he couldn't quite catch. The reaction was merciless. Two soldiers stepped forward and swung their sticks at the same instant, the riveted metal ends cracking hard into the man's ribcage. The sickening crack of snapping bone echoed through the night air as the bucket fell, the water spilling into the dirt.

The masked man was already swinging off the roof. But the sound he heard as he fell to the ground added speed to his movement – and stoked a fire in his heart that matched the inferno in front of him.

It was the scream of a child burning to death.

He hit the ground like thunder and judgement.

Roland Koch was a slightly tubby man of around forty years of age. Born in Bremen, he had never set foot outside that city until he'd boarded the zeppelin to Mexico and his post in Aldea. He was not one for zoos, and so had never come within fifty feet of a maddened tiger. But if he had, then the snarl of animal fury that met his ears – at the same time that a lashing foot kicked him ten feet backwards into the heart of the blaze – might have sounded familiar.

Still, it's probable that even then he would be too concerned with his own burning flesh to make the connection.

El Sombra was a whirlwind, a dervish, a demon of movement and motion and violence. His elbow cracked hard against the forehead of a new recruit and the young man crumpled dead to the earth. He spun without pausing and the heel of his foot slammed into the soft trachea of an eighteen-year-old who had joined the squadron the previous week and had, it was agreed by all, a glittering future in front of him. That glittering future was now two and a half minutes long and did not involve breathing. And now the sword – that terrible blood-tempered sword – slashed from the masked daredevil's belt with a terrible sound of razors and hate, plunging into the neck of a father of two who wrote letters to his family in Bonn every two days, leaving it a flapping, gushing ruin. A boy and a girl would not have their letter that weekend – instead there would be a cold telegram from the Führer expressing regret, and their dreams forever after would be haunted by the clang of steel and the crash of thunder.

Perhaps their names should be recorded for posterity, these doomed soldiers who only followed orders – but it is more fitting to leave them as ciphers. They were wheat in the thresher, sheep fed to the slaughterhouse. The sword flashed in the light of the flames, glinting red with the fire and the blood as it carved and chopped though the men as though they were kindling. He was a blur of speed – leaping over the swinging metal truncheons, spinning into kicks that cracked jaws and broke noses, a flurry of punches slamming into soft bellies. One by one, the soldiers fell back, unconscious or dead, bodies around the bonfire.

It was a massacre.

Climaco Aguilar lay on the ground, clutching his shattered rib, the empty bucket at his side, and he remembered how this had all started. For years, the old schoolhouse had lain empty and desolate and the children had gone without books, without learning, growing up as automatons for the glory of the Reich.

Children of seven and eight, who should have been laughing and bubbling with joy and life, were walking in step, marching, their faces blank and empty, their eyes glazed and dead. The townsfolk had survived only through capitulation – those who resisted, in word or deed, were killed. But the sight of their own children reduced to shells, stumbling on little legs as they hauled stone blocks to the statue, passing out at the end of each day through sheer exhaustion while their skin turned sallow and grey, was enough to bring back those forgotten thoughts of rebellion.

They began to meet after dark, no more than three or four at a time – any more and the soldiers might have discovered their secret. They could not give their children food, or clothing, or even heat in the winter – everyone was allocated the same resources, just enough to keep them from starvation. Any family caught sharing their rations went to the Palace Of Beautiful Thoughts for a session with Master Minus.

All they could offer was education.

Not much – an hour a week at most, stolen after dark. Tiny groups of children smuggled to the schoolhouse and given the very basics – reading, writing, learning to count. Sometimes as little as reading to them of the world outside – anything at all to counter the endless propaganda hurled at them by their new rulers. Isidoro the schoolteacher was long dead, but his wife Verdad was alive and more than happy to carry on her husband's work, despite the risk to her aged bones.

For two and a half years, it had carried on. Years of paranoia, almost constant fear of discovery, but the fear was worth it to see the children smiling when their minds drifted to the delicious secrets that Verdad had given them, counting to ten in their heads or thinking of Magna Britannia, that country far away where there was a mechanical man to serve every family and the children had sugar-drops when they were good.

Tonight, things had proceeded as normal – the children shepherded in, the lessons beginning as usual. Climaco was watching for any soldiers when the flames first started licking at the sides of the building – the fire had started from inside, God only knew how. And then, as if on cue, the soldiers had arrived, circling the building to make sure no-one escaped and no help came. It seemed an example was to be made.

Climaco tried to struggle to his feet. He had to fetch water. He knew what the masked man would do next. He wished he had the strength to do it himself.

Staffelkapitan Jonas Oswald charged, baton swinging. In the past seven seconds, he had watched his entire unit fall like rain, but he did not let that slow him. If he could take the madman by surprise, then he could end this here and now. The masked lunatic growled like an animal, and turned, swinging his sword with a devil's strength. Jonas felt the blade strike, like a hard punch in the side – felt something tear in his spine – and then he toppled sideways. He could no longer feel anything below the waist, and there was something blocking his vision. He understood, then, that the end had come.

He remembered how this had all started. A couple of shared beers in the officers' mess after a hard day of herding human sheep – two bottles for the whole unit, and those were supposed to last the week. They hadn't even had the chance to finish them before the call went out.

Some cretins, most likely El Sombra and his fellow terrorists – had managed to set the old schoolhouse on fire. The unit was to form a ring around the building to prevent the fire spreading, wait for help to contain the blaze, and prevent any of the workers from interfering. Those were their orders, and they carried them out.

The hardest part was ignoring the screams from inside. But there was no saving those people, if you could call them 'people'. If they'd wandered into a restricted building and set it ablaze, then they'd brought this on themselves through their own stupidity, as you'd expect from subnormal intelligence. There was no sense in risking the lives of his men to save the lower races from their own idiocy – besides, the unit was needed outside, to prevent any more of them destroying themselves, like that idiot with the bucket who seemed so ready to hurl himself into the flames.

They'd been following orders. And the masked killer had swept down and butchered them all for it. Didn't he understand that they were trying to help?

Jonas Oswald blinked twice and realised what the object was that was blocking his vision, as the lower half of his body toppled forward, the ragged end of his spine flapping, leaving his line of sight clear. Then everything went black.

"Estoy hasta la madre, pinche pendeja!"

The masked man hurled his sword at the last of them. The man – at nineteen, barely that – screamed as the point of the sword plunged through the open mouth and through the back of the neck in a gout of red blood. The nameless young soldier crashed to ground, eyes already rolling back in his skull, and El Sombra took back his property.

"Water! Now!" El Sombra's voice was like an oncoming storm.

The man who'd been beaten earlier limped forward, carrying his bucket, and hurled the remaining contents over the swordsman. Others in the crowd picked up the hint quickly and doused him with what little water they'd managed to collect, until he was soaked through, dripping wet.

He turned to face the blaze, an inferno now. There were still screams coming from inside, which meant that there was some hope at least. But he knew he had seconds at best. This was not like fighting – something he could do almost without thinking. This would be difficult. He had to save as many of the children as he could, and his true enemy tonight was not the soldiers, or even the flames. It was time. Every second that passed could mean the end of a young life, in fire and agony and horror.

Tick tock.

El Sombra dove into the fire.

The flames licked his face and burned at his neck and back, bringing back memories of the desert heat. He made for the stairs, trying to get to the screaming and weeping he could hear coming from above.

The wooden stairs were a mass of flaming timber, but they could still support his weight. He stilled his mind, shutting off all sensation, all pain. Then he ran forward, pushing through the wall of fire, the calloused soles of his feet hitting the red-hot wood as he took the stairs two at a time. Smoke burned his lungs and his throat was raw. He could barely see and his ears were full of the crack and hiss of blazing wood. He was on the same floor as the screaming now, but he might as well have been a thousand miles away. Every breath he took was soot and heat and the terrible stench of cooked pork.

He staggered forward, eyes swamped with tears, and saw the children.

Six of them were huddled together, not looking at him. They were looking at the seventh, a boy, perhaps six years old but certainly no older.

His name was Spiro Otilio Herrera, and he was on fire.

His flesh was melting, running off his body like tallow-fat, as he thrashed and screamed at the top of his lungs. There was a sizzling that filled the room, and the stench of cooking meat. But the smell wasn't the worst thing.

The worst thing was what had happened to his face.

The fire had burned away lips, nose and cheeks, and burst one eye. The hair had been consumed first. All that was left was a shrieking, blazing skull, resting obscenely on the candle-wick body.

The masked man looked down at the thrashing thing that had once been human and he knew there was no saving the boy. Even if he could get Spiro Herrera outside, there was no medicine that could save his life. He would scream and scream for hour upon hour, each gasping, tortured breath bringing even more pain, until he finally died. Still, he would have tried. But there were six others who needed him and he had no time. El Sombra could do nothing for him...

...but draw his sword.

In that moment, El Sombra knew himself to be no longer a man. He was, instead, what the ticking clock had made of him.

He was a monster.

Tick tock.

Erendira Herrera, worker number 2137, was twenty years old and one of the most proficient workers in all of Aldea. So proficient that she had earned a commendation from the Oberstleutnant himself. Like other workers who had been commended, her papers allowed her to walk the streets a full two hours after sundown, provided she caused no undue disturbance. She had earned that privilege through her obedience to the Führer. Stood at the back of the crowd, watching the building burning and inhaling the sickly-sweet stench of sizzling fat, she listened to the shrill screaming coming from the upper floor of the burning building and seethed.

She remembered how this had all started. The uneasy smiles of her parents at dinner when she expounded on the greatness of Der Führer. Her mother's look of worry and pain when she came back from another gruelling overtime session on the high scaffolding. The long arguments with her parents, as if being held up as an example by Master Plus himself was somehow not enough for them. The guilty looks when she mentioned how it would soon be time for little Spiro to begin his work training.

Once she had returned from overtime to find Spiro absent from his room, her mother and father refusing to allow her to contact the proper authorities, content to sit and wait. Eventually he was brought in by Mr Aguilar – a sloven who did not pull his weight on the statue and often needed to be beaten with a cane in front of the other workers – and her mother and father had said nothing about it to her, while Spiro babbled about pyramids and sphinxes and things which he had no business knowing.

She had not wanted to go to Master Plus about the matter. Not until she had all the facts. It was not her place to enforce law in Aldea and, besides, wasting Master Plus' time with gossip and scandal might tarnish her work record.

But she should have informed on them. She knew that now. It was perfectly obvious what had happened. They'd been having their little club meeting, learning their useless stories, and that doddery old witch Verdad had knocked a candle over and set light to all those useless books and bits of paper that should have been burned long ago. She'd started a fire and then fallen or something and not been able to lead the children out. She was stupid and old. In Berlin, they put stupid old women like her in chambers and gassed them, and then burned them in ovens.

She wished this town was more like Berlin.

It made her furious. Every breath she took was tainted with the smell of burning flesh and the blood of the dead. Because these fools could not accept things as they were, children were being burned alive. Good men had been butchered by a lunatic. And for what? So a few new workers knew that across the sea, there were pyramids? What would they do with that knowledge when they were ordered to get a half-ton block of stone up to the top of a hundred foot scaffold? Across the sea, there was discipline. There was *ordnung*. That was all that mattered.

She gritted her teeth, air hissing between them like the noise of a kettle. This would come back to her. When the soldiers investigated, they would find her parents and her little brother mixed up in this somehow, and that would be the end of her commendations and her special privileges. Number 2137 would be just one more troublesome worker from a bad family.

It wasn't fair. It wasn't right. This minority of rebels were spoiling things for everyone who did what was right. Someone had to teach them a lesson. Somebody had to show these criminals and thugs and their masked hooligan the difference between right and wrong.

She picked up a stone and hefted it in her palm.

The children stared at him for a second that seemed like an hour, and El Sombra looked back at them, unable to meet their eyes. The tears running under the mask were no longer caused by the smoke.

And that had been the easy part.

There had been only one choice regarding Spiro Herrera. Now there were more. There were six children in the inferno, and he promised to himself that he would save every single one of them.

And he knew he would break that promise.

A roof beam cracked and fell, blazing, superheated timber crashing towards his head, and he hurled himself forward. There were three girls and three boys. Two of the girls and a boy were awake and conscious. That might mean they could survive longer, but on the other hand, the still ones might need resuscitation. He could not trust that to the crowd, so it was likely he'd be performing it himself – spending vital minutes saving one child while the others burned. The awake ones first (Could he manage all three? He'd have to.) and then back inside for the rest.

All this ran through his mind in the split–second before the beam crashed through the floor behind him.

He grabbed two children in his arms and one by the hair, and twisted, his back smashing against the burning wall. The force of his momentum smashed through the weakened wood, propelling him and his three charges out into the night air on a plume of smoke. It was hard to compensate for the added weight, but he shifted his balance and turned a graceful loop in the air – a memory of jumping off the edge of a canyon while weighted with heavy rocks suddenly flashing into his mind – before landing hard on the pads of his feet, bursting blisters. The children were unharmed. Alive. Now for the rest.

The stone smashed hard into his left temple.

He winced in pain and his skull rang like a bell. He could not believe it.

Someone had thrown a rock at him. For saving three children.

And that was the least of it.

He was just one target. Rocks were hurtling through the air from all sides, at all comers. The crowd had turned on itself and become a riot. A part of him was relieved that he'd made the right decision – there was no way any of these people would be capable of resuscitating a burn victim – but another part was counting seconds. *Tick. Tock.* Every second that passed meant that the risk of another death was higher.

Tick. Tock. Tick.

If he left the children here they'd be trampled or torn apart by the mob. If he stayed, three more children died.

Tick. Tock. He heard screaming from above him. *Tock. Tick.* One of the unconscious ones had woken up. Probably because they were on fire.

If he moved these children away from the crowd and then left them, they'd be picked up by wingmen and taken to a torture chamber somewhere. *Tick. Tock.* He needed somebody who could get them home. But there was nobody.

Tick. Tock. Tick. Tock. Ti–

"Give them to me!" Climaco Aguilar lunged from the mass of bodies, one eye swollen, blood pouring from his nose, missing teeth. El Sombra recognised in him a kindred spirit, and gave thanks. "Get back in there! Get back..."

But El Sombra was already gone. Under a barrage of stones, Climaco herded the sobbing children towards the relative safety of the alleys.

Tick. Tock. Tick.

El Sombra's thudding heart was a stopwatch that counted down the seconds until the death of the next child. Every time his bare foot thumped down on the hard, hot timber, he left a sizzling footstep of blood. He tried not to think about the blood dripping from his sword...

Up the stairs two at a time and this time they could no longer bear his weight. He felt the third stair from the top give way underneath him, and he launched himself up, stabbing the point of his sword into the ceiling above him and letting it bear his weight for the split second he needed to swing himself over the gap to relative safety.

Upstairs things were much worse. There were large holes in the floor from where roof beams had crashed through or the wood had simply given way in the terrible heat. The smoke was thick and black, and the flames were raging out of control. He looked around desperately for the remaining three children. He couldn't hear anything from them. But he'd heard a scream. Was it seconds ago? Minutes? How long did they have to live?

He moved forward as quickly as he could, hoping that he wouldn't fall through the floor onto the bonfire raging below. The only thing he could do would be to grab the children and leave by the hole he'd made before. The smoke cleared for a moment –

– and he was looking at Verdad. Isidoro's wife. She'd been here all along, hidden from view by the smoke. Her old, wrinkled face was distorted in agony. She'd fallen and broken something, by the look of it. Her bones were very brittle and she had to be very careful now that there was no possibility of medical care for her. And she had been coming up and down the rickety steps and teaching the children by candlelight. How much courage did that take?

She looked at him with frightened eyes, then looked away, towards where the children had been. The meaning was clear. He had to leave her to burn.

He wished he had time to speak to her, even a few words. Could she tell him what had caused the blaze?

Did she remember how this had all started?

Tick tock. No time. He vaulted through the billowing smoke, and it was thick and black and tore at his throat and lungs with sharp needles. Nobody could survive more than a few minutes in this place... maybe not even a minute. He had heard once that in an environment like this you had perhaps three breaths before you passed out. How many did a child of five have?

Where were they?

He was in the right place. He was sure of that. Had they moved?

Tick tock.

He drew in a deep breath of smoke and flame and bellowed.

"Scream! Scream, damn you..." The shout broke into a hacking cough. There was a cough in response. *Thank God*. El Sombra dove forward, reaching, hands brushing against small forms. One. Two. A boy and a girl.

There was another one. Where? He didn't have time. That cough he'd heard had been the sound of a death rattle. If he didn't move now, the two children he had would die.

He wished he could see through the billowing smoke, just for a moment – one moment was all it would take. He hoped he remembered correctly which direction led to the outside. He prayed to anyone who might be looking down for some guidance.

His only answer was the pounding of his heart.

He hurled himself sideways, protecting the children with his own body as he crashed through one of the windows. He was too weak this time for fancy landings, and so he fell hard onto his back, glass digging into the meat of his shoulder as the wind was slammed out of him on impact. He looked at the two bodies cradled in his arms. Both dead.

Above him, he heard the screaming begin again.

He had made the wrong decision.

Around him, the crowd busily tore each other apart.

There were only a few left, less than twenty, the others having run or limped away to homes and families – those who were not simply beaten to death by the mob. Once upon a time, all of Pasito would have been filling buckets and pails, desperately doing everything they could to put out the raging inferno. Now the town reacted to trouble by turning on itself, the careful clockwork spinning quickly out of control. El Sombra did not have the time to stop them, or even to give a thought to how far his home had fallen.

The clock was still ticking.

He could either go into the burning building for a third time to rescue the screaming, agonised boy he had left behind, or he could perform resuscitation on one of the children with him. Most of the boy's flesh was charred and blistered, the larger part of his skin burned away. He was a ruin. But the girl was hardly marked. Evidently she had simply inhaled too much smoke. But if he didn't get her breathing again immediately–

With that thought, El Sombra condemned the boy above him to death by fire.

Leaning down, surrounded by chaos, he began to breathe for the girl. He had let down too many during those five minutes, but the clock was still ticking. He still had the power to claw back a life, one more life stolen from the jaws of death. In the distance he heard the sound of clanking metal wings somewhere above the roar of the flames and the howls of the crowd, but he did not stop. Let them come. Leaning back, he began to compress her chest. One more life. That wasn't much, was it? Not very much at all.

Above him, the screaming finally died. He gritted his teeth as his arms pushed, bullying her heart into beating again. Then he leant down to inflate her lungs.

Again. Again. She must breathe. She had to breathe.
  She would not breathe.

Alexis Eisenberg stood at the window of the humble
hovel overlooking the schoolhouse and watched as the
masked man tried to resuscitate the girl. Hopefully he
would fail – it would set the capstone on what had, all
in all, been a very good night indeed. He took a sip of
brandy from his hip flask, smiled, and remembered how
it had all started.

He had known about the 'education program' for
some weeks now. It was something he had permitted to
continue. Oh, he could have gone in – crushed the whole
enterprise under an iron fist, carted the ringleaders off
to the Palace Of Beautiful Thoughts, perhaps shot the
children in the street as an example. It would have been
a perfectly good way of dealing with the symptoms, but
it would not have cured the underlying disease; this idea
the lower orders had that they knew what was best for
their spawn.

He could shoot one hundred people, but that would
only create one hundred martyrs. The cycle would have
begun over again quickly enough. The only way to really
squash these little rebellions was to make them collapse
of their own accord. Have the people understand that
the system was there to protect them, and that to move
against it would only result in harm coming to those they
loved.

And so he had planted a very small, very potent
incendiary device.

It would be explained away as an accidental fire, caused
by a candle tipping over. He had already begun planting

the seeds of that conclusion, using his spies among the workers to amend the rumours that were circulating. And the results had been better than he could possibly have dreamed.

El Sombra knew who the power was now. Any rebellious elements would be dealt with. Not by the wingmen, but by the people themselves, who were all too eager to savage each other in the name of safety. His clumsy attempts to bring the people together under the banner of Old Pasito were doomed to failure. There was no Pasito anymore. Pasito had been a town of friends and good fellowship – but Aldea was a place of strangers and mistrust. And that made it easy to control.

And deep down, all that was nothing compared to one great triumph – Alexis had hurt the masked man. Where was his laugh now? He had seen innocents burn to death. He had, Alexis was certain, killed at least one child to save it from pain.

Later, Alexis would consult with Master Minus, the expert in mental distress, and find out how deeply he had managed to wound his enemy. For now, he simply watched. The girl was still not breathing, and his wingmen were getting closer. It would be the cherry on the icing if El Sombra had to let her die to save his own skin, or better, be shot dead as he fruitlessly tried to restart her heart.

Alexis stroked his fingertip lightly over the scar on his cheek and leant forward, grinning like a jackal, to watch.

As the clank and creak of wings filled the sky, El Sombra stood, cradling the little body in his arms. Time had run out.

"Move, all of you! Follow me!" He yelled it at the top of his lungs, but the crowd did not seem to hear. A couple of the battered rioters broke off from their fighting to look at him as he ran for the nearest alley, but most kept up their war without even turning around.

Running into the shadows of the alley, El Sombra heard the storm of creaking wings thunder over the burning schoolhouse. Something was shouted in German: An order to stop fighting or face the consequences. Before the sentence had finished it was drowned out by the clatter of machine-gun fire. More lives he had failed to save.

And then, in El Sombra's arms, the little girl coughed softly. Her name was Graciela and her parents were sitting in their dwelling and sobbing as they heard the shots ring out. They had lost all hope.

Graciela began to breathe gently, in and out, and despite himself, the man behind the mask smiled.

He did not smile as he ran his fingers over the burst blisters on the soles of his feet. He had failed the people when they needed him most. He had allowed three children and an old woman to die and run while others were gunned down. He had had no choice in any of this, it was true, and he had done the best he could in the situation.

But all the same, he had failed.

He had spent a great deal of time learning everything he needed to know to conduct a one-man war against his enemies – and virtually no time learning how to help his friends. Oh, he knew resuscitation, and the treatment of wounds, but he had had no idea that the people of the town were trying, against all hope, to give their children an understanding of a life beyond slavery and despair. Earlier, he had moaned to father Santiago like a cretin that there was no resistance. Father Santiago effectively lived in a cave – of course there would be pockets of resistance that would spring up without his knowledge. It would not have taken much effort for El Sombra to find out about them, and yet he had blithely carried on down his own path, like a train on a track, unable to deviate for an instant. He had amassed an arsenal of guns and ammunition for the people to enact his personal vengeance, but had not bothered himself with bringing them hope.

He had been a fool.

He looked towards the town and then stood and began walking in the opposite direction. He could not return to the priest's shack just yet. He did not need a bed or home-cooked food. He needed the desert, and heat, and solitude. He needed to think.

Things would have to change.

Alexis leant back in his bed and smiled. He had suspected it for a long time, but seeing his enemy's face lit by the firelight, seeing that look of grief and shame and horror... there could be no mistake.

Alexis knew who El Sombra really was.

In the morning, he would discuss his suspicion with Master Minus. Together they would work out a plan of attack, something to run parallel with his father's bumbling attempts to have him killed. Something to succeed where Herr Generaloberst had failed. He turned on his side and thought about children, burning in a furnace of flaming timber.

He slept like a baby.

CHAPTER FIVE

Zinnsoldat

Seven days later and the dawn was breaking. Jesus Santiago watched the desert sun slowly rising over the dust and the rock, turning both a bloody orange. He was taking a chance – he knew that leaving his basement was not to be taken lightly. His occasional trips to the town for information were risky enough. But to stand outside his home doing nothing – making both it and him a target for any desert patrol that might venture out of its usual pattern – well, that was sheer foolishness.

And yet, the sunrise was very beautiful.

Since El Sombra had come to the town, Jesus had found it easier to take joy in the small things. It was as though he'd brought hope itself back with him from the grave. Things that had been so easily forgotten in the name of survival – laughter, courage, defiance – found themselves embodied in him. Since the fire at the schoolhouse, Jesus had seen little of the masked man, but the reports still came to him of curfew-breakers saved from death, of soldiers and wingmen cursing lost shipments of ammunition. His friend had been busy – but his self-imposed task was now a private penance, it seemed, for imagined sins.

Jesus hoped the penance was over soon. He missed his friend.

There was movement behind him on the roof of the shack, and then the sound of a body hitting the dirt. Jesus turned to see El Sombra crouched, cat-like, the dust still swirling around the soles of his bare feet, his sword gripped in his hand. He smiled at the eyes behind the mask, and said the first thing that came into his head.

"They're going to kill you."

El Sombra looked up from his egg, tearing off a piece of the white with his fingertips. "That was a very pessimistic way to greet a friend, amigo."

Jesus shrugged, smiling as he leant back in his chair, a glass of good whisky in his hand. "I only repeat what I hear. I'd have told you sooner, but you've been in the desert for days, you know? Did what happened at the schoolhouse hit you that hard?"

El Sombra scowled. "What do you think?"

Jesus hung his head. "It's my fault. I should have known what Verdad and the others were doing. If I'd kept you informed, you could have..."

El Sombra shook his head. "No, it wasn't you. It's in the past now. Besides, I haven't been sitting around crying like a schoolboy. I've been waylaying as many foot patrols as I can – trying to starve their supply routes. It's like chess – they have six or seven routes, but they all need to go through shade at some point. If they march their men through the open desert all the way, their men die. But if I try and take them out in the open desert, their snipers are more likely to draw a bead on me before I get to them – so I die. So I have to guess where they're going and then find a shady patch along the way to hide in until they come. It's a science, my friend, but I'm getting much better at it."

"I hate to say it, but... that isn't like chess in the slightest."

"Well, I've never played chess. The important thing, amigo, is I'm starting to put a dent in their supplies again.

Crippling their Engine was a good idea, but I forgot that if generals have a problem, they throw human lives at it until it goes away."

"So they're using their soldiers as packhorses, marching them through the desert laden down with their guns and medicine?"

"And the strong drink. Don't forget the strong drink."

"They must be killing a dozen every trip."

The masked man shook his head. "They've shipped in trolleys infused with their special metal. If you kick an empty one, it floats into the air and keeps going for a mile or more. They're expensive and difficult to make, so I do that a lot. A similar principle to the wings – designed to lighten the load enough to make carrying it across the desert a little less impossible."

"So I suppose you're killing a dozen every trip instead?"

"One thing the Ultimate Reich is not short of is human lives, amigo. What were you saying about them killing me?"

Jesus sat down, leaning back in his chair. "The soldiers are making noises about dealing with you once and for all. After what happened at the schoolhouse, you've become a much more sympathetic figure to the people. It's just a shame you weren't around to capitalise on it, you know? Anyway, they have something cooked up that's apparently going to get rid of you once and for all... something called Der Zinnsoldat."

El Sombra's eyes widened. Jesus frowned. "Does that ring any bells?"

The masked man shook his head. "Zinnsoldat is bastardese for 'Tin Soldier'. It's not a name that strikes fear into my heart, amigo, put it that way."

Jesus tapped his fingertips together gently, watching as

El Sombra finished his egg and used a hunk of bread to mop up the remains of the yolk. The priest murmured a few halting, guttural syllables.

El Sombra frowned. "What the hell was that?"

"I was speaking English. It roughly translates as 'what does a name mean? A rose with a different name would have the same sweet smell'. A famous quotation from Shakespeare, who Djego would certainly have known all about."

El Sombra winced at the name, then growled, tearing into the bread with his teeth. "Let's keep him out of this."

"Look, I wouldn't be telling you about this if they were just saying they were going to kill you, you know? They say that every day. This is a lot more serious, my friend... more sinister. Whatever this Tin Soldier does, it's going to be bad. Keep your eyes peeled."

El Sombra nodded. "It's nothing, amigo. You worry too much. Listen, as long as I'm here, I have something I need to ask you. There are things I need to know in this town before I can be truly effective here. For example, there's a house near the centre of the town with all the upstairs windows covered in some kind of canvas. I need to know more about it."

Jesus nodded. "The House Without Windows? You know as much as I do. Master Plus lives there and for some reason he keeps the upper floor blocked off like that – that's everything. It's one of those secrets it isn't healthy to learn, you know?"

The masked man smiled. "Then I'll have to find out first hand."

As the sunrise hit the Red Dome, it seemed to wash the General's office in a sea of blood. As he looked out through the tinted windows, the sun seemed a boiling mass of fire, a pitiless red eye belonging to a terrifying monster, opening slowly onto the town and bathing it in a gaze that turned it to stone. He couldn't help but smile slightly at that idea, the great weathered face cracking a little. He turned to look at his imposing guest and let out a soft chuckle. There was such a monster stalking Aldea today, and he had its leash in his hand.

There was a knock.

The General grinned. "Come in, Master Plus. Come in and meet our new toy."

The door opened, and the fat man shuffled in, keeping his eyes lowered, as the General knew he would. Eisenberg said nothing, waiting with his arms folded for the little fat man's eyes to rise and take in the sight of his new friend. Slowly, Master Plus lifted his head – and then took two stumbling steps back, a gasp torn from the depths of his throat, sweat beading on his brow.

It was the reaction General Eisenberg had been hoping for. "Be careful, Mein Herr. You will give yourself a heart attack."

Master Plus said nothing, only panted, clutching his chest and regaining his feet, his eyes bulging.

Eisenberg smiled. "Master Plus, may I present to you – Der Zinnsoldat."

It was ten feet tall, and shaped roughly like a man.

The posture, however, was closer to that of a gorilla – presumably to allow it to fit into smaller spaces, such as the office. The two massive paws, like industrial diggers, clutched and flexed, metal joints squeaking as the network of hydraulic pipes that ran like creepers up and down the forearms hissed menacingly. It had no head, as such, but there was an approximation of a face in its chest, comprised of a pair of massive iron doors, locked shut, with small horizontal slits which glowed orange with the heat of the coals behind. Occasionally a bright ember would drop to the carpet, as though the creature was drooling in anticipation of the kill, and glow for a terrifying moment before dying away. Above the furnace apparatus were a pair of vents, which some enterprising engineer had fashioned into the semblance of eyes, giving it an expression of cold and merciless calculation. On the monster's back, there was a large metal dome, like the shell of some hideous beetle, and rising from this were six metal pipes, for the purpose of letting off and circulating steam within the massive robot, and a chimney that belched the occasional puff of tar-black smoke into the air as it moved. Underneath the shell could be heard a series of clicks and rattles, a constant ticking of clockwork that sounded like nothing so much as an army of devouring insects on the march, as the beast emotionlessly processed its latest directives. The final touch, rising from one shoulder, was a small hydraulic chamber, decorated with the swastika, like a brand to show ownership – or a tattoo to show allegiance.

It moved slowly, leaning forward and staring at Master Plus as though measuring the trembling fat man as a threat. The grabbers closed shut, forming into massive crushing clubs. The slowness of its gait was even more terrible, for it gave the impression that the monster was only storing its power, that any moment it might spring forward with the speed of a striking cobra, and crush the head of the fat man between its metal hands, popping the skull like a boil.

It radiated power, menace, and a cold mechanical contempt for all that could not be represented in numbers and statistics. It was the representation of all that the Ultimate Reich was and all it planned – the icy dominion of inhuman efficiency over the soul of man.

Eisenberg smiled, running his hand gently over the metal shoulder of the immense machine. "Isnt it wonderful? Berlin has only six of these. We're very lucky to be allowed to borrow one. I hope you realise how highly the Führer values this experiment."

Master Plus swallowed hard and took a faltering step closer. "What... what in heaven's name is it?"

Eisenberg looked over at the fat man, smiling. "It is a machine in the shape of man, Mein Herr. Or rather, in the shape of an assassin. This wonderful creation will solve a certain masked problem that afflicts us both; disrupting work, stealing valuable supplies, committing murder with impunity."

Master Plus swallowed gently. "El Sombra."

Eisenberg's cold grey eyes narrowed. "I do not need to be reminded of his alias, Master Plus."

The fat man looked at the floor. "My deepest apologies, Generaloberst, I did not mean..."

"Why has there been no salute yet from you, dog? Forgotten your place here already? Heil Hitler!" It was barked like a drill sergeant. Master Plus shuddered and snapped back a salute, almost crying.

"Heil Hitler!"

The General smiled and nodded. "That's better. It wouldn't do to make the wrong impression on my friend here... would it?" The immense robot hissed like a cobra, a cloud of steam filling the room as it moved forward a step, the grabbers creaking and flexing. It was all that Master Plus could do not to soil himself then and there. Eisenberg chuckled.

"Relax. It won't hurt you. It's just looking for food."

"Food?"

"It's not quite as efficient as an English robot. That furnace in its chest needs feeding, and often. Luckily, it's designed to find anything that can be burned in any environment and use it to fuel itself." He nodded to the machine. "Demonstrate."

It moved like lightning, the joints hissing as it whirled around. Two massive paws came down hard against the wood of the General's desk and smashed it into fragments. It was only the heavy reinforcement of the floor that prevented the iron fists from pounding the shattered remains through into the room below – as it was, the floorboards beneath the carpet were cracked and broken. Eisenberg smiled softly as the machine opened the huge mouth-furnace doors, the ingenious construction ensuring the flaming matter within did not spill out even as the robot shovelled broken, splintered shards of wood into it. The entire operation took perhaps fifteen seconds. When the robot was done, it turned back to face Master Plus, the slits in the furnace doors glowing with infernal light.

Eisenberg spoke softly. "That desk was solid mahogany. I wonder if El Sombra will prove quite as flammable when he is crushed by those paws."

Master Plus stuttered, fighting the wave of terror that crept through him. "I... It... it seems a shame, Herr Generaloberst, to lose such a fine desk..." He flushed crimson even as he spoke, hearing his own stupid banality loud in his ears.

Eisenberg nodded, unsmiling. "It was a present from my late wife." The fat man's eyes widened. "Do not look so shocked, Mein Herr. We must be prepared to sacrifice the things we love for the glory of the Ultimate Reich. Is that not so?"

Master Plus swallowed hard. "I... I don't see..."

"It is very simple. There is nothing you own that is so precious that it cannot be taken from you in service to the Führer. Love is a weakness, and weakness must be eliminated." Eisenberg reached forward, placing a huge hand on the other man's shoulder. "After the wedding, Master Plus, you will come to understand."

Master Plus lowered his head and hoped that the tears in his eyes would not condemn him, as the General reached into his pocket and removed a small roll of paper, studded with tiny bumps, like Braille, and various little punched holes in a complex pattern. He held it up for Master Plus' examination, although all his attention was concentrated on his mechanical creature.

"This represents all the information we have on the masked dissident. Recent sightings, movements, a full description, those he's been seen with, even things he's said. Der Zinnsoldat has already been fully programmed with information regarding Aldea, its history, and our mission here. Now watch closely..." He unfurled the roll of paper and began to carefully feed it into a small slot sitting next to the dome that protected the creature's thinking-machinery. "Our friend feeds on information as well. Hear that clicking? That's how it thinks. All those tiny little cogs and wheels and gears clicking together, falling into precise place..." The machine suddenly swung its arms around, following and smashed through the doorway of the office, bringing down the heavy wood door in its rush to be about its murderous work.

Master Plus cried out, and the General laughed, a mocking glee in his eyes. "There it goes! It won't stop now until the masked man is dead. Come on, Mein Herr. We must be quick if we're to keep up with our little pet."

Carina looked out of her window, as she often did, down at the fruit-seller on the corner. His name was Miguel – her father had told her – and his life was idyllic in its simplicity. He was always on the corner, leaning against the wall, with a basket piled high with oranges and a smile playing around his lips. She remembered seeing people buying fruit from him... well, she couldn't remember precisely when, but she must have, surely. He had a wife, two children – the youngest was just starting lessons at the schoolhouse, apparently. It must be nice, she thought, to mingle with other children. But that wasn't possible, of course.

Until the age of nine, she had been allowed out. She remembered splashing in the mud and climbing trees. There had been a boy named Hector – something had happened to him, she remembered – had he been injured somehow? She remembered a fire... but it seemed so distant, as though it had happened in a dream.

That was just before she was shown her rooms for the first time. Her father had explained how things had always been in Pasito. There came a time when women were locked away, for their own good, in palatial quarters such as hers, so that they could mature without distractions. She remembered being appalled at that. Even at the age of nine, and just back from the hospital – what had she been in hospital for? – even then, she'd felt that something about that was just... wrong. At first, she'd rebelled, running around, breaking things, crying for her playmates. But before long, she settled, as she had no other choice. Her father, who could be bought with a smile, was obdurate in this one matter. So she stayed, locked in her tower, taking her lessons, reading the books her father brought her, often sitting at one of her windows, looking out at the peace and quiet of the town – the peace and quiet that never ended.

Carina had never seen anyone arguing in Pasito. Occasionally she heard shouting, sometimes even gunfire, and there was always a strange clanking, hissing sound that she could never identify, like great iron wings beating far away. But when she went to the window, there was no sign of anything but peace and harmony. Sometimes that peace and harmony made her feel uneasy. Sometimes she'd sit, looking down the street, watching, biting her lower lip as she waited and waited for someone to leave one of the buildings, or cross the street. Scanning the scene, looking for something, but never certain quite what. Occasionally she would comment on the seeming strangeness of Pasito to her father, and he would laugh and dismiss her idle thoughts, making her feel stupid and silly and foolish for questioning the evidence of her eyes.

Somewhere under the earth, a few hours after such a conversation, an old man in thick glasses would listen to Master Plus' report and make a note in a leather-bound journal. And smile at the continuing success of the experiment. But of course, Carina never knew of that.

On a sudden impulse, she stretched out, leaning as far out from the window as she could, reaching forwards, fingertips stretching. She felt only the air. It was something she did more and more often lately, without knowing quite why. Or perhaps she did know why, deep down below the floor of her conscious mind. Perhaps the truth was simply too horrific to face without being forced to.

Perhaps, in the back of her mind, she did know that her outstretched fingertip had been less than an inch from the canvas, but probably not. It was, after all, canvas that had been decorated with the second most cunning optical illusion in the world. She would make the distinction herself at the age of sixty, when she saw the first in its museum in Marseilles and was heard to comment 'even if someone walked through that one, I'd still believe it'. And then the grey-haired woman would sigh and look to the ground, as though remembering a man she had lost in blood, a long time before.

But that was the future.

Carina turned to pour herself a glass of water from the carafe standing on the table by the couch, and that was when the shadow fell across the room.

Carina turned and what met her eyes was terrifyingly, vertiginously impossible. The shadow was hanging in the sky. The shadow of a man was in the sky. She felt a stab of splitting pain in the back of her skull, and felt a feeling of pure horror wash over her. Horror and something else, something indefinable. Why should this be making her feel so angry?

There was the sound of tearing canvas, and a man fell through the sky and clutched at her windowsill. He was half-naked, wearing a tattered, bloody mask and carrying a sword, and he had serious grooming and hygiene issues. None of which mattered.

All Carina cared about was seeing the sky for the first time.

The real one.

"Make that hole bigger." She heard herself speaking, but felt hardly conscious. The edges of her vision were greying, and something was rushing through her blood, through her brain – a pure, white-hot rage with her father's name.

The masked man kicked at the canvas as he clambered over the sill into the room, slumping on the polished-wood floor. Carina walked around him without a glance in his direction and stared out of the window, as she had done so many times before.

She finally knew what it was she was looking for. She'd found it.

It was impossible to describe – like a hole in space, onto a different world. A world that was darker, and crueller. The buildings were old and worn, neglected. Smoke hung lazily in the air, and occasionally a strange bird-man would wheel past in the long distance and a tiny little creaking, clanking sound would reach her ears. Something about the bird-man made her feel sick. The last time she saw one of those... she'd blocked it out, but it still made her sick. But only a little sick.

What really made her want to vomit up a tide of black bile was the thing in the very centre of the scene, that rose over the town, coated in scaffold, with human beings crawling like ants over it, working blindly and hopelessly and forever. The statue of the man with the nasty little moustache and the ugly hair and the arm raised in eternal salute. And the eyes, sculpted perfectly, as to the life. Eyes that seemed dead, all human emotion vanished from them. Eyes that had held no understanding of common humanity, windows to a soul soured and twisted beyond recognition. All those who bought the threepenny broadsheets with their alluring red banners and nodded their heads sagely at the carefully-tailored ignorance within, all those who were first to stand up and moan shrilly about the wave of 'social correctness' that was sweeping Europe, coveted and lusted for a pair of eyes like that. They were the idol and the template for all those who secretly believe that the world would be better if such silly concepts as 'human rights' were hurled into the incinerator. Along with a few dozen humans to really drive the point home. They were evil personified, cast in stone to gaze forever at the town which they had enslaved. Carina cast her eyes away, unable to stand the sight of them.

It was her first sight of Adolf Hitler.

She didn't feel the tears trickling down her cheeks, but she felt her teeth clench, and heard the terrible hiss of her exhaled breath as it burst from her.

It was El Sombra who broke the silence. He was staring out of one of the other windows, looking at a scene of perfect, pastoral calm.

"What the hell happened to the town? I've only been in here a minute!"

Carina turned and stared at him, then – despite herself – she began to laugh.

Father Jesus Santiago sat in his front room, enjoying the sunlight streaming through the window. He'd pulled the wooden boards down to allow the light in and was sitting at his desk, collating a list of the disappeared – one of the many tasks he set for himself every week. Someone had to keep track of these things.

He'd been afraid that the addition of sunlight would show up the old, broken furniture and layers of dust, but to his surprise the room still had a rustic charm, despite its abandoned quality. In the back of his mind, he knew he was taking another risk, but there hadn't been a soldier within a mile of the house in years. It was time for him to start enjoying life again – the small things that most took for granted, morning sunlight, fresh air. There was no sense in denying himself the most basic joys life had to offer because of misguided paranoia –

– there was the sound of clanking metal in the distance.

Jesus' eyes narrowed, and he turned to the sound, listening intently. The clanking and creaking of metal was nothing new in these parts, but there was something different about this. The sound was heavier, somehow. Louder, more insistent. As though made by something very, very big...

The adrenaline hit. Jesus leapt out of his chair, grabbing the paper he was working on and hurling himself at the trapdoor. He could hear his heart pounding in his ears, feel the blood rushing, his chest tightening as he burrowed under the rug. Working quickly, he levered up the catch with slippery fingers, lifting the heavy wood of the trapdoor enough for him to squeeze through, then letting it drop and hoping the rug stayed enough in place to fool the intruders. He couldn't breathe – he had to consciously work his lungs, trying to keep from panting, to keep as silent as possible. The sweat dripped down his neck and back and the scraping of the wooden door against the barely-healed scars had set them screaming once again. They seemed to burn as he lay with his spine pressing on the stairs just under the trapdoor, unable to move a muscle in case his shifting weight made them creak. Over his head, there were thudding footsteps and the sound of German being spoken.

Like a fool, he had dropped his guard – and they had come for him.

The floorboards overhead were creaking. Not just the floorboards, but the supporting beams in the cellar, as though they were being forced to bear some unimaginable weight. The noise was deafening. Not just the creaking and clanking, but a terrible clicking like a thousand insects trapped in a metal jar – all sandwiched between terrible claps of thunder, hard metal impacting on dusty wood. Occasionally he heard the crack of one of his floorboards breaking under the strain. There was a very real possibility that whatever thing was up there would simply crash through the floor under its own awful weight. If that happened, he would be discovered or, worse, crushed to death by the monstrosity above.

The thunderous footsteps shook the wood an inch from his head, making the trapdoor rattle under the rug – and stopped.

The seconds ticked by. Except for the ticking and clicking of the thing above him, there was no sound.

Jesus held his breath.

A drop of sweat slowly trickled from his hairline, running over his brow, down the side of his nose. His lungs began to burn with the effort of controlling his breathing, of staying so very still.

The clicking above him stopped.

Silence.

Very slowly, and with infinite care, Jesus allowed himself to breathe out, and then slowly breathe in.

The clicking began again, loud and fast, and then there was the sound of heavy metal cracking onto wood as the beams around him screamed in protest. The monster was taking a step. And another. And another.

Away from him.

Jesus breathed out again, silently, and allowed his body to relax.

Beneath him, one of the steps creaked.

A massive industrial grabber smashed down through wood to close on his left ankle, then jerked hard, dragging him through the splintered hole. The smashed, ragged edges of the wooden boards tore at his back and shoulder, raking down the flesh, tearing the half-healed wounds open as his body whirled up through the air like a rag doll, to be brought down hard against the floor with enough force to crack the wood beneath him. He felt two ribs snap like twigs and then something popped in his ankle as the monster tightened its grip on it. Then it swung him up again. This time it slammed him into the wall, his bandaged shoulder taking the brunt of the impact, and swung him around like a hammer to crash down into the centre of the great oak table he'd been working at. Another three ribs shattered and something in his spine seemed to tear as two of the table legs snapped off with the force of the impact. The priest rolled onto the floor, retching up what looked like half a pint of blood and black matter. The pain was indescribable and he could no longer feel his legs. He turned his head slowly.

Something from a nightmare was towering above him. An immense metal creature, hunched like an ape to fit into the room, the chimney on its back belching smoke as it scraped against the ceiling, mechanical paws already reaching out to grip him again. The terrible buzzing of a thousand trapped hornets was coming from a shell on its back' and, as he watched, it took hold of one of the legs of the shattered table and broke it up into pieces to stuff into the raging furnace located in the centre of its chest. But perhaps the worst thing about the monster was its eyes – or the burning holes that passed for its eyes. There was something horrific in that unchanging, fiery gaze, the unmoving carved slits constantly fixed in a look of cold concentration – in the way that the creature would crush him, tear him to shreds, without the slightest show of outward emotion.

"Wonderful, isn't it? We've spent years wondering where your bolthole is, and the machine works it out in seconds. Where is the one called El Sombra?"

The voice was deep, gravely, with a very strong German accent. Jesus had heard it before, but could not remember where. He coughed up more blood in reply.

The metal creature yanked his dislocated ankle again, and this time he screamed as his body arced through the air, the thing letting go and sending him crashing through the thin wooden panelling of a wall. He landed hard on the dusty floor of what had once been the kitchen, sharp splinters of wood sticking into his back, arm twisted beneath him, the shattered end of the ulna bone poking through torn flesh. He screamed again, the scream becoming a choking sound as he retched up more of his own blood.

The General looked down at him, face filled with contempt.

"Again. Where is the one called El Sombra?"

Jesus coughed hard, spraying a red mist over the floorboards. The General patiently waited until he found his voice, looking at the shattered man with his ice-grey eyes.

"I have... no idea what... you're talking about, Herr Generalob..."

The sentence ended in a scream as the mechanical horror took a step forward, the heavy metal foot coming down hard on the priest's wounded shoulder. The clavicle snapped, making a sound like dry kindling.

"We know he's been here, Priest. Der Zinnsoldat is never wrong. Where is the one called El Sombra?"

Jesus' vision was greying at the edges. The pain came in waves now, like knives tearing his flesh. He choked as more blood spewed from the back of his throat, blood mixed with bile. How much more was in him? He tried to speak through the agony, every syllable punctuated with little flecks of red on his lips.

"Te meto la... verga por el osico... para que te calles... el pinche puto osico hijo de perra..."

The General turned, looking to Master Plus, who was cowering in the doorway, staying as far from the immense machine as he could.

"You speak the mud language. Were those directions?"

Master Plus swallowed hard and shook his head. He looked sick, and the sweat was pouring from him as he bore witness to the torture. "No, Herr Generaloberst. Quite the opposite."

Eisenberg nodded, looking down at the mangled body below him. "I don't think pain is going to work here, and I don't want him to die of blood loss before he's shown us where to find our masked friend. I think we need more subtle measures with this one."

He turned, fixing his grey eyes on the fat man.

"Get me Master Minus."

"Okay. Okay... so let me see if I have this straight. Your father..."

El Sombra furrowed his brow.

"...is a massive, massive... massive asshole."

Carina nodded, pouring herself another glass of water. She did not turn around. She could barely look at the windows now. "I feel like such a fool."

"Don't. I know they aren't real and I'm still fooled. They almost seem like they're moving."

Carina laughed. It was without humour.

"They almost do. If you look at them long enough, you'll think you remember them moving... or someone walking across them... I don't know how they do that." She sighed, closing her eyes and burying her face in her hands. "Maybe it's magic. Why not? If I'm going to be locked up like a princess in a tower, it might as well be a magic tower."

El Sombra winced and pressed his fingers to his temple, as though he was developing a headache.

"Unnh. Unterschwellige... subliminal message. It's a signal or message embedded in another object so it passes below..." He winced again. This one had been buried deep. "... below the normal limits of perception. So the conscious mind cannot see it, but the subconscious mind perceives it and informs the conscious mind. In your case, it's a whole bunch of little messages in the picture telling you that it's real, and to stop thinking about it and accept it."

Carina stared at him in shock.

El Sombra smiled sheepishly. "Sorry. I must have picked that up somewhere."

Carina reached out and touched his temple with the tips of her fingers. "Do you... do that a lot?" He nodded, looking down at the carpet as though he'd been caught doing something embarrassing. Carina drew back, realising in that moment how little she knew about this El Sombra, this man who had come in through her window and revealed everything she had known to be a lie. "Who are you?"

He turned to look at her, and there was something in the eyes underneath the mask.

She understood then that this was a man who would never lie.

This was a man who would never stop fighting until ten minutes after he was dead – and even then, beware! Check the grave daily. Leave a candle burning in the dead of night and never turn your back on a shadow. Never again, for as long as you live.

This was a man who had lost almost everything he had, and would hurl the rest into the fire – even down to what little remained of his soul – if that would save one life.

This was a man who could never be stopped or bought or beaten. A man who could never be broken.

Because he had already been destroyed.

The reason he was what he was... was because his mind was damaged. Like a horse whipped with iron chains until it bled, he would plough on, hammering forward forever or until he died in the dirt, heart and soul burned to nothing in the inferno of his revenge.

So this is what a hero is, she thought. *This is everything my father, the bastard, the liar, is not. This is the woodcutter of the fairytales, the masked caballero, the knight, the man who can fight off an army with a smile, the one who will always be there for me if I ask but once. This is the hero. And he is mad.*

And he is in so much pain.

"I'm sorry."

"Sorry for what? I'm fine." He smiled brightly, his eyes not meeting hers, playing the reckless warrior as he did with everyone else. But she understood it was a front. There was an undercurrent of shame and anger in him that would never quite go away.

Carina shook her head and looked away for a long moment, out at the statue, almost calculating. Then she smiled softly and led him to the divan, sitting him down gently. "Come on. Take the weight off your feet for a minute; they look like they could use it. I want to hear your story."

"It's not something I like to..."

"None of that. I'm going to fix you, El Sombra. You want to save this town, fine, but I'm going to save you. It sounds like somebody has to."

He looked at her, blinking.

"Now tell me your story. And don't leave anything out."

Master Plus's voice cracked and quavered in the still air.

"Please, Herr Generaloberst. Please don't send that thing to my home."

The General's face was as stern and cold as steel. He was enjoying the way the fat man squirmed.

"What would you have me do, Master Plus? You heard what the man said. El Sombra is investigating the House Without Windows. Your house." He waved vaguely towards the shattered Jesus, who was desperately gasping for his next breath through a mist of blood. Next to him was Master Minus, dressed in his black hermetically-sealed suit, fiddling in his black medical bag. His truth serum had done its job adequately. It wasn't something he enjoyed using – it was clumsy and rarely gave good results – but it was tailor-made for cases like this, where the intensity of the pain and injury prevented the subject from resisting its effects.

Master Plus looked desperately around at the immense metal monster standing behind him. "Isn't there some chance that he could have lied? It might be a bluff..." Master Minus said, hopefully.

"If it is a bluff, we'll know after Der Zinnsoldat tears your dwelling apart and crushes everything that you love. Come now, Master Plus, stand up straight. This is your chance to show the Fatherland what a truly obedient servant of the Ultimate Reich you are. I'll be monitoring your reactions as the machine tears your home to splinters, along with anything else that gets in its way. You could really impress me, Mein Herr. It's quite an opportunity for you."

Tears rolled down Master Plus' cheeks as he fell to his knees. "My daughter..."

"... will have to pay the price for consorting with a terrorist. I'm sure Der Zinnsoldat will make it very quick." Eisenberg nodded, and the machine turned on its heel, marching forward on its huge crushing feet, one metal paw smashing a section of the wooden wall out and then flicking around like lightning to grab a length of wood for the furnace in its chest. Master Plus scrambled up, his chubby legs flailing as he tried to give chase.

Master Minus sighed. "It's a shame the experiment has to end this way. Carina was a very strong-willed child. I would have looked forward to seeing how the Lying Window technology could be applied in the Fatherland, on those less prone to questioning their surroundings."

Eisenberg turned to Master Minus. "I'm sure we have more than enough results to implement trials at home. Now, I need your professional opinion. What should we do with the priest? I was considering allowing Alexis another chance with him in the Great Square, but now I doubt he'd last the night."

The hunched figure in the leather suit breathed in and out, the awful hiss of his exhalation seeming like some giant cobra readying itself to devour its prey as he loomed over the broken, crippled shell that had once been Father Jesus Santiago.

"Allow me, Herr Generaloberst. It seems that poor Father Santiago has been severely injured by our rambunctious little toy."

The eyes underneath the mask glittered like black diamonds.

"I wish only to afford him... the very best of care."

"So... that's everything? Yes, you can eat that."

"Fankf." El Sombra nodded, teeth already busy tearing a large chunk from a yellow-skinned melon. While telling the story of what had happened to Pasito in the past nine years, he'd been fidgeting – exploring the palatial surroundings, examining the covered windows with curiosity, and eating fruit. Mostly eating fruit. A detailed knowledge of vitamins wasn't one of the things he'd picked up during his nine-year fugue state, but he had a vague idea that it was a good idea to get plenty of them. Who knew when he'd get the chance again?

He'd been amazed at how easy it had been to unburden himself. Usually the mention of Djego's name caused him terrible pain, but for some reason, Carina helped lessen that pain. When she asked, he could look at the past without the black bile crippling him. Ironically, it was probably something Djego would understand. He had had a vague knowledge of feelings like tenderness and love – albeit a crude, sophomoric one. Of course, with Djego, everything he knew about women was out of a book, or one of the old copies of The Pearl he had kept underneath his bed. A good thing he wasn't here now. El Sombra smiled and swallowed another chunk of melon.

"That's everything. Well, up until I decided to investigate this place."

"So you're saying everything I care about has either been torn to shreds or never existed in the first place?" Her voice was bitter as she lowered her head and wiped a tear from her eye. "I'm sorry. I don't usually cry, it's just... I knew where I stood. Even with that monster Alexis, I thought I had all the facts. Now... it's worse than just feeling stupid. I feel like there's not a single thing I can claim to know anymore. I was told the sun rises in the east. Is that true? I was told that two and two make four... God, it's horrible. Where does it end?"

El Sombra reached to place a hand on her shoulder.

"Well, I think once they're done here they'll just burn everything to the ground and everybody with it." He smiled. "But I'll kill them all before it gets that far. So you needn't worry."

She looked up at him, frowning. "How do you always know just the wrong thing to say? Any more pearls of wisdom up your sleeve? I could write them down for future generations."

He grinned. "I don't know. I was just about to ask if you were doing anything after I stab your fiancé through the heart and decapitate your future father-in-law."

She shrugged. "I think I might be washing my hair... oh for God's sake, you can't even wait for an answer before you go for the satsumas. It's ridiculous. If I ate like you, father wouldn't need to put a lock on the door, I wouldn't be able to fit through it."

He raised an eyebrow, chomping into the fruit, skin and all. "Mmmrpphhrm?"

She winced as a jet of juice sailed past her left ear. "Dear lord, you've got the eating habits of a vulture. And the smell. What am I going to do with you?"

"I dread to..."

Boom.

El Sombra snatched his sword. "Diablo! What in the hell was...?"

Boom.

"The walls are shaking! It's an earthquake!" Carina jumped up from the divan, running to flatten herself against the wall. El Sombra looked around for some kind of shelter, white knuckles gripping the sword.

Boom.

Carina felt the impact right through her. "Wait, I can feel something pounding into the side of the house. I think there's something climbing the..."

Boom.

A huge mechanical club smashed through the brick and plaster, three feet from Carina's head. She screamed, hurling herself forward into the masked man's arms – then looked back to see a terrifying metal giant tearing open the wall, masonry flying down into the street as it was peeled away by great crushing claws.

"What is it?" Carina screamed, her eyes wide with a terror beyond anything she had ever experienced. The narrow, emotionless eyes looked back at her, burning, promising death.

El Sombra breathed out, preparing himself. He muttered the name, almost under his breath.

"Zinnsoldat!"

CHAPTER SIX

Feed The Machine

The first thing El Sombra noticed was the smell.

Oil and hot iron. Hissing copper, brick dust and the intangible smell of steam, mingled together with the strong stench of blood, fresh-spilled, smoking and bubbling against hot furnace-metal.

The smell of efficiency in action.

All the numbers crunched, all the plans made, the blueprints drawn up, all led to this – the sickly-sweet, almost medical smell of blood and steam. When the bastards had done with the world, all men would breathe this air, every day of their lives. Blood and steam and the smoke of the terrible automated processing factories that clanked and belched human fat into the sky in the heart of the Fatherland. The conveyor-belt monstrosities that carried corpses to the fire – the dead bodies of 'them', the 'others', the different ones with their skin, their faith, their love that could not be allowed.

El Sombra occasionally gave himself a split-second for this sort of poetic reflection. But only one. He grabbed hold of Carina and swung her around to stumble back against the soft cushioning of the divan. An instant later, the monster charged, massive hands extended, fire blazing in its metal maw, the slits of its eyes glowing with an eerie light. For the machine, the brutal attack was simply the easiest means of completing its program. A quick, efficient strike. It was without rage, without malice. It took no pride in its ability to rend and tear. It was simply a tool.

El Sombra judged the moment carefully. The creature was almost on top of him when he pitched himself forward, hands moving to grip each side of the chimney that jutted from the back of the thing. The elegant high ceilings of Carina's rooms allowed the monster to stand almost to its full height, which meant that there was enough space for what he had in mind. The muscles in his arms strained to support his own weight as he pivoted himself upward and over the charging monster, swinging on the hot chimney and vaulting over the network of pipes as though they were balance beams. The machine crashed into the wall on the other side of the room, knocking out bricks and mortar, and barrelled through into the small kitchen beyond – where Carina prepared many of her meals.

El Sombra moved to the hole in the wall, watching the monster closely to catch its next move. Perhaps there was a way to shut the machine down now, before it did any more damage...

The massive engine seemed to lose interest in him for a moment, looking around the small kitchen. The infernal glow of its chest had softened to a dull orange, and the ape-like machine sought to remedy this, reaching out one of its gigantic paws and taking hold of a wooden chair – then crushing it into kindling. As the behemoth opened up the furnace doors in its chest, the masked man edged back towards Carina. He knew he had only a few seconds of grace left before the machine went back on the attack. That time would best be spent in trying to ensure Carina's safety.

He turned to face her. "Quickly – out the window!"

She looked at him without comprehension, and in that instant he heard a crash of thunder from the kitchen. His seconds were used up and the monster was awake again. Awake and ready to kill.

"The window! Jump for it!" He pointed wildly, then dived to one side as the immense robot plunged a pair of huge metal fists through the remains of the connecting wall. Carina rushed towards one of the painted scenes, caught herself, then dashed towards the ragged open hole that displayed the true face of the clockwork-town, only to come up short.

"It's so high up!"

"One storey! Just jump!" El Sombra launched himself up and back, the metal paws clanging like foundry hammers as they slammed together in the space where he'd been a split-second before. He threw himself backwards, tumbling in mid-air to land as a cat does on the Persian rug. "Just jump!"

Carina looked at him, fear written in her eyes. "I can't!"

And she couldn't, El Sombra realised. Carina had always been scared of heights, in the way that children are until they learn that not every fall will hurt you. But for nine years, there had been no falling. Before that, her idea of a dangerous drop had been around six feet – the distance from her father's shoulders down to the ground. And now she had to leap from a second-storey window and land without injury, with no time to judge, while the building shook from the blows of a rampaging mechanical titan. El Sombra cursed himself as he dived between the creature's legs, a brutal blow from the thunderous metal fists shattering the floorboards behind him. Stupid. *Stupid.*

All right.

Plan B.

Jumping to the side, he grabbed hold of one of the red drapes that framed the false windows, tearing it down and holding it in front of him to attract the attention of the monster. It was an unnecessary gesture. The attention of the mechanical creature was fixed on El Sombra, in the same way that the sights of the firing squad are kept fixed on their target. The machine turned, watching carefully, as El Sombra stepped back against the heavy oak door, the door to which only Master Plus held the key. It watched him as he fluttered the red material, as he spoke softly, in low, hushed, almost reverential tones.

"Toro. Toro."

The machine hissed, cold and calculating, letting off another burst of steam. It flexed one massive paw, the iron joints creaking slowly in the silence of the room. Carina pressed herself into the far corner, tensing herself as she saw the terrible potential in that coiled-spring form, as it wound itself up, ready to unleash its full destructive fury.

Then the monster charged.

Like lightning, it powered forward, one huge mechanical fist like a battering ram slamming through the red cloth and into the oak with enough force to crack the massive door into two halves and tear those halves off their hinges, sending them clattering and crashing down the stairs. The power of the blow was enough to pulverise El Sombra's ribs, snap his spine, reduce his internal organs to pulsing red liquid.

But El Sombra was no longer there.

"Hey, zurramato! Over here!" He made sure the creature had a good view of him as he stood, one foot on the windowsill, framed by the false vision of unbroken Pasito. Then he drew his blade and leapt, all in one motion – his sword carving the canvas as he swan-dived, somersaulting to hit the ground feet-first.

Der Zinnsoldat could not be angered, or aggravated. There was no emotion lurking within the heavy metal body and yet, something in the manner of the target – this human, this mass of flesh and organ, this inefficient skin of water and chemicals and bone – irked it. The mission of Der Zinnsoldat was to track this fragile flesh-thing and crush it into pulp. The capering and darting of the insect was preventing Der Zinnsoldat from fulfilling its mission. Its drive to live was disrupting the efficiency of the unit.

Inefficiency could not be tolerated.

The numbers crunching beneath the creature's metallic carapace dictated that the only correct course of action would be to do as much damage to the flesh as possible, in order to minimise the possibility of the target escaping and healing its wounds elsewhere. The weak bag of skin and muscle would be rent. The blood that flowed through the organs would flood onto the dirt. The eggshell skull that housed the fragile brain system would be crushed, its precious cargo pulped between steel claws.

Efficiency would be maintained.

Der Zinnsoldat crashed through the wall in a shower of debris and brick-dust, metal hands extended to crush, to tear, to kill. After that, the room was silent, but for Carina's breathing.

She was alone again.

In perhaps less than an hour her entire world – the cosy womb in which she had spent nine years asleep and barely stirring – had been destroyed, physically and figuratively. The wind that blew through the gaping holes in the walls was warm, but it chilled her nonetheless.

She looked around at her possessions. Most of the vases had been shattered, and the furniture was in pieces, but her most prized possessions – the books – were still on their shelves. Absently, she picked up a chunk of brick and looked at it before placing it neatly on top of a pile of other bricks. She reached for another and then stopped, the futility of the task overwhelming her.

She looked at the door. This was the door that had been locked for nine years, since a time she could barely remember, and now all that was left was a single torn and hanging hinge and a vista of empty space. Carina was not a fool. She knew that El Sombra had risked his life to open that door, to give her a means of escape.

Escape to where?

She picked up another brick, absent-mindedly placing it on the pile, and considered her options.

El Sombra ran, and a tidal wave of killing metal crashed and pounded at his heels.

His lungs burned and he measured the time he had left to live in seconds. Even if the wingmen hadn't been briefed on the deployment of this creature, the sheer noise of the chase would bring them swarming like flies. If he was still on the run when that happened, he would have no room to dodge without dancing straight into the arms of the beast. The bullets would ricochet off the iron gargoyle's body like the stings of a hundred impotent insects, but the masked man would be shredded like confetti.

The maximum response time of a Luftwaffe unit to a disturbance of this magnitude was – maybe – two minutes. This close to the statue, one minute.

That was if the General had not already informed them of his plans.

His bare feet slammed against the dirt. His lungs burned and his heart threatened to burst free from his chest. Behind him, he heard the echo of thunderous footfalls and the sound of clanking, creaking, groaning metal. He strained his ears, tuned out the panting of his breath and the sound of metal thunder at his heels, and the sound of the clanking and creaking seemed to come from the sky above his head. A creaking that could only be made by one thing in all the world.

Metal wings.

He was out of time. Any second now, the bullets would cascade down like a waterfall, filling the whole street. The few citizens who were taking the air on their brief break from their allotted tasks – and now found themselves flattened against walls and the ground in terror as they watched the violent, impossible spectacle pass them by – would be torn to pieces along with him. Gunfire would crash through the thin walls of the dwellings and take more lives, and it would begin in less than an instant. There was nothing he could do about –

– a man on a horse.

A Nazi. One of the grey-coat guards, the earthbound ones, riding on a horse, a man of rank trying to look big, but only looking confused and shocked as he took in a sight he was never given the proper clearance to imagine. El Sombra threw himself at the soldier. His name, for the record, was Klaus Haas, he was thirty-seven years old and, to his credit, he nearly managed to unholster his Luger and fire before the sharp edge of El Sombra's blade met his belly with enough force to unseat his spindly legs and fat bottom – even as the rest of him toppled to the ground in an entirely different direction.

The name of the animal was Karsten. Karsten had been bred in stables in Augsberg reserved especially for horses designated for military service. In the normal course of events, a horse possesses a natural aversion to the smell of blood and will bolt at loud noises such as gunfire and the crack of a severed spine – but Karsten had been trained for the battlefield, and so he merely stood still, barely shuffling as his owner was bisected on top of him. At the Augsberg stable, warhorses were trained to stand still if their riders were killed so that they could be of use to other soldiers. The flaws in this thinking would have been apparent to any stablehand of Augsberg, had one been there to watch El Sombra nimbly leap onto Karsten's back and swat his flank with the flat of his sword, spurring him to gallop.

This had all occurred in the space of perhaps two seconds. Der Zinnsoldat was not slow by nature, but the inertia that the heavy machine had built up in its headlong chase worked against it. It had assumed, based on the data it had collected deep in its clockwork mind, that the target would keep the same course until he slowed fractionally enough for Der Zinnsoldat to reach him. When the meat-thing changed direction so suddenly, the machine could not stop itself in time. Thus, instead of reaching to pluck its target from the back of the horse and crush him like a bag of kindling, Der Zinnsoldat flew past, a slave to its own momentum. It corrected the problem instantly. Metal feet and palms impacted against the ground, kicking up dirt and dust, forcing the mechanical behemoth to a slow skidding halt before it swung around and burst again into motion, chasing after the horse and its cargo, grabbers snapping like crocodile jaws.

El Sombra gunned the horse on with another swat of the blade. He had a better chance of keeping out of the monster's reach now, but he still tensed in anticipation of the hail of death that was about to erupt from the clear sky. He risked a glance upwards and saw a single wingman, armed with a pistol and not even aiming it, desperately signalling for backup with both hands. The meaning was clear – the wingman had not been invited to this particular party – either Eisenberg had forgotten to inform the troops or, more likely, he wanted to allow his mechanthrope to have the kill. There was a logic in that. Gunning a rebel down with machine-guns was effective, if slightly mundane, but having a rebel torn apart in the crushing paws of a giant metal ape had a certain style all its own. It would send a simple message – *you thought you knew the worst we could do to you, and you were wrong.*

Tactically brilliant, if you were a five-year-old boy who wanted to show off his new sparkly toy. El Sombra grinned. He had maybe twenty seconds before the sky came alive with the Luftwaffe, and he knew just how to use them.

He steered Karsten towards the statue.

Master Plus was in the doorway.

By this time Carina had built a small cairn of bricks, perhaps to mark the death of the life she had led. She was absent-mindedly tidying up, keeping her hands busy as she thought the situation through. She knew she had to leave. The question in her mind was where to go – or so she told herself. In truth, she had still not reconciled herself to the notion that the entirety of the world she inhabited was a house of cards that had finally tumbled to the ground around her. A part of her still believed that things could return to normal, that the holes in the walls could be repaired and everything could be made secure again. It was a part that had no say in her conscious thoughts, but it was strong. Strong enough to keep her stacking stones and pretending to herself that she did not need to act just yet.

And now Master Plus was in her doorway. He was a mess; his white suit stained, the fat on his body trembling like jelly. He ran forward and took Carina in his arms, holding her close to him, tears rolling down the fleshy mass of his face as he sobbed like a child. "Carina! Oh God, you're alive, you're alive! I saw the holes in the walls and I thought the monster had got you... I thought you were – oh, forgive me, forgive me, forgive me..."

Carina, who had rehearsed this moment in her mind a hundred thousand times since the moment the masked stranger had cut his way through her immaculately-designed horizon, found herself with nothing to say.

She held her father close, and the part of her that hoped so strongly that everything could be put back and made as it was curled up and died at the touch of her father's tears. There was no going back. Everything she knew had been broken and strewn about at random, and there was no power in creation that could tidy it all up now.

She sighed softly, her own tears coming now, as she held him close, and part of her burned with anger that she should be the one to comfort him.

"There, there, Father." she whispered. "There, there."

"Hi-yahhh!"

Karsten thundered forward, one step ahead of Der Zinnsoldat. The metal monster had almost caught up many times – for Karsten, as noble a beast as he was, was flesh and blood and thus could tire, or fall momentarily behind in the chase. But Der Zinnsoldat had a weakness too – one El Sombra was quick to observe. The monster reached out with one immense steel fist, slamming it into the side of a wooden house, not slowing down. The wall exploded into matchwood as the beast thundered forward, the fist opening to gather fuel, before thrusting it into the open furnace of its chest. The flames leapt higher, spurring it on, as the pipes on its back screamed in a geyser of superheated steam.

El Sombra grinned.

It needs to eat. But not drink.

He drove the horse forwards into the Great Square. For a second, in this vast and open space, he would be a target. He glanced up again, to see a trio of wingmen flying high above on plumes of steam, readying their weapons. The first response. He grinned again. Let them come. He had an answer for them now.

He swatted Karsten's backside, driving him on towards the base of the gigantic stone statue. At this time of day, there were more than a hundred workers swarming like ants over the immense idol, chipping and polishing at the stone. It was near complete, this great stone prayer to the gods of death and madness, and in just a few days the order would go out to dismantle it again. But El Sombra had other plans.

"Run!"

He shouted it at the top of his lungs, driving the horse around the edge of the scaffolding and between the tall wooden struts. At first, the workers only stared down at him, uncomprehending, but when Der Zinnsoldat crashed through into the square, pipes hissing with a semblance of terrible fury, they dived from the structure, bolting for any shelter they could find.

El Sombra ran his horse around and around the edge of the great stone effigy. Above, the wingmen who gathered with their guns ready were unable to open fire. To hit the workers with a poorly-aimed shot would be bad enough, but to hit the statue was unthinkable. And so they held their fire, flapping in great circles, watching helplessly as the massive mechanical engine of destruction closed in. There was nothing in its programming about the importance of either the great statue or the scaffolding around it, and so it swept the wooden struts to one side, collapsing the structure bit by bit as it followed the charging horse and its rider around the base. The faceless machine did not flinch as the heavy wooden beams and planks crashed down on it, or make any sign that it even noticed the inconvenience, beyond grabbing one of the thinner wooden beams and snapping it into pieces to feed its ever-hungry furnace.

El Sombra gritted his teeth and rode on, wood and metal crashing all around him before he burst free from underneath the toppling scaffold. Tugging the reins hard, he turned the beast around to face the wreckage. Broken slats of wood were strewn on the ground and piled against the base of the statue, leaving the bulk of it naked – Hitler in full salute, feet apart, immortalised in one hundred feet of stone. The very sight of it made the bile rise in the masked man's throat. Too often he had stared at the grotesque effigy, but no longer. If he accomplished nothing else before this monster finished him, he would at least bring this stone idol crashing down.

He spurred the horse forward, hooves pounding the ground. At the statue's base, the machine paused. The target was coming towards it. The best course of action would be to wait for it to come within reach and then lash out – disable it, crushing all organs and bones beyond recognition. It was simply a matter of calculating the best moment to strike.

El Sombra concentrated. This would be tricky. He eliminated all mental chatter from his mind, focussing on the moment. Time seemed to slow, then stretch, the hoof beats beneath him echoing, a slow drum-beat of war.

As the horse reached the base of the statue, he tugged the reins hard. Karsten jumped between the feet of the Führer.

Der Zinnsoldat analysed the move in a microsecond. The target had moved behind the sheltering protection of a wall of shaped stone, but it would not stand up to a serious blow. The robot swung a huge metal claw around, like a wrecking ball...

And struck.

The sound echoed across the clockwork-town. The sound of stone cracking and crushing under the terrible impact of metal. It startled Carina, making her pull away from her sobbing father, and look in the direction it had come from – towards the statue.

For a moment, the great effigy of Adolf Hitler seemed to shudder slightly, then began to list to one side. Something in the stern features suddenly appeared to suggest desperation as the sound of crumbling stone grew louder and the statue began to topple backwards. For a moment, Hitler seemed to be gazing up at the sun, the saluting hand pointing to the sky – and then the whole thing vanished from Carina's sight with the sound of a colossal thunderclap.

Carina blinked, realising how it already seemed as if the statue had always been gone. How much the lack of it made her feel that the old Pasito had returned. She smiled.

Master Plus screamed.

If Carina had spent the last nine years in a prison, then so had he. For nine years, his continued existence and the existence of everything he loved was dependant on his usefulness to the regime. The main part of that usefulness was in monitoring the workers of Aldea in their constant and methodical construction and destruction. The state of the central statue corresponded with his own state of health. If things were ahead of schedule and moving smoothly, he was secure and happy. But if something happened to the statue – some minor blemish, perhaps, or an imperfection in the quality of the stone – the blame fell to him. He was woken in the middle of the night, interrogated, occasionally beaten. Once, early on, he had been taken to visit the Palace Of Beautiful Thoughts. That was because the lower tip of the little finger of the saluting hand had crumbled away under an over-eager chisel.

Now, the entire statue was gone.

Master Plus saw all of his hopes and dreams fall with it.

"No!" he screamed, freeing himself from his daughter's arms and scurrying to the window on his fat little legs. "No! That monster, that cursed metal ape! I knew it would do something like this!"

"The metal monster? You knew about it?" Carina had not thought she could be shocked any more by what her father had done. But to hear him refer to the thing that had nearly killed her in such familiar terms sent a fresh wave of anger through her.

"Yes... yes, my superior, the General, he brought it in to

track and kill the insurgent – El Sombra. I told him it was too dangerous, but he would not listen. I swear, Carina, I never thought the terrorist would…"

Carina breathed deeply, then exhaled sharply. "You mean to say you set that killing machine to hunt him down? That… that thing that can tear through stone and brick and kills without pause, you sent it after a human being?" She closed her eyes. "I don't even know you, Father. Are you just going to stand here and let that machine tear the town to pieces?"

Master Plus took a couple of paces towards Carina, then stopped, looking down at the floor. In the floorboards beneath him, there was a deep gouge where the massive feet of Der Zinnsoldat had pounded and chewed up the wood in its rush to kill. As he looked at it, he remembered a human being writhing on a floor much like it, being slowly crushed by a foot like an industrial press, while he watched. While he watched. As if from a great distance, he heard himself speak.

"What can I do?" He sighed, shaking his head, and when he raised it, his eyes were filled with tears. "What can I do to stop it? They said they would brand a number on your forehead and make you a slave. I had to convince them I could be of use to them – I still do, every day. I grovel. Just to keep you safe for as long as I can. What else could I have done? Yes, I am guilty, I will always be guilty – but tell me, what else could I have done?"

There was silence, and then Carina turned to the doorway, looking at the empty space for a long moment. Then she looked over her shoulder at her father.

"Did you come here by foot, Father? Or on horseback?"

El Sombra's vision cleared.

Between his thighs he could feel the flanks of the horse, hooves still pounding the dirt. In his nostrils was the scent of blood and powdered stone. His vision was a slowly clearing blur.

He remembered now; a chunk of stone had impacted against his forehead, cutting it open and scrambling his brains for a second. Karsten had kept galloping on, bless him. He was still alive, which meant that his plan might have worked. If he could just get his vision clear...

He blinked...

...and saw what was left of the statue.

With one foot shattered by the blow, the immense construction had become unstable. The other ankle had slowly cracked under the weight, and the statue had swayed backwards, finally toppling with an impact that shook the earth like the fist of some terrible god. Now the great stone face stared impassively up at the sky, and the saluting hand rose vertically like some strange obelisk, flat palm facing the sun. The great stone head and shoulders had done the most damage, flattening a number of officer's dwellings on the edge of the Great Square, but the bulk of the statue had fallen in the Square itself, and thankfully none of the workers had been crushed.

Above, the wingmen flew in small, terrified circles, still reacting to what was, for them, an unparalleled tragedy. It was the perfect time to make his escape, just as soon as he knew that –

– Der Zinnsoldat had survived!

It stood, with its remorseless blazing eyes turned towards El Sombra, as though carefully examining him for injuries. The masked man had known that there was little chance of crushing the monster beneath the falling statue – but he had hoped. Der Zinnsoldat could not be allowed to survive. The machine had done far too much damage already.

The great mechanical beast watched the target closely. Destroying the human's hiding place had injured it, but not critically. From the previously gathered data, the computer underneath the metal shell made swift calculations of the target's future intent. It would attempt to escape the Square first of all, most probably heading towards the dilapidated shack where Der Zinnsoldat had encountered the secondary target earlier. Once the target had confirmed his intent by riding in a particular direction, Der Zinnsoldat would move to give chase, using the knowledge of the town layout that had been programmed into its memory to cut him off from his goal. Then the target would be destroyed.

Patiently, the machine stood waiting for El Sombra to make the first move. Had the monster been capable of expressing surprise, perhaps a gasp of shock might have emanated from the blazing furnace mouth, borne out on a tongue of flame. As it was, the monstrosity let off a vast burst of steam from the pipes jutting from its back, a sign of the sudden frenzy that its many cogs and gears had been thrown into. The target was acting in a way that defied probability, in a manner contrary to the dictates of survival. The numbers had been utterly wrong.

El Sombra had circled Karsten around and was now riding the horse at full gallop towards the waiting arms of the machine.

Der Zinnsoldat modified its stance, moving forward on its tireless metal legs, picking up speed. The most efficient course of action would be to drive one of its huge digger-hands into the rider, scooping him off the animal and then applying pressure sufficient to burst him.

Above, the wingmen held their fire, circling like vultures. It would not do to startle the horse at this stage. It might prevent the metal behemoth from making its kill, and then blame would be apportioned and punishment would be served. The best thing to do was to simply wait for the metal creature to act.

Karsten's hooves thundered in the dirt. If El Sombra had underestimated the metal monster, it was all over and done with. He swatted Karsten's backside again with his sword, focussing all his attention on the robot.

Der Zinnsoldat, in turn, watched the masked man approaching, the massive grabber flexing, pistons sinking into place. Then the target came within range, and the arm lashed out, lightning-fast, to snatch the rider from the horse.

The metal scoops clanged together on empty air.

El Sombra had launched himself from the saddle, turning a forward somersault in mid-air as the crushing, killing machine arm sliced the space less than an inch below him. Karsten, trained to ignore shells whizzing an inch from his flanks, paid no heed to the metal brushing his back, not stopping or even slowing as the masked man completed his flip and landed back in the saddle.

Der Zinnsoldat whirled, one arm whipping around in an attempt to connect, but the target was already beyond his reach. Deep in the mass of cogs and wheels that formed its clockwork mind, something very much like anger was building.

El Sombra leant sideways in the saddle, reaching for his own target – a metal bucket that was half-full of muddy water. It had been part of the construction equipment, abandoned in the workers' rush to evacuate. Now it was a weapon. The masked man gripped the handle and carefully eased himself around on the saddle, facing backwards at the metal giant lumbering after the horse. He grinned, a slow easy smile.

"Getting a little tired, amigo? Need a tasty snack? Lookie lookie! Delicious wood! Get it while it's broken and scattered around!" He laughed. Not the great, rich, booming laugh which the occupying force had learned to fear, but a soprano cackle like unto a castrated hyena. Had the machine been gifted with understanding of such matters, it may have taken offence at the mockery.

But der Zinnsoldat had no understanding of mockery, of course. It had no understanding of anything that was human, or warm, or alive. Perhaps it took the suggestion at face value, but more likely it was only coincidence that the creature chose that moment to lean one of its massive grabber-arms down and scoop up a shattered length of wood, the furnace-door mouth yawning wide to receive the offering. El Sombra grinned and gripped the metal of the bucket, readying himself to hurl the water and put out the flame –

– and that was when the bullet grazed his shoulder.

Fire tore through the muscles of his left arm, the bucket jerked, and the payload of water splashed harmlessly into the dirt. El Sombra cursed himself. Overtaken with the triumph of bringing down the statue, of being alive to see it happen, he'd forgotten the wingmen circling overhead. Just because they hadn't fired yet didn't mean they weren't ever going to. Stupid, overconfident *pudrete...* that could have been your head!

He flipped back and jerked the reins as more bullets streaked down from above, impacting against the ground all around him. Small arms fire, but undoubtedly the big guns were on their way. The question was, would they follow him and pick him off once and for all? Or stay in the Square and take control of the citizens? There was quite a crowd now, creeping back to examine his handiwork. And were those cheers he was hearing?

Herman Becker, a mere private in the great and powerful army of the Ultimate Reich, heard the cheering and knew that his time had finally come. He was a small, withered, timid man of forty-seven years, who could barely do two push-ups and needed glasses to read with. Originally a book-keeper from the small, sleepy town of Delmenhorst, he had woken at the same time each day to a grey sky, taken the same bus every day to his grey job, utilised the same half-hour every day to eat his grey liverwurst sandwiches and drink a cup of grey tea, and walked back in at the same time to kiss his grey wife. And then he had seen the posters advertising a career in the Ultimate Reich, and colour had come to his grey little world.

The recruitment officer had attempted to impress in him the need for book-keeping in the Reich, the subtle glories of the administration posts, which kept the Fatherland running smoothly. Becker would have none of it. He wanted action! Adventure! Excitement! Heroism! He wanted to be able to stand in front of the Führer and say that he had done his best for the great dream of German purity! And then perhaps after that he would be able to summon the courage to tell his grey and fleshy spouse that he was finally leaving her for good.

The opportunity came sooner than expected. Herman Becker had a choice of whether to serve in his sleepy home town or to take the great zeppelin across the sea to the faraway town of Aldea, to keep the peace among subhuman savages. An adventure in far off lands – the great white hero taming the mud people, like a story from one of the chapbooks Becker read when he was a child. Becker would be like his boyhood hero, Nick Führer, Agent of S.T.U.R.M., a jet-setting secret agent who fought against the coloured and the subnormal in far off climes, consorting with beautiful Aryan women. So he rode that great zeppelin to the new world.

And what did he find?

He wore grey clothes, and carried a grey pistol that he never fired, and a little grey hand grenade allegedly of the incendiary type, and he stood in a desert of grey under another grey sky and watched grey people build a grey statue. And every day was the same.

Until El Sombra had arrived.

Suddenly here was a villain to match those in the chapbooks of his youth – evil men like Lex Luthor and the Red Rabbi – an enemy feared and despised by his fellow soldiery, a foe worthy of the man of adventure and passion that Herman Becker knew he really was. The lowly private had come running from his post at the thunderous crash of masonry and wood, and now stood ready at the edge of the Great Square to meet the foe.

The villain thundered towards him on a stolen horse, sword in his belt, clutching an empty bucket in one hand – liberated for some nefarious purpose that could not be guessed at – and pursued by a massive mechanical marvel, doubtless a secret gadget created by a weapons specialist working for his beloved Führer. He had outwitted the machine, but he would not outwit Herman Becker. Herman Becker had an answer to villains of his shadowy stripe! Herman Becker did not believe in the half-measures adopted to mollycoddle those who would attempt to poison the values of the Ultimate Reich!

And with that thought, Herman Becker pulled the pin on his hand-grenade and attempted to toss it into the bucket that El Sombra was carrying.

It missed, of course. A swaying bucket held by the rider of a charging horse is a notoriously difficult target, and Herman Becker's hands were shaking with the nervous tension that is all too common in the dangerously unhinged. The grenade banged against the side of the bucket and rebounded to fall at the luckless private's feet.

El Sombra saluted as he charged past on Karsten, and the booming joyous laugh filled Herman Becker's ears. He stared for a moment, dumbfounded, and then drew his Luger, pointing the pistol at El Sombra's back, mouth opening to shout something about destiny and heroism and righteousness. And then the swinging claw of Der Zinnsoldat smashed into the side of his head, knocking him against the wall and fracturing his skull. All of his noble dreams of heroism and chapbook nobility, every second of his grey little life, all of it was boiled down in that instant to one simple truth: Herman Becker was in the way.

The grenade exploded at the machine's feet.

Carina had been lucky. While she'd seen soldiers in both the streets and the sky, they'd all been too preoccupied with the falling statue to take much notice of her riding her father's horse. She was controlling the old white stallion more through luck than good judgement, but still she had managed to avoid drawing too much attention, although it would be difficult to draw a great deal in the current situation. The soldiers of the Ultimate Reich were responding to an emergency unimagined since Pasito had been claimed by the Nazis. With the statue fallen every soldier was needed to restore order and get the citizenry away from the Great Square by any means necessary. To stop for anything less than that would not be conducive to their continued health. Still, she kept to the alleyways. There was no need to take unnecessary risks.

She considered her next move. To head towards the Square would be to invite disaster. But that was where El Sombra had been. He might be dead now, crushed beneath tons of stone, or in the grasp of the robot. She had no choice but to...

The sound of hooves filled the little alleyway. Hooves and the thunder of iron feet.

Carina's eyes widened as she saw El Sombra gallop past the end of the alley on a brown charger, decked out with the livery of the Ultimate Reich, his sword seemingly replaced by an old tin bucket. She was on the point of calling out to him when she saw what followed.

It was the monster. The machine-thing with its furnace jaws and its terrible slitted eyes, enshrouded in fire. The inner workings of the beast were far too well shielded to feel the blaze, but the incendiary gel from the grenade clung to it like a cloak of flame, making it even more terrifying. Before, it was fearful in its inhumanity, in its crushing power. Now, as it surged forward inside its own inferno, it looked like a creature crawled up from the depths of hell.

Carina gasped as her father's white horse reared back, away from the threat. She swallowed hard. El Sombra would have no chance against that. No chance at all. Her own words came back to her.

"I'm going to save you. It sounds like somebody has to."

No time like the present.

She shook the reins and sent the white horse forward, following the trail of smoke and destruction.

Karsten's hooves bit into the earth. The animal was tiring now, barely keeping ahead of the monster's paws. In front of him, the desert stretched out, a vast expanse of sand and rock. El Sombra knew the desert like the back of his hand, and he'd taken this direction for a reason. The sand was thick here, almost forming dunes. There was enough of it for what he had in mind. And then Karsten's hooves were thudding hard against the sand, and there was less traction for them to grip on. And Karsten slowed by a fraction of a second.

The sound was like a sledgehammer bursting a watermelon, but magnified a dozen times and flavoured with the stench of blood. The heavy digger-hands, closed into clubs, crashed together, catching Karsten's rear between them. The impact shattered both hips, bursting the fragile meat between. Karsten shrieked and El Sombra came flying off his back, crashing into the dirt a metre away. Then the robot dealt a second hammering blow to the animal's skull and it fell silent. The legs and hooves of the beast continued to twitch for several minutes, writhing obscenely in the bloody sand. Even dead, it still ran.

El Sombra picked himself up from the ground, grasping the hilt of his sword in both hands, steadying himself for the battle to come. Then he turned to face the music. The monster stood in front of him, looking at him almost quizzically with those burning headlamp-eyes, huge arms readying themselves for the final strike, the flames enshrouding it beginning to die down.

The moment stretched. Time stopped.

And then the creature moved.

It swung one paw in a semicircle, aiming to slam it against the masked man's head, then swung the other a half-second later and three feet lower. Like a chess player, it thought several moves ahead. El Sombra could not launch himself backwards out of the monster's reach, nor could he duck the first blow without being hit by the second. And he had less than a fraction of an instant to dodge the attack.

Any other man would have died, skull split and smashed, brains spattered and flung across the sands, ribs crushed, body caved in and distorted by the force of the blow. But El Sombra was standing on desert sand. This was his place of power, where all the things he had learned and stored away were fresh in his mind and waiting for their moment of use, bubbling just under the surface. He did not need to think. His mind was stilled, reduced to the simple mechanics of reaction. In his own way, he had become as much a creature of efficiency as Der Zinnsoldat.

He threw himself forward, inside the reach of the metal arms, then gripped the hot pipes and gears that made up the monsters body, scampering up its face and flipping over its back. The flesh of his hands were burned by the flames and the heat the creature generated, but he did not feel pain. As the monster swung around to face him, arms swinging around to cave his skull and crush his bones to powder, the masked man dived between its metal legs. It was a game – a merciless game of tag, where the opposing player had the power to cripple or kill with a touch. And El Sombra was the loser before he had even started to play.

A robot would not tire. A man of iron and steam would not flag, or stumble, or make any mistake. Out here there was nothing to distract the monster from his business, nothing to disrupt the efficient schedule of murder it had charted in its clicking, ticking brain.

Until a white horse ran into its field of vision, the rider leaping from the back of the beast to run in front of the target, shielding him with her own body.

Carina looked into the headlamp-eyes. "Stop! Stop right there! I am the daughter of Master Plus and in the name of the Ultimate Reich I order you to shut down!"

Der Zinnsoldat's clockwork mind clicked and whirred furiously. While most of the words flowed over it without recognition, the distinctive syllable clusters of Master Plus and the Ultimate Reich were enough to get its attention. It processed the new data.

Carina swallowed. She had made the monster pause. She could not back down now. "Do you hear me? I said shut down! Now!"

Carina's plan was sound. She had a connection to the Ultimate Reich, perhaps one that was important enough to stall the creature, but almost certainly a connection that would protect her. If she could put herself in harm's way – make sure that there was no way the monster could kill or injure El Sombra without hurting her – then she could stop it. It was a sound plan, but a risky one. If Der Zinnsoldat had not been programmed to consider Master Plus, or the family members of the Reich, or if it had been instructed to take orders from only one source, she would be dead. It was a gamble.

And she lost.

Der Zinnsoldat examined her closely. She was of almost no consequence... however, it would be foolish to simply crush her when there was one role she could still perform. The firebox that powered the mechanical monster was dangerously low, the chase through Aldea had exhausted the bulk of its power.

It needed to eat.

One arm snapped out, the grabber taking hold of Carina's waist, the pressure enough to make her cry out as the great furnace clanged open, revealing the leaping flames within. El Sombra knew what was about to happen and knew that he had perhaps a second to react before Carina was stuffed alive and screaming into the firebox.

His hand reached out and grasped the bucket, still lying where it had fallen. He filled it with the desert and then charged at the machine.

Der Zinnsoldat registered El Sombra's approach. The target was once again rushing towards him, but this time on foot, and lumbered with a heavy weight. It paused in its business, waiting for him to come close enough for its empty grabber to slam shut on his neck and sever his head. It did not lower Carina to the ground.

Nor did it close its firebox.

El Sombra hurled the bucket with all of his strength. It described a short and graceful arc in the air before striking the open firebox and jamming there, the sand within cascading out to cover the burning embers. The flames were already low, but it still took all of the sand to smother them completely. The furnace died, leaving only smoke and smoulder.

If Der Zinnsoldat could feel such a thing as panic, it felt it then. It tossed Carina to one side like a sack of grain and charged, both paws extended in a final attempt to fulfil its programme. Its life could be measured in seconds now. Can a machine panic? Can a machine hate? The meaning of Der Zinnsoldat's existence was in tearing and crushing and killing the target, in rending El Sombra like cloth, in wiping the masked man from the face of the Earth. It had been sentenced to die, yet its final movements were for the purpose of killing its foe.

If that is not hate, what is?

El Sombra was within range. Der Zinnsoldat brought up a metal paw, achingly slow.

The masked man took a single step back. And Der Zonnsoldat crashed to the earth, no more than a heap of old and broken metal dotted with flame.

El Sombra rushed over to Carina. She had struck her head against one of Karsten's hooves when she fell, and was rubbing the back of it in obvious pain. "Are you okay?"

She looked up and smiled, then winced. "I will be. You know, I was meant to be the one to save you this time."

The masked man grinned. "If you hadn't turned up when you did, I'd be a dead man by now. You saved my life."

"Fine... we'll call it one each. But next time I get to save you properly."

"We'll see." He smiled again and leant down, lips close to hers – and then she fell back, unconscious. El Sombra touched the back of her head, and his fingers came away bloody.

It looked like a serious concussion, maybe even a skull fracture. Not to mention the bruised ribs she would have sustained in the monster's grip. He could take her back to the shack and try to fix her up, but what then? She'd be on the run with him. They'd go out of their way to hunt her down. Every nook and cranny of every house would be searched, anyone suspected of hiding information would be shot, any suspected revolutionaries would be tortured and, meanwhile, Carina would probably be brain damaged because he didn't have the resources or the knowledge to treat a serious head injury.

Taking her with him would get the whole town burnt to the ground and probably kill her.

Of course, the bastards had the best in medical care. And she was the daughter of one of the top bastards in the land, the traitor Rafael, alias Master Plus. Her father was obviously a highly regarded man, by his dazzling white suit and the jewels that dotted his person. If El Sombra took her back to him, she'd doubtless be in the lap of luxury before an hour had passed.

He frowned. There was a flaw in the logic somewhere that bothered him. But the girl in his arms could be dying. He had no time to debate with himself.

It was time for El Sombra to make his deal with the devil.

"...and then, when I had lost all hope, he rode up on my white horse, with my daughter in his arms. She has a concussion and needed medical care... and so you were the first one I called on. That's what happened, General."

General Eisenberg raised an eyebrow. The expression on his face was one of cold, unremitting contempt.

"He brought your daughter back to you, Master Plus? That seems strange. You say he was the one who kidnapped her in the first place, yes? Well, then, why would he bring her back, even if she was ill? Unless, of course, she was in league with him. That would make her an enemy of the Reich, would it not?"

Master Plus swallowed, feeling the noose tighten. "General, with all due respect, my daughter would never, never consort with an enemy of..."

"I'm very glad to hear you say that, Master Plus. Very glad of that indeed. Because if she had... consorted, as you put it, with an enemy of the Ultimate Reich... well, steps would have to be taken. For both of you." He smiled and nodded towards Master Minus. Who smiled and nodded back. The General turned, his eyes twinkling, and suddenly the two men seemed like nothing so much as a pair of hungry vultures circling a hunk of rotting carrion. "You understand that, don't you?"

Master Plus' throat was dry. He breathed in and then out. If they did not believe his story... he thought back to the moment when El Sombra had ridden up to him on the white horse. He was sitting outside his destroyed home, with a pair of guards stationed to keep watch. He had told them nothing. What was there to say? He could not condemn his own daughter with the truth.

He had let his head fall into his hands, and when he had raised it again, the guards were gone, without a sound, and El Sombra was in their place, riding his horse, and carrying his daughter. Master Plus had screamed bloody vengeance, called him every name under the sun, and the masked man had taken a tin bucket, of all things, and slammed it down on his head. And then he had told him to take care of her, to get her medical attention, everything the Ultimate Reich could provide.

El Sombra was a good man, it seemed. But he did not understand. He honestly believed, like Carina, that Master Plus held sway in the Generaloberst's office. And why shouldn't he? It was precisely that impression that the little fat man had spent nine years attempting to cultivate.

A pity, then, that nothing could be further from the truth. Master Plus knew what the penalty for his daughter and himself would be if the facts of her involvement with the defeat of Der Zinnsoldat were made known. Now he sweated grotesquely, pinned like a butterfly on a board by the General's mocking stare, as he searched desperately for a way to make his ridiculous fairytale believable.

"General... the... the only way she would have received such a head injury would be in trying to escape his clutches. You... your own experience on the battlefield... Herr Generaloberst, you must have left many enemies wounded, in order to slow down their fellows..."

"Not a one, actually. I shoot to kill." Eisenberg stared for a long moment, watching the fat man squirm. "All right, Master Plus, I believe you."

Master Plus' eyes widened in shock and relief. "Yes, Herr Generaloberst! Thank you, Herr Generaloberst!" He made a start towards the door and then stepped back, shuffling his feet and giving a quick and shoddy impersonation of a salute. "H-Heil Hitler, Herr Generaloberst!"

"Heil Hitler, Master Plus." The Generaloberst paused, almost for effect, and then turned slowly to stare the fat man directly in the eye, his grey orbs turning frosty. "Of course, that still leaves us with another matter."

Master Plus looked at him as a gazelle might look at a lion slowly stalking closer.

The Generaloberst's voice was soft and infinitely gentle. "The matter of the statue, Master Plus."

Master Plus stepped back, one hand clutching at his chest, his skin suddenly as pale as the flesh of a corpse. He staggered, then swallowed hard, letting out a shaky breath. He could not speak. All that came from the pallid throat was a low, strangled sound of terror and despair.

The General nodded. "I will call on you to discuss that at length, Master Plus. In the meantime, you may return to your quarters. I strongly suggest you remain there until you are summoned."

Master Plus nodded, the glazed look of purest horror in his eyes unchanging, and slowly staggered towards the door. It seemed as though he was still having trouble breathing as he gripped the doorframe, looking back at the General as though he was about to say something – but then he turned away, back bent like an old man as he made his way through the door. Master Minus smiled wryly as the fat man shuffled out, then turned back to Eisenberg.

"Herr Generaloberst, on the matter of his daughter... why pretend to trust such an obvious fabrication? You are a man badly in need of a scapegoat." His voice was soft and sibilant, crackling like dry old leaves.

Eisenberg turned, and all good humour was gone from him. The twinkle in his eye, the confident air of command had been replaced by a rage born of stark fear. "There is no scapegoat, you fool! Der Zinnsoldat was in my care! It was signed over to me! Now the only way we're going to get it working again is to ship it back to Berlin and have it repaired, and if that happens, and this lunatic hasn't been caught, I will be going back with it, and you will be, and my psychopath of a son will be, and we will all be gassed and thrown to the wild dogs! Do you honestly think Berlin wants human robots if it means that every nine years we can expect terrorist attacks? We have to crush this El Sombra like the bug he is and we have to do it now!" He began to pace, growling under his breath like some wild beast.

Master Minus looked curiously at him through the faceplate of his leather suit. "You will do yourself an injury, Herr Generaloberst. Stop and think for a moment. This El Sombra is only one man, and even madmen have weaknesses that we can exploit. Is the girl being cared for?"

Eisenberg snorted contemptuously. "She's being kept under guard in her rooms, or what's left of them. El Sombra needn't have bothered bringing her home, there was barely anything wrong with her. A cut head, minor concussion and a bruised rib or two, nothing remotely serious. He must have panicked like a schoolboy." The Generaloberst allowed himself a chuckle. "For such a bloodthirsty insurgent, El Sombra has a weak stomach when it comes to sacrificing those he cares for."

"Then we have a weak spot, Generaloberst. He cares. We can use that, I think."

Eisenberg smiled. "Quite so, Master Minus. We can use the girl as bait for..."

"Of course, Generaloberst, but I was thinking more that it was time to test one of my own humble experiments in the field of robotics. It isn't quite as... self-sufficient as Der Zinnsoldat, but it has a psychological edge all of its own. The prisoner Santiago is still alive, thanks to my... committed care. I would like your permission to feed him to Projekt Drehkreuz."

The old man smiled softly.

"It is time the fly met with The Spider."

CHAPTER SEVEN

Drehkreuz

"Hear ye! Hear ye! The wedding of Oberstleutnant Alexis Eisenberg and Carina, daughter of Master Plus, shall take place this very day at noon in the Centre For Social Advancement! All are invited! Come one and come all to the wedding of Oberstleutnant Alexis Eisenberg and Carina, daughter of Master Plus!"

Ten minutes later, El Sombra burst into the dilapidated shack that belonged to his best friend.

"'Carina, daughter of Master Plus'? She was Carina Contreras when I knew her, when did they take away her name? And what's this Centre For Social Advancement? And what's this wedding?" He stopped, looking around. "Hello?"

The only response was the air whistling through the old boarded-up windows. The shack was exactly as it had been when he had last seen it, every rotting beam and splintered board in place, the table standing sturdy and strong by the window, catching the sunlight.

On the table was a note.

Gone for a walk. Back soon. J.

El Sombra picked it up, turning the paper over and over in his hands. A note on the table, left in front of the window for all to see. Madness. He turned the paper over again, read the message once more, folded it and slipped it into his pocket to dispose of later. Then he looked around again, eyes roaming over the walls and floor. Without knowing quite why, he reached out, fingers brushing the wood, almost as if to make sure it was actually there. There was an itch in the back of his mind, and for some reason he could barely fathom, the fact that the layout of the shack was exactly as he had last seen it... disturbed him.

He moved to the rug that covered the trapdoor, lifting it up and then knocking out a prearranged rhythm. No response. He hooked his fingernails at the edge of the trapdoor and it came up easily, without the slightest squeak from the hinges, without even a whisper. The silence of it unnerved him.

Descending into the darkness he held his breath, unsure why his hackles were up. What was he expecting? A skeleton to rear out of the darkness and bite him? Jesus to appear and say that he had left that note as a practical joke?

Something was... wrong. There was no other word for it.

He searched twice through the dank recesses, not quite sure what he was looking for, and then blew out the candle he'd lit and went back up to the surface. Evidently, he had to take this at face value. Jesus, in his infinite wisdom, was out on a morning walk. He'd see if he could spot him in the desert. If he did, he'd knock him unconscious and carry him back to the shack, and then chain him to the basement wall.

El Sombra shook his head, looking around at the inside of the shack, and then walked out into the sunlight, still troubled. There was something nagging at him, but it was not until far, far too late that he realised what that something was.

Everything in the shack was in its place... except for

the cobwebs strung across the corners of the ceiling and between the beams.

They were gone.

"You had that eyesore rebuilt? Isn't that a little extreme?"

Master Minus shook his head. "No, Generaloberst, it is not. We cannot put surveillance on the house, because he will see it and never go there again. If we had left it as it was, with holes in the floor and blood on the walls, El Sombra would have known that his fellow insurgent was dead or in our keeping, and his reaction would have been completely unpredictable. By spending a small part of our resources on making a tumbledown shack in the middle of nowhere look slightly less tumbledown, we keep our mouse running in the maze of our choosing."

Eisenberg shrugged, looking out of the window over the town.

"We could have used his friend as bait. That was my plan, and it's a plan that's worked in the past. Hold a big, flashy execution in the Great Square."

"And what happens when El Sombra swoops in and rescues him and humiliates you as he did your son?"

Eisenberg bristled at the mention of Alexis. The boy had never been quite right in the head, but since his defeat at El Sombra's hands he had grown far worse, if such a thing were possible. The General would have been afraid for him if his own position were not so precarious. "Let me assure you, Master Minus, the insurgent could never..."

"He finished Der Zinnsoldat. Can you take the risk?"

The silence filled the great, plush office. Without the

mahogany desk, the place seemed empty now, as though the Generaloberst had already packed up and moved out. Eisenberg felt exposed here. He hadn't felt exposed when he'd crawled across the fields outside Kiev in full moonlight, inching forward, waiting for something with black leather wings and ripping teeth to swoop down and drain the blood from his body. There, he had focussed on the mission, and his duty to inspire the men who followed behind him. But now the men who followed him had sharp knives ready for his back, and his office was a stark emptiness that echoed the hissing, clicking, scraping voice of the Führer. In his mind, he could already hear that voice pronouncing a sentence of death upon him.

He was afraid.

"This scheme of yours, it seems a risk in itself. How can we be sure that the terrorist won't destroy your Spider the way he's destroyed everything else we've thrown at him?"

Master Minus smiled, a dry chuckle emanating from somewhere within the loose confines of the leather suit. "I fully expect El Sombra to defeat our Spider, Generaloberst. In fact, I look forward to it. The moment when he plunges his blade through the Spider's beating heart will be very sweet to me."

Eisenberg looked up, outraged. Master Minus chuckled again, amused at the reaction.

"For at that moment we finally destroy El Sombra."

Master Plus sat on the steps of the House Without Windows. They might as well call it the House Without Walls now, he thought, as he played with the rings on his fingers. He shook, twitching involuntarily, beads of sweat creeping down beneath the collar of the white suit which was no longer quite so pristine. The streaks of dirt and dust that had found their way onto the fabric mirrored the sudden fall in status of the man who wore it.

He had been relieved of his duties.

The statue had fallen, and the workers were swarming to clear it from the Great Square, starting with the shattered remains of the feet and working up. It would take two weeks, if not longer, and there would be little need for reward to spur them on. Failure to keep to the schedule would mean death. And so Master Plus sat on the steps and fiddled with his useless finery and waited for his own end to come.

A pistol dropped into the dirt at his feet.

"I took it from a soldier on the way here. I thought you might have a use for it. There's still a bullet left, so... feel free."

Master Plus looked up at El Sombra, then back down at the gun. He sighed.

"For God's sake, get inside before someone sees you."

The two men entered the house, moving towards the small kitchen that Master Plus kept for himself on the ground floor. It was where he did his drinking. He pulled a bottle of whisky from the shelf and sat down, motioning to El Sombra to take a seat. The masked man looked at him distrustfully.

"What is this? You're offering me a drink now?"

"They took my daughter because of you."

El Sombra blinked, then sat down. "Say that again."

"They took her. Because of you. Because you came bursting in through the window of my home. Because you just had to see what was inside. Because you told her everything so now she hates me. Because when the consequences of your actions bounced back on her, you couldn't at least keep her out of their hands."

El Sombra's stomach lurched and he felt a terrible fear overtake him. "Why wouldn't she be safe in their hands? You're part of the machine here and you're her father."

Master Plus pointed a finger angrily. "How naive can you possibly be? I'm expendable at best! After what happened yesterday, they're just waiting for an excuse to finish me. They pretended to tolerate me because they had a use for me, but you've ruined that. It's on your head if anything happens to her!"

"You're the one who kept her locked away for nine years!"

"I was trying to protect her!"

El Sombra slammed his fist down hard on the table. "Well congratulations, amigo! You did a brilliant job!"

There was a silence between the two men. Each dearly wanted to attack the other, to take out their fury and frustration on the enemy. To mask their own guilt with righteous anger. Instead, they simply sat there and watched each other. Master Plus had not shaved, and his white suit was grubby and stained, but he seemed to have gained some small measure of strength over the last twenty-four hours. If only the innate strength of one who understand that he has nothing more to lose.

The masked man exhaled. "Fine. I screwed up. I should have taken her somewhere safe and tended to her myself. And you screwed up by being a mula. There's no point going over it any more, it's done. What's important now is that we fix it and get her back. What's this wedding?"

Master Plus closed his eyes tight. "The town criers are privates dressed up. God knows why. To catch attention, but I can't imagine any of the workers being that thrilled when they're being forced to pull fourteen hour shifts. But now you know as much as I do. I wasn't informed about any of this, I just heard the announcements. Needless to say, no leaves have been granted to the workers or the lower ranks, so I assume it'll be just officers there. Again, God knows why they're doing it that way. Their original plan was to make a big public spectacle out of it, a little dazzle for the drones." He buried his head in his hands.

"What was your plan? Beyond marrying your daughter off to a psycopath?"

Master Plus gave a great, racking sob, the tears pricking at the corners of his eyes before rolling down his great cheeks.

"I don't know. I remember her seventeenth birthday, looking at her... I thought to myself, I still have time. I still have time to think of something. Anything. And I never did think of anything, I just kept on, and on, doing as I was told, hoping I'd come up with an idea. She'd have been better off with a brand on her forehead and no thoughts in her head. She wouldn't have been noticed. But I had to 'protect' her, turn her into an experiment, put a target on her... oh, Jesus forgive me, forgive me!"

"Jesus isn't here. He's gone for a walk." El Sombra sighed and pushed his chair back. "Where's this Centre For Something Something?"

Master Plus wiped his eyes, drawing in a great hitching breath. "It's the church. The Old Church. It can't be a chuh-church any more, but they've always liked the building. They have events there for visiting dignitaries."

El Sombra nodded. He had never managed to get much information on the old church – Jesus had a superstitious fear of going too near it, thinking he would be recognised if he dared to step through the doors – but this was no surprise. It would be just like the bastards to turn a place where good men worshipped God into a place where bootlickers worshipped the next rung of the ladder.

Master Plus interrupted his reverie. "What will you do if it's a trap?"

"What will I do if it isn't?" he shrugged. "I can't sit back and allow it to happen. If the Church has the same layout I remember, there should be a side exit for the vicar. I'll just grab Carina and run."

"You'll be killed."

"She's dead if I don't get her out of there. You know that."

Master Plus had nothing to say. El Sombra sighed and lifted himself from his chair.

"It's ten to eleven, by your clock. I'm going to see if I can't disrupt this wedding they're having and get your daughter somewhere safe. I'm going to be taking the pistol, so I suggest if you do decide to end it all you use a rope."

Master Plus stared at the bottle. "Thank you."

El Sombra nodded. "You're welcome."

Carina stared at the wall. The only features in the cell were a thick metal door, a wooden shelf that acted as a bed, and a bucket, which was emptied twice a day. The only light came from a small candle placed in one corner. She'd considered starting a fire with it, but all she had to burn was her bed, and that would take too long to catch light. And if it did catch light – what? She'd die of smoke inhalation. A great moral victory, no doubt, but nothing she was interested in doing.

From what El Sombra had told her, there should have been a yellow mist in the air to drive her out of her mind. She wasn't happy by any means – she hadn't been since she'd awoken from a sound sleep to find herself here – but any anxiety she was feeling wasn't artificially produced.

She frowned, remembering the stories of Conan Doyle. Eliminate the impossible, and what is left must be the truth. So, she hadn't been harmed, or even questioned, and she wasn't being held in the Palace Of Beautiful Thoughts. Which meant that she wasn't going to be interrogated or questioned, assuming that El Sombra had told her the truth about what her father's friends did to people.

So she was being kept in storage. It was a similar prison to her rooms in her father's house – only considerably less lavish. What were they keeping her for?

The wedding.

They'd invested a lot in her, and they wouldn't see any of it back if the wedding didn't take place in some form. So they'd keep the plates spinning a little longer, have their royal mock-celebration behind closed doors, make proclamations and give out photos and souvenir teacups after the fact... then see how it affected their workforce and tabulate the results. And when they had collected their data, she would, if she was lucky, be shot twice in the back of the head and left in a ditch somewhere.

Smoke inhalation might be more pleasant.

She sighed and leant back against the wall. The best thing she could do would be to sit tight and wait for her chance to escape. That chance would most likely not arrive until the wedding, so she would have to stay alert and hope she could seize it when it finally came.

She had no daylight, and no clock to tell the time, but if she had – and if the dank cell in the basement of the Red Dome had been within earshot of the town criers who had paraded in the streets and lent their voices to the dawn chorus – she would have known that it was three minutes shy of noon.

Her wedding was about to begin.

El Sombra made his way through the back alleys towards the church.

The Old Church had been built in the early eighteenth century; the work of zealous Spanish missionaries who believed that the first thing a tiny colony like Pasito needed was a place of worship. Its construction had been sponsored by a wealthy philanthropist of the time, and thus it was built of stone rather than wood, and sported an impressive circular stained glass window, depicting the Crucifixion around the circumference. The building had been allowed to remain standing at the request of Alexis Eisenberg, who enjoyed the irony of holding formal receptions for the Ultimate Reich in what had once been house of God.

El Sombra looked up at the old, grey stone, listening to the sound of the organ playing within. It was the Wedding March. Obviously the ceremony was just starting. There were two guards posted outside, one on either side of the double doors that led within, but they seemed shiftless and preoccupied, kicking pebbles to one another and chatting about who knew what. El Sombra watched them carefully from the shadows, then turned away. They looked like bait, and besides, there was no point in coming from the direction the bastards expected. Surprise was the key.

He scanned the sky quickly for wingmen before leaping at the church wall. As his fingers and toes found holds in the stone, his mind flashed up images of sheer rock faces in the desert sun, cliffs without handholds, overhangs of desert rock that could not be climbed, that he had climbed regardless. In comparison, the wall of the church was child's play, and he scaled it silently and swiftly, reaching the roof in less than a minute. The organ was still playing, a loud cacophony that seemed more sinister than celebratory. He would look forward to shutting it up once and for all.

The masked man took a deep breath and stilled his mind. Then he began to run towards the far end of the rooftop, past the silent bell tower with the old weathercock slowly creaking and spinning on top of it, sprinting almost to the edge before hurling himself into space. His body twisted in mid-air, hands gripping a stone gargoyle leering over the edge of the roof, using it to swing himself down, bare feet aiming towards the circular stained-glass window.

The force of his impact shattered the glass, sending hundreds of razor-sharp fragments pouring into the church, slashing at his legs and back, spotting him with shallow cuts as he descended to land like a cat on the altar, the coloured glass shimmering down around him and tinkling against the cold stone.

It took him less than a second to see that his plan was doomed from the start. Rescuing Carina from her wedding to Alexis was a noble goal – but there was no wedding taking place in the church.

Instead, El Sombra had landed in front of a firing squad.

Ten machine guns opened up as the masked man dived behind the stone altar, the bullets ricocheting off carved saints and crosses. A squad of ten wingmen had been waiting in readiness for at least an hour for him to come crashing through that very window. When their moment had arrived, they had not flinched or hesitated. It was only the lightning reflexes that the masked man had cultivated over nine long years that prevented him from being chopped into mincemeat by the rain of gunfire.

El Sombra considered his odds. Since this was a trap

the Reich would have sent their most efficient killers, men who worked well with each other. If they'd been prepared for him to enter through the large stained glass window, then that meant they were skilled tactical planners with an understanding of his psychology. Some had duelling scars, which indicated a mastery of aerial sword fighting. Not that they'd need that with the machine-guns they were carrying, but it meant that even if they were disarmed, they would still be more than capable of ending his life.

Ten highly-trained assassins, six of whom were even now moving around the sides of the altar to box him in. And as a final touch, they'd brought along an organist to serenade them. El Sombra grimaced as the music soared to a new and screeching crescendo, and wondered what kind of mind would think to provide such a distraction. The man at the organ was hunched over, wearing a black, hooded robe, his fingers whirling over the keys as he played a series of savage, half-human melodies that seemed to resonate with murder, malice and death. He looked more like a worker than a soldier. Doubtless some poor fool who had been tortured beyond the limits of his endurance until the pillars upon which his sanity had rested snapped like dry twigs. And now, on the whim of one of the bastards, he was set at the organ like a monkey in a travelling sideshow. It was doubtless meant as a distraction. It was a good one. El Sombra saw the men taking their positions to catch him in their crossfire, as if in slow motion, and the constant screeching and wailing of the thing in the corner meant he could barely think at all, much less come up with an escape.

Think, damn it. Think! He was hiding, behind an altar, from ten men armed with wing-packs and machine guns. Four were moving around each side of the altar, two by two, to pin him in a crossfire, and two more were rising into the air to take the advantage of height. The great vaulted ceiling of the Church was perfect for such a manoeuvre. The remaining four – including the commanding officer, he assumed – hung back, taking up the rear. He needn't worry about them just yet, but that still left him facing odds of six to one.

El Sombra had a sword and a pistol in his belt, but nothing that could take care of six armed men, all firing from different angles. And there was no way he could leap out of the way of this. If he couldn't think of a way to murder six armed men in less than a second, he was going to die.

He was in serious trouble, and the worst of it was, no matter how he looked at the situation, there was no way that it wasn't his fault.

Hauptmann Aldous von Abendroth commanded Eagle Staffel.

He was forty-one years of age, he stood at six feet and four inches, and he had less than three per cent body fat. Each day with his breakfast, he drank a glass of tiger's milk and royal jelly, which he had imported from his castle in the Bavarian Alps. After breakfast, he would do one hour of T'ai Chi – a system which he had developed a grudging respect for, despite its origination among the mud men of the East – and then challenged whichever of his men had distinguished himself the day before to a wrestling match. It was considered a great honour among the men of Eagle Staffel to be allowed the chance to wrestle with Aldous von Abendroth.

After the wrestling, he spent another half-hour in fortifying his mind by reading Goethe, or Schiller, or one of the court epics of Heinrich von Veldeke. By that time, the other soldiers, who rose with the dawn like the sluggards they were, were stumbling to the mess hall, perhaps casting a glance at Eagle Staffel as they engaged in some rousing callisthenics, followed by a shared snack consisting of nature's miracle, the grape, with a little goats cheese that he had flown from Tuscany.

And then Eagle Staffel dressed.

Hauptmann Aldous von Abendroth had been awarded the Knight's Cross with Golden Oakleaves, Swords and Diamonds. He was a celebrity in Germany, with a range of chapbooks based on his many exploits in the service of the Fatherland and at least one film, but he was mainly known for his range of health magazines, in which he endorsed a rigorous regimen of callisthenics, T'ai Chi (which he renamed The Abendroth Discipline out of respect to his audience's sensibilities) and of course, nature's miracle, the grape.

Despite these eccentricities, he was a very dangerous man. He was an expert in both armed and unarmed combat as well as a master of planning and strategy. When backed up by his Eagle Staffel he was unstoppable.

Most recently, the Staffel had been called away from rest and recreation in the cafes of Rome to a small Mexican outpost of the Fatherland, in the hope that they would assist in solving the thorny problem of insurgency in that colony. A vast amount of damage had been done by a single man. A specialist in bladed and unarmed combat who was making it his business to disrupt and destroy as much of the good work being done by the Ultimate Reich as he could. Hauptmann von Abendroth had dealt with nihilists of this stripe before. They set themselves against the Fatherland's doctrines of ordnung because they were too weak to survive under the Führer's gaze. Well, Aldous von Abendroth knew something about strength, and he intended to teach that something to the anarchist who cowered before him now.

This 'El Sombra' would find that the lessons of Eagle Staffel were short, and sharp, and very final indeed.

El Sombra narrowed his eyes, looking at the sharp pieces of stained glass that littered the altar and the ground around his feet.

This was going to be tricky.

He moved like a streak of lightning. His hands flashed out to the top of the altar, reaching out to take a large sliver of stained glass in the space between each of his fingers – then he leapt into the air, spinning around once, both arms extended, and let them fly. The razor sharp chunks of coloured glass sped through the air like shurikens.

The effect was impressive, to say the least.

The Church echoed with the wet sounds of glass meeting and piercing flesh. A long chunk of brilliant emerald glass, like the feather of some magnificent bird of paradise, jutted from the eye of a man on his left. On his right, there was a soldier with a long gash running along the side of his neck, the jugular already pumping out a cascading waterfall of rich, red blood as clutching fingers desperately attempted to stem the tide. El Sombra held his stance, muscles tensed, eyes flickering around the circle of men that surrounded him. Everywhere he looked, he saw a fatal wound, a pair of eyes glazing over. He allowed himself to exhale. None of the six shards had missed its target.

Aldous von Abendroth listened, speechless, as the heavy organic thud of four slumping corpses echoed in the confines of the Church – followed by the crash of metal and flesh and hissing steam as two wingmen fell out of the air to crash onto stone.

And then the sound of the organist spurring his instrument on, as though relishing the scent of death.

"Spread out! Random directions, random courses! If you get a shot – take it!" Aldous von Abendroth barked the orders quickly to the three men who remained, not allowing himself to think about the six lying dead on the ground – men who had been his responsibility, who had followed his orders and died because of them. He had trained them, taken care of them, taught them everything he knew, and because he had underestimated the animal squatting in front of him, they had died.

He would not make the same mistake twice.

El Sombra didn't allow himself time for such reflection. He had cut the odds against him by more than half, but that was only because he'd been allowed one free shot. Now he had three people ready to kill him and one more in command, and he should really deal with the damned organist as well. The echoing, screeching music was buzz-sawing through his brain, making it difficult to concentrate. He vaulted the altar and dodged left – and then his eyes lit up.

On a small plinth next to the pulpit, there was a two-foot wide iron collection plate, decorated around the edges with a chorus of trumpeting angels.

Perfect.

He somersaulted forwards, a stream of bullets crossing through the space he had vacated, and snatched up the iron plate, lifting it in time to block another burst of fire from above. He sprinted forward, running between the pews as the bullets chewed up the stone in front and behind. Spinning the plate in his fingers, he gripped it like a discus, aiming upwards, targeting Lieutenant Johannes Trommler, a smart young man of twenty-five who had risen in the ranks quickly, impressing the Hauptmann with his quick reactions. On this occasion, those reactions would not be quick enough. Even as Johannes aimed his rifle to fire a killing shot, El Sombra was already flicking his wrist, sending the iron plate spinning upwards, speeding towards its target. Johannes Trommler made a hideous gurgling sound as the iron plate buried in the front of his throat, penetrating deep enough to lodge between two of his vertebrae.

Hauptmann von Abendroth shouted more orders as another of his charges crashed to the ground, choking and coughing blood. "You two – stay low, for God's sake! Get in close, don't give him room to dodge!"

The masked man's lips twitched, but he did not allow himself the smile. It would not do for the Hauptmann to realise he had taken the bait. If he'd kept his soldiers in the air, with their height advantage, they would most likely have picked him off before he'd managed to target another of them. Now their noble commander had ordered them to clip their own wings.

Well, when they shook hands with the Devil, they could tell him that they had only been obeying orders. Doubtless he wouldn't have heard that one before.

Aldous von Abendroth watched his two remaining men carefully. They were good boys, both of them, and they would know what to do in this situation. The fighting men of Eagle Staffel had been trained to react to any contingency, and von Abendroth was confident that this grim scenario would prove no exception. The insurgent could not be allowed to escape, nor could he be allowed back near the shards of glass. Once had been far more than enough.

He narrowed his eyes and nodded almost imperceptibly at the two remaining men. They returned the nod and began Manoeuvre Vierundzwanzig. Both of the young Lieutenants began to carefully creep in opposite directions, neither too quick nor too slow, Lieutenant Bauer moving to one end of the central aisle that ran the length of the Church, and Lieutenant Ritter heading off the other, blocking El Sombra's access to those remaining glass shards. Once the two were sure the insurgent was trapped between them they would open fire, aiming for the head and upper torso – a classic pincer movement. It was von Abendroth's role in the manoeuvre to keep the masked man's attention focussed on him for the vital moments, taking care to draw his fire without spooking him enough to make a run for it. In von Abendroth's eyes, the procedure was much like luring a dangerous animal – a tiger, perhaps – into a trap, ready for the hunter's bullet. The Hauptmann believed that in comparing his foe to a tiger rather than an ape, he was respecting the danger El Sombra represented.

But there are more dangerous animals in the world than tigers, and they walk on their hind legs.

Aldous von Abendroth ostentatiously aimed his gun as though to fire, and watched the prey carefully through the rifle sight. As was expected, the masked terrorist crouched, readying himself to spring at him as the two trusted Lieutenants moved into position. Unseen by the insurgent, they raised their guns, aiming, tracking...

And then El Sombra took a step back.

Von Abendroth blinked. He was surely about to spring, to attempt a frontal attack – why would he step back? Unless he knew about the two guns on either side. Unless he wanted them in the perfect position to–

"Don't fire!" von Abendroth screamed.

Too late.

Two fingers squeezed two triggers at the exact moment that El Sombra threw himself flat and the two remaining men of Eagle Staffel found themselves staring down the barrels of each other's guns. The thunder of machine-gun fire filled the old stone building, echoing across the pews, mingling with the sound of lead piercing vulnerable organs and the screams of dying men. The organist added the final touch in a crashing minor chord.

As the bullet ridden corpses hit the cold stone floor, El Sombra picked himself up and made a little show of dusting himself down. "And then there was one. Any requests from our musical friend before I send you to join them, amigo?"

Aldous von Abendroth could only stare. In less than two minutes, this scarecrow had destroyed nine of the finest soldiers in the Reich – men he had considered his own sons. Eagle Staffel had been annihilated. The boyhood dream of every young man in the Fatherland had been crushed at the hands of this greasy, unshaven, bloodthirsty maniac.

His voice boomed through the empty space like cannon fire as he fought to control his fury. "You! You don't even know what you've done today, do you, schweinehund? Those were the finest young men I've ever known! We wrestled together at sunrise! Well, now Hauptmann Aldous von Abendroth will avenge their deaths! Come closer, you grotesque abomination! Come closer that I might crush you as easily as I would crush nature's miracle, the..."

El Sombra cut him off. "You're flying low, amigo."

Von Abendroth choked on his words and instinctively glanced downwards. "What?"

The ball of the masked man's foot rocketed up into von Abendroth's jaw, sending him tumbling backwards against one of the pews, the constant churning wail of the organ providing a musical counterpoint to his humiliation. He snarled, recovering quickly and moved into a fighting stance.

The older man feinted a punch to the insurgent's belly, then dropped without warning into a sweeping kick aimed at the ankles, sending the masked man tumbling to the floor to smack hard against the tiles. As El Sombra attempted to raise himself von Abendroth stepped forward to stamp the heel of his leather jackboot down hard against the centre of his back. The fight would go out of the terrorist once von Abendroth had snapped his spine and left him convulsing on the stone floor like a gutted fish.

El Sombra rolled over, putting up his hands to catch the boot as it sped downwards, then twisting hard, sending von Abendroth off his feet to slam into the ground. There was a sickening crack as the Hauptmann's head hit the wood of one of the pews, and his eyes squeezed tight for a single agonised moment – and that moment belonged to El Sombra. He launched himself forward, bringing an elbow down against von Abendroth's throat, his other hand pinning his arm. He repositioned his weight, bringing his centre of gravity down hard on his elbow, attempting to use his own body weight to crush the Nazi's throat.

Aldous von Abendroth growled through gritted teeth,

his breath sounding much like the whining of a deflating balloon, and brought a knee up hard, catching the insurgent where it hurt. It was enough to make El Sombra relax his grip for a second, and Von Abendroth took his chance. He gripped the masked man's shoulders, shifting his weight backward as the knee followed through, driving the masked man's body over his head. Then he swung his other leg up, kicking El Sombra hard in the belly, the momentum driving the terrorist onto his back as he desperately tried to take in a breath. Von Abendroth was on him in less than a second, gripping his throat and slamming his head back down against the stone as he wound his thickly-muscled neck back, like a coiled spring. Von Abendroth might have been the Hauptmann of Germany's most prestigious Staffel, but he still knew how to deliver a dirty blow when he had to.

There was a hard cracking sound as von Abendroth threw his head downward, mashing his forehead into the bridge of El Sombra's nose and banging the back of his head into the floor – once, twice, blood spurting and flowing down over the masked man's moustache and into his mouth. One more would see him finally go under, and then Von Abendroth could finish the job by twisting his head all the way around on his shoulders, and finally consign this ragamuffin to the pit of devils he belonged in.

El Sombra would not give him the chance. He twisted savagely, bringing his legs up underneath von Abendroth's belly, then pushing upwards, launching the Hauptmann over his head to sail into the altar.

The top of his head smacked hard against the carved face of a baby cherub, and all he could see for a moment was a pulsing red light, building and dying away with the agony that radiated from his cracked skull. He'd received worse injuries. All he needed was a moment – a split-second. He concentrated his mind, willing away the pain, readying himself to uncoil. Even over the tumult of the organ, he could hear the terrorist's bare feet as they slapped the stone floor behind him. He would wait for the masked man to get closer and then, when he was within reach, von Abendroth would spin, aiming the heel of one palm into the centre of his forehead. The rock smash blow would drive the brain against the skull – and that would be that. All he had to do was wait for El Sombra to come closer... closer still...

Now, thought Aldous von Abendroth.

And then a single bullet tore through the back of his head, spattering his brains and fragments of his skull across the front of the altar and stilling such thoughts for all time. El Sombra tossed the smoking Luger to one side.

"I had a feeling that bullet would come in handy today."

He Sombra looked around the church at the carnage he had created, and felt a sudden wave of tiredness wash over him. What had this been for? He was spent and aching, covered in cuts and contusions, and Carina was still missing. He decided to head back to the shack and see if Jesus had returned yet. He needed to talk things over and work out some sort of plan of action. It was clear he was going to get nowhere if he continued charging into situations like a raging bull. He smiled softly. Jesus would know what to do. He was a good friend, his only real friend in this terrible place.

He shot a glance at the organist, still playing merrily away. The music of choice was now a funeral dirge, sombre in tone but played with a manic, disturbing glee. It sent a shiver through El Sombra's spine, but he could not find it within him to confront the organ player on the matter. The figure at the instrument seemed so wretched, a deranged madman endlessly pounding his keys, one more victim of the bastards and their tortures. Instead, El Sombra simply turned to make his way out through the front door.

The double doors of the church were locked tightly. He should have expected that. Presumably the keys were with the –

The organ screamed.

El Sombra whirled around, unable to believe what he was seeing. He watched, wide-eyed, as the brass pipes began to peel themselves off the wall, clanking and shrieking and blowing steam, clicking together, reconfiguring themselves. It was like watching the skeleton of some grotesque metal animal building itself from the ground up.

Within less than four seconds, the organ had fully transformed from the musical instrument that had provided such sinister accompaniment to the deaths of Eagle Staffel into what looked like a large mechanical spider, scuttling forward, steam hissing in sinister clouds from the brass legs of the beast. In the centre was a cockpit of sorts – the keyboard formed a semicircle around the organist as he played on, discordant notes flowing from the spider-creature as it obeyed his commands. What El Sombra had taken for the hood of a monk's habit was actually an executioner's mask, and behind it, a pair of bloodshot eyes glittered with a mad passion for murder and death. This was Master Minus' own experiment combining human and robot technology. A terrifying apparition torn from a mind devoted to pain and misery. This was das Drehkreuz!

The Spider.

El Sombra scowled. Trained soldiers were one thing, but this was definitely his cue to leave. He somersaulted forward, aiming to flip onto the altar. His next move was to jump, reaching upwards to catch the edge of the shattered window and haul himself through it to the relative safety of the outside world.

It was a move he never got to make.

The Spider moved with impossible speed, scuttling across the floor of the church and up the wall to block the circular stained-glass window with its body. Suction pads cunningly concealed at the end of the brass legs held it in place as the organist hung horizontally, strapped in his chair, merrily playing his frenetic melody of destruction. El Sombra paused, disturbed by the sheer strangeness of the creature that hung there like its arachnid namesake – and that instant's hesitation was enough. The Spider brought up two of its eight brass legs and sent a hissing jet of scalding steam down to engulf the altar. El Sombra hurled himself back, barely escaping being boiled alive by the thing that hung from the window, and fell hard against the stone with a sickening thud. He'd taken too much punishment in recent weeks, and now every such impact seemed to jar right through him, awakening old hurts and pains.

He swallowed hard and drew his sword. Escape was impossible. It was going to be all he could do simply to stay alive in the face of this threat. Der Zinnsoldat had been bad enough, but that, at least, had been predictable. Its computer brain made it easy to out-think. This was being controlled by a human being. A mind sent far beyond the edge of madness by the devilish practices of the Ultimate Reich. There could be no predicting it, and evidently no avoiding it.

The only way to survive would be to kill it.

He began to step backwards, slowly luring the Spider down from its perch. If superheated steam was its main weapon, it would want to stay close enough to kill. And it wouldn't want him to get hold of the key to the main doors.

He took a single step sideways, reaching for Aldous von Abendroth's corpse.

The Spider pounced.

It was on him in less then a second. The hot brass pipes, dripping with condensation, swiped at his feet in an attempt to send him tumbling to the ground, the organist's eyes alive with a demented glee as his fingers ran up and down the keyboard in a frenzy. But El Sombra had been expecting the attack. He leapt into the air, landing on one set of pipe-legs and then hurling himself at another, using them to swing away towards the pulpit and landing, cat-like, atop it. He could feel the blisters forming on his hands and feet, but the machine reacted the way he hoped, the spider-legs clanking into each other as the machine tried to spin round, almost toppling over. The look of glee on the operator's face was replaced by one of berserk hatred, as his fingers cascaded over the keyboard, urging the monster on after its prey.

El Sombra dived down from the top of the pulpit, rolling between the thing's legs as it let off another thick cloud of scalding steam. The Spider was impressive, even fearsome, but for all that, it was only as good as its pilot. It might have seemed like a wise move to Master Minus to put this lunatic in the control seat. After all, he would have needed someone who was unlikely to be troubled by the deaths of Eagle Staffel, should they fail in their mission –but now that the machine had lost the element of surprise, El Sombra knew he could defeat it.

As the massive monster machine swivelled around in

an attempt to get at him, the long metal legs banging against each other hopelessly, El Sombra darted to the Spider's left, towards the altar, before pushing off it to the right as though part of some human game of bagatelle. He moved quickly, and for a moment the simple joy of action overtook him and he let out his familiar, joyous laugh, so that it echoed through the church, mingling with the crashing chords and wild stabs made by the organ-creature. Wherever the maddened organist directed the terrible engine of destruction, he encountered only empty space, with El Sombra laughing merrily and challenging him with a swipe of his sword, sometimes a few feet away, sometimes across the room. And then the Spider would turn, and sway, and tilt, and lash out crazily with the brass pipes that were its legs, all the time coming closer and closer to toppling completely.

When it finally did, it seemed a mercy.

El Sombra ran at it and, at the last second, let himself fall into a skid, the moisture that had collected on the smooth, cold stone of the floor aiding him as he flew underneath a pair of clashing, crushing spider-legs. Maddened with hatred, the spider desperately tried to reach beneath its own body to catch at him. The mechanism was already severely off-balance from his last few manoeuvres, and this proved to be the final straw. Brass legs clattering against the stone, the suckers at the ends clinging in a terrified attempt to right itself, the Spider slowly toppled sideways, crashing down like a house of cards.

El Sombra saw his moment, and took it.

He hurled his sword like a javelin. The blade sliced through the air before plunging deep into the heart of the organist. The eyes under the executioner's hood bulged in pain, and as the music sighed away with a final screech of indignation, he turned, fixing the masked man with a look of terrible accusation.

El Sombra smiled grimly. "You signed up for the wrong side, amigo. Don't start crying now."

Those were the last words the hooded organist heard. He slumped forward, the look in his eyes freezing, becoming the terrible stare of a corpse.

El Sombra waited, expecting a trick. He'd been foolish to disregard the organist while he was alive, he wasn't about to make the same mistake just because he was dead. He waited a full minute, muscles taut, ready to spring if there was the slightest danger. But there was none. Eventually, he relaxed, breathing out slowly, letting his heartbeat return to normal. It was time to retrieve his sword and get out before anyone came to check for his body – or bring in backup.

He walked forward and gripped the hilt of the sword, readying himself to tug it free from the chest of the dead man. On an impulse, he took hold of the executioner's hood. No harm in seeing the face of the poor bastard underneath.

He tugged the black cloth upwards – and then fell back, pale as death, a strangled cry stillborn in his throat.

The face under the executioner's hood belonged to Jesus Santiago.

His expression was a grimace of fear and terrible sorrow, as though even in death he was begging his only friend not to take his life. In brutal counterpoint to that look of terror and despair, El Sombra's sword jutted from the centre of his chest, evidence of guilt. He took another step back, his silent, cold accuser staring at him, with eyes that would never see again.

And then the Spider reared forward once more, all the more terrible now for its silence, as the cruel metal legs struck with a ferocity they had lacked before, the brass pipes smashing one after another against his skull, slamming into his sides to crack already bruised ribs, blasting him with scalding hot steam.

He put up a token resistance, but the once mighty El Sombra now stumbled where he once leapt, trembled when he once held fast, and the joyous laugh that had once boomed from his throat had been replaced by a shattered, broken whimper of defeat and despair.

Within seconds of this unequal combat, he slumped to the ground, mentally and physically broken.

And the last thing El Sombra saw, before the darkness claimed him, was the face of the friend he had murdered.

"The church is a wreck. But I've pulled all the workers off cleanup in the Great Square to get to work on it. I'm confident it'll look perfect for the proper wedding tomorrow."

Master Minus raised an eyebrow as he spoke into the telephone. "One night is not a great deal of time to restore a church, Herr Generaloberst..."

"Nonsense. I've had them working on fixtures and fittings a week in advance. You didn't think I was going to leave the place as it was, did you?" The voice on the other end of the line was as stony as ever, but there was a warmth in it now, a sense of self assurance that had been missing since El Sombra's arrival. "I have a new stained glass window ready to install, and an altar to go with it. God is dead, Master Minus, and we have killed him. It's time we redecorated his ugly little house to show that off."

Master Minus shared Eisenberg's relief. His own fortunes were bound to his superior's, and while he could be very useful to the Führer even if the clockwork-town proved a failure, it was doubtful Hitler would remember that while in the full flower of his wrath. He allowed himself a soft chuckle at the Generaloberst's little joke. "In that case, we are back on schedule. I'll be taking a little time away from my interrogations tomorrow to catalogue reactions to the wedding. I'll need six or eight of the workers delivered to me for study by late evening."

"Ah yes, the interrogations. One in particular, I imagine." Eisenberg's voice was genial, but there was an edge to it. "If he does not break, kill him. After the wedding tomorrow I want to see him either on a leash or in a coffin."

"My dear Generaloberst, the man is already broken. My wonderful Drehkreuz has done more than a hundred advanced robots ever could have. Even if Der Zinnsoldat had been successful, it could only have crushed his body. My creation has shattered his very soul."

There was a pause before the General spoke again. "Take no chances with him. If he should show even a flicker of resistance... bring me his heart." Master Minus heard a soft click as Eisenberg hung up his end of the line.

Master Minus leant back, and smiled, taking in a deep breath of the yellow mist that swirled around his head. The wonderful tang of it filled him, made him eager to begin the day's work. He smiled, running his withered tongue over his yellowed teeth, and rose to greet his newest charge.

El Sombra still wore his mask.

Master Minus approached the prisoner, casting an eye over the selection of tools he had prepared for use. This one would no doubt prove difficult... had the battle not already been won.

The old man grinned as he looked into the opening eyes of his captive.

"Welcome, El Sombra. Welcome to the Palace Of Beautiful Thoughts."

CHAPTER EIGHT

Psychological Warfare

"We are in an age, Mein Herr, where creativity is forced to find new means of expression.

"Look at the world. In the theatres of London, we see slum children elevated to the status of theatrical players and writers, men like Stamp and Micklewhite debasing the stage in their bawdy attempts to accurately reproduce the squalor and misery of the boarding house and the kitchen sink. In Russia, the Kinema becomes the stomping-ground of the subhuman, with vampires slathered in greasepaint so they may be captured for the camera sinking their fangs into innocent young girls. Werewolves and the risen dead trained to jump through hoops for the amusement of braying, indolent, popcorn fed simpletons. In the Jew held dystopia of New York, the deviant Warhol enamoured the gallerias with infinite reflections of soup cans. Soup cans! They call National Socialism evil, but by God we don't deify packaging.

"What does that leave? Novels by dilettantes about drug addicts, music broken and crushed into three minute chunks for easier digestion, fashion chasing its own tail through a sea of signifiers and shock value. What is left? What medium is there for the artist to explore? The animals have taken the flag of civilisation and they have wiped their ugly bottoms with it. They have been shown the shining canvas that unites creation with Creator and they have torn it to shreds! How is the true man to seek the path of art? How are we to know the mind of God?

"I will tell you, my friend, that there is only one medium remaining with which to create true and lasting art, and that is torture. Torture is all we have left.

"Don't you agree? Which reminds me, how is my Mexican? Adequate?

"Not talking? Well, I can hardly blame you for that. You were badly beaten. Scalded. Bones were broken. I certainly understand if you don't feel like conversing at present, Mein Herr, but never fear. I shall do the talking for both of us.

"All you have to do is breathe."

The voice scuttled and clicked across the stonework, a beetle voice for the beetle man. He was old and withered and bent but still possessed of a terrible potency, unless that was simply the gas. Yellow taint in the air and in his lungs, whispering hideous things in the depths of his mind... how long had the masked man been there, chained to a great iron 'X', hanging, naked and spread-eagled for inspection?

How long had those glittering tools waited to be used?

Scalpels and spurs, barbed wire, a metal ball that separated with the turn of a screw into ever widening segments, to tear and split the orifices of the captive. Soft, wrinkled fingers stroking over sun baked flesh, measuring places to cut, caressing, cupping and gently squeezing with the practiced, shameless ease of a doctor. Or a father at Christmas, smiling and proud, taking his time, waiting to carve.

El Sombra breathed in, and felt something intangible at the core of him begin to pitch and roll and begin to tear apart. Master Minus continued to speak.

"Where were we?

"Ah yes. We were discussing torture and its relationship to art. To appreciate the connection, we must first disconnect the concept of torture from the tiresome notions of morality so often attached to its practice.

"In the chapbooks, the films and the junk novels devoured in their hundreds by the general public, torture is only practiced by the morally corrupt. If this was a scene from a pulp novelette, doubtless I would be cast in the role of the villain. My intention to torture you would signify to the reader that I was the blackest, most evil creature to inhabit the face of the planet. Their sympathies would be drawn to you. They would be... excuse me a moment, I need to make sure this blade is sharp enough to cut bone... They would be on your side. They would weep for your tragic death.

"But let us now assume that this is a different kind of novelette altogether. This one is based on the gritty events of the real world. It has a title designed to rouse the male ego, perhaps Hostile Zone or Spectre Force. It is about agents of the government dealing with terrorists determined to undermine their very way of life.

"Here we are again, on the page, at the torture scene. But now you are a merciless killer, responsible for the deaths of dozens of government troops who are working to bring order to a troubled region. You are a terrorist whose goal is to destabilise everything the government has built here. I do not know who else is operating in your network. I have no idea of what plans your people may even now be carrying out. Allowing you to keep your secrets could result in the deaths of hundreds, perhaps thousands. You will not see reason. You will not talk.

And here I stand.

"I am willing to do whatever it takes to wrest your secrets from you. I am willing to dirty my own hands, to sacrifice my own moral high ground, in order to save the lives of the innocent. Now the reader is with me. He respects my integrity, my courage, my unwillingness to play by rules written by liberals and politicians. And there is a part of him – no small part – that wants to see me prove my masculinity by dominating the cowardly villain in front of me.

"And so, with a simple shift of perspective, you become the villain, and I the hero. And torture, that most morally corrupt of practices, becomes right and proper, a thing of justice, the beloved tool of the righteous and benevolent.

"Torture, Mein Herr, is neither good nor evil in the final analysis. It simply is.

"Allow me to demonstrate."

The blade was a tanto, an antique Japanese dagger. It had not drawn blood since the late fifteenth-century, but the razor edge was still keen and quite capable of cutting through flesh as easily as butter. The old man held it reverentially, testing its edge as he spoke, then gently dipping it in a bowl of vinegar, to maximise the pain of the wounds. Stepping forward, he ran one fingernail over the chest of the chained man, selecting a spot just over the heart. The cuts were slow. Deliberate. Methodical.

There were seventeen in all, small, deep cuts into the flesh. It was only on the thirteenth cut that El Sombra even gritted his teeth. By the fifteenth, he allowed a sound to slip – something halfway between a grunt and a snarl.

At the seventeenth cut, he cried out, and his head fell forward.

The old man washed the cut with a sponge dipped in vinegar, admiring the effect. The scars, once healed, would display the Japanese kanji 'kage', meaning shadow. A nice touch, the old man thought. After all, he didn't intend to leave the chained man his face. How would his new masters recognise him without the proper identification?

He chuckled, the sound of a thousand beetles skittering over a sheet of glass. And then he began to speak again.

"So. We have established that torture is a concept outside the realm of morality, to be classed as right or wrong depending on who wields the reins of power. If it makes you feel better, we can use a different word. Interrogation, perhaps, or questioning.

"Or art.

"After all, an artist is one who shapes a particular medium to suit him, whether it is as a statement or merely for aesthetic pleasure. That medium might be stone, or clay, or porcelain. It might be canvas or celluloid, words on a page or actors on a stage. But the artist shapes the medium and recreates it to his wishes with the tools at hand.

"In this case, the medium is your flesh and soul, which have been given to me to reshape according to my will. The tools I use are laid out before you, scalpels and skewers, vices and clamps, one hundred little gadgets that I have collected over the years, each one serving a specific purpose in sculpting you to meet the needs of my superiors. But these are crude tools at best. What is the pain of cut flesh compared to the agony of knowing that you murdered your only friend? What is the ache of a broken rib compared to the ache in your heart when you remember how you ate and drank with him, how you shared his home and hospitality, and then drove your blade through his heart because you just couldn't be bothered to save him?

"Breathe in, my friend. Breathe it in deep. You'll come very quickly to understand, I think.

"That is the true purpose of this torture – of this art. To open your eyes. You must learn to see things as I do. I am not doing this to you as punishment. I am doing this to bring you your salvation, to rehabilitate you, to make you understand your place in the scheme of things. When I am done with you... when you have breathed in your fill of these wondrous airs of humiliation and despair... you will see that the way of the Ultimate Reich is the way forward for humanity.

"And you will see it of your own accord."

And then the chained man began to laugh.

Softly at first, then louder, the sound rolling through the quiet, cold room like the skeletons of winter leaves in a chill and bitter wind. It was not a laugh of joy, or of hope, or of strength, or of anything associated with sunlight and clean air. It was a laugh that belonged in these dank and fetid conditions, a snide chuckle, a sneering, contemptuous snicker. A laugh like a thousand beetles marching across a sheet of glass.

It was a sound that would have been sickeningly familiar to anyone who had once been a guest of the

Palace Of Beautiful Thoughts. The old man started back, looking at the features of his chained captive, breathing in sharply as the handsome face of the terrorist became foreign and strange, warped by the noise emanating from it. He recognised the sound too, recognised the dry, hollow chuckle. And it chilled him.

The chained man turned his head, as though on aged bones, and smiled, a dry and sinister grin. And then he spoke. And the voice that came from his throat did not belong to El Sombra at all.

The chained man spoke with Master Minus' voice.

"Very good. Very well done. You're almost there now, my friend.

"Tell me, how did it feel to make the incisions? Was it stimulating to carve helpless flesh as though it were meat in a butcher's shop window? Did the experience make you feel in control? Dominant? Like a true man? Very good, Mein Herr. Very, very good.

"You even spout my doctrine as though it were your own. We've really made some marvellous progress in the last few hours. I think we might put you to work as a soldier when we're done..."

The old man stepped back, straightening as he breathed in deep. He could taste the tang in the air, the yellow mist that coiled around his head. He looked towards the mirror, at the aged face, the lines and wrinkles and deep canyon-folds etched into the flesh.

For some reason, he did not recognise his own eyes.

"Poor El Sombra. Poor hero, poor monster. You still haven't learned the true meaning of shame, have you? After all you've done...

"I told you that I wanted to make you understand how things truly are. How can you understand stretched on a rack? How can you see the truth when your eyes are blinded by pain and shame and the depths of your despair? It is not enough to understand helplessness and suffering – you must know the savage joy that comes with inflicting these things upon others.

"In order to truly be brought to our way of thinking, you must know what it is to be the torturer."

The old man's hands shook, and he turned towards the chained man for a moment with a look of helpless terror. Then he summoned his authority – the authority of the torturer – and attempted to force words from his throat to overtake the dry, whispering insinuations that emanated from the man on the rack.

The chained man's smile froze him in his tracks. It promised terrible cruelty, a mephistophilean love of manipulation, and the eyes sparkled with fire from the depths of Hell itself. The old man sucked in another breath scented with sickly yellow and looked desperately away, to find himself staring once again at the mirror, at the face that was surely not his own...

"That's right, Mein Herr. You are the torturer. The self-made hero, El Sombra, finds himself reborn into the body of the villain, Master Minus – or is it the other way around? Is the despised terrorist now finding a new lease of life as a noble hero of the Ultimate Reich?

"How many have you tortured today, Master Minus? I saw the glee in your eyes while you delved and hacked and sawed. I heard the whispered words you spoke, almost lovingly, into the ear of that father of three, the one you warmed up with. You've done well in your new role. It's hard to believe the heroic El Sombra ever existed... although now I think of it, he was always fond of tearing his enemies apart with that sharp sword of his, wasn't he? I suppose Master Minus was always there, just waiting to get out. In many ways, this must be a dream come true for you..."

"It isn't true."

The old man was shocked to hear the voice come from his mouth. Was that the soft-spoken rasp of Master Minus? Had those words been spoken by the man who had studied the works of Freud and Jung in the forbidden libraries of the Reichstag, who had had long discussions with Adolf Hitler – not the frail flesh portrayed in the destroyed statue, but the towering majesty of the true Führer – on the nature of the self? Or was this a cracked and pale imitation?

He swallowed and spoke again, hoping against all hope that this time the voice would sound more like Master Minus, less youthful, less... less Mexican. But deep down, as he tasted the yellow poison on his tongue and felt it unlocking the dizzying, vertiginous trapdoors of his soul, he knew that the voice of Master Minus was the voice that came from the man who hung in chains with blood trickling slowly over his belly and a familiar smile lighting up his face.

He closed his eyes, listening to his own words echoing hollowly.

"It isn't true..."

"Oh yes it is.

"Look in the mirror, Master Minus. Look at the rubber face hanging loosely over your own. Feel the way your back aches and strains from being stooped over in an imitation of age. Here is the truth, El Sombra. You've been Master Minus for hours. Perhaps this was who you always were.

"If the conditions are right, then a cheap theatrical mask is all that stands between the noble hero and the torturer. Take off the mask, El Sombra. Let yourself see how far you have fallen."

The old man, who suddenly felt neither old nor a man, raised his hands, fingertips touching the aged, wrinkled face with the unfamiliar eyes. Could he fool himself that his fingertips travelled across soft, worn flesh, lined with years of service? Or was he feeling sterile plastic, soft, loose latex? He shuddered, the motion travelling up his spine, his hands shivering and twitching as he tugged ...

"Take off the mask."

❦   ❦   ❦

... and the old, wrinkled, false face was torn away, coming off in long strips, pulled away bit by bit to reveal another face underneath. His eyes were wide, unblinking, unable to close as he stared at the face underneath, the face that had been there all the time.

Behind him, the thin beetle-voice spoke once more.

And this is what it said:

"APRIL FOOL! QuiÈn es el hombre? QuiÈn es el hombre? I'm the hombre! I'm the hombre! Now all I need are some pants."

El Sombra grinned down from the vertical rack at Master Minus, slumped on his knees in front of the blood spattered mirror, staring without eyelids at the remains of his face. He had succeeded in tearing all of the flesh from it, and all that remained were a few scraps of muscle clinging to a crimson, bloodstained skull, with two grotesque eyeballs gazing mercilessly at their own reflection. El Sombra smiled and did the voice, again while he made another attempt to work his left hand free of the shackle that held it in place.

"Creatures of the night... what music... they make... I vant to suck your bloooood... yeah, you keep looking, amigo. Intense shame boosted by mind-warping drugs, hey? That's very original, I wouldn't know what that's like at all... ah, these bastard cuffs!" He was babbling, a result of the endorphin rush from the intense pain and the thrill of victory. The yellow mist coursing through his veins – the mist Master Minus relied on so heavily – had been counterbalanced by the Trichocereus Validus already in his system, the desert cactus that had destroyed and rebuilt his mind. But while El Sombra was in a stronger position than the torturer realised, Master Minus was weaker than he knew, far too used to the easy victories the mist brought him, not realising that his own exposure to it made him ripe for psychological attack. The old man had spent years claiming that he was immune to the yellow mist, but nobody had ever been in a position to test that claim – until now.

That didn't mean El Sombra was immune to the mist either. The strange fog was slowly starting to make his head swim, bringing up memories of his brother's curse and Jesus Santiago's final accusing stare. He hadn't torn his own face off just yet, but he could feel his mind slowly breaking under the pressure. It was time to check out.

He grunted, teeth gritting again, as his hand tore free of the manacle, raw and bloody. It felt like the edge of the metal cuff had taken off most of the skin, and he was lucky his thumb hadn't been dislocated. He flexed it a few times before reaching for the cotter pin he kept fixed at the back of his mask and starting work on the other shackle, trying not to breathe in more than he had to. The sooner he was out in the fresh air, the better he'd like it.

"So... where are you keeping her?"

General Eisenberg admired his dress uniform in the mirror, adjusting his cufflinks carefully. "In the basement. We still have some holding cells there from the days before we built the Palace. I wouldn't go down there, though. It's bad luck to see the bride the night before the wedding."

"It's a quarter to eleven, Father. The wedding's at noon. I'm sure it wouldn't do any harm to look in on her. Just to share a final sweet moment together before we meet at the altar..." Alexis busied himself brushing his shoes, which had arrived in the post that morning from Milan, where they were currently proving the height of fashion. This was one of the few pairs of shoes Alexis had ordered in recent weeks that had actually arrived in any fit state to be worn. He had lost eight pairs of suede loafers – hand-crafted in Tuscany – when the Traction Engine had toppled over the cliff, and attempts to have other pairs brought across the desert on the trolleys had been stymied by El Sombra's one-man raiding parties. Once, he'd been fortunate enough to receive a pair of brogues from Saville Row that had allegedly managed to find their way through. He'd opened the box to find an 'E' carved onto one toe and an 'S' onto the other.

Alexis shook his head. "I'm sorry, Father, what were you saying?"

"I was running through the schedule for today, Alexis, if you could take your mind off your footwear for a moment. Carina and her father have both been dressed and are being gathered for the ceremony. They'll be waiting by the main doors by 11:30 hours. By 11:40, I need you to – where are you going?"

Alexis looked back at his father as he sauntered to the door, flashing his angelic smile. "Well, I've got almost an hour. I thought I'd borrow a wing–pack and head over to the Palace. Maybe check in on my best man... show him my new sword." He grinned and hefted the recently-acquired blade, twirling it a little before placing it in a sheath at his waist.

The Generaloberst closed his eyes and pinched the bridge of his nose, trying to control his anger. "You don't need another reason to talk to Master Minus, Alexis. You pay more attention to that withered corpse of a man than you do to your father. I told him – and I told you – there is no way in hell that El Sombra is going to be your best man. I don't care what sort of message it sends, we're not dropping a random element like that into a controlled experiment! We either have him publicly executed or we have him put to work on the latrines–" He looked up from his tirade and lapsed into angry silence.

Alexis had gone.

El Sombra hadn't had any luck finding anything to wear, but he had found a Japanese katana to match the tanto. The twin swords had been a gift from the Japanese emperor after the recognition of Manchukuo in 1938, and had been subsequently passed on to Master Minus in recognition of his service. They were a good pair of swords – finely balanced and very sharp. As El Sombra had had no practice fighting with a dagger, he took the longer one and left the tanto behind. He wasn't too fond of that blade anyway. The blood was still dripping down over his belly.

His left wrist was still throbbing and stinging, and the yellow mist was hardly helping his composure. The maze of tunnels and cells that composed the Palace Of Beautiful Thoughts was ghoulish and confusing enough in the ordinary course of events, but with Master Minus' drugs coursing through his veins and lungs, the cold and sterile concrete felt like the inside of some hideous mausoleum. The walls loomed in oppressively and the echo of each footstep convinced him that there were enemies on all sides, waiting like tigers to spring at him. In fact, nothing could be further from the truth. There were no guards stationed inside the Palace Of Beautiful Thoughts. Soldiers were required to enter only to escort prisoners to their cells. Once in their cells, any prisoners were swiftly made tractable and easily directed by the mists, and Master Minus could generally move them from place to place himself without any trouble.

Those few prisoners left in their cells did not reassure El Sombra in the slightest. When he worked open their cell doors and attempted to give them their freedom, most simply continued lying on the floor as they had been. One or two burst into tears. One man of around thirty walked towards the grey concrete wall of his cell and began to rhythmically bang his head against it, until El Sombra knocked him unconscious to keep him from fracturing his skull.

Carina, thankfully, was not among the prisoners. To see her in that state would have most likely driven El Sombra over the edge.

Eventually, the masked man opened an airtight metal door to find himself in a small room with leather jumpsuits in a variety of sizes hanging on one wall, and another larger airtight door on the other. As he closed the smaller door behind him, extractor fans in the ceiling pumped slowly into life, drawing the yellow mist from the room and replacing it with clean, fresh air. El Sombra felt his head begin to clear immediately, and allowed himself to stand for a moment, taking in deep lungfuls, relaxing as the artificial wind slowed around him.

The outer door began to open.

Hans Bader had been guarding the outer door to the Palace Of Beautiful Thoughts for a little over three years. In many ways, he was the perfect candidate for such a duty, for Hans Bader had lived in a state of almost constant fear and anxiety for most of his adult life.

His first memory was of seeing his father's pipe in a pipe-holder in the study, and reaching up with tiny little fingers to take hold of the fascinating object. His father had not had the chance to clean his briar-bowl that day, and the ash had, quite naturally, gone everywhere, most of it scattering on an antique rug that his father had brought back from Turkey. Hans Bader vividly remembered how his mother had grabbed his shoulders and shaken him roughly. "You're a stupid, stupid, stupid little boy!" she had screamed, as he bawled in uncomprehending terror. His father stood by, shaking his head, and at the end of his mother's outburst he had simply muttered that he was very disappointed. Then he left Hans Bader to sit in his room and think about what he'd done.

It was a pattern that repeated itself throughout his childhood. There would be some minor infraction – a bottle of milk accidentally tipped over perhaps, or an egg dropped on the floor, or simply a word out of place – and his mother would grab at his shoulders, shake him roughly, and bellow that he was stupid and useless and had no common sense whatsoever. His father would simply repeat, in his low, slow, sad voice, that he was extremely disappointed. And Hans would be sent, shaking at the ferocity of the verbal assault, to his room, to think deeply about what a useless and pathetic creature he truly was.

He began to jump at shadows, staying in his room constantly to avoid the verbal attacks, spending his time there trembling and twitching with an unnamed dread. His father, having already proved himself an expert on the rearing of children, took his listlessness and depression for indolence and resolved, after caning the boy several times, that the best thing for him would be the army.

And thus, Hans Bader was enlisted with the Ultimate Reich.

Naturally, by this time his confidence had been not so much damaged as razed to the ground. He was utterly incapable of using his own initiative by this point, and as a result, stood frozen and trembling while his fellow soldiers rushed about their tasks, petrified lest he make some tiny, insignificant error. He was deathly afraid of his drill instructor upon first meeting, and memorably wet himself on being asked his name, which sealed his fate with regards to his fellow soldiers. 'Wetpants Bader' had a career that mostly consisted of being shuttled from one place to another, screamed at for being almost completely incompetent, and then dismissed, to be moved on to the next hellhole that awaited him.

Eventually, his travels took him to Aldea. By this stage, he was heartsick, barely able to eat and had developed a severe nervous twitch in his right eye. When other soldiers stood stiffly to attention, he hunched his shoulders, quivering like an autumn leaf.

It was in such a state of nervous exhaustion that he was first taken to meet Master Minus.

Master Minus had never had more enjoyable company.

Soon, Hans Bader was given a new task, one he was told that he could not possibly fail at. He would stand outside the door to the Palace Of Beautiful Thoughts and prevent anyone without the proper clearance from entering – a simple matter of remembering the faces of three people. And whenever he heard the telltale whine of the fans, that was his cue to open up the door and allow Master

Minus to leave, lest the old man strain himself turning the heavy iron handle.

Almost shockingly, he found himself happy in this work. It was so very simple, and Master Minus was the only person he had ever met who truly liked him for who he was. Slowly, he began to feel more self-assured. Which, for Hans Bader, meant fewer episodes of bed wetting and more nights spent sleeping rather than staring at the ceiling and shivering in cold, stark, fear.

For a little over three years, Hans Bader had guarded the door, protecting the Palace Of Beautiful Thoughts against any threats that might come from outside. He was finally somewhere close to being happy, and had even grown almost proud of his three years of service. He felt that he could finally call himself competent.

Unfortunately, he couldn't. In guarding the door against outside intruders, he had made another grievous error – his last.

He had never considered that a threat might appear from within.

His end was mercifully swift. The keen edge of the katana cut through Hans' side, slicing through organ, muscle and bone until it exited through his shoulder; along the way, it split his heart into two unequal segments, ending his life in an instant.

The body slid into two chunks as El Sombra stepped back, nimbly avoiding the gore.

As he stood, breathing heavily and trying to get the remains of the drug out of his system, a small burst of applause erupted from the sky above his head. He looked up.

There, smiling angelically in a wing-harness, steam-wings creaking softly as he slowly glided towards the ground, was Alexis Eisenberg. El Sombra looked at him, and then looked at his right hand. Suddenly he could no longer hear for the sound of blood pounding relentlessly in his ears.

Clutched in Alexis' hand was the sword that had belonged to El Sombra's brother, Heraclio.

The Generaloberst walked around the Old Church slowly, casting a critical eye over the new decor. Finally he paused, and turned to Oberleutnant Odell Strauss, who had masterminded the workforce in transforming the place in a single night.

"Most satisfactory, Oberleutnant. The pews could perhaps have used a little more work, but the new altar is perfectly serviceable. And I particularly like the new stained-glass window. It's simple yet bold."

The window that had been shattered by El Sombra on his entrance had been replaced by a gigantic swastika, in black on red. It cast the whole church in a baleful, bloody glow, making it look like a place more suited to satanic rituals than a wedding. The altar had also been remodelled, the angels originally pictured on its sides replaced by soaring eagles flying though fields of sculpted fire, and the wooden pews were now decorated with more swastikas, tastefully carved into the wood at regular intervals. The only part of the Old Church untainted by the Nazi emblem was the creaking old pipe organ. It had been dismantled to create a space for Das Drehkreuz to lurk in, but now it was back in its old familiar place, as though it had never left. Ironically, under the infernal light it looked like nothing so much as an ancient torture device.

Oberleutnant Strauss nodded. "Thank you, Herr Generaloberst. Under the circumstances, I feel it would be wise to discipline the workers who recarved the pews, since their craft has proved somewhat lacking."

Eisenberg nodded. "Shoot them. Master Minus is far too busy to be interrupted with trifles. My son is no doubt delaying him with foolish requests as we speak." He looked down at his watch – twenty minutes to noon. He sighed, and walked to the open double doors, looking out at the street. Over a distant rooftop, he could see a single stone hand where once there had been the reassuring figure of his Führer, standing in proud dominion over the town.

He sighed and shook his head.

"Where is that boy?"

Alexis smiled as he touched down in front of the masked man. He wore a tuxedo which had cost slightly over 2,000 Marks, a pair of shoes hand-stitched by Salvatore Ferragamo himself, and a necktie made by McLaren and Westwood of the King's Road, a black silk affair with a single blood-red swastika imprinted on it where a tiepin would normally stand. Even the creaking pack on his back fitted perfectly, the straps holding fast without ruining the line of the suit. He looked – and felt – truly angelic. The perfect couture in which to slaughter his greatest enemy.

The trick would be to avoid getting blood on the tuxedo. Although perhaps a little would offset the fabric nicely.

He examined his enemy. El Sombra trembled slightly as he stood, like a leaf in a light breeze. His eyes were red and bloodshot, his knuckles white as they gripped the handle of the katana. He looked feverish, occasionally shaking his head slightly as if to clear it. Several fresh wounds were bleeding down over his right nipple, arranged in a pattern the significance of which escaped Alexis entirely. And he was completely naked except for the mask.

Alexis ran his finger slowly over the scar that marked his beautiful face, then grinned like a wolf.

The mask would have to go.

He lunged forward, aiming the point of Heraclio's sword at El Sombra's shoulder. The masked man, still disoriented from the yellow mist, and reeling from the sight of his brother's most prized possession in the hand of the man who had murdered him, failed to block the blow quickly enough, and the point of the sword grazed his shoulder, drawing fresh blood.

El Sombra grimaced in pain. Paradoxically, his first thought was not to the two inch gash in his shoulder, but rather to his brother's sword. Bad enough that it was in the hands of Alexis, but the katana was by far the stronger blade. El Sombra knew from the heft and the sharpness that it was capable of snapping Heraclio's sword in two, like an axe chopping a sapling. Perhaps he should have done just that – ended the threat before using a second slash to divest Alexis of both his wolfen smile and the head that went with it. But this was his brother's sword. It was more than just a weapon. It was all that remained of Heraclio. It had been handed to him with his brother's dying breath. It was not a possession, but rather a sacred relic.

It would be wrong to say that for El Sombra, losing the sword was like losing a limb. It would be like losing the very heart beating in his breast.

Alexis knew this, of course.

He had not spent years visiting and conversing with Master Minus simply for the company. He had always been adept in spotting the physical weaknesses of his

foes, but with the insights the old torturer had provided
him, he knew where to search for psychological weakness
as well. His father, for example, had a deeply buried fear
of the Führer – something Alexis suspected was common
in those who had actually come face to face with Adolf
Hitler in his later years. A simple phone call had been
enough to arouse the Führer's interest in Projekt Uhrwerk
and inform him about the new element attacking it, and
suddenly the great General Eisenberg was concentrating
less on controlling his son than on saving his own neck,
which had allowed the younger Eisenberg the freedom
to play his own games. As a result of which, Alexis
had discovered El Sombra's own hidden weakness. He
grinned, darting forward again, forcing the renegade to
parry his brother's blade as it aimed for his heart and
then for lower organs. Then he spoke.

"What's the matter, Djego?"

El Sombra stumbled back as though he had been
struck. Alexis stepped forward to fill the gap, keeping
Heraclio's sword moving, forcing the masked man to
continue parrying to avoid being skewered. "Oh, I see..."
He chuckled, his right arm a blur of motion. "This is the
way your brother was killed, wasn't it, Djego? While you
watched? As I remember, you were crying at the time,
like a little child, so it's always possible you didn't see
very much. But you saw plenty of him afterwards, didn't
you, Djego?"

It was like being punched in the stomach. The name.
Again and again. The shame of it. The man he had been,
and as the yellow mist sparked and hissed inside his
brain, the man he was again. Dirty and ashamed and
alone in his brother's blood.

He swung the katana, but it was with Djego's strength,
and Alexis easily blocked the clumsy strike. El Sombra

– if it was El Sombra and not Djego, that foppish, foolish young man who had let his brother die – blinked, trying to marshal his thoughts. He was being taken apart like an amateur. He was an amateur. He was weak and hopeless and useless...

"You've failed him again, Djego. Poor Heraclio. It's a good thing I killed him. Imagine how he'd feel to see this." Alexis was, frankly, having the time of his life. This was utterly perfect. It was everything he'd wanted since the first time he'd been humiliated by the man in the mask. It was perfect. The perfect wedding present.

"And that reminds me; in a few minutes I'll be marrying the lovely Carina, who I believe you've met. This sword is going to be my wedding gift to her. Don't get me wrong, it's of no particular sentimental value, in fact–" He lunged, slashing at El Sombra's belly while the other man clumsily attempted to parry. "– in fact, when I sliced its original owner apart like so much wurst, I felt... well, I felt less than nothing, really." Another lunge. This time the blade gashed the masked man's cheek, and Alexis grinned with petty vengeance. "I mean, for me, this is just a souvenir of a particularly dull invasion. I fought a halfwit and subjugated a city of mindless sheep. Hardly one for the history books."

El Sombra snarled, and there was blood in his eyes. Alexis smiled. Almost there...

"Still, I'm sure my lovely wife will appreciate it. By the time it severs her neck, I'd imagine it'll come as something of a relie–"

El Sombra charged.

He was angrier than he'd been in a long time. There was rage in him, hot and righteous and blazing, and he was ready to carve his brother's killer into bloody chunks with the heavy blade of the katana and then go on and cut every member of the Reich to pieces, to keep cutting and chopping and hacking until every last one of the bastards was dead at his feet. He wanted to soak the streets of his childhood in their blood, to cleanse the rotten sewer that his town had become.

Alexis flicked Heraclio's sword forward with machine precision, the point slashing through the skin and muscle of El Sombra's forearm. The masked man's fingers flared involuntarily and the katana clattered to the ground at his feet. Alexis kicked the sword away with the point of his immaculate shoe.

He smiled, eyes narrowing, savouring the moment. "Look at you! You've met the woman once and suddenly you fly into a rage over an idle threat. This is exactly like you, Djego. Didn't you try to ruin your brother's marriage the same way?"

He levelled the point of the sword at his enemy's throat.

"Take off the mask, Djego. It's time to grow up a little."

Djego looked up at him, swallowing hard, clutching his injured arm. Suddenly he felt very small and weak and foolish. Alexis' smile widened.

"El Sombra is dead."

Master Plus was dead. He knew this to be a certainty as he stood in his place by the altar, dressed in a spotless new white suit, tugging at the tight collar and feeling, not for the first time, as though he would suffocate. He shuddered inside as the first few bars of the Wedding March played on the creaking organ and he saw his daughter, dressed in a beautiful white gown and veil, led down the aisle by Oberleutnant Strauss. He had been judged too much of a risk to play that particular role in this farce, and he found himself glad.

A disinterested observer might have thought that Carina was looking around at the new decor of the Old Church. Actually, she was checking possible escape routes and examining the congregation. A crowd of sixty men were stood to attention in the pews, all of them wearing gleaming wing-packs and armed with some form of automatic weapon. She wasn't sure which possibility was more frightening – that this was a trap, or that such an armament was part of their uniform. Actually, the latter was the case. This was the officer class of Aldea. The highest echelon. For the most part, they were pen-pushers and desk-warmers, long absent from any form of real combat. The wings on their backs were dress models, plated with gold and silver to catch the eye, rather than the more powerful combat models. And the machine guns were purely for the occasion. A show of strength that seemed almost comical coming from this crowd of armchair warriors.

Failing to find any immediate way out of the situation, she turned her eyes to her father, and felt a pang of sympathy for him. It confused her.

Master Plus saw the look of compassion in his daughter's eyes and looked away. Anger or bitterness he could have dealt with, but the look of pity on her face was far too much to bear.

Oberleutnant Strauss led her to the altar and then stood stiffly as the Wedding March played on. And on. It was five minutes to noon, and the groom was still nowhere to be seen. The congregation continued to stand stiffly to attention, looking straight ahead. General Eisenberg, in full dress uniform and his own pair of dress wings, stood at the pulpit, looking out on the scene as it descended further and further into a parody of itself. He hissed through his teeth like a teakettle and muttered the same words over and over again.

"Where is that boy? Where is that boy?"

Djego reached behind his head and untied the knot that had bound the red wedding sash to his face for nine long years. It took several tries to pick apart the blood encrusted knot, and when he lifted the mask from his face he was left with a strip of paler brown across his eyes, where the sun had not baked his flesh. Alexis could not help snorting with laughter at the sight.

"You look like a raccoon. Was it worth it, Djego? All you've really done is make things worse for the people you allegedly care about. We might have shipped them back to the Fatherland for cheap labour if you hadn't stepped in, but now – well, we'll be killing them and bulldozing their bodies into pits. Entirely because of you." He smiled genially. Djego had already sunk down onto his knees, and was looking at the ground like a contrite schoolboy, the long wedding sash cradled in his hands. It was too perfect. Alexis slowly drew back Heraclio's sword. He was satisfied. It was time for the coup de grace.

"Goodbye, Djego. I'll put your brother's sword to better use." He smiled, slashing Heraclio's sword forward, aiming to bury it in Djego's worthless throat.

The blade passed through empty space.

Djego was already moving, springing up and spinning out of the way of the blade – performing a backward flip and sailing over the head of his enemy. He came down like a cat behind Alexis, wrapping the wedding sash around his throat and pulling tight. Heraclio's sword clattered into the dirt as Alexis desperately reached up, scrabbling helplessly at the tightening material. Djego leaned in and whispered into the other man's ear as he tugged the sash tighter still, and there was something in his voice as cold and unyielding as a gravestone.

"Amigo... that's my sword."

Alexis could only gurgle and gasp, mouth flapping like a fish, eyes bulging and rolling into the back of his head as the man behind him pulled with a devil's strength, the red cloth burying into the flesh of his neck, cutting off both his air and the blood flow to the brain.

His hands continued to scrabble at the cloth cutting into his throat for a few more seconds before they fell limply down to hang at his sides. The strength left his legs and he slumped, held up only by the sash that was strangling him. His feet began to twitch and writhe and in a final indignity, his bowels and bladder let go, drenching the inside of his expensive, immaculate suit with filth.

It was ten minutes before Djego let go of the wedding-sash and let the body crash to the ground.

The organist dutifully went into the Wedding March for another time. It was almost twenty minutes past noon. The congregation were still standing to attention, albeit with visible effort. Master Plus was still looking at the ground. Carina, in her wedding gown, continued to look carefully around at the windows and the double doors. And General Eisenberg paced back and forth in front of the altar, lips pulled back from gritted teeth, staring furiously at nothing at all.

"Where... is... Alexis?" He barked the words like a snarling dog.

His son would pay for this humiliation. The El Sombra business may have called unwelcome attention to Aldea at a crucial moment, but it was Alexis who was the loose cannon now. All eyes were on the project, and while this wedding was, at best, a minor experiment, it had become symbolic of a return to business as usual, a sign that the Generaloberst's grip on matters was still as firm as it had ever been. Alexis would not sully that. He would not be allowed to drag his father down through his own flippant attitudes. Alexis would be brought down to the level of Obergefreiter. He would be forced to clean the latrines in the town for seven months. He would be disowned.

There was a knock at the door. Or rather, the hilt of a sword pounding against the wood, three times.

The Wedding March stopped. General Eisenberg cursed, and stepped quickly back to his place behind the podium, thankful that his wretched son had at least thought to give the assembly some warning before he sauntered in from whatever jaunt he'd been on for the past hour. Perhaps it would not be necessary to reduce his rank to Private after all. First Lieutenant would be quite sufficient.

"Come in and take your place, Alexis. We need to get this wedding back on schedule."

There was silence. Eisenberg smashed his fist down hard against the pulpit and screamed.

"Alexis! Get in here now!"

Slowly, the wooden double doors creaked open, to reveal a dead man. Wilhelm Brandt had been happy to be picked to stand guard on the Old Church and ensure none of the curious workers stepped near it until the wedding was finished with. He had felt it an honour, after years of being passed over for such duties, to finally be picked to add his strength to an important venture for the Ultimate Reich. He saw guarding the Church almost as a sacred trust.

So the last emotion that passed though him after the hilt of the sword seemed to come out of nowhere to smash hard into the back of his head was a feeling of crippling shame. The knowledge that his unconscious body was to be stripped before his throat was slit, in order that his killer might get a clean pair of trousers, would have been unlikely to alleviate that.

El Sombra stepped into the Church, his mask firmly in place, Alexis' wing-pack strapped tightly to his back. In his right hand, he held his brother's sword. In his left, he held a human heart, freshly hacked from its owner's chest. He smiled.

"Your son couldn't make it, Herr Generaloberst. But he asked me to convey his apologies and to assure his bride that his heart, at least, will always be with her."

He tossed the bloody organ into the Church and it skidded along the stone floor, tumbling over and over to rest a couple of inches from Carina's white dress.

"How thoughtful of him," she said softly.

After that, there was silence for a while.

And then the congregation turned, levelled their automatic weapons, and opened fire.

CHAPTER NINE

Gotterdammerung

The noise hit like a bomb.

Sixty heavy-calibre machine-guns opening up as one, spraying a torrent of lead at the entrance of the Church. Stray bullets impacted against the heavy oaken doors, splintering them, tearing them off their hinges so that they collapsed to either side of the yawning entrance. There was the tinkling sound – like a thousand tiny bells – of cartridges bouncing off the stone tiles. The overall noise was deafening – a hundred storms rolled into one, a barrage of thunder and final judgement, a hymn of murder and destruction that echoed around the stone arches above.

The barrage lasted a total of eight seconds, and in that time two thousand three hundred and eighty-seven bullets were blasted towards the figure standing in the doorway.

None of them connected.

El Sombra was no longer there.

Carina took her hands from her ears and looked through the crowd of soldiers and the thick, pungent fog of cordite. She took a sharp breath at the sight of a riddled, punctured corpse laying in the dirt – and then remembered Wilhelm Brandt, the hapless guard who'd died a few moments before the tide of bullets had torn his body into shreds. Of El Sombra, there was no sign. Slowly, the soldiers crept forward, inching towards the doors, ready for the masked man to appear from whatever point of ambush he had chosen.

In the expectant silence, she heard a slight creaking sound, far above her head.

The soldiers heard it too. One by one, they cast their eyes upwards, towards the ceiling.

Silence.

And then the stained glass window exploded once again, the swastika shattering into a thousand shards as El Sombra flew through it on the wings he'd taken from Alexis' corpse. He'd stolen more than a pair of trousers from the luckless Wilhelm Brandt. He'd also stolen the guard's M30 machine-gun, secreting it on top of the church roof in case the numbers inside were too much to handle. Now he made use of it, squeezing the trigger to let off long bursts of fire, sending streams of ammunition into the crowd below him. While the masked man had had problems with guns in the past, the congregation in the church was so densely packed together that he couldn't help but hit one of them no matter where he fired.

Oberleutnant Strauss reacted instantly to the carnage unfolding in front of him. He was confident that his position next to Carina would shield him from the attack, and so, ignoring the tiny slivers of glass that cascaded over his head, he pulled his Luger from its holster and aimed carefully. Odell Strauss might have been a dab hand at interior design, but as a marksman he was even better. He was confident that, from this position, he could hit the masked man's femoral artery, causing him to bleed out over the assembled company within the space of a few brief seconds. He smiled softly. It would certainly be a wedding to remember.

That was the moment when the jailer, Rafael Contreras – who had spent the last nine years as Master Plus, manservant and dogsbody to a regime that considered

him less than human – finally found his courage. Seeing
the Oberleutnant levelling his pistol, he took two quick
steps forward and drove his elbow hard into the man's
teeth, a move he had first learned to use against the
drunks and hopheads in his father's jail when he was
sixteen. Now the jail that his father had built was the
Palace Of Beautiful Thoughts, and somehow he had been
so concerned with keeping his daughter 'safe' – fattening
her for the slaughter – that he had never made anyone pay
for that. And so it was a blow with the pent-up rage and
humiliation of nine years behind it, and it sent Strauss
flying backwards, broken teeth tumbling from between
split, bloody lips, the pistol skittering across towards the
empty pulpit. Rafael felt the impact run up his elbow,
his ulna nerve stinging and pricking with pain. It felt
liberating.

Carina looked at her father in shock, and then reached
out to take his hand, shouting to be heard over the
gunfire:

"Papa! We'd better get behind the altar. I don't want
you killed."

Rafael smiled, tears pricking at the corners of his eyes,
running the words through his mind again and again. *I
don't want you killed.*

Those might have been the sweetest words he had ever
heard his daughter say.

Having spent the bulk of their ammunition firing wildly
through the double doors at the unfortunate corpse of
Wilhelm Brandt, the amassed officer class of the Ultimate
Reich found themselves unable to effectively return
fire as El Sombra emptied almost the entirety of his
ammunition into them. As was often the case with the
military, the men further up the chain of command had
little understanding of the realities on the ground and,

as was also common, they had wasted their resources without thought for the long term. As was somewhat less common, they paid the price for their mistake – despite their heavy wing-packs, the bullets from the M30 were more than powerful enough to punch through one human body and into another and thus El Sombra was able to reduce the congregation by half before they even began to fire back.

Once the assembled Oberstleutnants and Majors began to return fire, the masked man dropped down into the very midst of the crowd, hovering in place to lash out with both his feet, spinning and kicking in a quick circle and using the butt of his gun as a club to smash the skulls of those closest. The congregation were unable to return fire for fear of hitting one of their own – the punishments for gunning down a fellow officer were severe – and so El Sombra found it easy to reduce the congregation to a mere handful of men, standing dazed and bathed in the blood of their colleagues.

Noting that there was now more than enough room in the crowd to fire on the masked man without risking hitting each other, the remaining officers raised their guns – but it was already too late. With a cheery wink and a wave, El Sombra flew out of the double doors and into the cloudless sky above, leaving the officers left standing after his bloody assault no choice but to follow him out and into the heavens.

The entire bloody battle had taken, in total, perhaps ten seconds. Sheltering behind the stone altar, Carina and her father were left to gaze out onto the bloody remains of dozens of men littering the floor. The cream of the Ultimate Reich, leaders of men hand-chosen to make the mission in Mexico a success, now stacked atop one another like cordwood. The lucky ones were still alive, bleeding out from ragged holes ploughed through their flesh and organs, and their groans and pleas for aid echoed through the empty space, along with the remnants of the gunfire. She exhaled hard, the adrenaline still raging through her system. "We should... we should get away from here."

Rafael nodded. He was sickened at the sight of the carnage, and at his own part in it. "You're right. I think this might be how it ends."

And then General Eisenberg stepped out from his hiding place behind the wooden pulpit, Oberleutnant Strauss' pistol in his hand, and shot Rafael squarely in the back.

He looked down at the writhing man, and hissed curtly between his teeth. "Master Plus, you are dismissed from your duties." Then he shot him again. Carina lunged forward, smashing a fist hard into the bridge of the Generaloberst's nose, breaking it a third time, a cry of hatred torn from her throat.

The Iron Mountain was unmoved by the gesture. He barely noted the blood that trickled over his lip as he gripped her wrist, pointing his gun at her belly. "I was stabbed in the chest with a hunting knife on the Russian Front, Carina, and I didn't even notice the wound until a minute after I finished killing my opponent with my bare hands. A punch in the face is hardly going to slow me down. Think yourself lucky I still have need of you." His teeth were still clenched, and his eyes glittered like chips of cold, grey ice. He had walked into this church secure in the knowledge of an almost spotless victory over the last enemy of the Reich in this misbegotten country, and in just a few minutes, he had lost everything he possessed. His only son had been murdered, and now the same man had, in the space of ten seconds, torn apart the vision he had spent nine years building. And somewhere inside him, like a goad spurring him to greater violence, was the nagging thought that it was his own overconfidence that was to blame.

Safe in the knowledge that he had quashed all resistance, General Eisenberg had allowed his top men to form the congregation at his son's wedding. These were the military minds he had hand-picked to aid him in his work, the cornerstones of the clockwork dream, the most integral parts of Projekt Uhrwerk. He would never have allowed all of them in the same room if there had been even a shred of doubt that resistance in Aldea was finished for all time.

And that was the final thing he had lost. He had come to the town of Pasito as the warlord of a thousand campaigns, one of Hitler's most trusted lieutenants. He had come to the Project as a success – and one man had stripped that from him. He had lost the most valuable resources of the Ultimate Reich – the Traction Engine, Der Zinnsoldat, Daz Drehkreuz, mostly likely Master Minus, not to mention countless weapons, supplies and men – and he had lost them all to that one man. He had lost the respect of his Führer to that one man, and with it his life, for there was no way he could escape punishment for such a titanic failure. And finally – cripplingly – he had lost respect for himself. The tactical skill that had won him his position had been exposed as hopelessly, fatally flawed in his own eyes, and the taste of that knowledge in his mouth was bitter beyond description. He was sick inside with it, black bile hissing and scalding his soul. He burned.

He would cleanse that shame. He would excise the foul, black matter from his being and then go to the execution chamber with at least some tattered piece of his dignity intact.

He would see El Sombra's corpse at his feet. Or he would die trying.

Above the Church, El Sombra flew on his borrowed wings, pursued through the sky by the highest echelons of the Ultimate Reich. He squinted against the rushing wind, performing a tight loop as bullets singed the air inches from his feet. He had had some small amount of practice with the wings on the way over from the Palace, and he had spied on a training session once or twice during those nine years he had spent in a fugue state, learning what he needed to know. It wasn't much at all, but he could at least manoeuvre without crashing into the ground.

The assembled officers were more adept with the wings, but not by much. For one thing, these were dress models – designed for their looks more than for actual use. For another, these were men used to a position of leadership and command – in other words, the rear. Perhaps three of these men had ventured out from behind the safety of their desks in the Red Dome during the past nine years – apart from the occasional leave, of course, which was generally spent getting fat on German beer and imported champagne in one of the beerkellars or underground cabaret clubs in Berlin. To put it bluntly, these were not the lithe troopers who swooped and soared through the sky like swallows on the recruitment posters, but rather, for the most part, a selection of fat robins, blustering their way through the warm air as they attempted to shoot down their prey with guns they had not practiced firing in months.

They had the advantage of numbers, and that might have forced a quick end to the combat had they deigned to work together. But these were men used to barking orders in the heat of battle – or at least the heat of administration – and being quickly obeyed without question, and so they flew their own courses yelling directions, which were ignored by any within hearing. Birds without a flock.

Their disorganisation cost them dear. El Sombra knew that, with his limited skill with firearms, he had to get in close in order to do any damage with the machine-gun, and so he allowed as many as possible to get on his tail, waiting until the bullets almost brushed his cheek before flipping back in a tight turn. As they attempted to swing their guns upwards and pick him off, he flashed over their heads, firing tight, controlled bursts with his weapon into their wing-packs. The masked man managed to rake four sets of wings with the gun before the ammo ran dry, their owners crashing into the ground or, in the case of one whose bright painted wings were torn completely off by the blazing assault, tumbling up into the sky, the cavorite infused into the main harness lifting his body against his will so that he resembled nothing so much as a slowly-rising helium balloon with kicking feet.

The machine-gun El Sombra had stolen was now little more than a club, and so he hurled it downwards with all the force he could manage, the heavy metal object smashing into the elbow of an aged Oberstleutnant who, until today, had been in charge of requisitions and the many different types of forms that needed to be filled out for such matters. The lower end of his humerus was shattered by the blow, and he dropped his own weapon, veering helplessly towards the ground as the pain caused him to lose all control over his flight. Like many of the aged and out of shape men who formed the officer class in Aldea, he was unused to wearing wings in anything other than a ceremonial situation, and so failed to pull out of the dive before the earth rushed up to meet him and crack the rest of his old bones like fine china.

One of the few who was used to wearing wings in combat was the elegantly named Major Dieter Faust, a sixty-year-old veteran of the Ultimate Reich's unfortunate adventures in the jungles of Vietnam. After a long and gruelling career in the Luftwaffe, he had been posted to the clockwork-town for the purpose of training new recruits in the use of the steam powered wing-packs that gifted the Reich with the power of flight. Now he saw his fellow officers, seemingly unable to engage in a simple aerial combat with a single amateur foe, and he was horrified. Was this what they had been reduced to? Granted, they had lost Eagle Staffel, and such gifted impresarios of flight as the younger Eisenberg and Hugo Stahl, but when he thought that officers of the Reich could be reduced to such a shambles... he shook his head, fuming. He would finish this ragged upstart himself, and then once he was back in Berlin he would be submitting a full report on the combat–readiness of the officer class. He would submit it to the Führer himself, in triplicate. That would show them.

El Sombra noted the grey-haired man pursuing him, and angled his flight down towards the Church, picking up speed. He could tell that Dieter Faust was going to be a problem. For a start, he carried a Luger in his grip rather than one of the cumbersome M30s. The others had fired off their machine-guns as though they believed that, if they fired enough bullets into the air, by the law of averages one of them was bound to hit the target – but Major Faust was evidently a believer in a single accurate shot. He was not firing his weapon randomly. He was tracking El Sombra carefully, aiming at where he was going to be, and accelerating to bring himself in range so as to shoot to kill. El Sombra smiled grimly. This one actually had a chance of bringing him down.

The masked man flipped onto his back, letting Dieter come closer, hovering in place as he kept his eyes on where the other officers were. Then he turned his attention back to Major Faust, and drew his sword.

And stilled his mind.

He closed his eyes, feeling the sword in his grip, opening them to see Major Dieter Faust aiming the pistol carefully. Time seemed to slow. Somewhere in the still, silent desert that he had become, El Sombra calculated the exact trajectory Major Faust's next shot would take. And the one after that. And the one after that. He listened to where in the air the other officers were, buzzing around, raising their own guns in a bid to catch him in a crossfire. He smiled, relaxed and content, and looked Dieter Faust square in his furious green eyes.

The Luger fired three times.

One by one, the bullets struck the sword, ricocheting off at angles as El Sombra brought it slashing through the air at exactly the correct moment.

Major Dieter Faust was shocked. For the first time in his entire ordered life, there came into the piercing green eyes a look of uncertainty, as though all of his most cherished assumptions about the world had been brought crashing down. This was the fear to be found in the eyes of the parish priest on coming, in a single horrific instant, to understand that there was no God.

Then he heard the first screams.

To his left, he saw the accountant, Major Heinrich Mahler, who kept the books for the Project and probably had not known which end of the gun shot the bullets, screaming and clutching at his eye, pulses of rich red blood flowing between his fingers, before he went still and tumbled out of the sky. One of the bullets had burst the jelly of his eyeball and travelled deep into his brain, bringing him death in one single white-hot instant of unendurable agony. How could something like that have happened?

He looked to the right, and there was Gustav Vogel, the Oberstleutnant who coordinated the supply routes, a good friend who knew how to fly, how to shoot, and yet there he was, clutching his throat and gasping like a dying fish, with blood coursing down his chest...

And then Dieter Faust realised that he was no longer holding his pistol, and that he would never hold anything in that hand again. The final ricochet had taken off three of the fingers on his right hand. He look at the hand, the thumb and little finger wiggling obscenely, bookending three lumps of torn, bloody meat, and then he looked at the masked man who was swooping down towards the Church roof.

He realised then that he was looking at Satan himself.

No normal man could have done such a thing. This was a creature with death and vengeance coursing through his veins where other men had blood, a creature born not of flesh but of some infernal flame of damnation. Where order was brought to the world, this one would bring bloody chaos. First the scene in the church, service reduced to a riot of dead and wounded men, and now this – this final insult, this demented fluke that the monster had used to save his wretched life. Dieter Faust knew that this ragged, ungainly creature was the enemy of everything he held dear.

A new resolve took hold of him in that moment. He might not have a gun, but he could deal with this abomination, this grotesque untermensch, with his own bare hands. Swooping down, he kept hot on the heels of the ragged swordsman, reaching to grab hold of the flapping trouser-legs. At these speeds, he could do serious damage if he could only force the masked man down onto the roof.

El Sombra looked back at the last enemy, keeping his course straight, heading towards the bell tower with the weathercock standing proudly on top of it. He swung his sword at the thin metal spoke that held the bird up, chopping it in two, and then reached out quickly to catch the tumbling piece of flat metal. He looked at it – perhaps a quarter of an inch thick, the metal rusted and weathered over the years to a blunt edge. He smiled, gave a swift backward glance, and then simply flipped the weathercock backwards over his shoulder.

Major Dieter Faust saw the motion but had no time to consider its significance before he felt something hard strike his face, smashing the cartilage and bone of his nose and splitting his lips. He felt his front teeth rattling on his tongue, loose, but he could not seem to work his jaw to spit them out. Blood coursed down over his neck and into his throat and something grey obscured his vision – something he could not quite define. He reached up, wobbling in his headlong flight, and felt the flat metal of the weathercock, his fingertips feeling back until they reached the point where it had embedded itself vertically in his flesh, splitting his face into two grotesque halves...

That was the moment when Dieter Faust, who was a man who believed in a rigid order, who had no patience for any who lost control of their wings no matter what the circumstance, fully understood the true meaning of chaos. His scream as he lost control and veered madly towards the bell tower was long, barely human and wracked with impossible agonies, and it was cut suddenly short when he impacted against the heavy iron bell, tolling his own demise.

El Sombra hovered in place, looking quickly around for his next opponent. The sky was clear.

Slowly the sound of the bell faded away to silence.

He exhaled.

And then General Eisenberg roared out of the shattered window of the Church below, bellowing at the top of his lungs.

"El Sombraaaaahhh!"

The General's dress wings gleamed in the sunlight, and El Sombra could see from the way he rocketed through the air that these were far more powerful than the wing-packs he was used to, or even the one he was wearing. It could move faster, turn tighter. Every twist he made in the air on his way up seemed effortless, a fact even more astonishing given that he was holding the struggling Carina by the waist, in one hand, using her as a human shield while he aimed the Luger at the masked man with the other.

The Generaloberst grinned, although it was less a sign of good humour than the baring of teeth common to predatory animals. The wings he wore were a prototype, fresh from the offices of the Messershmitt company. Mass production was not due to start until the following year, and so, with Project Uhrwerk in its final stages, he had had the new wings repainted to serve with his own dress uniform. This happy accident meant that he was now able to outfly and outfight his enemy – El Sombra had a sword and an inferior set of wings, while Eisenberg had a gun and the finest flying apparatus in Mexico. It would be no contest. He flew directly for his enemy, keeping his Luger trained on the space between the masked man's eyes despite the struggling efforts of his hostage.

El Sombra saw what he had to do. He rolled, pitching downwards, the metal wings on his back clanking as they folded in. He hurtled down towards the earth, picked up speed, the ground rushing up to meet him. Eisenberg took his opportunity and followed close behind, keeping on the masked man's tail as he aimed the pistol and readied himself to put a single bullet into the back of El Sombra's head. He looked forward to the sound the lifeless corpse would make as it smashed into the dirt.

At the last second, El Sombra triggered the wings and they unfolded out to either side, spreading wide to catch the air. He turned upwards, shooting into the blue sky with the speed of a rocket – the speed he needed to outfly the faster foe. The Generaloberst's bullet thudded into the dirt below him, and Eisenberg cursed, once, before he replicated the masked man's manoeuvre effortlessly, swinging himself up into the air, keeping on El Sombra's tail, aiming for another shot. He was grimly confident that he could keep up such a chase indefinitely. He had the faster machine. He was the better flyer. And he was armed. All it would take would be one mistake on El Sombra's part and the terrorist would be a dead man.

Carina was holding onto her captor for dear life. She was terrified – her fear of heights made her queasy with vertigo at every turn the General made – but she held back her fear, keeping her focus on the possibility of escape. She knew that if she could claw free of his grip when they were close to the ground, she would have the best chance of survival. The only flaw in that theory was that, when the General had been close to the ground, he had been travelling at such speed that she would very likely have broken her neck had he chosen that moment to let go. On the other hand, at the height they were at now, she did not have the slightest hope of surviving the fall. Whether she liked it or not, she had no chance of getting away. So she held on against death, praying through gritted teeth that there would come a moment when she could break free without killing herself in the process.

Eisenberg held onto her tightly and lifted his pistol, aiming once again for El Sombra's back. This time he would shoot to wound, and then perhaps shoot to wound again, until the masked man was finally no longer able to avoid the fatal shot. This plan had the advantage of cruelty, and the thought of the agony a bullet could inflict when boring through the soft offal of the gut made the Generaloberst smile to himself. Even as he squeezed his trigger, El Sombra flipped backwards in a tight loop, suddenly facing downwards again and aiming himself directly at the General. The bullet whispered past his temple.

Eisenberg clicked his tongue, growling low in his throat. A quick death, then, instead of the planned torture – whatever it took. He had patience. El Sombra could dodge as many shots as he liked, but he would die in the end as surely as a pig fattened for the slaughter. Eisenberg sighted the pistol directly between the masked man's eyes, making sure that Carina protected as much of his own body as possible.

El Sombra hurled his sword straight down.

Carina's eyes widened in shock as the sharp, flashing blade seemed to come straight for her. Eisenberg gritted his teeth and his finger began to squeeze the trigger – only to feel the gun jerk in his hands, suddenly heavy, off-balance. He looked at it, and his own grey eyes grew wide at the sight.

The barrel of the Luger was split down the middle and

blocked solid. El Sombra's sword was securely wedged into it.

The masked man smiled and allowed himself a single instant of pride.

It had, perhaps, been the best throw he had ever made.

The Generaloberst snarled like an animal and reached to tear the sword free from his gun and in the process he let go of Carina with no more thought than you or I might let go of, say, the handle of a heavy suitcase in order to reach into a pocket for a key. Carina had finally outlived her usefulness, and now Eisenberg needed both his hands free more than he needed her alive.

She did not scream as she fell. But her face grew pale as gravity took hold in the pit of her stomach and her own death rushed up to greet her.

El Sombra, diving downward like an eagle sighting prey, had already reached terminal velocity, while Carina had a few moments left before they were falling at the same speed. He sped past the hovering General, reaching, hand clawing at the air. At the same time, Carina reached upwards, kicking with her legs as though that might slow her fall, straining with all of her strength as though attempting to break gravity's hold through sheer force of will. Underneath, the ground rushed at them both like a barrelling freight train, as the masked man's hand finally found hers, tugging her into his arms before he allowed the metal wings to spread wide once again, lifting him and Carina back up towards the blue canopy above.

The pack on El Sombra's back was calibrated to support one person, and, unlike the General's, it was incapable of supporting two easily. El Sombra felt the momentum he'd picked up from his headlong dive quickly running out as they swept upwards, passing the General once again as he tugged fruitlessly at the fused sword and gun.

"Hold on." The masked man spoke softly, unbuckling the pack from his back at the apex of their upward flight, and then, in one sure movement, quickly swinging it around the two of them and locking the strap around Carina's waist, holding her with one arm as he secured the shoulder straps with the other. There was only a slight lurch, and within seconds, Carina went from clutching El Sombra to keep herself from falling to being the one holding him up. It was a welcome change, although she was still trying to recover from the shock of her earlier near death experience. Thus, when he chose that moment to kiss her softly, his lips finding hers with a sure confidence that would have shocked his old self, she did not return the gesture, but only blinked in stunned surprise. Events were, in all senses, moving slightly too quickly for her to be comfortable.

"See you later." El Sombra smiled genially, and let go, tumbling away from her as she floated up into the sky. Carina cried out, dumbfounded at the act, and reached after him as a reflex action, before closing her eyes to avoid the sight of the man she had come to trust falling to his death on the dust below.

El Sombra looked at her, wind whipping at his hair, and grinned. She was in for a shock.

Below them both, the Generaloberst continued to tug at the sword embedded in the pistol. The pistol might still be of use at short range, and the sword had a keen edge, but fused together in their current manner they were little more than a club. Finally, with a grunt of triumph, he yanked the damaged pistol free of the blade, looking around to see where El Sombra had gone in the few seconds he had managed to distract him.

El Sombra slammed into the Generaloberst with all his weight, knocking the air from the other man. The sword went flying from Eisenberg's hand to tumble through space, finally embedding itself in the hard ground beneath them. The remains of the pistol, however, became a crude bludgeoning weapon as the General smashed the butt of the gun hard into the side of El Sombra's head.

"Let go of me!" he snarled, spittle flying over his chin as his face contorted into an expression of pure, unfettered hate. In the depths of his rage, he came close to losing control of the wings, and the combined weight of the two men caused them to veer crazily across the sky, missing the rooftops by inches as they swooped and soared. Again and again, the General brought the gun down, pistol-whipping the masked man brutally. Carina had been forgotten, the survival of the Project had been forgotten, even his dead son was forgotten as every part of Eisenberg's being focussed on one goal – the brutal murder of the enemy who had destroyed everything he had once taken pride in.

El Sombra attempted to block the blows from the pistol butt without letting go of the General, but there was already blood coursing into his eyes from a serious gash in his forehead and he was having difficulty seeing through the film of red that covered his vision. Desperately, he reached up to grip Eisenberg's wrist, stopping the gun butt from smashing into his skull yet again, pushing the arm back as Eisenberg roared at him like a maddened bear. Then he snapped his head forward. Hard. The masked man's forehead slammed into the bridge of General Eisenberg's already broken nose, smashing it flat against the face. At the same time, El Sombra twisted the General's wrist, forcing the fingers open and letting the broken Luger drop down into the burnt-out remains of the schoolhouse far below.

The General spat blood and his eyes burned, a savage, bloodshot glare filled with the utmost loathing. Cursing, he brought his knee up hard into the masked man's groin. El Sombra gasped, clutching at the General as he felt his stomach turn over in that very personal agony, and his weight shifted the wings once again, sending them diving down in a wide turn towards the Great Square. Below them, the workers looked up from their duties at the air show put on seemingly for their benefit. The statue had already been dismantled and was being carted away from the waist down. Now all that was left was Hitler's torso, the stern stone head gazing up into the sky above, and the arm raised heavenward in salute. Those few guards left to oversee the operation shouted abuse at the workers, trying to force them to continue, before they were distracted by what was going on above their heads. Was that really their Generaloberst, in full dress uniform, battling like some demented beast as he swung madly through the clear sky? What in heaven's name was going on?

El Sombra punched upwards, his fist cracking against Eisenberg's jaw, knocking his head back and loosening a tooth. In response, the Generaloberst let loose a slavering cry of animal hate and wrapped his hands around the masked man's throat. He began to squeeze with a strength born of madness, gripping hard, choking the life from the man he hated most in the world. There was nothing in his eyes now that resembled the man he had been. The cold air of command had been burned away in the blaze of his fury, and the glitter of his ice-chip eyes now suggested a psychopath rather than a tactician.

El Sombra gritted his teeth, grabbing hold of the

General's wrists and shifting his weight. Though unable to turn his head under Eisenberg's merciless assault, he was nonetheless able to judge their location in the Square by the position of the surrounding buildings.

They were nearing the most sacred spot in all of old Pasito. The spot where his brother's blood had stained the ground, where his curse had been uttered, where El Sombra had been born in a night of fire and blood. It was where El Sombra would finally die.

But not before he'd done what he was born for.

The masked man grinned even as he was throttled by the General, continuing to shift his weight subtly, to steer the two men through the warm air. The Great Square had gone through many changes since his brother's death, but he remembered what it was that stood on that spot now. It was a great stone shoulder, connected to a long arm and a flat palm raised in eternal salute, up into the sky, like an obelisk, or a monolith to mark the dead.

Heraclio, he thought. *I came back. I came back to fight them. And I won.*

You can rest now.

He let go of the General's arms, dangling limp from Eisenberg's grip, and then brought his fists up, the knuckles of his index fingers raised to jab hard into the undersides of the elbows. A sharp stinging pain flashed up the General's forearms, into his hands, and the fingers lost their grip, letting the masked man plummet down towards the unyielding stone beneath.

General Eisenberg, the Iron Mountain, looked up to see the flat stone palm hurtling towards him at incredible speed, and he mouthed the first thing that came into his mind.

"Heil Hitl–"

He smacked into the stone hand like a bird flying into

a windowpane. The impact pulped his face and cracked his skull open like an eggshell.

El Sombra saw the impact, and felt a great sense of peace descend on him. The Ultimate Reich was finished. The head had been cut off, and now the body would die. He had finally won.

He smiled, feeling the wind whipping through his hair.

Then his back smacked hard into cold stone and everything went black.

CHAPTER TEN

The End, And After

Djego opened his eyes.

He was in a comfortable bed in an unfamiliar room. The walls were painted a soothing shade of peach, the sheets were clean and fresh, the sun was shining and the general atmosphere was one of relaxation, rest and well-being. It made him nervous.

As his awareness slowly returned to him he found himself looking at a painting on the opposite wall. It was a picture of what appeared to be a group of dogs, sitting on chairs around a table as though they were men, in a room with ugly blue wallpaper. The dogs were playing a game of cards. One was smoking a pipe. Another had a cigar. One was cheating, an ace held in a paw under the table. All of them had expressions of relaxed joviality, which sat well with their canine features. The whole effect was, quite naturally, unsettling and terrifying to Djego, and he was about to bolt out of the bed and try his luck in a fall from the window when he became aware that there was someone sitting at his bedside.

"It's called A Friend In Need. A man named Cassius Coolidge painted it some hundred and thirty years ago, and somehow it found its way into the hands of the Reich. You wouldn't believe some of the treasures we've found since they left." The voice was warm, rich and reassuring, with a soft musical lilt to it. Hearing it was like sitting next to a roaring fire on a cold and lonely day, and Djego sank back into the pillows, breathing a slight sigh of relief. He looked towards the voice, heart lifting as the name came back to him from far away.

Carina smiled.

"Welcome back, Djego. You were out for a long time."

Djego's hand lifted to his face, and he gently felt under one eye. There was nothing there. Where his fingers would once have touched the bloodstained fabric of his brother's wedding-sash, now all they touched was his skin.

"The mask..."

"It's safe. And the sword is too. They're both locked up safe and sound in the cupboard over there." Djego looked at her, brows furrowed. She took a deep breath, and carried on. "And... that's where they're staying. You've been through a lot, Djego, and I don't..." She blushed, smiling at the ludicrousness of what she was about to say. "I don't want you leaping out of the window and running off to hit somebody. There's no need for that anymore and... I wanted to meet you. The real you. I wanted to see the real man underneath that piece of cloth."

Djego nodded slowly. "... okay."

He felt naked without the mask, exposed. El Sombra was gone, and there was only Djego left. But somehow... the sky was not falling. Carina was smiling at him, she was taking care of him. He attempted a smile, and it felt comfortable. Perhaps... perhaps it would be enough to be Djego, for a while. The hated name did not have the same power when it came from her lips. It sounded like the name a man might have, instead of a dog. And he had a sense that he would not need the other name – that other man – for a long time. He looked up at her, groping for something to say, to cover the silence of the moment.

"Where am I?"

"A guest room in the Red Dome. We moved you here as soon as you could be moved. It's a lovely place, once you get past all the swastikas. We're going to keep it standing." She smiled softly, as he groped for another question.

"How... how long was I out?" He smiled sheepishly up at her, and something in the sheer mundanity of his own responses pleased him. Djego was beginning to register the aching of his muscles and bones, but still, he felt good. He felt like... Djego was someone he could live with now. Someone he could live with being. Still, there was a nagging itch at the back of his skull, a barely perceptible tingle.

Carina smiled. "About seven weeks, on and off. You came out of it long enough to tell us where you were keeping all the guns, which was nice of you, as it meant we could fight back properly instead of just hurling stones at them. And occasionally you'd start shouting about the bastards... but once they'd gone –"

Djego sat up, staring uncomprehendingly. "They're gone? You drove them out?"

"We drove them out." She smiled. "You'd killed so many of them, and then the General, and his son, and the High Command... their nerve broke, and ours... you should have seen it. When the general's head splattered like that, the crowd just roared. There were only a couple of guards armed with little pistols to keep them at work. They were lynched. By the time I got back to the ground, it was open warfare. Anybody who'd even thought about taking a hand against the bastards was hurling rocks and beating on them with hammers, and the brainwashed ones who didn't want to make trouble were just hiding in their homes."

Djego was shocked. This was what El Sombra had wanted, but the thought now made him feel sick. "Oh my God. How many died?"

Carina shook her head. "Not many at all, considering. Fourteen people, thank the Lord no children. But the soldiers... their hearts just weren't in it, like I said. There wasn't any chain of command anymore. It was just the grunts left, kids and old men who were only there because they'd been told to be. When we attacked them with the guns towards the end, they scattered like rabbits, and they always used to shout the same thing in German – 'I was only following orders! I was only following orders!' Isn't that funny?"

Djego rubbed his forehead. It seemed as though he should be able to know what the German for that was, but somehow he couldn't remember. "I suppose."

Carina sighed, reaching out to tease her fingers through his hair absently. "Anyway. They fought a holding action for a couple of weeks, trying to keep us away from their supply depots, but when we took hold of the guns... well, there and then the orders must have come from across the sea. They ran away, Djego. They're gone."

Djego was silent for a very long time. He stared at the picture of the dogs playing cards, and something uneasy stirred in him. "Gone. Gone across the sea." He shook his head, as though clearing it, and then turned to Carina again. "So what happens now?"

Carina sighed. "I'm in charge. Or rather, a committee that I'm part of is in charge. They didn't leave us any infrastructure to work with, unfortunately. We were mindless cattle to them, they weren't worried about providing things like hospitals and – well, you saw what happened to the school."

Djego nodded. Once, mention of what had happened at the schoolhouse would have made his blood boil in his veins. Now, that was someone else's anger. Djego only felt sadness that so much time and so many lives had been wasted for so little reason. "You said there were people who'd been brainwashed... what happened to them?"

Carina was silent for a long moment, then she stood up and moved to the window, looking out. "It took them a while. It was only when the bastards were finally gone for good that they came out. They were so scared... I think they really believed that they were going to be taken in the night at any moment. Some of them still do." She shook her head. "After nine years of this... some people just don't have any hope any more. The best we can do is give them work. You know that some of them are building a statue of you?"

Djego looked at her as though she'd gone mad. "A statue of El Sombra?"

"It's all they know how to do. They're incompetent and unqualified for everything else, but if I don't give them work, they just sit in their homes and have panic attacks. So they're working on a big statue of you." She smiled wryly. "Hopefully, once they're done, I'll have weaned them on to farming. They do have a good work ethic."

"I'm amazed they're doing anything at all that might offend their beloved Führer." Djego's voice was tinged with a deep bitterness. It offended him that his town should have been brought so close to the brink of destruction by a little man, far across the sea, a man he'd never even met. The itch in the back of his skull intensified. "How do you get them to do anything you say?"

There was a soft chuckle from the doorway. "You have me to thank for that." The voice was soft and earthy, with a pleasant rasp in it that made all the difference to the doughy, tremulous tone it had had before. That was the doing of the bullet that had partially collapsed the owner's left lung. The other had entered his back between two of his ribs, miraculously passing through without harming any of his internal organs in the process and lodging in the floor of the Church.

Rafael Contreras, who had once worn another name that was now mercifully forgotten, stood in the doorway, with tea.

"Father!" Carina's voice carried a familiar note of anger, but it was anger born of concern, and Rafael cherished it. "Father, what are you doing? Give me that, you're going to hurt yourself!" She took the tray of tea from him and set it on the side table, turning to Djego with a tight smile. "He has to do everything around here. I have to keep reminding him he had a serious trauma. He could have died. You could have died!" She turned to her father again, shaking her head in disbelief.

"What happened to you?" Djego was taken aback by the change in Master Plus. It was as though he'd become a completely different man but then, he understood how such changes could happen. Again, he felt a nagging feeling at the back of his skull. But the bastards were gone.

They were gone.

"Eisenberg shot him twice in the back and then left him to bleed on the floor. He could have died; he would have, if I hadn't gone back for him. I had to tear the wedding dress up for bandages."

Rafael smiled. "The best use that could have been made of it. It's a good thing you knew a little about how to deal with something like that."

"You were the one who let me read so much." She smiled, but there was an edge to the banter. Carina and her father were on good terms, better than they had been since she was a little girl, but there would always be that edge there, an area of darkness that he could never atone for, and she could never forgive, no matter how much they both tried. Carina quickly turned back to Djego. "Books on first aid and medicine. I wanted to be able to help if anything happened to him." She winced, and Rafael looked away. "Anyway, it doesn't matter. I could help him, that's all that matters. And I could help you too."

Djego raised an eyebrow.

"That fight... the torture... the fall," she shook her head. "You came close, Djego. I thought you were going to die. To have you talking again after just a few weeks..." She smiled, reaching to take his hand and squeeze. "You're a tough guy."

Djego shook his head, looking up into her eyes. "You must be thinking of somebody else. Although you did keep your promise. You saved me, Carina." He smiled and gave her hand a squeeze.

Carina laughed. "I haven't saved you yet, my friend. But I will. Trust me. And now, I have to get my stupid father to sit down before he injures himself. Enjoy the tea."

She stood up, and gently guided Rafael out of the room and down the stairs. Djego was left to lie on the bed, propped up on the pillows and sipping the tea reflectively.

It was all over.

Aldea was gone, and in a few years Pasito would again be a good place to live, with only the Red Dome and a statue of a ragged man in bloodstained wedding trousers and a mask to mark the darkest period in its history. All the bastards were gone.

He frowned at that. Something about the notion didn't seem to fit, but Djego couldn't put his finger on it.

He began to scratch at the back of his skull.

"... so Octavio says that if they're going to be locking up drunks, they need uniforms, which we have, but obviously the uniforms can't be grey and we should change the cut of them as well... are you listening?" Rafael looked at his daughter quizzically. They were both sat in the small room that had become their kitchen since they had moved into the Red Dome.

Carina nodded. "Just thinking about Djego. He's going to have a lot of adjusting to do. More than we do. It's like we've been waiting all this time for our lives to have purpose again, and now they do... and he is gone. There's nothing left for him."

Rafael nodded. "Is that what you meant when you talked about saving him?"

She sighed and nodded slowly. "The first time we met, he just seemed so... so sad. He was in pain and lashing out against it like a rat in a cage. I want him to be a man. I want him to be happy, but he's never going to be happy so long as he's got that mask on... he needs to learn how to live again now it's all over, anyway. He's been out in the desert for god knows how long, thinking about nothing but fighting Nazis. What's he going to do now?"

Rafael shrugged. "Go to Germany and kill Hitler?"

"Don't even joke about it, father." Carina smiled softly, shaking her head. Then she looked up with a start. "What was that noise?"

Rafael looked up at the ceiling. "It sounded like breaking wood."

Carina was up and out of her chair in an instant. Heart pounding, she ran up the stairs and grabbed the handle of the door to the guest room.

"Damn it, he's locked the door!" She hammered on the wood with her fists, and Rafael came running close behind her, his breath ragged and short.

"I could... break down the door..." The last word was barely audible over his coughing fit. Carina looked at him in exasperation and ran back down the stairs, heading towards the store cupboard in the basement where the master keys for all the rooms in the Red Dome were kept. She moved quickly, but she already knew she would be far too late.

Sure enough, when they finally managed to open the door, all that they found was an empty cupboard with the door torn off. The window was wide open.

Djego was long gone.

The man walked through the desert.

And the desert brought strength to the man.

El Sombra was at home here. It was his element, his place of power. He relished the heat of the sun on his back, and the way the sand warmed the soles of his feet as he trod. The familiar weight of the sword was in his hand, and he clutched it so tightly, so gratefully, that his knuckles were white with the strain, and that felt so good to him that he laughed, the sound of joy carrying over the sands. The mask was back where it belonged, covering his eyes, the knot of the cloth riding against the back of his skull in the way it used to.

He felt bad about leaving Carina so suddenly, and without saying goodbye. He'd hurt her, he knew, and he'd hurt himself at well. Djego had had a chance for something good in his wretched life. A chance to help his hometown heal from the horrors that had been inflicted on it. But El Sombra could not let him rest just yet.

As far as Carina and Rafael and all of Pasito cared, the bastards were gone, but they weren't gone. They'd only left his town. His country.

They hadn't left his planet.

They had gone west, across the sea, to use the lessons they'd learned on Pasito on their own people. But that wasn't the worst part. The worst part was that the man in the statue was still alive. He'd destroyed El Sombra's home from the comfort of a government office somewhere, sitting in a comfortable leather chair as he signed forms to authorise the death and degradation of everything the masked man loved, without ever meeting the people he was condemning, without looking into their eyes. The man in the statue was the orchestrator of every sorrow and shame he and the people of Pasito had ever suffered - and he had never paid the price for it. At best, all Pasito was to him was a cross on a balance sheet, a failed experiment. And that wasn't good enough.

El Sombra wanted the name of Pasito to wake him up in the night, sweating and shaking. He wanted the thought of what he'd done to burn in the coward's heart until the day came when he thrust his brother's sword through it. He wanted the man in the statue to suffer until he ended his wretched life.

It was too bad about Djego. El Sombra regretted little, but he regretted denying Djego that one small chance at happiness. But it couldn't be helped.

Until Adolf Hitler was dead, El Sombra could never rest.

The man walked west, towards the sinking sun.

EPILOGUE

The Man In The High Castle

Walter Hopfenkecker was neither a strong nor a brave man. Built like a strand of straw on a riverbank, he had often been picked on as a child, his face pushed in the mud by older, stronger children as they screamed into his ear "Walter Haufen Kacke! Walter Haufen Kacke!" He remembered vividly how they took his brand new mathematics book that his father had slaved eight hours overtime to buy him, and threw it in a river. He remembered sitting on the riverbank, sobbing into his hands and thinking that he had never felt so helpless. He wanted control over his life. He wanted the power to stop them hurting him. He wanted them to fear him, wanted them to be punished.

It is from such tiny acorns that great oaks grow. Now Walter Hopfenkecker was the Chief Administrative Assistant to Adolf Hitler, and his power was vast indeed. And men feared him.

Or he punished them.

There was only one man who did not fear Walter Hopfenkecker, and only one man who Walter Hopfenkecker truly feared. And he could not truly be called a man at all.

Walter paused at the great oaken door that let to the Führer's study, trying hard not to allow his hands to shake as he reached to turn the iron key that would allow him access. He bit his lip, almost drawing blood, and then uttered a soft and silent prayer as the key turned and the door slowly swung open.

Then he stepped into Hell.

Steam and smoke filled the massive chamber, scalding the skin and choking the lungs. The art treasures adorning the walls had to be protected by boxes of glass, the temperatures carefully regulated to prevent the toxic atmosphere from destroying what lay within. Human beings who entered the office of the Führer were afforded no such protection.

In the centre of this hideous miasma there was a machine.

It was more than three storeys tall, a terrifying construction of iron, copper and glass. A noxious green liquid coursed through tubes running up and down the structure, exiting a grille in the top as vapour, a grotesque mist that would burn at the eyes and lungs and kill any man who breathed it in. Vast pistons pumped and shifted, creating a constant, eternal shriek of metal scraping against metal. It was horrific to look upon – a vast industrial nightmare that seemed designed for no purpose beyond torture and death.

It was formed roughly into the shape of a man, and at the top, there was a great bronze head, motionless, with eyes that burned a terrible green. In the centre of the chest, there was a tank of reinforced glass, filled with the bubbling green poison, and hanging in the very centre of this, in a web of copper wire, was a human brain.

It was a brain that had once attempted to excise an entire people from the face of the planet. It was a brain that possessed an uncanny ability to incite hatred, fear and violence, to turn a crowd of ordinary people into a mob, to create an entire country dedicated to the deaths of the innocent in the name of their own twisted notions of purity.

It was the brain of Adolf Hitler.

Slowly, the Führer reared up to his full height, leaning over to gaze down at the tiny little man who'd dared to intrude upon him. The eyes in the great bronze mask – the mask of Hitler, an idealised Hitler, more like an Apollo than the shabby, ugly man with the awful hair who had once stalked these halls – stared down at Walter, merciless and cold. From Walter's perspective, he seemed like some terrifying iron god, ready to pronounce judgement on all those whose names were not written in his Book. When he spoke, the voice that projected from speakers located in the brass head's throat was a screaming symphony of needles scraping slowly across sheet glass.

"Greetings, Herr Hopfenkecker. You have the final report on Projekt Uhrwerk?"

Walter nodded, stifling his coughing. "J–Jawohl, Mein Führer. I am pleased to report an eighty-three per cent success –"

"Eighty–three per cent. Does that sound acceptable to you, Herr Hopfenkecker?"

A chill crept up Walter's spine, and he gave a tiny shudder. No, it did not sound acceptable to him. "Unfortunately, the... the actions of the terrorist network forced us to bring the Project to a premature end..."

"One man is not a network, Herr Hopfenkecker. Do not try to diminish your own execrable performance by conferring special powers upon your enemies. I will not tolerate it." The terrifying, screaming machine leant close and Walter took a half-step back, his gut lurching. "One man, who single-handedly destroyed our work in Mexico, in the process destroying hundreds of thousands of Marks' worth of property and ending the lives of several dozen of our finest troops. What do you think my reaction would be, Herr Hopfenkecker, if a similar man were to arise here in Berlin?"

"Mein Führer, with the greatest respect, those were special circumstances, we were an invading force and we had barely occupied the town for nine years. Under the circumstances, we did brilliantly. If Project Uhrwerk Phase Two were to begin operating in Berlin – where we control both the government and the media, and there are no outside influences to interfere with the programme – my people calculate a one-hundred per cent chance of total success."

There was a pause. Slowly the head of the immense machine tilted, as though studying Walter for some small sign that would indicate whether or not one of the huge machine-fists should close about him and burst him like a poisoned boil.

Then, the structure shifted back in a storm of shrieking metal and glass. Walter breathed a sigh of relief. "Danke, Mein Führer. Danke."

"We have better things to worry about than a tiny town in a backwater region. When the glorious Reich sweeps through Mexico again – as it will cover the entire world – I will take great pleasure in crushing the town of Pasito and leaving the population's heads on poles to serve as a lesson in obedience. In the meantime, we shall continue with the programme as it stands."

Walter nodded. "I will attend to it directly, Mein Führer. The terrorist will be destroyed with the rest of his town when the great day of our conquest comes."

There was something not unlike a dry chuckle from the machine. It sounded like a handful of broken glass being slowly crushed by the turning of a thumbscrew.

"Oh no, Herr Hopfenkecker, you misunderstand me. We won't be leaving El Sombra to live out his pitiful existence without retribution. Nor will we have to. Anyone who can destroy a man like Eisenberg and everything that he loves will not be content living out his days in some cow town in the desert. Not when there are people like you and I still waiting to be murdered. He will come to me, Herr Hopfenkecker. He will walk into my waiting arms.

"Have our people in the Tsar's Empire watch out for him. If he shows his face, report back to me. I want him alive, if at all possible. I want the pleasure of snuffing his miserable animal existence out like a candle. I want to see this miserable urchin who did us so much damage suffer as nobody has suffered before."

The chuckle slowly built into a laugh, and the horrific echo the machine produced to attempt it was the sound of a blitzkrieg of shrapnel tearing through an orphanage of screaming glass children.

"I promise you, Mein Herr... El Sombra has not heard the last of Adolf Hitler!"

THE END

Al Ewing was born in 1977, three days before Elvis died on the toilet. Indoctrinated into the loathsome practice of comics at an early age by his disreputable brother, the child progressed from his innocent beginnings to the loathsome depths of sin represented by the British comic *2000 AD*, long known as a haunt of depravity. He remains ensconced there to this day as a writer of the bizarre and fantastic, when not involved in even more sordid past-times. *El Sombra* is his first penny dreadful.

Now read the exciting new short story from the creator of Pax Britannia, Jonathan Green...

PAX BRITANNIA

FRUITING BODIES

Jonathan Green

SEPTEMBER 1997

I-Have His Carcass

The Thames. Thick and sluggish as treacle. The foul waters of the ancient waterway oozed between the detritus-strewn mud banks bordering the river at Southwark. The river that had spawned the sprawling metropolis was now being smothered by its obese offspring. Londinium Maximum drained the eternal Thames of all it had and then regurgitated it again, a diseased open sewer, polluted by rapacious industry and the waste of the teeming millions that called the urban sprawl home.

Scummy waves lapped at the tarry shoreline, regimented lines of flotsam and jetsam – flood-borne sticks, unidentifiable twists of rust-red metal and all manner of broken Bakelite or ceramic waste – showed where the still tidal river had marked its own rise and fall. Its own unique aroma of oil and excrement rose from its sludgy surface, carried along with whatever detritus had found its way into the surging effluent current of Old Father Thames. One gaseous wave could provoke involuntary vomiting in one not used to the noxious odour. However, the vagabond now combing the mired beach, searching for any forgotten finds, was not troubled at all by the stench.

His battered hobnail boots caked with mud, a filthy woollen hat pulled over the untamed mess of his hair – his wiry, grey beard just as bad – he puffed on a clay pipe clenched between tobacco-yellowed teeth. With his right hand he held a rough hemp sack over one shoulder and in the other he gripped a pole for support when traversing the sucking mud.

Old Samson might smell as bad as Old Father Thames, and be inured to the Stink – as it was called – but how his ratting terrier Jip ever managed to sniff out one scent amidst that miasmic stench, God alone knew.

The old man paused in his scouring of the mud flats, lent back, legs braced, unbending his crooked back, and took in a great lungful of London air. It was laced with the tarry smell of the pollutant smog that shrouded the city from the early autumn sun. That same sun still warmed the land, drawing the stinking smog from the streets until it hung over the capital, a gargantuan squashed mushroom cloud. To Samson, the river's unique smell was as familiar and as reassuring, in its own way, as the stale baccy aroma of the Dog and Duck, as welcoming as the rosewater and sweat scent of a two shilling whore.

The beachcomber gazed at the jaundiced haze streaking the lightening sky, and absorbed the sounds of the city, the rattle and clatter of the Overground, the blaring horns of the traffic filling the thoroughfares of Southwark and the steam horn voices of the tugboats on the river.

A broad, near-toothless smile spread across his crab apple face and for a moment he closed his wrinkled eyes, enjoying the warmth of the September sun on his weather-beaten skin. All was right with the world. This was the best time of day to be out, combing the shoreline for anything that had been disposed of by the city that might be of value to someone still, and so furnish Samson with another bottle of gin or perhaps even a tumble with Nancy. If he were really lucky perhaps their union might take place in a bed this time, upstairs at the Dog and Duck, rather than up against the wall behind the chandler's. Thoughts of Nancy filled his head, sweet as sugarplums.

Jip's urgent barking roused his master from his reverie.

Focusing on the yapping, Samson saw the dog worrying at something down by the water's edge. At first it looked like a bundle of black cloth, exposed by the retreating tide. Putting his weight on his stick, Samson pulled his mud-caked boots out of the sucking mire.

"Give over there, Jip. What's got you bothered as a Whitechapel street-walker?"

The terrier was growling, tugging at the cloth gripped in his teeth. It wasn't just a piece of cloth though; something was bound up within it, something that shifted with the push and pull of the waves.

"What is it, you daft bugger?"

Samson was practically standing over the terrier now as it wrestled with the bundle. Under the relentless worrying of the dog something flopped loose. Samson saw the sodden cloth of a sleeve and the pallid, waterlogged flesh of what was left of a hand, after the eels and other murk dwellers had had a go at it.

It was unmistakeably a body – a man, partially smothered by the other detritus that had been washed up with him, face down in the stinking shallows. Lank tresses of black hair moved in the sudsy surf, moving as if blown by a gentle breeze.

"God's teeth!" the beachcomber swore, the colour draining from his cheeks. He prodded at the corpse with his stick. "Get away from there, Jip!" he suddenly snapped, giving the dog a kick. Whimpering, the terrier released its hold.

Dropping the sack and bracing himself with the pole again, Samson leant down. With one strong hand he grabbed the collar of the dead man's suit and heaved. As the surge of the river lifted the corpse, Samson turned it over.

"Bloody hell!" he gasped, seeing the dead man's bloated features. "Poor bugger," he breathed, turned away and threw up.

II-Inspector Allardyce Investigates

"Not another one," Inspector Maurice Allardyce said with a sigh, giving the body a cursory visual examination. "So, what do you make of it Sheldon?"

"Well, she's dead, sir," the Sergeant said, an anxious look on his face as he tried to fathom what type of game the Inspector was playing.

"I can see that, smart arse. In fact, I can safely say that I have never seen anyone in the rudest of rude health look like that. Have you?"

"No, sir."

"So, what killed her?"

"Well," Sergeant Sheldon hesitated again, not sure whether this was some kind of test Inspector Allardyce was putting him through. "Her body appears to be riddled with mould... Fungus, sir."

"But that couldn't have killed her, surely? The rot must have set in after she died. How long did your witnesses say she'd been missing for?"

"She was last seen last night."

"Looking like this?" Allardyce exclaimed. They both looked down at the corpse of the ageing prostitute slumped in the alleyway.

"That's when she was last seen alive, sir, at around 9 o'clock outside the Dog and Duck."

"You mean she wasn't in this state at nine last night?"

"No, sir."

"Your witnesses - drunk were they?"

"No, inspector. At least twelve people saw her at that time. She was leaving the pub with a vagrant called Samson. Lives down by Southwark Bridge."

"Then he's our man. He's the one who..." Allardyce tailed off, unable to find the words.

The Inspector wasn't happy. He had been called to the scene of the crime – if crime it were – by the local beat-bobby Sergeant Sheldon, who was flummoxed as to exactly what had happened to the gin-sodden old tart, and even whether a crime had been committed at all. And now Allardyce found himself here, in the stinking slums of Southwark, with, if he were honest, no better idea of what was going on than the grizzled copper. Surely the old tramp had something to do with it, but then what could the vagrant have done to the old whore for her body to have become host to some kind of virulent fungal infection? The exposed skin of her arms, legs and face was covered with the grey-green swellings of puff-ball mushrooms, their own epidermal layer like shrivelled human skin. The curious growths crowded in on each other, one fungus sprouting on top of another, bursting from the cleavage of the woman's tarty blouse. Others had ruptured through the mesh of her stockings. The area had been cordoned off with tape as a precaution, a young constable standing by, just in case.

"Who did what, Inspector?"

Hearing the voice – dripping with disdain and with an air of aloof amusement – Allardyce stiffened.

"Oh, it's you," he said, turning, trying to affect his own air of aloof disinterest. "You're back from your jaunt around the South Seas then?"

"If you could call it that," Ulysses Quicksilver replied, giving the shorter man in the beige trench coat an appraising look with his sparkling brown eyes from behind the foppish flop of his fringe. "Yes."

"What brings you sniffing round Southwark? Looking for some lady action are you? The charming dandy routine getting a bit tired, is it?"

"Oh you know, I just happened to be in the area. Any witnesses to the death?" the dandy asked, brashly ducking under the police line – ignoring the young constable's blurted command that he stop – with no sign of respect for the authority of the Metropolitan Police.

"Are you trying to tell me how to do my job again, Quicksilver?"

"You have asked for witnesses haven't you?" Without waiting for an answer Ulysses Quicksilver turned to the steadily encroaching crowd and addressed the downtrodden and dispossessed of Southwark. "Good morning, ladies and gentlemen. Did any of you happen to be present when this poor lady here died? Did any of you see anything?"

There were nervous mutterings from among the crowd. It wasn't common practice in these parts to trust the police, let alone offer them assistance. But that said, with a nervous cough to attract attention, a thickset man emerged from the gathered stickybeaks, wringing a cloth cap in his large hands.

"Ah, yes, sir. Don't be nervous, old chap. Come forward and have your say."

"Well it was me that called Shelly here," the man said, nodding at Sergeant Sheldon. "And there was a whole load of us what saw it."

"Saw what, my good man?" Ulysses asked, flashing his most ingratiating smile.

"What happened to Nancy, the poor old soak." The man didn't take his eyes from the cap twisted into a tight knot in his hands.

"Would you care to elaborate?"

Allardyce looked on aghast. The slimy bastard could charm the knickers off a nun.

"It was this morning. She was lying here, empty bottle hugged to her breast. Thought she was asleep. No one was surprised to find her bedded down in an alleyway. It wasn't unusual. Anyways, then she comes to – head thick as London smog – and then she starts coughing. Terrible hacking cough it was. I thought she'd caught pneumonia. Then she was on her feet. Comes stumbling into the street, gasping like she's choking, eyes mad. It was just like she was being throttled, only she wasn't. And then, before anyone could help her, she collapses and those things start popping up all over her body."

"You mean the puffballs?" Quicksilver asked, seeking clarity.

"If you say so, sir. I wouldn't know," the man confessed.

Allardyce looked again at the dead woman's face. One eye had been forced shut by the oppressive pressure of several bulbous eruptions whilst the other was protruding unpleasantly – almost accusingly – from her head, the white of the eye and iris discoloured by the verdigris pigment of the fungi.

"After that, no one would go near her. She was good as dead, already. But then I said someone should do something, should tell someone. So I dropped in on Shelly at the station."

"What a fine upstanding citizen you are," Quicksilver said, without a hint of sarcasm in his voice. The man stopped crushing his cap in his huge hands, and looked directly at Ulysses, a proud smile of self-congratulation appearing on his face. "And you were right not to go near her."

"What did happen to her?"

"We don't know yet. But that's why I'm here. Don't worry we'll have this sorted out in no time. Trust me."

The smartly-dressed dandy looked entirely out of place, in his emerald green crushed velvet jacket, paisley-patterned waistcoat and plum moleskin trousers. He was also wearing his trademark cravat, held in place with a diamond pin, and held his bloodstone-tipped cane, almost casually, in one hand. He turned to Sergeant Sheldon, the earnest young constable now at his superior's shoulder like some eager puppy. "Sergeant, we need to seal off this whole area – the alleyway, the pub, the street – and put the body into quarantine. We're going to need to send in clean-up crews to decontaminate the area."

"We?"

Quicksilver turned to the Inspector for the first time since the eyewitness had spoken.

"Whose crime scene is this?" Allardyce challenged, reddening.

"I'm sorry, Inspector. Please, carry on."

"Right... well..." Allardyce looked at Sheldon, the bobby, at Quicksilver and then back at the Sergeant. "Do what he said."

Sergeant Sheldon paused, shooting Quicksilver an uncertain look. It was only when the dandy had nodded his consent that the policeman made a move to obey.

"And only let automata-Peelers handle the body or move it," Ulysses instructed, but in the tone of one doing no more than making a helpful suggestion. The sergeant shot him another anxious look. "Just in case."

Sergeant Sheldon and the bobby moved the gathered crowd of curious onlookers back. "Come on, ladies and gentlemen, there's nothing to see here. You know what curiosity did to the cat."

"Not her, Sergeant, if you don't mind," Quicksilver said, picking out one old woman from the throng of peering faces. "She's with me. Penny," he said, now addressing one onlooker in particular – an ugly, wart-nosed and toothless septuagenarian – "your assistance, if you would be so kind."

"Right you are, guv'nor."

"Cause of death appears to be extreme fungal infection and subsequent cellular degradation of the host body. You know what needs to happen now. I want you to ensure that no one goes near the cadaver. God only knows what could happen if those fruiting bodies spore."

"You're putting this slattern in charge of my operation?" Allardyce exclaimed, his voice rising in pitch with his growing disbelief.

"It's all right, Inspector, Penny here's used to dealing with this sort of thing."

"I've cleared up all sorts of messes, guv'nor."

"You?"

"You'd better show him your ID," Quicksilver said, nudging the wizened old crone. She pulled out a worn carpet bag from under her shawl, opened it and extracted a crumpled card. She held it out for Allardyce to see.

"Not another one," he said wearily. "She's one of your lot?"

"Agent Penny Dreadful, at your service, sah!" the old woman said, struggling to stand to attention.

"Penny Dreadful?"

"It's a codename, sah."

"A codename. I don't bloody believe you lot. All this cloak and dagger crap. What's the point? What's your real name?"

"I could tell you, but then I'd have to kill you, guv'nor."

"And she could too," Quicksilver said, unable to stop himself from grinning.

"Just think of me as the fixer, sah, and we'll say no more about it."

"Anyway, to work." Quicksilver knelt down beside the body.

"I thought you said only automatons should go near the body from now on," Allardyce pointed out, keeping a good distance from the corpse himself but doing nothing to stop the dandy.

"Do you know what species these mushrooms are, Inspector?"

"Well... I was going to wait for the lab boys –"

"I thought not, and neither do I. So I'm going to take my own small sample. I need an expert to tell me what we're dealing with here. Don't worry, I'll be careful."

"Do I look like I care?" Allardyce sneered.

The dandy agent of the throne withdrew gloves, a scalpel and an evidence bag from the capacious pockets of his jacket and very delicately cut one of the puffballs from where it had taken root within the dead woman's flesh, manoeuvring it into the bag with the scalpel blade. He then cut another sample before sealing both specimens and the contaminated blade inside the bag.

"That should just about do it," Quicksilver said, straightening. He turned to Allardyce. "I'll get out of your hair now."

"If only you would."

"Not that there's that much of it to get into," Quicksilver threw back. "Things to do, people to see. You know how it is? Besides, I missed breakfast this morning and for some reason my stomach's hankering after one of Mrs Prufrock's mushroom omelettes. I'll be seeing you, Inspector, I'm sure," he said, turning away and giving

Allardyce a jaunty wave.

"Not if I see you first," the policeman muttered under his breath.

III-People Who Live In Glasshouses

The Mark IV Rolls Royce Silver Phantom rolled to a halt outside the entrance to the Royal Botanical Gardens. Ulysses Quicksilver looked out of his window at the twisting wrought-iron leaves and the glittering glass structures of the grand greenhouses beyond. The leaves of the many trees dotting the park were on the turn now, copper and gold spreading among the green of summer. "You have the sample?" Quicksilver asked his manservant sitting in the driver's seat.

"Yes, sir."

"Drop that one off with Dr Methuselah. Tell him I'll pay his usual fee."

"Yes, sir. And then shall I return for you? Or should I wait for you to call?"

"We'll see, shall we Nimrod? It's such a pleasant day, and the sky is such a warming shade of yellow today, that I might make the most of this Indian summer and enjoy a stroll along the river. I can always take the Overground from Kew. I'll let you know."

"Very well, sir. You think you'll find the answer you're looking for here?"

"Where else would one come with a question about plants other than to the botanist boffins at Kew Gardens?"

Ulysses exited the Silver Phantom and, engine purring, the sleek automobile pulled away from the kerbside. Passing through the vine-leaf wrought gates he approached the visitor turnstiles. Flashing the contents of a leather cardholder he was admitted immediately and, on asking for the Director, was directed towards the newly constructed Amaranth House. The construction work on the latest of Kew's majestic glasshouses was complete, as was much of the internal planting. All that remained now was for the last coat of gleaming all-weather emulsion to be applied by the team of gardeners and automata that had been set that task, and for Director Hargreaves and his cadre of loyal horticulturalists to finalise the arrangement of the specimens exhibited within.

Since the chaos and near-anarchy of the Queen's 160th jubilee celebrations, a matter of only a few months ago, all appeared to be well within the realm of Magna Britannia once again. The greatest world-spanning empire the world had ever known still held firm, thanks in no small part to Ulysses Quicksilver himself. With the apparent wiping out of the Darwinian Dawn, official functions were continuing again. The latest was to be the opening of the new Amaranth House, which would contain some of the world's rarest and most specialised plant specimens. The press was full of it: in two days' time, a whole host of the great and the good were due to attend, including the new Prime Minister. Ulysses' own invitation had been waiting for him when he returned from the first and last voyage of the sub-liner Neptune. Queen Victoria herself would not be attending on this occasion and, considering what had happened the last time he had taken up such an invitation, Ulysses was thinking of giving the event a miss as well.

Passing a battered tanker that, from the pungent reek coming from it, contained an enormous quantity of weedkiller, Ulysses crossed the threshold of the grand glazed double doors and entered Amaranth House. He found Professor Hargreaves, the current Director of the Royal Botanical Gardens inside, directing his staff in their positioning of a potentially deadly – and hence currently bound – Patagonian Mantrap. He was a bean-pole-thin man in later middle age, his thinning grey hair parted in the middle and slicked down with a generous amount of hair lacquer. His twirled grey moustache had been equalled carefully tended and he observed the world through blue-tinted spectacles. It was humid inside the glasshouse and, having removed his jacket and rolled up his sleeves, the Director was really getting stuck into the work himself. Picking his way past wheelbarrows of compost and busily painting automata-drudges, Ulysses approached the team of horticulturalists seeing to the re-positioning of the large spine-mawed plant.

"And make sure its trapper tendrils have been pruned right back before the opening. We don't want the new PM becoming a tasty morsel for Audrey here, do we? This is one auspicious event we don't want going with a bang," he was saying as Ulysses approached.

"Do you name all your plants, Director?"

Professor Hargreaves turned at Ulysses' interruption and glowered at him in annoyance. "What? No, of course not. Only the larger specimens. The gardeners simply bastardised the Latin name of this one and, well, it seems to have stuck. She does appear to have something of a personality, as do all the semi-sentient carnivorous specimens."

"It seems to me that you're making rather a fuss of what is, as I understand it, in South America considered to be a pernicious weed."

"This isn't simply some common or garden triffid or vervoid, I'll have you know. The Patagonian Mantrap is on the verge of extinction, thanks to Man's total disregard for the green heart of this planet. There are only two that I know of in the entire country. The work we do here at Kew is vital to the ongoing survival of these rare and most beautiful –"

"And deadly," Ulysses threw in.

"– plants in existence." Hargreaves went on without breaking his stride. "Anyway, who do you think you are butting in here like this? Who admitted you?"

In response, Ulysses dextrously took out his leather cardholder, flipped it open and, just as deftly, put it away again.

"Oh," Hargreaves said in surprise, despite himself, "you. I've read about your exploits in The Times. Rather a lot of fuss over some attention-seeking derring-do, if you ask me."

"Yes, that would be me. Ulysses Quicksilver at your service."

"Mr Quicksilver, I am sure you can appreciate that I am a very busy man. There is still so much to do in preparation for the opening and so little time to achieve it all in."

"I appreciate that, Professor," Ulysses said, a fixed smile on his face, "but you must understand that I would not trouble you if it were not a matter of the utmost importance. This won't take long."

"Very well then, what can I do for you?"

"I have need of your expert knowledge." Ulysses delved into a jacket pocket and took out a plastic evidence bag containing one of the two puffball fungi he had taken from the dead prostitute. "Can you tell me what species of fungus this is?"

Professor Hargreaves took the bag from Ulysses and examined it intently for a few moments, turning it over in his hands, pulling at the plastic to examine the pockmarked skin of the specimen more closely. After a few moments consideration, he handed it back to Ulysses.

"Where did you get this?" he asked sharply.

"Have you ever seen anything like it before?" Ulysses asked the Professor.

"No, I have to confess that I haven't."

"Would any of your staff be able to help?"

"No," Professor Hargreaves answered far too quickly. "If I can't help you, they most certainly won't be able to. My knowledge of plants is unsurpassed."

"Would you like to keep the sample for a closer examination?"

"No, Mr Quicksilver, I would not. As I have told you already, I am particularly busy at present and do not have time to follow wild goose chases. If you won't tell me what's so special about this specimen then I'm afraid I can't help you any further. It must be some kind of aberration, a mutation, that's all I can tell you."

"Thank you, you've been most helpful." Ulysses turned to leave but then paused, taking in the wonders of the new glasshouse around him. "I hope the opening goes well."

Professor Hargreaves watched the dandy leave, an unflinching scowl knotting his features. Sure that the nosey intruder had gone, he left his men filling in the soil around the writhing Audrey's snaking roots and hurried off to another part of the glasshouse.

He found Assistant Director Mandrake working, as always, in the semi-gloom of the fungus beds in the basement level of the Amaranth House. Here plants which thrived on the forest floor beneath the light-blocking canopy of the rainforest or in the dark sinkholes of the South American jungle plateaux, were tended in conditions that mimicked their natural environments. It was hot and dark down here, the atmosphere heavy with the smell of leaf-mould and wet loam.

"Mandrake, a word."

"What is it, Director?" the younger man asked, putting down his trowel. He too was in shirtsleeves as he worked in the stuffy heat, his black hair plastered to his head with sweat.

"We've had a visit from one Ulysses Quicksilver, an Imperial agent."

"Why would one such as he be interested in our work here?" the other asked innocently.

"He isn't. He wanted my opinion on something. He showed me a specimen – a fungus. I don't know where he got it from but it looked very familiar. Greeny-grey with an epidermis like dead flesh."

Mandrake said nothing, but simply looked at Hargreaves with something akin to mild curiosity.

"You know what I'm talking about."

"Do I, Director?"

"You damn well know you do. It looked very like the specimens I've seen you working with recently down here." Hargreaves scanned the dark, dank space. "Where are they? What have you done with them? Where have you moved them to?"

Mandrake fixed him with piercing pearlescent green eyes. They seemed almost luminescent in the gloom beneath the glasshouse. His skin was pallid and white from a lifetime working away in the darkness where the necrotising plants grew.

"You're right, of course, Director. It's time you knew everything."

"What is it you've been busying yourself with down here while the rest of us have been striving to get everything ready for Friday's official opening?"

"Let me show you," Mandrake said, moving towards an iron door at the other end of the sub-basement. "This way."

Professor Hargreaves joined his assistant at the iron door. The smell of damp and mould was even stronger here. Mandrake forcibly pushed the handle down and opened the door. "Please, after you."

Professor Hargreaves stepped through into humid darkness.

"Where's the light switch?" he asked.

In place of an answer, the door slammed shut behind him and he heard the grate of bolts being thrown on the other side.

"Mandrake? What the hell are you playing at?"

Hargreaves froze as something wet and spongy to the touch grabbed hold of his hand in the darkness. Then the screaming began.

Without any warning, without any wailing of sirens, the fire brigade arrived within the warren of slum tenements and decaying wharfs of Southwark. A gleaming brass and red-painted fire engine rumbled to a halt outside the Dog and Duck and its crew silently went about their business, extending the ladder atop the vehicle and unrolling hoses with practised efficiency.

One of the helpful individuals from the crowd who had aided Ulysses Quicksilver earlier that day approached a fireman kitted out in full protective gear – fire-retardant coat, re-breather helmet and protective boots. The fireman went about his business, ignoring him.

"Where's the fire?"

The hulking fireman remained silent and quietly carried on unrolling the hose in his hands, giving nothing away.

IV-Scorched Earth

On the morning of the eighteenth of September, Ulysses Quicksilver returned to the scene of the prostitute Nancy's demise, but things were not as he had left them the day before. He had returned in hope of finding more clues to help him resolve both the mystery of her death and of the curious fungus, but something else entirely that he had not anticipated was waiting to greet him.

The area had been ravaged by fire the night before. The Dog and Duck was nothing but a blackened shell, the streets around it sooty and blackened by flames that had been hot enough to melt the surface of the road and crack the bricks of buildings. Southwark was thick with a bitter charcoal smell. Wisps of grey smoke still rose from the burnt-out tenements. The fire had been intense but short-lived.

The area had been cordoned off in the wake of the fire, just as it had been following the prostitute's gruesome death. The eager young bobby, who had accompanied Sergeant Sheldon the first time Ulysses had passed this way, was protecting the ruins from looters and heedless passers-by. It seemed that Sheldon was not prepared to entrust this task to the automaton-Peelers that had been drafted in from Scotland Yard.

"Good morning, constable," Ulysses said, beaming despite the obvious devastation around him. "What's been going on since I was last here?"

"Good morning, Mr Quicksilver, sir. It happened last night, when everyone was in the Dog and Duck."

"Everyone?"

"All the regulars, I mean."

"Everyone who might have come into contact with Fungoid Nancy, you mean."

"Well... I hadn't thought of it quite like that myself, sir. But now you come to mention it."

"A bad fire was it?"

"I think the fire service described it as 'intense'. They were here in no time and got it under control as quickly as they could."

"Good to hear you can rely on London's noble fire brigade, eh?"

"Yes quite, sir."

"What of the prostitute's body? Was it moved before the fire broke out?"

"It's funny you mention that, sir. The fire swept through the area not long after you were last here, Mr Quicksilver. There hadn't been time for the arrangements to move the body to be completed."

"Is that so?"

"Yes, sir," the constable went on, the word 'confidentiality' apparently missing from his copy of the Oxford English Dictionary. "Strange case, wasn't it?"

"Indeed," Ulysses agreed, "and getting stranger all the time." Ulysses cast his gaze around the wasted ruin of the street, as if somehow a more intricate inspection would give him some further insight into solving this mystery.

"And who'd have thought it? Two in one week, like that."

Ulysses' gaze fixed on the affably smiling policeman.

"I beg your pardon, constable. Two?"

"Yes, sir. The first one was pulled from the Thames down by Southwark Bridge last Sunday. A man it was, well, what was left of him."

"I don't believe it," Ulysses muttered to himself. "Allardyce must have known about it. Two cases in a week and he didn't think to share that little nugget of information."

"I'm sorry, sir. Would you be meaning Inspector Allardyce?"

"Know him do you?"

"Well, of course, sir, but –"

"What can you tell me about him?"

"Inspector Allardyce, sir?"

"The first body. You said it was a man."

"Oh, yes, sir. Sorry, sir. Well, seeing as how it's you, Mr Quicksilver, I can do better than that. I can let you see the body if you like. It's still in cold storage down at the station. I'm guessing no one informed your bosses to come pick it up."

"Then take me there forthwith, constable!" Ulysses exclaimed, the grin back on his face, excitement sparkling in his eyes. "It would appear that the game is afoot once more."

"Do you have any idea who it could be?" Ulysses asked, staring down at what had once been a man of medium build and medium height with shoulder-length black hair, dressed in an unremarkable black suit.

"No, sir. No one's been in to identify the unfortunate gentleman."

As far as Ulysses could see, physical identification would be a near impossible task. It seemed that every square inch of skin was covered with the same grey-green puffball growths that had ravaged Nancy the prostitute.

"And no autopsy has been carried out either?"

Ulysses' breath clouded in the chill air of the morgue. The atmosphere was thick with the clinical smell of formaldehyde and disinfectant that Ulysses equated with death. Wisps of misty vapour spun in the vortices of air currents created by the cautious movements of the constable, Sergeant Sheldon and the dandy.

Sergeant Sheldon had left Ulysses to open the body bag himself, which he had done with incredible care and only after donning medical gloves and mask. However, none of the puffballs spored on opening. In fact they appeared to have already spored and were now entirely shrivelled, looking even more like dead flesh, as if they were dying back, their rapid development having consumed every nutrient provided by the host body, like a malignant, rampaging cancer.

"Far as I'm aware, he's not even been reported missing," Sergeant Sheldon said, "so I doubt anyone's looking for him anyway."

"Most interesting," Ulysses said, using a pair of tweezers to pull open one side of the dead man's river-ruined jacket. "And no one thought to check the dead man's body for any personal effects that might reveal his identity?"

"His pockets were checked. He had nothing on him."

"Then what do you call this?" Ulysses challenged, extracting a sodden, folded piece of paper.

"Well I'll be damned!" Constable Harris swore.

"I thought you said you checked the pockets!" Sheldon snarled.

"Exactly how incompetent is Her Majesty's Metropolitan Police trying to be? Is there some incompetence award you're going for?" Ulysses flashed the constable a look of contempt that made him physically recoil. "Most Appallingly Slack Police Procedural Practice in a Borough Station?"

"I... I don't know how that was missed, Mr Quicksilver," Sheldon apologised, a look of thunder on his face.

"Because nobody dared look that closely, fearing that whatever did for this poor wretch might be the end of them. That's how! Let's take a closer look, shall we?" Ulysses said, his anger abating and his natural curiosity coming to the fore again.

With the aid of the tweezers he managed to separate the sodden sides of the folded vellum. Despite the efforts of the Thames, the ink of the handwritten missive was still just legible.

"What does it say?" Sergeant Sheldon asked.

"Well, the gist of it is this," Ulysses replied. "The addressee is one Garic Mandrake, and it is signed by – if I am not mistaken – the eminent botanist and out-spoken critic of Magna Britannia, Auberon Chase, condemning the former's immoral work. He doesn't go into details, unfortunately, but he does state that he wants no part in Mandrake's brand of, and I quote, 'botanical terrorism.'"

"Bloody hell," was all the ashen-faced constable could manage, reeling at the revelation that, like as not, the forgotten corpse in the cold store was mixed up in some plot against the stability of the Empire. In the wake of the Wormwood Affair, everyone took talk of terrorism very seriously, from members of the public to those in authority over them.

"It seems likely to me that for the dead man to be carrying such a letter about his person, until it may be proved otherwise, we should take this corpse to be that of Garic Mandrake. Would you not agree?" Without giving Sheldon or the constable the chance to reply, Ulysses went on, into his rhetorical stride now. "And, by extension, one could safely surmise that perhaps Auberon Chase had something to do with his death, or at least knows more about it than we currently do."

Sergeant Sheldon simply looked at him, opened mouthed.

"You might well be dumbfounded, Sergeant. This station managed to miss two potentially crucial pieces of evidence."

"T-two, sir?"

"Firstly, the letter from Auberon Chase, and secondly," – he now used the tweezers to separate the matted locks of the man's hair behind what had formerly been his right ear, revealing angular ruddy petals caught between the fibres – "this seemingly innocuous scarlet flower."

V-A Rose By Any Other Name

The Rolls Royce pulled up outside the Suffolk country house, practically the only noise made by the car's arrival being the crunch of the gravel drive under its tyres.

The Old Vicarage was all steeply-pitched roofs, arched stained glass windows, black iron guttering and faux battlements. The extensive gardens were shielded behind high hedges and a red brick wall. Several acres of beech woodland held all within its arboreal embrace.

"So this is the home of the eminent, not to say curmudgeonly, botanist and orchidologist Auberon Chase?" Ulysses said, looking out of the window at the imposing gothic residence.

"Is that a rhetorical question, sir?" his ever-faithful manservant enquired, his voice a cut-glass emotionless monotone at odds with Ulysses' excitedly upbeat attitude.

"Of course it is, Nimrod," Ulysses replied flashing his retainer a wicked grin. Nimrod responded with a condescendingly arching eyebrow. "And as we're here, I think it would be rude not to pay our respects."

Having exited the car, the two men approached the front door, the ostentatiously dressed dandy leading the way, his immaculately turned out manservant a pace behind. When the third ring of the doorbell still produced no response Ulysses decided to investigate.

Passing through a gate into a walled flower garden, with ornamental lawns, carefully clipped topiary bushes and the rhododendrons of an arboretum beyond, Ulysses and Nimrod found their way to the extensive conservatory attached to the back of the house.

Cautiously pushing open the unlocked door, Ulysses paused on entering.

"Someone's been here before us," he said darkly, "and I don't mean our errant botanist." He pointed out the broken pane of glass in line with the door handle, the shards lying on the tiled floor inside.

"So I see, sir," Nimrod assented.

"We should proceed with caution."

"Understood, sir," Nimrod said, taking a pistol from its hidden holster inside his tailcoat, as Ulysses took out his own gun.

Plants filled the conservatory. Some were in the middle of being re-potted into larger terracotta containers. A half-open bag of spilled potting compost and a trowel lay as if they had only just been put down, as if whoever had been at work here had just stepped away for a moment. There was everything from tall-reaching bamboo and primeval cycads to a magnificent aspidistra and creeping grape vines. Along one glass-panelled wall was Chase's prized collection of rare and exotic orchids: everything from the magnolia-painted petals of the Butterfly Orchid to the Devil's Tongue.

But the orchids were not the only rare plants that had a home here; there were a number of specimens that would not have been out of place within the newly completed Amaranth House at Kew. These included a Patagonian Mantrap, a six-foot tall specimen residing in a massive ornamental Grecian urn.

It was this plant that Nimrod was examining when he made the pronouncement: "Sir, I think you should take a look at this."

"Ah, Auberon Chase, I presume," Ulysses said with macabre humour as he approached the mantrap himself.

All that Ulysses could see were a pair of trouser clad legs and two feet, one missing a shoe, protruding from the thorn-fanged maw of the mantrap amidst the spiny leaf-pseudopods of the plant.

Ulysses turned before the woman spoke, his uncanny sixth sense giving him prior knowledge almost akin to prescience, pistol held level at waist height.

"Don't move!" Despite having the bravura to challenge the two of them, she could not hide the undertone of nervous anxiety. "And put your hands up, where I can see them."

"Which is it to be? Don't move, or put our hands up?"

The young woman – in her mid to late twenties – stood at the entrance to the glazed plant house. She was holding a garden fork firmly in both hands, prongs pointed towards the dandy and his manservant. The look on her face suggested that she was prepared to make good use of it if needs be.

She looked like she would have been more at home trekking through the jungles of Borneo than stalking Ulysses in the Suffolk countryside. Her petite, lithe, and richly-tanned body was contained within long cargo shorts and a positively disgraceful, tight-fitting brown vest top, under a sleeveless khaki jacket. Her choice of wardrobe was too daring and modern, even for the more progressive and increasingly permissive attitudes prevalent across the Victorian empire of Magna Britannia at the end of the twentieth century. Her dark, shoulder-length hair was tied back in a stubby ponytail.

Her outfit obviously favoured the practical but to Ulysses' mind it merely served to accentuate the pert curve of her buttocks, the hollow at the small of her back, the subtle swell of her bosom, her small breasts pushing against the tight material.

"Well, hell-o," Ulysses smarmed. "And who are you?" He ignored Nimrod's tut of disapproval, drinking in the vision of loveliness before him.

"Never mind that! Who are you and what are you doing in my uncle's house?" she snapped, glancing at the bloated bulb of the Patagonian Mantrap, a film of moisture covering her eyes. "What was it that caused you return to the scene of your crime?"

"Madame," Ulysses said, his most endearing smile shaping the chiselled features of his face, "you are mistaken. We are not murderers returning to the scene of what would appear to be some heinous crime. We have only just now stumbled upon this unfortunate scene. But, I might ask the same questions of you. Who are you and what brings you here?"

"I asked first," the young woman said stepping boldly into the conservatory, adding emphasis with a thrust of the fork.

Ulysses reached into his jacket and pulled out his leather cardholder, flipping it open with a flick of the wrist. "I am Ulysses Quicksilver, Madame, agent of adventure, agent of justice, and agent of the throne of Magna Britannia, recognised for my valorous actions by Her Majesty Queen Victoria herself. I find myself here in my capacity as an investigator into two particularly unpleasant deaths." Ulysses returned his ID to his pocket. "Now, Madame, if you would be so kind as to return the favour."

The young woman remained tight-lipped before relenting. "I am Petunia Chase, and Auberon Chase is... was... my uncle." Ulysses glanced at Nimrod, that one look full of meaning for the two of them. They had become embroiled with supposedly grieving female relatives before, and didn't want to be duped again. He had used to think himself a good judge of character – now his confidence in his own abilities had been shaken by the events of not so long ago.

"And what brings you here at this inauspicious time, Miss Chase?" Ulysses asked, his tone measured.

"It's Doctor, actually," the woman said, interrupting.

"Really?"

"Yes, I possess a doctorate in botany. I'll have you know that I am very well qualified."

"I'm sure you are. Very well endowed," Ulysses added, smiling despite himself. "Academically speaking, of course."

Cheeks reddening and nostrils flaring in annoyance, the woman persisted in her explanation regardless. "I have returned, only this morning, from my latest expedition to Java, collecting and cataloguing new and rare plant species. But when I arrived there was no reply to my rings. So I came around the back, found the conservatory open and..." Tears subsumed Petunia's words as her overwrought emotions overcame her at last.

After the accusations, the recriminations, the confessions, the explanations, the sudden emotional empathy and the change from cold indifference to sympathetic understanding, Ulysses found himself sitting on the step to the conservatory, with one arm around the girl, the floodgates of emotion having failed before the tidal wave of grief that finally overwhelmed her.

"Now – and I know this is hard – but I have a question for you. How can you be certain that your uncle's death wasn't an accident?" Ulysses made sure that he kept his eyes fixed on the young woman as he asked the question, and that he most definitely did not look towards the broken pane of glass.

"A world-renowned botanist, who worked with plants all his life, eaten by his own Patagonian Mantrap – a plant that, I might add, he raised from a cutting? Do give me some credit, Mr Quicksilver. He had tended that plant for the last fourteen years without coming to harm. Don't try and tell me that this was an accident. And if you didn't break that pane of glass to get in, who did?"

"Very good, Petunia – I can call you Petunia, can't I? – very good," Ulysses said, a winning smile on his lips. "I have to say, I am impressed. And, as a result, I want to help you."

"You do? But we've only just met."

"And yet I have already taken your plight to heart. I want to find the one responsible for your uncle's death just as much as you do. And, finding myself a little short of leads, it strikes me that you could be my best bet when it comes to unravelling the knots of this mystery. There may be something you know, the import of which you are, as yet, unaware. Failing that, I could do with someone of your background and expert knowledge on my side."

"What can I do?" Petunia asked, a look of earnest intent in her wide brown eyes.

"Come with me," Ulysses said, dramatically seizing her hand in his. "Come with me to Southwark."

VI-A Gruesome Discovery

The party stood at the edge of the Thames – the dandy, his manservant, the police sergeant and the grieving niece. Ulysses Quicksilver watched the swirling current of the churning brown water, listening as the water lapped at the tarry mud of the shoreline, considering the case in hand.

"You're certain this was the spot?" Ulysses quizzed Sergeant Sheldon for a second time.

"Like I said, sir, this was where Old Samson found the body."

Ulysses had hoped that if he could visit the place where the first body had been washed up for himself, he might uncover something that had so far been missed. But there had been no such obvious revelation. With a sigh, he turned from the river.

"Nimrod, any thoughts, old chap?" he asked.

"Well, sir, I was just considering how the body must have been carried here from much further upstream."

"How much further?"

"A body could be carried from as far away as Hammersmith or Chiswick. Perhaps even Brentford and beyond."

"Is that right?"

The high-pitched yapping of a dog abruptly interrupted their discussion.

Ulysses led the party towards the barking and into the shadow of Southwark Bridge. There before them was a ramshackle hut cobbled together from rusted corrugated iron plate, and reclaimed pier supports. A terrier, its fur coloured brown and filthy white, stood before a sack-cloth-draped entrance, Ulysses unsure whether the dog was warning them away from its territory or trying to attract their attention.

"Hello, fella," Ulysses said, crouching down and scratching the dog behind the ears. The terrier gave its own unintelligible greeting, tail wagging. "What are you doing down here all by yourself? What is it you're protecting so very well?"

Stepping past the dog, moving aside the sackcloth curtain, Ulysses entered the shack. The smell was the first thing that hit him – the stink of fungal decay and something much worse. Then his eyesight adjusted to the gloom.

Ulysses staggered from the shack, face pale, trying hard not to gag. "Sergeant Sheldon," he managed, "who did you say found the first body?"

"Old Samson the beachcomber," the police officer replied.

"And he was one of Nancy's regulars?"

"I believe so, sir."

"And he's not been seen since Nancy's death."

"No."

"Well we've found him now, Sergeant."

His curiosity piqued, Sheldon bustled past Ulysses and into the tumbledown hut, the terrier growling at him as he did so. "God save us!" he gasped as he too caught sight of the mouldering, fungus-eaten corpse. "Just like the first one. Like Nancy."

"I think it's time we followed this trail of corpses back upriver to find its source," Ulysses stated with cold finality.

The pensive silence that followed his words was broken by a yapping bark that was sounding more and more like a canine cough.

Petunia looked at Ulysses, her own face paling. "What's wrong with the dog?"

Later that same day, at the station, Sergeant Sheldon was completing the unfortunately necessary incident report relating to the discovery of Old Samson, a lukewarm mug of tea on the desk in front of him. The vagabond's body was now resting in the morgue alongside the other fungus-riddled corpse, having been brought back by the robo-Peelers still on secondment from Scotland Yard. But for the time being Sergeant Sheldon was alone with his paperwork.

The first inkling he had that anything was wrong was when smoke began to seep under his door. He was on his feet in seconds, the report and his tea forgotten, yanking the office door open to make his escape and raise the alarm. As he stumbled down the passageway to the front of the station house, covering his mouth with a handkerchief against the choking smoke, he could see shapes through the frosted glass of the main door, even as the flames licked higher, cracking the glass.

Blinking back tears brought on by smoke and heat, he could make out a... What was it...? An engine, yes, a fire engine, already there, the heat-distorted silhouettes of firemen dousing the burning police station with the hoses held in their heavy gloved hands. And yet, it seemed to Sergeant Sheldon that as the firemen swept their hoses back and forth across the front of the burning building, the higher the flames rose and the quicker the fire took hold.

Wracking coughs seized his body and he fell to his knees. He reached out and grasped the handle of the door with one hand, immediately and instinctively pulling it back as the hot metal took the skin from his fingers.

The smoke was overcoming him, he knew it. But, even as his vision blurred, he couldn't help wondering why the liquid pumping out of the firemen's hoses looked like fire.

VII-Three 'Men' In A Boat

The steam launch chugged onwards casting a bow-wave of ripples in its wake, as it steamed its way upriver, towards the setting sun. The purple orange cloudscape of the evening sky stained the tireless Thames, the water this far from the centre of the capital noticeably less discoloured and polluted. The sun appeared to be dropping closer and closer towards the tree-dotted distance with every mile the party travelled.

Ulysses Quicksilver sat at the bow of the boat, his steely gaze focused on the horizon, while Nimrod sat at the back, keeping the launch on course. Petunia's sharp eyes scoured the banks for the one vital clue that might tell them they had found the source of the dread devouring fungus.

Dusk was drawing on, bringing moonrise in its wake. The trio had set out on their endeavour late in the day, partly thanks to Nimrod having to make a stop at the residence of Dr Methuselah to collect a package which he had then dutifully delivered to Ulysses before they boarded the hired launch at Putney.

It was becoming increasingly difficult for Petunia to make out anything very much within the shadows of the riverbank. If she didn't find what Ulysses had asked her to look out for soon, their journey might prove to have been a hopeless venture. And then there it was, a flash of scarlet beneath the drooping boughs of a willow at the water's edge.

"Ulysses!" she called. "We must be near."

"You're sure?" he queried, not taking his eyes off the darkening horizon.

"Absolutely. It couldn't be anything else."

"So the first fungally finished fellow ended up in the river somewhere around here?" Only now did Ulysses turn to face Petunia.

"It's only circumstantial evidence I know, but it's as good as we're going to get. Considering our situation it's got to be as good a place to start as any."

"But where is here?" Ulysses mused.

"To our right, sir, is Syon House," Nimrod spoke up from the back of the boat.

"Of course. Spent an absolutely awful evening there once at a masked ball."

"Which means that to our left are –"

"The Royal Botanical Gardens at Kew."

"Precisely, sir."

"Then take us into the bank, please Nimrod."

Cutting the engine, the ever-capable Nimrod steered the launch in towards the bank, the hull of the vessel bumping against the muddy slope.

The three of them alighted in the dusky darkness, Nimrod pausing only to make sure the boat was secured. Cautious as a cat burglar Ulysses approached the perimeter fence of the ornamental gardens, visible beyond the railings as shadowy shapes against the velvet blue of burgeoning night, cane in hand. His footsteps crushed the fiery red flowers growing there amongst the lush grass, the same species Ulysses had found caught in the first victim's hair.

"So, here we are again," Ulysses said.

"It would appear so," Nimrod agreed, joining Ulysses at his side. Neither of them looked like they were really dressed for a night's reconnaissance.

"I knew there was something fishy about Professor Hargreaves."

"You've been here recently?" Petunia asked.

"Yes, and I knew then there was something funny about the Director's attitude, although at the time I naively put it down to the stress of the opening..." Ulysses' words trailed off as the veracity of what he was saying sank in. "Of course!" he hissed. "Whatever he's got planned, it all hinges around the opening of the Amaranth House tomorrow."

"So what do we do now?" Petunia asked. "Contact the police?"

"We haven't got time for that. Besides we don't want the likes of Inspector Allardyce generally cluttering up the place and getting in our way," Ulysses stated firmly, then flashed Petunia a grin, the sparkle of thrill-seeking excitement in his eyes. "I rather suspect we have to act quickly and decisively before things get out of hand. Nimrod," he addressed his manservant, "please help Dr Chase over the fence and then stay close. We don't know what we might find in there." He glanced at the dark silhouettes of the glasshouses again.

"Very good, sir," Nimrod assented, "but before you proceed any further, you do have Dr Methuselah's package about your person, don't you?"

"Indeed, Nimrod. Secreted away safely." He patted the breast pocket of his jacket.

"What is it that was so important we had to make

a detour at what is, according to you, such a crucial time?" Petunia challenged.

"It's just a precaution."

"Against what?"

"A lethal, fungal pandemic outbreak," Ulysses said with a dangerous, shark-like grin. "As you have so rightly pointed out, there is no time to delay. The game is surely afoot."

Having clambered over the fence and entered the botanical gardens in such a clandestine way, the trio skulked their way along the night-shrouded pathways. But as they neared the Amaranth House, Ulysses' prescient sense began to flare.

A shadowy figure detached itself from the darkness before them. Ulysses' nostrils were instantly assailed by the earthy odour of rotting compost. Then the figure spoke.

"Why, good evening, Mr Quicksilver," it said, the voice strangely familiar, and took another step closer. Wan moonlight fell across the stranger's face.

"Director Hargreaves," Quicksilver said, making a vain attempt at ignorant foppish bravado. He could see other man-shapes emerging from the looming shadow of the Amaranth House now, a mob of gardeners and visitors, or so it seemed. "Fancy meeting you here. Are you out for a pleasant evening's stroll as well?"

The Director said nothing.

His sixth sense screaming, Ulysses heard the whoosh of displaced air behind him too late as a heavy object connected with the back of his head. Muscles relaxed, his body folded up, and he crumpled onto the carefully manicured lawn.

VIII-The Mandrake Mandate

Darkness enveloped him, a cloying blackness redolent with peaty decay. Ulysses struggled to consciousness and blearily opened his eyes. This did little to dissipate the murk but slowly his eyes began to adjust to the green gloom. Blinking away his concussed stupor, every movement of his eyelids causing the obvious lump on the back of his head to throb horribly, Ulysses struggled to make sense of his surroundings.

He was underground, of that he was sure, and it seemed that the only light came from some photo-luminescent plant source. Growths of a curious algae covered what Ulysses could now see were riveted iron beams and pillars, supporting some structure or other above.

Stretched out on his back, he was staring up at a ceiling. Cautiously he moved his hands and feet – they were not restrained – and felt the edges of the table, or whatever it was he was lying on. Slowly he turned his head to his left. Lying on a wooden worktable next to him was an unconscious Petunia; eyes closed, breathing deeply. Beyond her the gloom thickened again, a mass of inseparable shadows. Ulysses turned his head to the right, half expecting to see Nimrod laid out like Petunia but there was nothing but the dark shapes of freestanding shelves, the kind one might expect to find in a greenhouse.

It was quiet in this place, but not silent. An unsettling sound, a fizzing-crackling noise, filled the gloom: it was as if he could actually hear things growing in the darkness. And then the skull-splitting pain distracted him again, deadening the information being relayed by his other senses. Despite the throbbing ache at the base of his skull, Ulysses sat up and leant towards the comatose young woman. "Petunia," he hissed, "can you hear me?"

The girl stirred in her sleep, making a semi-conscious moan, but her eyes remained shut.

"Petunia," Ulysses tried again, daringly loud, his voice carrying in the stillness. "You have to wake up." He put out an arm to shake her. Behind the headache, Ulysses became aware again of the desperate itch of precognition at the back of his skull. As if he hadn't worked it out for himself already, they were in danger.

A sooty bulb hummed into life. Smudged yellow light bathed the chamber. Ulysses winced under the sudden illumination.

"Let her sleep," came a voice. "It will be much less painful for her that way."

"What? Who is that?" Ulysses challenged, shielding his eyes against the light with one hand. "Show yourself!"

There were figures moving close by, not ten feet away. He squinted, trying to make out features, discern differences, but there was something frustratingly indistinct about many of the lumpen forms. Then he saw someone he did recognise.

"Director Hargreaves. I might have known."

The Director said nothing but continued purposefully towards Ulysses, a curiously benign, almost drugged, expression on his face. Hargreaves looked like he had been interrupted about his business, missing his jacket and with his shirtsleeves rolled up. He was holding something in his left hand. Its tip glittered under the glare of the artificial light and Ulysses recognised it immediately: it was his bloodstone cane.

"Oh, you disappoint me, Mr Quicksilver," came the voice from the shadows again. It was not the Director who had spoken.

"Whom am I speaking to? Show yourself!"

At Ulysses behest, another man stepped into the wan

pools of light cast by the naked bulbs. He was of medium height, medium build, with greasy black hair swept back from a widow's peak.

"Do I know you?" Ulysses asked disparagingly.

"Apparently not. But I know you," the man replied, almost taunting him. "Everyone knows Ulysses Quicksilver – dandy, rogue, sometime agent of the throne. You're notorious, something of a celebrity in the wake of your adventures at the jubilee celebrations. A man of some standing, it would seem. An ideal subject, in fact."

"Subject? What are you talking about?" Ulysses swung his legs off the table.

"For replacement."

"Replacement?" Ulysses repeated. If only he could keep his apparent captor talking then he might yet be able to get them out of this predicament.

"Yes, Mr Quicksilver. Replication and replacement."

"Assistant Director Mandrake. Who did you have to do away with to earn that title?"

Ulysses couldn't help glancing round in surprise, hearing Petunia's voice behind him. He had thought her still unconscious.

"I remember you," the man said, his smug expression vanishing in a moment. "Yes, Petunia Chase."

"Jolly good, so everybody knows everybody now. Introductions over, would you kindly explain what is going on?" Helping Petunia down from the wooden table Ulysses whispered, "I rather feel it's time to leave."

With a sudden, deft movement he spun on his heel and lunged for the Director. Seizing hold of the bloodstone tip of the cane, he twisted and pulled. The rapier blade sheathed within slipped free with a razor ring.

"If you had fun and games in mind, then you should have restrained us."

"Why? What's the point?" the Assistant Director said, unimpressed. "Where are you going to go?"

His prescient sense burning like a blowtorch flame, Ulysses darted glances around the subterranean chamber. His eyes fully adjusted to the change in light levels, Ulysses could see his surroundings quite clearly now. On either side of both he and Petunia stood the stacks of mushroom beds. Swollen fungal shapes emerged from rich compost, their flesh pallid and grey-green: the colour of rotting human flesh. The fungi were at varying stages of development, the very newest growths nothing more than bulbous white heads pushing up from beneath the dark soil. But there were other trays next to these that contained much more advanced growths. Where Ulysses would have expected to see fat stems topped by dark-gilled heads, these fruiting bodies were vaguely humanoid in shape. And they just kept increasing in size, from one stack to the next.

Beyond the planting trays a host of figures were moving towards Ulysses and Petunia, tightening the noose around them. There were both men and women, dressed in all manner of garb, from that of high class ladies and gentlemen to the practical overalls of lowly gardeners. But there were other things shuffling between them, like ill-formed clay figures with clumsy limbs and thick-trunked bodies, hairless and with only the merest suggestion of features, like folds of flesh in their blank faces.

Petunia gasped, eyes wide in horror as she caught sight of another of the assembled throng: "Uncle? But – no – it can't be!"

"Oh, but it can," Mandrake stated bluntly.

There he stood, renowned botanist and outspoken critic of the Empire, Auberon Chase, as large as life when the last time Ulysses had seen him he had been very much dead.

"Keep back!" Ulysses warned the advancing mob. They moved as one. Director Hargreaves was closest. "I told you to keep back!" the dandy bellowed in both fear and rage. Hargreaves reached for him. Ulysses swung his rapier blade, savagely bringing it down on the Director's arm. The keen edge cut into the exposed flesh and sliced through it cleanly.

The Director made a curious keening sound, looking in appalled horror at where the limb had been severed below the elbow. Petunia's scream was more full-bodied. Ulysses was shocked himself. He had not intended to slice the man's arm off. The severed limb lay on the concrete floor, still holding the sheath of his cane. No blood pumped from either the wound or the stump of the arm. In fact, where Ulysses' blade had cut through the flesh it appeared dense and grey, like the meat of a fungus.

"What the hell's going on here?" Ulysses cried, pulling Petunia close to him, ready to ward off any other further attacks.

"Revolution, Mr Quicksilver. A change to the world order." The advancing crowd of people and fungoid things halted in their advance.

"But... why? How?" Ulysses' mind was racing as he tried to see a way out. Where was Nimrod? If only Ulysses could keep this Mandrake talking, perhaps they might yet get out of this situation alive.

"You have the arrogance to ask why?" Mandrake railed. "Or is it sheer bloody-minded ignorance? Are you not aware of what the rapacious society we live in has done to this planet? We are the custodians of Mother Earth and yet all mankind does to her is rape and pillage from the very thing that he should be striving to protect. This is called the Great Steam Age by some but such power and progress comes at too high a price. Irreparable deforestation is taking place on a global scale causing untold environmental damage. The Amazon rainforest is being depleted on a daily basis, all to feed the hungers of the infernal machines Magna Britannia is so beholden to. Policy must be changed. Attitudes must be changed.

"Untold thousands of species have been destroyed, thanks to the thoughtless harvesting of the rainforests for fuel. Thousands of cures for all manner of diseases have quite possibly been lost. Plants were among the first living organisms to rise to prevalence on this planet and practically all other forms of life owe their existence to them. Plants were once the dominant kingdom on Earth and they shall inherit this world again!"

"But what do you hope to achieve here that will make any difference?" Ulysses challenged.

"Replication and replacement."

"So you keep saying, but what do you mean?" Petunia shrieked, her desperation at her own plight vying with her desperation to understand.

"Let us show you." The throng began to advance again. Ulysses swept around him with his blade but there were too many. Feeling a hand on his shoulder, he turned and looked into the amorphous face of one of the fungoid creatures. The fungus-being's mouth opened and it exhaled a cloud of spores into Ulysses' face. He stumbled back, coughing, but the plant-thing maintained its hold on him.

He felt woozy, drowsy, and inclined not to fight back. The rapier fell from his open fingers. Cold, damp, probing digits sought out bare flesh, enclosing his left hand in their succulent grasp. Petunia's screams became muffled and then turned to a hacking cough. Ulysses suddenly felt so tired; he just wanted to sleep.

But somewhere, deep inside himself, Ulysses Quicksilver the hero, the struggler against adversity, the champion of Magna Britannia, could sense what was happening and fought to be free. With his right hand he fumbled inside a jacket pocket. Fingers closed around the small inhaler pump that had been Dr Methuselah's gift to him. Fighting to keep his eyes open, Ulysses put the pump to his mouth and inhaled deeply – once, twice, three times.

His head already beginning to clear, airways free of the soporific spores, Ulysses shook the stupor from himself and looked into a face that was re-moulding itself into a visage that was looking more and more like his own by the second. At the same time, the bulk of the fungoid creature was changing, becoming leaner and growing in height to match his own.

Ulysses took the inhaler from his lips and sprayed it into the face of the creature. The fungus-Ulysses recoiled, wailing in pain, parts of its altering face dissolving on coming into contact with the fungicidal-spray as if eaten away by acid.

Petunia was limp in the grasp of another of the shapeless plant-men, which with every passing moment was becoming more and more like her in form and appearance. Ulysses pushed away from his own squealing attacker and sprayed the second metamorphosing creature, with the same consequences. As the shrieking fungus dropped Petunia, Ulysses put the inhaler to her slack mouth and let her inhale the antidote. Dr Methuselah had done his job well, creating a means by which to fight the necrotising spores of the fungal infection.

Having swept up his sword-cane, with one arm around Petunia to support her, Ulysses seized the initiative and advanced. Their attackers now found themselves under attack as Ulysses strode towards them, spraying the last of the pump's dose into the throng.

Men and women fell back, giving voice to the same unearthly screams as the fungoid things, suffering the same injuries as the two that had tried to assume the forms of Ulysses and Petunia.

Then they were past the throng, an iron door in front of them. Ulysses pulled it open and threw the two of them through. Up a steel spiral staircase and they found themselves inside the Amaranth House, what little starlight that penetrated the smog layer of London setting the myriad glass panes glittering in the reflected light of the distant city.

The two escapees staggered and stumbled along the set cobble paths between the planting beds, lungs heaving, the debilitating effects of the spores still lingering within their overwrought respiratory systems.

They were no longer alone either. The recovered throng emerged from the subterranean level of the glasshouse and poured after them, moving as one body again. It would be only a matter of moments before they caught up. And then the doors to the Amaranth House were before them and harsh, white light blazed into the building.

Ulysses threw the two of them bodily aside, tumbling into a bed of cacti, uncaring of the pricks of the spines as, engine roaring throatily, the tanker truck smashed through the glass doors and into the Amaranth House. Razor sharp glass shards chopped through leaves and lanced into the mud of the planting beds. Dark liquid fountained from the ruptured drum of the tanker and rained down on everyone and everything inside the glasshouse.

Creatures screamed as the fungicidal agents of the weedkiller broke down their mushroom bodies. The seemingly human men and women suffered the same fate, their true fungal forms dissolving into a grey sludge. The battered door of the driver's cab creaked open and Ulysses' loyal manservant jumped down from the vehicle.

"Just in the nick of time, eh, Nimrod?" Ulysses said, managing a wry smile despite being drenched in stinking fungicide and feeling drained from the effects of the fungus-thing's attentions.

"It would appear so, sir," Nimrod agreed. "Now, might I suggest that we make our getaway post-haste?"

"Indeed! I couldn't agree more."

Nimrod assisting Petunia in as gentlemanly a manner as possible, Ulysses picked himself up out of the cactus patch.

"Not so fast!"

Ulysses' flopped back into the prickly plants as his feet were pulled out from under him. Twisting round he looked into the manic face of the Assistant Director. Mandrake looked back at him with only one eye, the other dissolving along with the spoiled half of his face that had been splashed with the potent weed killer. "What have you done?"

"Hah! I knew it! You're one of them!" Ulysses exclaimed.

"I was the first," Mandrake snarled through liquefying lips. "The first of many."

The mimicking fungoid creature began to claw its way up Ulysses' legs, but he kicked out, freeing himself from the clutches of the bizarre plant-human hybrid.

"That may well be the case," Ulysses replied, "but whatever you are, you're still dead!"

In a flash the rapier blade was out of its sheath. Ulysses thrust, the slower Mandrake caught with his guard down.

Mandrake gasped and staggered backwards. Ulysses' blade came free of the body, the fungus flesh leaving a milky residue on its surface.

Ulysses, Nimrod and Petunia watched as whatever it was that had passed for Assistant Director Mandrake stumbled backwards over the guard wire surrounding the recently re-planted Patagonian Mantrap and toppled into the gaping maw of the incongruously named Audrey.

"Now," said Ulysses, suddenly overwhelmed with exhaustion. "Let's get out of here."

IX-Bad Seed

"It was him, wasn't it?" Petunia said, gazing into the middle distance.

"Don't think on it anymore, my dear," Ulysses said, hugging the shocked young woman around the shoulders. "It's over now. He's gone."

The three of them were sitting on the neatly tended lawn outside the Amaranth House. With the Mandrake-thing's demise, the last of the fungus-creatures had fallen too. It had been as if the plant-men mimics were all part of one gestalt consciousness: with the first destroyed, the repository of that consciousness went too.

"But it was his body that was washed up at Southwark, wasn't it?"

"Yes. I rather think it was. But, like I say he's gone. It's over."

"One of those... things... took his place. But how did he end up in the Thames? When they tried to take me I just wanted to sleep."

Ulysses took a deep breath, gazing to the horizon, the sky purpling with pre-dawn light. "I suppose the original

Mandrake managed to fight off the effects at first, at least long enough to get away. He must have fled and then fallen into the river as he tried to escape, but the spores overcame him in the end. And it was exposure to those same spores that eventually did for Old Samson and Nancy the street-walker."

"While the mimic-Mandrake continued his work under the Amaranth House. But why?"

"In preparation." It was Nimrod who spoke. "Today is the nineteenth."

"The day of the official opening," Ulysses expanded, bringing Petunia up to speed, "of the Amaranth House. The great and the good will be here in a matter of hours – politicians, industrialists, foreign ambassadors –"

"And Mandrake's fungi would have been ready to greet them... Become them."

"Indeed."

"But where did they come from?" Petunia asked. "I've never seen their like before."

"I rather suspect they were grown, genetically-modified in a lab somewhere." Ulysses gave Nimrod a look heavy with meaning. "Could this be connected to Professor Galapagos' work? Could someone be selling his secrets on?"

"It doesn't bear thinking about," Nimrod said darkly.

"So what happens now?" Petunia asked, all emotion drained from her by her recent experiences.

"Now? We wait for my old friend Inspector Allardyce, unfortunately. The Met can take it over from here."

The three survivors fell into stupefied silence again. From their roosts in the arboretum the birds began to greet the coming dawn with their massed singing. Faintly at first, distance muffling the sound, so that it was almost melodic, another voice joined the dawn chorus: a claxon wail. As it came closer, the siren became more strident.

Ulysses looked at Nimrod, bemusement written large across his features. "Who called the fire brigade?"

"So, doctor, explain to me again how the hybrid takes on the form of its victim," the visitor asked as they walked the length of the dungeon sub-level. Illumination was kept low in this place, but there was enough light for the visitor to gain at least a passing impression of the things kept behind steel bars and reinforced glass.

Something amphibian croaked, huddled in a gloomy corner of its damp cell. In another a droid – constructed after the neo-industrialist fashion – stood motionless, only the faintly pulsing glow of its eye-lamps indicating that there was any artificial life remaining within its metal body. In the next, a red-haired simian, as tall as a man, snorted and howled, gnawing at its own wrist and the manacle attached to it.

"Well, sir, it would appear that once fully mature the hybrid possesses a basic sentience. However, once introduced to its subject it assimilates characteristics of that subject, in terms of intellect and purpose as well as physical make-up, somehow assimilating and replicating all of this from the target's DNA."

"Fascinating," the visitor pronounced in his rich baritone.

"In order to subdue a subject, and make it susceptible to replication, the fungus produces modified spores. The spores themselves are highly toxic, as well as having potent narcotic qualities. Exposure to them ultimately results in death, a symbiotic sub-species of necrotising fungus breaking down the host body. I suppose the original reason for this development was to provide the hybrids with nutrient-rich compost. But, even away from its hybrid parent, this symbiotic fungus continues to reproduce itself by sporing."

"As we saw for ourselves in Southwark."

"Yes, sir," the lab-coated scientist confirmed.

They passed another cell, and the small terrier contained within growled at their passing.

"The dog's still alive, I see," the visitor commented.

"We're continuing to monitor it, sir, and considering a more thorough examination by means of a live dissection."

"Excellent. And here they are."

The two men stopped in front of the last cell, the visitor peering into the gloom. Inside the maximum-security containment unit was nothing more innocuous than a stack of planting trays, small white bulbs poking through the thick mushroom compost.

"Do you have a name for them yet?"

"Well, sir, they've been classified as a plant-human hybrid. As well as the human-animal element and the obvious fungal components, we have identified another half dozen plant species used in their bio-engineering."

"Yes, doctor, but do they have a name? Something like this needs a catchy name, don't you think?"

"Well, the team and I have been referring to them as mandrakes, sir."

"I like it. Mandrakes," the visitor mused, the moniker lingering on his tongue. "Yes, why not? And it's amazing isn't it," he went on, pointing at something else, almost missed at first, rooted in the muck and slime at the back of the cell. "That one looks just like him."

The partially altered thing stared back at them, silent and motionless, pearlescent eyes glowing green in the semi-dark.

THE END

Don't miss the further adventures of Ulysses
Quicksilver in *Pax Britannia: Leviathan Rising* by
Jonathan Green. Coming in 2008...

PAX BRITANNIA

UNNATURAL HISTORY

Jonathan Green

Price: £6.99 ★ ISBN: 1-905437-10-2

Price: $7.99 ★ ISBN 13: 978-1-905437-10-8

THE AFTERBLIGHT CHRONICLES

The
CULLED

Simon Spurrier

Price: £6.99 ★ ISBN: 1-905437-01-3

Price: $7.99 ★ ISBN 13: 978-1-905437-01-6

THE AFTERBLIGHT CHRONICLES

KILL OR CURE

Rebecca Levene

Price: £6.99 ★ ISBN: 1-905437-32-3

Price: $7.99 ★ ISBN 13: 978-1-905437-32-0

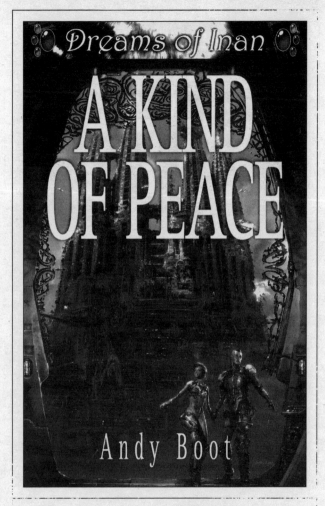

Dreams of Inan

A KIND OF PEACE

Andy Boot

Price: £6.99 ★ ISBN: 1-905437-02-1

Price: $7.99 ★ ISBN 13: 978-1-905437-02-3

Dreams of Inan

STEALING
LIFE

Antony Johnston

Price: £6.99 ★ ISBN: 1-905437-12-9

Price: $7.99 ★ ISBN 13: 978-1-905437-12-2

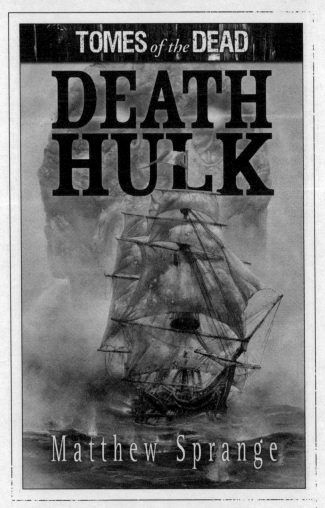

TOMES *of the* DEAD

DEATH HULK

Matthew Sprange

Price: £6.99 ★ ISBN: 1-905437-03-X

Price: $7.99 ★ ISBN 13: 978-1-905437-03-0

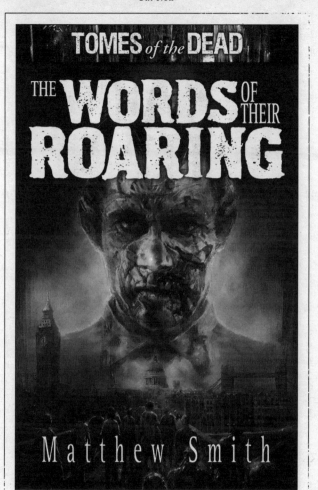

Price: £6.99 ★ ISBN: 1-905437-13-7

US Release: JULY 2007 Price: $7.99 ★ ISBN 13: 978-1-905437-13-9

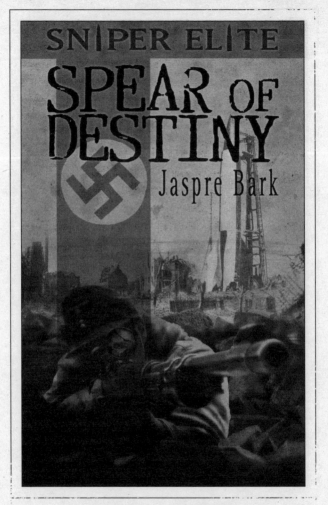

Price: £6.99 ★ ISBN: 1-905437-04-8

Price: $7.99 ★ ISBN 13: 978-1-905437-04-7

THE AFTERBLIGHT CHRONICLES

SCHOOL'S OUT

Scott Andrews

AUGUST 2007 Price: £6.99 ★ ISBN: 1-905437-40-4

OCTOBER 2007 Price: $7.99 ★ ISBN 13: 978-1-905437-40-5

Abaddon
Books

WWW.ABADDONBOOKS.COM